FLAME IN THE PALACE

LADY OF AVALION: I

SELUNA DRAKE

SELENITE PRESS

Flame in the Palace

a novel by
Seluna Drake

Lady of Avalion

part 1

Copyright © 2022 by Seluna Drake

ISBN: 978-0-9894685-6-5

Selenite Press

www.selunadrake.com

Cover Artist: Koletta Anastasia

Editor: B. K. Bass

for myself—

You did it.

NOCTURNUS

Nightson

Goldeport

Dawnmourne

Elmground

ROSENFORD

Westhaven

Thitis

Silver Coast

STIRLING

Ilona

Kinggrove

Oakhaven

Fairthorne

VALENRENCE

Talking Tree
Forest

Everhaven

RUNEWELL

Honeyridge

BRAMBLE

THE MAP OF
AVALION

CONTENTS

1. Midnight   1

2. Costume   15

3. Dance   29

4. Meeting   45

5. Points   57

6. Favour   73

7. Political   91

8. Toasts   105

9. History   119

10. Strength   133

11. Appearance   149

12. Pearl   165

13. Vulnerable   181

14. Memories   191

15. Honor   203

16. Self-Awareness   217

17. Bargain   227

18. Blood   237

19. Seasick   245

20. Hunting   255

21. Treason   267

22. Art   277

23. Tears   289

24. Compromise   297

25. Summons   307

26. Midnight Flame   313

27. Epilogue   317

Acknowledgments   325

About Author   327

I

MIDNIGHT

AT JUST BEFORE MIDNIGHT, the night sky shrouds the Morning Glory in a velvet blanket of summer humidity and gleaming starlight. It is the time when patrons eventually find their way to their beds or their horses, slowly emptying the dining room. Myria hurries through the inn, collecting empty tankards and abandoned plates. She deposits the dirty dishes in the basin where Grandmother Iris scrapes off leftover food for the compost bucket. They will wash the plates in the morning when the sun illuminates the path to the river. Before heading to bed, Myria's last task for the evening is emptying the compost bucket in a barrow beside the tavern. In the morning, Edgar will wheel this to his home and feed it to his pigs. Eventually, the favor will be returned with a delivery of salted pork and smoked bacon to the Morning Glory.

She finishes closing chores before midnight, her stained shirt clinging to every dip and crevice of her torso with the sweat of flushed skin. Myria ignores the minor discomfort, quite used to it in her usual rush to finish everything. She bustles outside with the scrap bucket in hand, the thick, breezeless night air offering no reprieve from the hot inn. As the bell from the nearby town of Everhaven rings the new day with twelve strikes, she enjoys the small victory of finishing the last of her chores so quickly.

The victory is short-lived. Before the last strike rings out, the sound of hooves clatters on the cobbled road, alerting Myria to horses approaching the tavern. The voices of men drift to her ears. A few moments later, she makes out their faces in the dim moonlight.

"Are you sure the innkeeper is still awake? I would hate to trouble them at this hour."

An exuberant voice addresses the concern of his companion. "Of course! I know they have wild celebrations here that last until dawn. It's why it's called the Morning Glory."

Myria's stomach sinks at the prospect of these new patrons, but the practiced barmaid smile rises easily enough, even in the darkness. The realization that they are all men, multiple men at that, makes her shoulders tense automatically, her free hand reaching for a reassuring grip on the concealed knife at her waistband. Fortunately, she's had very little reason to reveal it, but the reminder of its presence is a slight comfort for Myria who dealt with her fair share of thieves, drunks, and other, more nefarious, pests.

A new, dubious voice cuts across her thoughts, "And if you're wrong?"

The exuberant voice returns. "Then I know the owners. Everything will be fine."

"Somehow, Geffrey's definition of *fine* troubles me."

"Geffrey?" This time it is Myria's turn to question the four riders. The men, seeming to only now notice her standing there, freeze suddenly. The one named Geffrey, a distant cousin of hers, recognizes his name, perhaps even the sound of her voice. He jumps from his horse to embrace her.

"Myria! It is so good to see you. Please tell me you are still serving customers."

A moment's indecision grips her, and she stiffens in response. She isn't quite sure of what to make of her cousin, one she hasn't seen since childhood, embracing her and asking if the inn is open. A small wave of defiance swells in her chest, wanting to refuse him just for his audacity.

The thought reminds Myria of her grandmother's ever-present frown, and the inn's struggling ledger that causes it. They do not have the luxury of turning away customers, even if she cannot imagine the reason behind her cousin's presence now.

"Of course," Myria says, forcing a cheery, inviting voice to accompany her smile. Geffrey releases her. "Go pick your table. I'll take care of the horses."

Once they are all inside and she is alone, her body relaxes, but only briefly. Anxious about leaving her grandmother alone with them, she makes quick work of the food bucket. As she leads the four horses to the stables, Myria thinks back to the last time she saw her cousin. Years at least, perhaps when she was still a teenager. She knows Geffrey belongs to a prominent family, distantly related to her on her mother's side. She doesn't quite know how; she only knows that Grandmother Iris does not take very well to the thought of Myria's distant family members.

With the horses stabled, Myria brushes her hands against her apron in a crude attempt to clean them. She collects her abandoned slop bucket before returning inside to find the four men crowding around a table in the corner of the inn. Grandma Iris has already discovered their presence, eyeing them warily from the bar. Myria follows her gaze and realizes these are not ordinary men. Their jackets are silk, with wide, billowy sleeves and elegant gold threading. Their shirts are white—too white to belong to common laborers. Nobility.

The bucket nearly falls from Myria's grip as she realizes what that means about her cousin. Her mind grapples for the few memories she has of Geffrey: Their fleeting visits as children. His clean clothes and hair that never smelled. His parents, always overbearing and bossy. Myria realizes she has never seen Geffrey's home. Each memory is a fleeting moment, all restricted within her grandmother's inn.

Grandma Iris doesn't move from the bar, maintaining her vigilant, suspicious watch. Taking a deep breath, Myria approaches the table. She maintains a relaxed smile, hoping they will at least tip well. "What brings you to the Morning Glory, gentlemen?"

The three strangers look her over as Geffrey answers for them. "Bring out your best bottle of wine, cousin."

Myria does her best not to grimace, aware of the worn nature of her baggy wool pants, her stained shirt, and her messy hair. "We don't have any wine. It's just ale on tap, brewed fresh from Mossy Boulder down the road."

A man with dark hair and a pale complexion and sharp eyes frowns. "Do you not know who we are?"

The condescending words ignite a flash of annoyance that courses through Myria, compounded by exhaustion. Patience depleted and tip be damned, her smile never wavers as she turns to him. "I barely know who Geffrey is, to be quite honest. You can have ale, or nothing."

Another man with dark hair and olive skin interjects in a clipped voice. "Ignore Aryn. He's in a foul mood after the long ride Geffrey forced us on. We'll take four pints of ale, please."

Myria nods, hurries to the kitchen, and gathers four clean tankards. The kitchen door creaks open and closed as Grandma Iris follows her.

"You've got an opinion about our new guests," Myria says without turning. "Go on, share it."

Grandma Iris doesn't move from the doorway as Myria pours the ale. "They're nobility."

"I can see that for myself. How come I never knew that about Geffrey?"

"His parents used to try to take you back to their world. I wouldn't let them. Eventually, they stopped trying; especially when they saw how you'd become a headstrong barmaid."

Myria pauses to look up from her work. "Take me back? Does that mean my mother was noble as well?" Her heart leaps at the potential of being noble blood.

Nobility brings privilege, like the right to learn magic—a lifelong dream of hers. Only the highborn can learn such things.

Realistic pragmatism smothers that fleeting hope threatening to lift through her chest. The sweat-drenched clothes clinging to her are a stark contrast to the luxurious silks of the men in the other room. She is far from such privilege; she should not forget her place.

Grandma Iris falters, a reaction Myria has never seen in the woman before. If her grandmother is anything, it is strong and certain. Nothing ever gives her pause, until now. "Your mother gave it all up when she married my son."

Myria is about to push for more information when Aryn calls impatiently from the other room. She gathers the drinks and, balancing them on a tray, heads back to the dining room.

"Sorry to keep you waiting," she says, hiding the anger from her voice as she hands out the drinks. "We had already put our dishes away for the evening."

The final man, with honey-colored hair, seems to be embarrassed by the entourage. "We're very sorry for putting you out this late. Geffrey struggled with our navigation."

Geffrey's mouth falls open as if he is about to protest, but the dark-haired man shoots him a withering look that would silence any fearsome beast. "All right, I concede my methods were a bit unorthodox—"

"You lied about having a map!" dark-hair exclaims.

"But I knew where I was going. We ended up in the right place."

Dark-hair looks as though he wants to argue further, but honey-hair raises a hand to interrupt him. "It's fine, Emiri. Just enjoy the experience. We're here, drinking, with a beautiful bartender to keep us company."

Myria grins, attempting to appear shy, but most likely—in her mind—looking foolish. It is not the most forward flattery she has ever received, but she supposes noblemen couldn't be that much different from common ones. It is better than intrusive whispers asking about the state of her marriage bed when she turned twenty-two this last winter. "Will you gentlemen need any rooms for the night?"

"None," Geffrey exclaims. "Tonight, we will be hunting in the Talking Tree Woods."

Myria looks the men over, scrutinizing their fine clothing and smooth hands, and can't imagine them hunting anything. Well, *mostly* smooth hands. The dark-haired one named Emiri has callouses on his fingers. Perhaps he is not a noble after all.

As if noticing her eyes on him, Emiri cocks his head to the side and folds his arms across his chest, hiding those hands from view.

Myria drags her attention from Emiri and pulls up a chair to join their table as she quickly recalls the nature of their conversation. "May I ask what you're hunting?"

Geffrey's grin turns devilish. "The minotaur."

Myria can't help herself. Despite it harming her chances for a decent tip, she laughs in her cousin's face. "I'm sorry, and why are you hunting the minotaur?" she asks after composing herself.

Geffrey frowns. "Why is that funny?"

Emiri and honey-hair both chuckle, also finding amusement. "She's imagining you hunting the minotaur, Geff," Emiri points out.

"You really plan on hunting the minotaur?" Myria asks, looking at each of them to gauge their commitment to this outlandish scheme. "No one's ever been able to find him, much less navigate their way through the dark."

"We are going on one last adventure before the demands of the social season start," Geffrey answers, leaning back in his chair. He nods toward honey-hair. "Leor is about to become too busy for the rest of us. We thought we would make this night memorable."

For a moment, the image of the four of them stumbling through the dark forest coaxes an amused smile to her face. "And I suppose you're going to lead them on this adventure?"

Aryn laughs, and everyone looks at him. "That job is mine."

Myria's eyes travel down his frame once, finding nothing noteworthy of his features other than the customary sneer. Still, she is not convinced. If anyone in their group is likely to find the minotaur, it would be Emiri with callouses, but even then, his fine clothes would do him no favors. "Do you even know how to calm an angry minotaur?" she asks no one in particular.

Aryn's sneer deepens. "We do not have to worry about calming it if we kill it."

Geffrey hides his wide, nervous eyes with a sip of his ale, his silence enough of an answer for the rest of them.

Leor offers a thin smile for them before draining the contents of his own tankard, then turns to Myria. "Do you know where the minotaur is? You seem quite capable of handling yourself. Perhaps you would like to be our guide."

Myria considers the offer for a moment as the others bicker about it.

"We do not need *her*," Aryn protests.

"Of course we do," Geffrey insists. "Myria is perfect. She knows the forest better than anyone. You do not want to get lost in the forest with *me* as your guide, right?"

Emiri arches an eyebrow that appears dubious at best. "You don't think that's too dangerous?"

Myria ignores all their remarks, her eyes locked on Leor. His smile is inviting and charming, and there is genuine respect and kindness in his words that Myria knows is rare from anyone—nobility or not.

She grins mischievously. "I have conditions."

Aryn rolls his eyes while Geffrey cheers. Leor's smile only deepens, as if enjoying her assertive charm. "Sensible. I am listening."

"I will take you straight to the minotaur and give you this memorable night you've been wanting. *But,* no one is killing it."

This surprises them all, and their mouths hang agape in awe. "You've seen the minotaur?" Emiri asks.

"Of course," she says, beaming with pride. "What sort of guide would I be if I hadn't?"

Leor raises his brows and purses his lips as he sits back, seeming to take a measure of her, then nods in agreement. "Lead the way."

Myria's neck and cheeks warm as a flush flows into them at his approval. "If you gentlemen will excuse me, I'll prepare for the journey."

Before leaving, Myria goes to her room to grab a few items, including her traveling cloak and the wooden flute gifted to her by a traveling bard years ago. She takes an extra moment to tie back her hair before she returns to the kitchen and packs a few peaches in her bag. Grandmother Iris waits for her there.

"You're going out with them," she observes.

"I can't just let them hurt themselves. I'll be back in the morning."

"I would be more afraid of them than the minotaur. Nobles always take what they want, no matter what they have to do."

Myria sighs, resigning herself to let the argument go, and turns to her grandmother for a quick hug. "I'll be back in the morning," she repeats.

Outside, the night is dark, but her experience with the forest guides her path. She spent her youth in endless explorations of its depths, until as a teenager her excursions were limited to help her grandmother in the inn.

Myria pauses outside the stables when she hears the others saddling their horses. "You won't need those. They should probably rest after your journey anyway."

Leor steps out into the yard, the dim moonlight casting his face in shadow. His head tilts, as if continuing to size her up. The honey hair that shifts across his eyes appears blue in the night. "Do you have a horse?"

It is an innocent question, but something akin to pride—or humiliation—thickens her tongue. It is a struggle to not look at the ground, so Myria settles for glaring a spot on his nose, thinking it unlikely he could see the exact direction of her gaze in the darkness. Her reply is curt, monosyllabic. "No."

He retreats a step, as if recognizing he has offended her. His next question comes in the form of a peaceful offer. "You could always ride with me."

The gesture pairs well with his previous flattery, so Myria forces the coy smile. She combats the sudden rise of her temper with a steady breath. "Thank you, but horses would only be clumsy in the forest. There's no trail, and I am quite familiar with our path."

He seems to consider her in silence for a few moments, then looks over his shoulder. "Leave the horses."

She does not doubt that the responding growl of disgust is from Aryn.

Emiri steps out of the stables, stretching out his arms, and for once, his voice is not gruff or annoyed. "Walking? Should be fun."

Myria leads them down a worn, winding footpath through the forest, carved by herself over the years. Their only illumination comes from a sliver of the moon shining overhead. However, the dull light struggles to gain ground through the cloying fog. Chirps and buzzes set the forest alive with nocturnal life as they tread along. Deeper and deeper they penetrate the forest. After nearly an hour, the men behind her traipse with clumsy footsteps on the uneven forest floor, grasping at trees and each other for balance. The thick canopy of leaves all but obliterates the faltering moonlight reaching the ground, but every step Myria takes is sure and steady—she relies on instinct to guide them.

"How much further?" Emiri asks from behind. He is not as winded as the others.

"We're nearly there," she calls over her shoulder.

Someone steps closer to her, and it isn't until he speaks that she recognizes him as Leor.

"Is there a reason you do not want us to kill the minotaur?" he asks, keeping his voice low.

"He is the only minotaur I've ever seen in this forest. It would be a shame if he disappeared. What if he's the last of his kind?"

"Is he not dangerous?" Leor asks, a tone of fascination coloring his voice.

"Of course. Anything can be dangerous. But the real danger is when you don't recognize its potential. Proceed cautiously, and everything will be fine."

Leor gives a small chuckle. "I wish I shared your brave optimism."

Myria shrugs, realizing he cannot see it. "You can, as long as you see the world for what it is and what it can be. Tell me, why do you need to go on such a glorious hunt for a minotaur? Why will you become too busy for your friends after tonight?"

Leor hesitates, the lingering air of uncertainty hanging between. He finally manages, "I will be taking over my father's responsibilities soon. Much is expected of me, including starting a family."

"Starting a family?" Myria repeats. "Does that include arranging your marriage?"

A clipped breath escapes his nostrils. "Yes, it does." Leor sounds rueful, regretful.

"I am sorry to hear that it burdens you with such responsibility. My mother escaped a similar life so she could marry whomever she wanted. I couldn't imagine being forced into something like that, and I don't envy you for it."

He emits a soft chuckle. "Then I envy your mother for having the courage to take her future into her own hands."

"I really wouldn't know," Myria admits. "I never knew her. My parents died when I was very young."

Before Leor can respond, Myria slows her pace. Ahead, there is a break in the trees where the moonlight shines brighter on a small clearing filled with long, lush grass that sways with the night's breeze. Myria hisses for the rest of the party to stop as proceeds forward.

"I'll go on ahead. The rest of you should stay behind."

Emiri's voice is close. "Are you sure? Isn't the minotaur dangerous?"

"Yes, on both counts, but I know what I'm doing. It would be more dangerous to bring four new humans into his home without him expecting it."

"Is there anything we can do?" Leor asks.

"Keep calm."

Geffrey's voice cuts in behind the others. "So dark! How can we see anything?"

Myria rolls her eyes. "And keep quiet."

She creeps forward, keeping low as she scans for movement in the darkness. At the opposite end of the meadow is an opening to a cave that reaches deep into the cliffside. Myria has been here before, so she isn't afraid. However, there is something about the expectant audience behind her that makes her nervous. She shakes a tingling sensation from her fingers and stops in the middle of the clearing, fishing in her bag for the wooden flute. She mimics a few fingerings before beginning to play.

Music can indeed soothe any beast, smooth stones, or bend trees. When she first learned about the minotaur's presence in the forest, she spent many hours spying on it, wondering what sort of creature it could be. She found he was usually lonely, and the first time she tried playing for him was an experience that was as reckless as it was informative. Luckily, she discovered the minotaur *did* like music—a fact she never shared with anyone before, not even Grandma Iris.

Myria starts with a low-pitched lullaby, something soft and gentle to the ears. She does not know if the minotaur is already asleep. She considers as she plays, *If he is, it is best to wake him with something easy on his ears.*

She gradually increases the tempo of her tune, and the flute rings out to silence the night's buzzing. Everything is listening to her now. She focuses on not flubbing her fingerings. Minor chords or harmonies would do her no favors right now.

Within a minute, she hears a deep rumble stir within the darkness of the cave. She plays a little louder, yet keeps the melody soft and inviting. The men behind her whisper anxiously, causing her entire body to tense.

The minotaur reveals himself at the mouth of the cave. He is taller than any man she has seen, with the chest and arms of a human covered in dense fur. The bull shows in his cloven hooves, horned head, and elongated face. He must not have been asleep yet, as he watches her with alert and wary eyes. He is always careful. And she is careful to finish her music to the end of a major chord—careful to remain still for him.

When the last note fades, she lowers her flute and smiles.

"Hello there. I'm sorry. I know it is rather late. I hope you forgive me, but I brought some people who are keen to meet you." She doesn't know if he understands her, but she always speaks to him as if he can.

The minotaur raises his snout and sniffs the air before creeping to her. Myria remains still and waits for him to finish his inspection. Other humans have probably not been so kind to him as she, so she is patient with his trepidation. When his face is inches from hers, the minotaur stops and gazes at her. The anxious whispers of the men grow louder, distracting the minotaur. He snorts out a powerful breath with an uncertain grunt, blowing the hair out of her face. She senses the minotaur tensing in front of her, and her body coils like a spring.

She slowly reaches into her bag to break the tension and offers a peach. "Here," she whispers, a slight tremble in her voice. "I know how much you like them."

It is enough to refocus his attention. He is no longer cautious as he reaches for the fruit and bites into it eagerly. Myria breathes a sigh of relief and strokes his long snout.

"I am sorry for my rude friends. Can they come closer? I promise they won't hurt you."

The minotaur seems to consider her question for some time, chewing on his peach with his head cocked to the side. Then, amazingly, he nods.

The others draw near with less certainty than Myria. The minotaur's ears flatten back, but he appears no more imposing than that as he waits for the men to approach.

Myria introduces each man by handing them a peach to give to the minotaur. "This is my cousin Geffrey, and his friends: Aryn, Emiri, and Leor."

They stand in line, awaiting their turn to give their offering of peach as they gape at the towering minotaur. Myria steps back to provide them with space, crossing her arms and smiling at her handiwork. Emiri steps back with her as Geffrey hands his peach to the minotaur.

"Do you do this often?" he asks as he spins the peach in his hands.

"Do what?" she asks coyly.

"Make friends with dangerous, magical creatures," he replies with a snort.

"No, the minotaur is the only one I know."

"You know it's crazy, right?" His spinning peach increases in speed. "Geffrey has us hunting a minotaur, and some barmaid takes us right to one, plays music for the beast, and feeds him peaches."

Myria smirks, remembering his calloused hands. "*Some* barmaid? Is it as crazy as a commoner dressed up as a noble?"

Emiri chuckles, a husky sound that dissipates as he explains, "You are right; I am not a noble."

"But you ride around with them searching for minotaurs? Do you do *that* often?" she points out, echoing his initial question.

"Looking for minotaurs? No. Ride around with them?" He gestures to the group before them, where Aryn is offering his peach. Emiri hesitates. "Yes, it happens occasionally."

"How did you get so lucky?" Myria sighs.

Emiri tenses beside her. "I'm not sure if I would call it luck. How did you even know I was just a commoner?"

"I wouldn't call you *just* a commoner, but if you must know, I saw your hands." Myria reaches for one and holds it between the two of them. She traces the rough edges and lines with two fingers. "You have callouses, which means you've had to work hard in your life at some point. I have plenty of my own. Your friends don't have any."

Emiri says nothing about the sudden, forward gesture, and merely watches her. She maintains his piercing gaze with a shy smile. It is an expression that earns her many tips with the inn's patrons, but that is not why she smiles now. The inn and minotaur are far from her mind as she puzzles out Emiri's role among his noble friends.

"You never answered my question," she points out.

"I—" Suddenly, a small gasp from the others cuts him off. Myria drops Emiri's hand and races back to the minotaur, only to be greeted with a strange sight. The minotaur kneels with his arms outstretched, offering a hollowed-out horn to

Leor. It appears to be a minotaur horn, weathered and more ancient than those crowning her friend's own head.

"What happened?" Myria asks. "I've never seen him do this."

"Nothing," Leor hastily explains. "I just gave him my peach, and then he kneeled."

"Do you think it is because Leor is the prince?" Geffrey asks.

"Wait, the *prince*? You're a prince? *The* prince?" Myria repeats in confusion. *The King of Avalion is King Uriel and his wife is Queen Eloria. They have a son... Crown Prince Leor.* She shakes her head, not knowing how she missed the connection before.

Leor sighs. "Yes, I am the prince." There is sadness in the words.

Myria composes herself. "So when you say that you're taking on your father's responsibilities..."

Leor nods. "Yes, it means I will be king one day. I am sorry; I did not intend to deceive you. I simply did not want you to treat me differently."

"I'm more embarrassed that I didn't realize it sooner." She shifts her weight to one leg. "You should probably accept his gift," she says, nodding toward the horn still on the outstretched hands of the awaiting minotaur. "I've heard that minotaurs keep the horns of their fathers, but I've never heard of one being given as a gift."

Leor glances at the minotaur's gift as his face pales and his hands tremble. "I am not sure if I feel comfortable taking this from him."

"Best not to offend him by refusing it."

Leor takes her advice and holds out his hands to cradle the offering. "You honor me with this gift, Sir Minotaur. I will treasure it always." A long, braided cord hangs from the horn's tip. Leor slips this over his shoulder and lets the horn hang at his hip.

The minotaur rises to his feet, snorts, and gathers his bounty of peaches before retreating to his cave.

"That went much better than I could have expected," Geffrey beams.

Aryn scoffs. "I think anything would have been better than what you would have expected."

"We should head back," Myria says. "Are you sure you don't want to stay at the Morning Glory? It's pretty late, and we're the closest inn you'll find."

Aryn's expression curls in disgust. "Stay at an inn, like a commoner? You probably have fleas in your beds."

His words hang thick in the air as Myria frowns. She would not typically value the opinion of someone the likes of Aryn, but the insult stings in front of the prince. She forces a placid smile. "The bed I have in mind for you? Yes. For everyone else, I assure you that our beds are clean and comfortable."

The others laugh at her remark, and Leor says, "There is no other inn I would rather stay at tonight."

They gather their horses and head back through the dark forest. Myria estimates that dawn is only a short few hours away. She would get at least two hours of sleep before needing to start breakfast for the inn. Grandma Iris would probably disapprove, but this would not be the shortest night's sleep she has ever had.

When they return to the Morning Glory, Myria gives them directions to the available rooms upstairs as she checks on the horses one last time. As the men enter, Geffrey exclaims, "I cannot believe we are actually roughing it here, and without even a fresh change of clothes."

Aryn grunts in response.

It isn't until Myria settles the horses and heads back out toward the stable gate that she realizes she is not alone. Leor lingers outside, a hand scratching the nape of his neck as he seems to search for the right words among the packed dirt ground.

"Leor?" she says, her voice trembling, before correcting herself. "Or, I'm sorry, Prince Leor? Your Majesty?"

"I prefer just Leor, if it is all the same to you," he chuckles, still staring at the ground, but now fiddling with the hem of his sleeve.

"Okay, Just Leor." She laughs. "Is there something on your mind?"

He hesitates, opens his mouth, stops, and then starts again. "Myria, at the risk of sounding like your cousin, tonight has been undoubtedly splendid. I am sorry again if it appears I deceived you. I find it refreshing to go out in anonymity, where others do not know I am the prince. People treat me differently that way. Yet, spending this evening with you has been the most magical, the most *fun* I have had in a long time. It felt nice actually to *live* for once."

Myria shrugs and a smile tugs at her face. "You didn't need me for that. Not many get to meet a minotaur."

Leor laughs, but it's strained. "Believe me, it was not just the minotaur. Tomorrow, I will go back to being the prince of Avalion. I will choose a woman to be my wife by the end of the summer."

Something unfamiliar knots in Myria's belly and her breath catches in her throat. She gulps down a mouthful of air, holds it a moment, then says, "That sounds like you have a pretty big decision to make. I don't know if I could handle that."

"On the contrary," Leor disagrees. "You seem pretty fearless to me. You know exactly who you are and what decisions you are going to make. I... admire that about you."

"Admire?" she repeats, looking away into the distance as a heat rises in her cheeks.

Leor looks into her eyes and takes a step forward. "If you could have anything you wanted, what would it be? What do you want out of life?" He leans in, lowering his face inches from hers. "What drives you every day?"

It is such an intense, personal question, one that she is in no way prepared for. Myria stutters as his eyes bore into hers, his breath hot on her cheek. She looks down and fumbles through her words as she works out an answer that can compare to the levity of his questions.

"Right now, it's just the inn with my grandmother. It's the only thing I've ever known, and she's been the only one who has been there for me my entire life. I've never thought of anything different for myself, but I suppose I enjoy seeking out the small adventures every day. Like with the minotaur."

Leor smiles, and Myria breathes a sigh of relief that he seems satisfied with her answer. "I wish I could be more like you and have the freedom to do what I wanted."

Myria arches an eyebrow. "You're the prince. Surely you can do whatever it is you want?"

"There are privileges, of course, but I am duty-bound to put Avalion first. The needs of the kingdom come before my own, and so there are choices I am not free to make."

"Well, tonight—right now—you are far from the Ilona palace. You are Just Leor, so what does Just Leor want right now?" Myria asks, flashing him a smile.

"Right now, I would only ask for the perfect end to an unforgettable evening with you." He leans closer, posing an invitation.

Feeling emboldened, Myria stretches on her toes and presses her lips to Leor's. He smiles against her mouth as his hands cradle her face gently. When she pulls away, he touches his forehead to hers.

"And once more, you surprise me by being absolutely perfect."

Myria's grin is wide as she decides not to argue with him. "You should head back inside. I'm sure Just Leor needs his sleep."

Leor does as she instructs, and she hurries to shut the gate and extinguish the outside lantern hanging by the door. Finally, she heads back into the inn through the kitchen door and locks it behind her. Inside, the inn is completely dark, so Myria feels her way through the kitchen, heading for her room.

She stops at the bottom of the staircase when voices drift down from the corridor above. Pausing, she strains to listen, recognizing Geffrey and Emiri speaking just outside their doors.

"So, what do you think of Myria?" Geffrey probes eagerly. "She seems to get along pretty well with Leor."

For a strange, inexplicable reason, Myria holds her breath; her heart thrumming as she waits for his answer.

To her surprise, Emiri sounds curt, impatient. "She's just another dirty barmaid, right? She's probably waiting to take advantage of him."

Her chest steels itself and blood thunders through her ears, drowning out any response Geffrey might have. She tries to make sense of Emiri's words, thinking back to their brief exchange in the forest and wondering how she had given him such a poor impression. The exhilaration of kissing Leor wholly vanishes as an unfamiliar heat rises to her face. She forces herself to breathe evenly through her nose before sneaking back toward the kitchen.

Once there, she slams the door, signaling her presence, and stomps upstairs. The noise does its job, because by the time she reaches the second floor, it is empty. She takes refuge in her room, locking the door behind her before throwing herself on her mattress. To her dismay, the night passes without much sleep as thoughts of Leor and Emiri plague her mind.

2

COSTUME

IN ALL HER YEARS of childish daydreaming, Myria never imagined herself kissing a prince. The actual event proved blissful as she remembers: The feel of Leor's lips on hers, his hands on her face. She shared plenty of other kisses before, but there was something about kissing a prince, about kissing *Leor*, that was different. He is charming, reserved, and respectful.

The whole moment of euphoria was only marred after overhearing Emiri. *A dirty barmaid? Taking advantage of Leor?* That is not her. At least the second part isn't. She would never take advantage of anyone. Perhaps she took advantage of his kindness when she kissed him? Misreading the moment as something else?

Myria pushes out of bed to examine herself in the mirror. Dirt and grease smudge all over her clothes, and her hair is tied up in a tangled mess. To quickly remedy her reflection, she splashes her face with the ice cold water from the washbasin and scrubs herself with the nearby bar of lye soap. She does not stop until bright red splotches cover her entire body. Untying her hair and brushing out the harried tangles does not improve its wild and untamed appearance. With little recourse, she twists it into a long, tight braid before changing into a dark green dress, as opposed to her usual choice of pants. Then she returns to her reflection for a new inspection.

It is a considerable improvement, but Myria cannot help but still feel lackluster. *Inadequate.* The dress is one of the nicest things she owns. But even then, it does not compare to the likes of nobles, or a *prince*. Her face is clean, but pink from furious scouring.

For a moment, Myria hides her face in her hands. She rarely obsesses over her appearance. The romantic moment she shared with Prince Leor is long gone. She never expected to pursue that fantasy with him. Besides, Leor was not the one to call her a *dirty barmaid*. Why should Emiri's words mean so much to her?

Myria peeks through her fingers at her reflection again. Green eyes as bright as forest leaves stare back sheepishly. Emiri is a commoner, like herself. Perhaps that is why his opinion cuts deeper. She cannot imagine how she gave such a negative impression after their shared moment, but maybe she crossed an unintended boundary when she took his hand last night.

Whatever the case, it all matters little now. The prince and his friends will leave the Morning Glory and head back to their lives at the palace. More than likely, she will never see them again—except perhaps Geffrey. Life will go on at the Morning Glory, as it always does.

With that comforting—if desolate—thought, Myria heads downstairs. When she gets there, she sees Grandma Iris sitting across from Geffrey at a table. Myria puzzles at the strange sight, unable to recall when Geffrey and Grandma Iris have ever spoken to each other. Any previous meetings of theirs was eclipsed by the disagreements with her aunt and uncle. Even Grandma Iris quietly sitting while the morning chores await is an anomaly.

"Good morning," Myria says. She tries to sound cheery, but trepidation sneaks a subtle tremor into her voice. "I didn't expect to see you up so early, Geffrey."

He grins at her, a grin not unlike the one Myria remembers from their childhood. "Yes, the others have already returned for the palace. I wanted to spend some time with my family before I followed."

Something strange pricks at Myria's throat when she hears that Prince Leor and the others have already gone. "It's a shame I didn't get to say goodbye," she sighs, looking away for a distraction.

Grandma Iris clears her throat, drawing Myria's attention. "Your cousin wants to ask you something," Iris says. "He's just too polite to get to the point."

Myria meets her cousin's eyes with a raised eyebrow.

"Yes. Thank you, Grandma," he falters.

Grandma Iris sighs and rolls her eyes. "I'm not *your* grandmother."

"Yes, of course. Forgive my mistake—"

"Geffrey," Myria prods. "Your point, please."

Geffrey clears his throat. "Do you remember what Leor said last night? He needs to pick a bride by summer's end. The entire process requires all the noble families to put forth an eligible lady for his consideration. It is a tremendous social event, full of festivities all summer long. We call it the Summer Courtship. In the end, the prince picks someone to be his wife and the future Queen of Avalion."

"An entire summer spent trying to impress the prince?" Myria chuckles. "That sounds fun."

Geffrey, apparently misreading her sarcasm, perks up at her words. "If you really believe so, you can join. My family—*our* family—has no other eligible lady to enter as a suitor. I have no sister or any other female cousin. I could sponsor you."

Myria's humor vanishes as she gapes at him. "You want me to marry Prince Leor?"

"Yes. At least, I want to give you that chance."

Myria is stunned, unable to form words. Finally, she manages in a sharp hiss, "*Why?*"

Geffrey is confused. "Why what?"

Words flood from her mouth. "Where to start? Why sponsor me? I'm not a noble. I've never been to the palace. I know *nothing* about that life—"

"We are related, that is noble enough, and I could help you, train you."

Myria points to her dress. "You see this? This is the nicest thing I own, and it's not fit for a palace of any kind."

"We have money. Part of sponsoring you is getting you all the best and beautiful gowns."

"Why *me*? Why would you even think the prince would pick a lowly, dirty barmaid like me to be the future queen of Avalion?"

Geffrey clicks his tongue and takes a sharp breath. "Oh, you heard that? I would not worry about what Emiri says. Nothing impresses him, ever."

"So, why do you think you've got a chance by sponsoring me as a suitor?"

"Leor likes you. The two of you got along pretty well last night, right?"

Myria tries to hide the blush rising to her cheeks at the thought of kissing Leor, but feels the warmth of it betray her. "So why are *you* doing this?" she hastily redirects. "What's in it for you?"

Geffrey's animated face falls. "I will be honest with you. Our house will benefit if he chooses you. Even if he does not, being in the prince's favor still helps us. Money, gifts, titles, and honors. The primary reason I ask? Leor was happy with you last night—the smile he had when he walked inside after talking to you. I know Leor is the prince, but he is also my friend. I would like him to have some semblance of happiness."

"What better way of getting to know him than at court?" Geffrey beams. "Sure, there will be other ladies vying for his attention, but you can really see him work in his natural environment. Besides, the Brambles—our family—can help you and your grandmother financially. You would not have to worry about running this tavern anymore."

Myria looks to her grandmother. "I don't know. I've lived here my entire life; I can't just leave."

"All the more reason to leave," Geffrey says. "We could travel all over the kingdom, visit the other noble families, go on fresh adventures—even meet new minotaurs."

Myria feels the critical gaze of her grandmother, but refuses to meet it. Then she asks, "But why should *I* agree to this? Leor is nice and charming, but I don't know if I want to *marry* him. I can't just leave my grandmother to run the Morning Glory by herself."

Before Myria can say anything else, Grandma Iris interrupts. "What about magic? Can someone teach her magic if she goes?"

"Grandma!" she protests.

"Of course. I could teach her myself, even." Geffrey hesitates, apparently considering the offer. "Actually, it would be best to find her a better teacher, but it *can* be done."

Grandma Iris fixes her stern eyes on Myria. "The choice is yours, my sunflower. But I think you should go."

Myria is stunned. Her grandmother never pushes her to do anything, much less leave the Morning Glory. "Why?"

Grandma Iris turns to Geffrey. "Would you give us a minute to talk privately?"

Geffrey nods and nearly stumbles over his own feet as he hurries outside. Grandma Iris pats the seat next to her, and Myria sits down slowly, her eyes trained on her grandmother.

"You want me to marry the prince? I thought you hated the nobility."

"When you asked about your mother last night, I realized I kept many things from you, whether or not that was my intention. Your mother was indeed a member of House Bramble, and she abandoned her station to marry my son. She displeased many with this decision since she was already engaged to marry someone else. When Geffrey's parents came to take you away, I wouldn't let them. I thought I was protecting you. Your mother told many stories about how dangerous the nobility could be, so I never trusted them. I still don't, and I don't think you should either. *But...*"

Grandma Iris pauses as her voice cracks with obvious pain. Myria reaches for her hand and folds it between her own.

"But I realized last night that I've not done you any favors. A tavern is no place to raise a little girl. Despite this, you have grown up to be a strong, resourceful, and generous person. I should have done better for you, and I would be foolish to let this opportunity slip by. You should not bind your future to this tavern just because I am here. You should pursue a life that makes you happy. You don't have to marry the prince or join the nobility. But I know how much magic fascinates you, and this is a chance for you to pursue it. You shouldn't have to worry about the Morning Glory staying in business."

Myria's nose stings and her eyes burn. She tries to rub the sensations away with the back of her hand. "I don't want to leave you alone here. You're the only one who's ever been there for me. How can you run the inn on your own?"

Grandma Iris smiles, stretching the minuscule creases in her cheeks. "You should try being there for yourself for a change. And if your cousin is true to his word, I might have enough money to take on some hired hands. Don't worry about me, sunflower."

"Are you sure?" Myria asks, her throat dry. "You must promise me you'll tell me, or write to me, if you need me to come back."

Grandma Iris chuckles briefly before turning grave again. "Only if you promise me something in return. Don't let your guard down around *any* of those nobles, not even the charming prince or your cousin. Those types of people only care about themselves, and they'll just as soon put your neck on the line if it protects them."

Myria nods. "I promise to be careful, then."

"And keep up your mother's heritage. Do *not* marry someone you don't want to. Here..." Grandma Iris reaches into the folds of her dress, pulls out of a gold chain with a pendant, and hands it to Myria. "This was your mother's. Someone at court gave it to her, I think. It has her name engraved on the back."

Myria examines the necklace, a sprawling sun icon on one side. Flipping it, she sees the name *Callia Bramble*. She puts it on and stuffs the pendant inside her dress. "Thank you, Grandmother."

She leans close and gives Grandma Iris a tight squeeze before going to alert Geffrey of the good news.

Her cousin whoops with glee for several minutes before informing her they need to leave as soon as possible. The first event of the Summer Courtship is a masquerade that very night, and they still needed time to outfit her costume. Geffrey assures her she does not need much in the way of clothing, so Myria packs only a few personal items. She bids her grandmother one final farewell before riding away on Jadis, a stunning black mare and the first of Geffrey's gifts to her, toward the city of Ilona, and the palace.

Geffrey uses the time to drill her on the customs of noble life, such as addressing others and the royals, and proper titles for each duke, duchess, lady, and lord. He gives a quick rundown on how to curtsy properly, when to curtsy, who she should curtsy to. Myria does her best to focus on the nuanced details. The names are difficult to grasp without faces to attach to them.

After some time, Geffrey sees her attention waning and chuckles nervously. "Nothing you cannot handle. The most difficult bit will be the formal dances you have not learned... and potentially dealing with Olympe."

The name strikes recognition for Myria, but she can't quite remember how. "Who's Olympe?"

Geff's smile is too wide and toothy to be reassuring. "My mother."

The few memories Myria has of Geffrey's mother are fleeting images of her arguing with Grandma Iris. She cannot remember her face precisely, much less what she sounds like or what sort of person she is. "Why will meeting your mother be difficult?" she asks, then realizes, "She won't approve of me, will she?"

"Nonsense," Geff blurts out. "Mother always wanted to bring you into the family. She has only... lost some of her humor since my father passed away."

"Oh, Geff, I'm sorry to hear that. How long has it been?"

"Enough years have passed where the mention of his name no longer gives me sting." Geffrey glances at her before laughing at her concerned face. "Smooth your face over. Mother is not bad. She remains opinionated and honest, especially honest about her opinions, which can make her seem a bit... insensitive."

"Right."

"If you have lived with your cold grandmother all this time, I am certain my mother will seem the angel."

Myria frowns. "My grandmother isn't that bad."

"To *you*, but she clearly hates me."

"If she hated you, she wouldn't have encouraged me to go with you. She would have been against it altogether."

Her cousin spends the last hour of the ride speaking about his family and reminiscing about his late father. Geffrey assumed the title of Duke Bramble when he was only a teenager. The Bramble duchy is the largest expanse of land on the map, rivaled only by the immense Kinggrove of Runewell. Unlike the dense forest to the west, Bramble lands boast of numerous farmers and fields that provide the bulk of the food—grain, vegetables, and livestock—that sustains the entire kingdom. Counts acting as vassals on his behalf often report common problems with drought, pestilence, and other issues of production to Geffrey. As he describes the duties and expectations, there is a note of uncertainty in his voice that instantly clears once they are in sight of Ilona.

The massive capital city of Avalion sprawls before them, with the royal palace of polished white stone at its center; surrounded by sparkling fountains, luxurious gardens, and manicured lawns. The curtain walls of the city loom over Myria and Geffrey as they approach the main gate. Two guards flanking the portal step forward to meet them, but seem to recognize Geffrey and respond with some hasty "M'lord"s and stiff bows.

After passing through the gate, the two make their way through the market streets. Smells of baking bread and cooked meat fill Myria's nostrils, reminding her she has not eaten yet today. She clutches at her stomach as it rumbles. As Geffrey leads the way to the palace gates, many recognize his noble stature and part ways for him before whispering at the sight of Myria. Even here, amidst the common folk of the city, she feels out-of-place with her rustic dress. Myria looks away from them and focuses on keeping close to Geffrey.

After passing through the palace gates, their horses follow along the paved stone path until they enter a large courtyard in front of the palace. Trees surround the courtyard, with a circular fountain at the center. The remainder of the space is paved with the same cut stones as the path, broken here and there by marble planters brimming with flowering plants. Myria is assaulted by the pollen and scents, reminding her of a time she spilled a vial of perfume she found tucked away in Grandmother Iris's room.

As they dismount, attendants suddenly appear to take their horses. Geffrey asks one of them to notify his mother that he's arrived.

"What do you think?" Geffrey asks when he catches her staring at their grand surroundings.

"It's all very... big," she says finally. "Do you live here?"

Geff laughs. "No, the official House Bramble residence is an estate called Fairthorne, not far from your town of Everhaven. This is the royal palace, where the king, queen, and *prince* live. The entire court will stay here during the summer as well, including us." He leads her through the massive, polished wooden doors into a wide entrance hall lined with elegant paintings and gleaming statuary. The clicking of Geffrey's riding boots on the marble floor echoes from the vaulted ceiling above them as Myria stares at the artwork punctuating the walls, many of them royal portraits of past kings and queens.

Geffrey heads for the grand marble staircase in the center of the room, and Myria rushes to catch up as he explains, "The royal family lives in the east wing, and all the guests stay in the west wing. All the suitors, including you, will be staying there. House Bramble has its own suite."

They climb the flight of stairs, taking the left corridor toward the west wing. The hall stretches to an enormous length, dotted with multiple doors. Geffrey leads her almost to the end of the hall before opening a door on the left.

It opens up to a cozy sitting area with a fireplace on one side of the room and large glass windows overlooking the lawn on the opposite wall. Four new doors connect to the sitting area, which Myria suspects are the bedrooms.

"Mother," Geffrey calls, closing the door behind him. He crosses the room to a table where an abandoned decanter of wine sits. He picks it up, weighing it in his hands. "It is still pretty full, so she must be close." He gives a strained smile at his attempt at humor.

"Does your mother drink during the day often?" Myria asks.

Geff doesn't answer as he approaches a bedroom door closest to the fireplace and knocks.

"Mother? Someone is here to meet you."

A confident, alto voice belts out from behind the door. "The masquerade is tonight—*tonight*, Geffrey. Sunlight still mocks me through this window, which means I am not socially obligated to talk to anyone for hours yet."

"Good news," Geffrey announces in his cheeriest of voices. "House Bramble has our suitor."

There is a pause, followed by, "And who would be addled enough to agree to that?"

"Mother, do not be so sour," Geffrey snaps. "Come. Officially meet your niece, Myria."

There is shuffling on the other side of the door, then Olympe Bramble steps out of the bedroom in her full glory. She is tall, taller than Myria even. Her face is long and narrow with high cheekbones, and her golden hair is tied back from her face. She leans against the doorframe, studying Myria with severe eyes, swirling a goblet of what Myria assumes to be wine.

"Myria," she repeats with a sigh. "Myria, Myria, *Myria*. Hawthorne, is it? It has been a long time. You look almost exactly like your mother."

"Thank you," Myria mumbles under the scrutiny. "Aunt Olympe?"

"Please, spare me the family courtesies. My name is Olympe so I expect you to call me as such. My formal address is *Dowager Duchess* Bramble. However, if I hear you calling me such a thing, I will take great pleasure in ripping your eyelashes off of your eyelids. I do hate the sound of it, as if I were some sort of old crone. Lady Bramble will suffice otherwise."

Olympe turns to scrutinize her son.

"And *why* did you convince this unfortunate girl to work for us? Do you think the prince is going to pick a commoner? Our presence here is humiliation enough without keeping abreast of the harpies. Do you believe she is cutthroat enough to make it here?"

Myria frowns. "Olympe, I'm right here. I can hear you."

"Oh, I am sorry, Myria. I did not intend to exclude you from this conversation." Sarcasm flows from Olympe's lips as surely as the wine flows into them as she pauses to take a sip from her goblet. "Do *you* think the prince is going to pick you, a commoner, over a noble lady who has perfected her poison since the cradle?" Olympe's tone is flat and unimpressed. Oddly enough, Myria finds something humorous in it.

Geffrey is not dissuaded. "All the more reason my plan is going to work. Prince Leor cares not for all the politics and deception everyone is so fond of here at court. He values the genuine, and wants something *real*. Myria is best for that. Besides, we have already got an edge." He wags his eyebrows at his mother, as if hiding a great surprise.

"Go on," Olympe says, more bored than impatient. "Keep us not in suspense."

Geff leans close to Olympe and whispers, "Prince Leor has already kissed our dear Myria here."

Heat floods Myria's face. "Geff!" she hisses. "How do you even know about that?"

He turns to her and says, "I apologize. It is possible I was spying on you last night."

Olympe suddenly seems intrigued as she blinks at Myria. "Is this true, then? Have you already kissed the prince? No need to be shy about it now. Soon the prince's romances will be public affairs, anyway."

Myria's cheeks continue to burn and her glare locks on Geff as she nods. "Yes, Geffrey's right."

Olympe takes a long draft of her wine, sets the goblet down, and claps her hands together. "What good news. Who knew House Bramble could have a secret advantage up our sleeve? I doubt it will be enough to win his hand in marriage, but what the hell? Why not give it a real shot?"

She hurries across the room and opens the door nearest the window. "Welcome to House Bramble, my dear. I will not promise you anything except this lovely bedroom in our royal suite. I assume you are not hiding a costume in your bag?"

"Costume?" Myria repeats. Then it strikes her: the masquerade. In all the excitement, she forgot it is tonight.

"I cannot say I am surprised. Go in and undress. We have no time for a new fitting, but I will see to the details to avod as much embarrassment for our house as we can tonight. In the meantime, someone will bring in some hot water for a bath."

"I've already washed," Myria insists.

Olympe studies Myria from head to toe before laughing. "Of course you have. I shall be right back."

As soon as Olympe storms off, Myria turns toward the newly-opened room. The interior is bright, with the light of the afternoon sun streaming through the large window. An immense, canopied bed sits in the middle of the room, surrounded by an array of rich, dark furniture; including a desk, a chair, and a large wooden chest at the foot of the bed. Another fireplace adorns the wall opposite the bed. Myria marvels at the polished marble and gilded inlays of the mantle.

She doesn't have long to gawk, as a servant knocks before bustling in to help her undress. More attendants file in the room, dragging a large wooden tub into the middle of the bedroom.

"I don't think that's necessary," Myria says, but her protests are ignored as the attendants pour steaming jugs of water into the tub. They make quick work of her dress before discarding it on the floor, along with her shoes and undergarments. Then, Myria is unceremoniously plunged into the bathwater.

It is a new, though not unwelcome experience as she crouches low in the water, her hair swirling about her in long tendrils. She thinks she might soak in the warm water for hours, but the servants waste no time before scrubbing every inch of her scalp and body with soft, sable brushes and lavender soap. Then she's pulled out again, and the tub is drained and dragged away as she's dried with wool towels. By the time Olympe enters the room, they are adorning her in a shapeless chemise that falls to her knees and a maidservant is ruthlessly brushing out her hair. Myria's knuckles are white as she grips the bedpost to keep from falling over every time the brush catches a knot, and grits her teeth to keep from crying out in pain.

"You look and smell quite the improvement. I expect everything was to your liking, was it?" Olympe asks, though Myria doesn't think she expects an answer.

She turns to see the older woman draping several dresses across the mattress. A seamstress waits behind her, arms full of multicolored fabrics.

"Tonight is the costume masquerade. An elaborate costume is not necessary as long as we have enough details to promote the general idea. Since Geffrey could not find you sooner, you will be wearing an altered gown of mine."

As the maidservant ends her torture session and pins Myria's hair to the back of her head, she says "I'm sure that anything you have will be far more beautiful than anything I've ever owned."

Olympe chuckles before raising her voice to call to the other room. "Geffrey, get in here. Myria is decent enough to be seen by her cousin, and we could use your input."

Geffrey slides into the room, focusing on the dresses his mother indicates. "Yes, I think the first thing we should focus on is what color we want to present her in. Something bold, either on the light or dark side, like white or red."

"Why is my wardrobe a committee decision?" Myria asks, her stomach turning as they critically analyze Myria's frame against the dresses displayed before them.

"Is that a serious question?" Olympe asks, frowning at her choices. "As your first introduction to court, you will need to make a grand impression. Everyone will be there—the prince, king, queen, and all the other ladies vying for the royal attention. They will make statements with their attire, and you should be no different."

"Didn't Geffrey say Prince Leor doesn't care about the politics?" Myria complains.

Olympe's gaze bores into Myria's face, and it takes everything in her to not shrink. "You should still maintain a certain appearance. If you want to win, you've got to prove yourself not just to the prince, but to the king, queen, and the entire court. And despite all his niceties, the prince is still a *man*. He doesn't always think with his head."

Myria sighs, yielding to Olympe's logic.

Olympe smirks. "How perceptive of you. Now, I *love* the red or white suggestion. Red gets the blood racing, passion and flames. White evokes innocence; I imagine feathers and gold. The question is, which would the prince prefer?"

"A red nymph?" Geff muses with a devilish grin. "It would attract attention. Plus, red is the color of lust. Make it seductive, like any man's fantasy."

Olympe frowns. "We need *Leor's* fantasy here, not yours. Counter idea—we make her look like an angel. Leor is sweet; angels are sweet. Besides, if we dress her up in white, it gives the prince a glimpse of how beautiful she would look in a wedding dress."

"What do you think, Myria?" Geff asks. "What would he prefer?"

"Need I remind both of you that I've only had a handful of conversations with him?" Myria asks, her stomach continuing to turn as she contemplates the massive endeavor before her.

"Yes, but you are the only one in this room that has kissed him," Geff points out with a smirk.

She sighs, unable to counter the point, then crosses the room to look at the dresses. The red one looks tight, like a sheath, while the white one seems less restrictive, flowy, and more comfortable.

"I choose white."

Olympe rejoices at the decision with a victorious laugh before Myria is shoved into the gown and instructed to stand absolutely still by the window so that the seamstress can do her work. Of course, a corset accompanies the outfit, and when secured tightly around her frame, it proves immensely uncomfortable. It holds her body upright, constricting around her like a vise, completely negating the desire for comfort that guided her choice of the white dress.

Noticing Myria's exhaustion, Olympe instructs Geffrey to retrieve water and bread for her. By the time he returns, the dress is hemmed to fit Myria's height and Olympe discusses alterations with the seamstress to make the gown unique. They talk of gold and crystal embellishments, replacing the sleeves with loose straps, and possible feathers to attach to the accompanying mask. Myria contributes nothing to the conversation as she nibbles on her bread, trusting Olympe's judgment in these matters better than her own. Even Geffrey's input seems to be disregarded at this point, and while his mother is distracted, he slips out to make his own preparations.

The sun sinks below the horizon by the time the seamstress finishes the dress to Olympe's satisfaction. A sudden terror grips Myria. She turns to Olympe and says, "Geffrey said someone would teach me to dance before the masquerade."

Olympe clucks her tongue. "Do not fret, child. You need only follow your partner's lead. Now, take a look." With this, her aunt fastens the mask over her face and gestures to a tall, wood-framed mirror in the corner of the room.

The dress is magnificent beyond anything in Myria's imagination. Gossamer, white tulle makes up the skirt, giving it a light and breezy feel as it whispers about her feet like a magical cloud. The bodice is lined with sparkling crystal embellishments, and the silk sleeves are cut to expose her shoulders, draping down to her elbows. The mask covers the upper half of her face in a beaded and feathery swath that curves and swirls around her eyes.

Perhaps the most astonishing transformation for Myria is how her aunt's servants tamed her once-unruly hair into long, soft waves curling to the center of her back. Any lingering strands are pinned away from her face to accommodate the ornate mask. The only remaining vestige of her previous life is her mother's pendant, which hangs from her neck. In the mirror's corner, above her shoulder, Olympe looks on with a smug, self-satisfied grin.

"Let us show your cousin," she suggests. Olympe's voice and eyes betray her eagerness. As Myria gazes at her aunt's reflection, she realizes her own transformation is mirrored in Olympe's demeanor. The coarse, bitter old dowager seemed to be replaced by an excited, doting matriarch.

Myria follows Olympe into the sitting area, where Geffrey waits in tight black pants, flowing white shirt, black velvet jacket with gold brocade, and matching silk mask. His mouth hangs open in shock.

"At least, Myria is appropriately dressed," he blurts out. "What about *you*, Mother?"

Olympe waves off his concerns. "My dress is waiting for me in my room. You two go on ahead. Your entrance is *far* more important. Go prepare her for the vipers."

Geffrey leans closer to Olympe, locking her eyes in a commanding glare. "You *are* coming, right?"

She grows impatient. "Believe me, I have more intention to attend now than I did this morning. Hurry!"

Myria takes Geff's offered elbow and he leads them down the expansive corridors toward the ballroom. Already she can sense a difference from her arrival that morning as voices drift upstairs from the event below. People now fill the palace.

"What do you think?" Geff asks. "Mother is not so bad, is she?"

"No," Myria agrees. "I quite like her."

"What about all this?" he waves his hand around them as they march down the corridor. "The masquerade, the palace? I know this is quite a change from the inn."

"Yes, it is quite a bit to take in. The other suitors aren't all terrible, are they?"

Geff clears his throat and fumbles with his collar, pulling it away from his neck as if it were suddenly choking him. "Don't worry. You're a barmaid; you can make friends easily. Besides, your focus tonight will be Prince Leor. Seeing you again ought to be a delightful surprise for him."

"He doesn't know I'm here?" Myria asks, wondering if she should panic.

Geffrey, undaunted, merely grins. "No. Everything was rather last minute." Without further hesitation, he guides her down the grand staircase.

The entrance hall fills with a sea of nobles dressed in all sorts of regalia, a rainbow of colors with masks of various sizes, textures, and decorations. Myria picks out a few costume themes from the ladies, such as an ocean-blue gown and a fire-red one. She doesn't see another woman in white, which seems to earn her some curious gazes. Myria grips Geff's arm even tighter, and he pats her hand in response.

The nobles line the hall outside the grand ballroom. Myria waits her turn to be heralded in alongside her cousin.

"This is your first meeting with the royal family. All the suitors will have a brief introduction with Leor. Your objective is to dance with him, find a moment alone with him. Secure as much time with Leor as you can. Everyone else will be trying to do the same."

"How many suitors are there?" Myria asks, looking around.

"Including you, there should be at least six, one for each of the duchies."

Geffrey leaves momentarily to inform the herald of their titles. The lady in front of them waits alone. She looks back to wish Myria a shy word of good luck.

Myria thanks her, admiring her lilac dress decorated with a multitude of pink florals. "Your dress is beautiful," she adds.

The lady smiles at her before proceeding into the ballroom with an announcement of, "Lady Eulalia Runewell of Oakhaven."

Geffrey returns in time to lead Myria inside.
"Duke Bramble and Lady Myria Hawthorne of Fairthorne."

3

DANCE

THE BALLROOM IS MUCH larger than any room Myria has ever been in. The tiled floor gleams beneath the chandeliers, and the ceiling reaches to a two-story height with tall windows revealing the evening sky. Tables line the far wall, laden with an array of foods and drinks unfamiliar to her. But the mass of swirling gowns sweeping that polished floor overwhelms Myria the most. She has never seen so many people gathered in one place.

"Duke Bramble and Lady Myria Hawthorn of Fairthorne."

Geffrey leads her, stunned, to a new line. When Myria cranes her neck, she can spot Leor through the throng of ladies in front of her. The sight of him makes her cold cheeks flush. He remains as stunning as he was last night at the stables, his smile polite and blinding for the suitor in front of him. His crimson jacket and its silver threading are much more regal than the plain silk one he wore at the Morning Glory. Myria does not understand how she ever mistook him for anyone other than a prince.

After a few minutes, the line shrinks, and it is Geffrey steps forward to introduce Myria to the prince.

Leor recognizes Geffrey easily enough. His shoulders relax and his voice adopts an eager pitch. "Geff! I am pleased to see you this night. My father speculated if House Bramble would secure a suitor for the Summer Courtship. Please, introduce me to the lovely woman accompanying you."

The prince turns his warm gaze to Myria, and it chases away some of the anxiety burrowing in her stomach. His eyes, his expression... He has the blinding light of a fallen star, and it is an endeavor to not burn up in his fiery corona as he brushes his lips against her knuckles. Attempting to match some of that brightness, she smiles, stretching her lips to flash teeth. "Don't you remember?" she teases. "I might have been another passing commoner, but surely the minotaur was at least a bit more memorable."

Recognition passes through Leor's face, his plastered demeanor falling away like a mask. His grin returns, more genuine as he leans closer to her. The formality in his voice gives way to surprise. "Myria? Is that really you?"

She curtsies in response. "The very same."

"I feared I would never see you again, but I am grateful to be mistaken. Why do I owe this delight?"

Myria falters as Emiri's words flash through her mind, ringing with some level of accuracy as she remembers the deal she made with her cousin. *I'm here to help Grandma Iris; I'm here to finally learn magic.* She doesn't want to think about taking advantage of anyone, and it makes her feel ashamed. She maintains her smile, holding on to how Leor sets her nerves at ease. It makes the lie easier. "Isn't it obvious? I'm here for you."

Leor's eyes soften at the remark as he leans closer. "I wish we had more time to speak. For now, I must welcome the others. Your beauty surpasses them all, Lady Myria. Perhaps you could honor me with a dance later?"

When she nods, he kisses her hand again, much more intimate as he presses his lips to her palm. The next family's approach ends the moment and Myria cradles the hand as Geffrey steers her away.

"Excellent first impression," he praises. "Leor is happy to see you."

"Is that enough, though?" Myria asks, uncertainty welling to a lump in her throat as she looks at the group of other suitors.

"Yes, this is a brilliant start. Worry not, Mother and I will be here to help you for the rest of the summer. For now, use this time to acquaint yourself with the other suitors. Make some allies. I shall introduce you to the king and queen within the hour."

Myria scans the room and recognizes the floral gown of Lady Eulalia from just before they entered the ballroom. She is alone in the far corner with a crystal chalice of golden liquid. Myria approaches and curtsies in greeting. "Hello there, Lady Eulalia. I'm sorry I had little time to introduce myself earlier. My name is Myria."

Eulalia smiles, and despite the lavender mask covering most of her features, Myria can tell how beautiful she is. Her chestnut brown hair falls just below her shoulders, and kindness fills her dark, almond eyes. "How lovely to meet you so that I can return the favor. Your dress is divine and you may call me Eulalia. Is tonight your introduction to court?"

"Thank you. And yes, it is. Am I that obvious?" Myria asks.

Eulalia giggles. "Only because I have never seen you. However, my court appearances are also rather sparse at my parents' behest. They prefer me to stay home at Oakhaven, whiling away my hours with knitting like a spinster."

"What is Oakhaven like? I haven't traveled very much from my own home."

"My home is the white beacon in the Kinggrove, visible for miles out above the treetops," Eulalia drawls. Her eyes fall to the goblet in her hands as she considers her answer. "It can be difficult to compare to the castle here where we are not surrounded by forest."

"Are your parents here tonight?"

Eulalia laughs. "Not at all. They prefer not the social activity of the summer and have instead remained in their refuge at Oakhaven."

Myria turns to see the lady with the fire-red gown approaching them. Her gown shifts with each of her steps, shining with an iridescent material that mimics the movement of flames. Red ribbons tie up her black hair to frame her pointed features. Her lips pull back as she flashes her teeth, but given the sharp lines of the woman's face, Myria senses the gesture is more predatory than congenial.

"Lady Eulalia and Lady Myria, is it?" she greets with a nod. "Your costumes are almost comparable to mine but I should not be so hasty to share my good opinion. Allow me a formal introduction. You have the current privilege of gazing upon the illustrious Duchess of Dawnmourne; I am Cressida Nocturnus."

There is a pause, an expectation in her voice, and Myria quickly recalls from Geffrey's lessons how the duchess title outranks most. She follows Eulalia's lead and curtsies to Cressida. "It's a pleasure to meet you."

Cressida smirks. "May I steal a moment of Lady Myria's time?"

"Of course." Eulalia throws a warning glance toward Myria before disappearing into the crowd of dancers. It is all Myria needs to prepare herself for the moment alone with Cressida.

"You are new to court," Cressida says. "While I have never seen you among our circles, you were so familiar with the prince. You know each other."

Myria is unsure if she should withhold the details of her relationship with Leor or flaunt them to Cressida. She decides to proceed carefully with a mere confirmation. "Yes."

"As a charge of House Bramble, there are things you should know. I have great sway with the royal family. Because of this, I consider myself most fit to teach you these things

"Oh?" Myria waits to see what Cressida intends to share.

"All the other suitors here were born for this summer, groomed to be a potential queen for Prince Leor. I doubt someone like you has a similar experience. You should be practical and prepare yourself for the most likely outcome of this Summer Courtship."

"Which is?"

31

A muscle feathers in the duchess's cheek, as if stating such an obvious truth annoys her. "The prince will not pick some *newcomer*, an unknown variable, when he has all the political machinations of Avalion to contend with. A familiar face is not enough to be his future queen. Do not allow your hopes to rise, Lady Myria."

The words, while pragmatic, do little to hide Cressida's ambition. Myria flashes her most diplomatic smile, wondering how difficult politics can be if this duchess is so open with her thoughts. "Thank you very much for your concern, Duchess Cressida."

Cressida's expression twists at Myria's saccharine tone, perhaps frustrated she has not reached the desired effect. "I commend you, Lady Myria. You do not scare easily. Do not succumb to arrogance." The duchess turns away, disappearing onto the dance floor just as Geffrey materializes next to her.

"I see you have experienced the joy of meeting Cressida," he says. "What are your thoughts?"

Myria shrugs. "I can tell she likes to throw her power around to make a point. Not the scariest person I've ever encountered."

"Good to see you so composed about it. Keep that composure as I introduce you to the king and queen." Geffrey takes her elbow again and steers her to another receiving line in front of a raised platform.

"What do I say to them?" she whispers.

"Simple platitudes are best. This is a pleasant exchange; an introduction. A simple 'good evening, Your Majesties' will suffice."

Myria nods, keeping her firm grip on her cousin. The closest she ever came to the king and queen was seeing them through the tales of others. Some of the Morning Glory's patrons would mention getting a glimpse of them from a distance. They said King Uriel always exuded dignity as he stood still as a statue, wearing a frown that could have been chiseled from marble and just as silent. Beside him, Queen Eloria smiled and waved to the people, sometimes beckoning a chosen few forward to ask them how they fared.

As the line shortens, Myria gets her first good look at the royal couple in person. The king's black velvet jacket is trimmed at the shoulders with an elegant red cape that sweeps the floor. The heavy, jeweled crown sits upon his head as if it weighs nothing. Dark brown hair, streaked with silver, frames his broad face. Queen Eloria looks significantly younger than her husband, with only a few fine lines fanning from her eyes. She shares Leor's honey-colored hair, only hers is pinned into a tight bun beneath her crown. Her silver dress matches the streaks in the king's hair.

Myria swallows past a dry lump in her throat, forcing herself to relax. Geffrey doesn't seem intimidated. Surely, she could handle a few pleasantries.

"Ah, Geffrey," King Uriel says as they step nearer.

Myria is shocked to hear the king neglecting the formal title entirely. Perhaps her cousin's friendship with Leor affords him such familiarity.

The king continues in his baritone voice, "You are always a welcome sight at the palace. How does House Bramble fare?"

Geffrey seems to thrive under the royal flattery as he bows at the waist, bending low in an expression of humility despite the proud grin plastered on his face. Myria follows suit with an equally humble curtsy. His words are smooth as he gestures toward Myria. "Thank you, Your Grace. House Bramble soldiers on as always." He clears his throat. "Allow me this opportunity to introduce you to our suitor for the Summer Courtship—Lady Myria Hawthorne."

Myria seizes her opportunity, inclining her head at both monarchs before her, and repeats Geffrey's suggested line. "Good evening, Your Majesties."

King Uriel offers a polite smile. "I am glad to see House Bramble submit someone for my son's consideration. Might I inquire..."

King Uriel hesitates as his eyes catch something. Myria follows his gaze to her mother's pendant, the sun resting against her collarbone. She has an urge to hide it from him but knows he already recognizes it.

Queen Eloria nudges his shoulder. "Darling, is everything okay?"

King Uriel quickly recovers, straightening his shoulders. He rephrases whatever question he had been preparing. "Do you bear any relation to Callia Bramble?"

"Yes, Your Majesty. She was my mother," Myria answers.

A grim expression twists the king's face, but it vanishes so quickly Myria might have imagined it. The strong tenor of his voice suggests nothing is amiss. "Was? I am very sorry to hear of her passing. Welcome to court, Lady Myria. I look forward to learning more about you throughout the summer."

They bow again to the royal couple, then Geffrey steers them away.

Myria halts their steps, turning to pin Geffrey with narrowed eyes. "Does the king know my mother?"

Geffrey waves off her concerns. "Is that so surprising? Your mother and my father were young nobles when King Uriel ascended the throne. They were significant members of the court. It would be more nonsensical if they did not know each other."

"Geffrey, he recognized my pendant," she insists.

"And if she wore that pendant all the time, she would have been known for it."

Myria narrows her eyes. "You don't think the king was strange about anything just now?"

"Strange? No. He was cordial and diplomatic as always, personally welcoming you to court. We could not have hoped for a better outcome." Geffrey sighs in resignation when Myria's pointed glare does not waver. "Myria, your mother disappeared from court before I was even born. I would know not if something happened between them."

"Your mother might," Myria realizes, scanning the room for any sign of Olympe.

"Yes, go talk to her, but remember: Dance with the prince tonight."

Geffrey slips away as Myria spots Olympe drinking wine by the banquet tables. Her dress represents House Bramble through its gold and black silk, much like Geffrey's outfit, and her entire ensemble is topped off with enormous feathers sticking out of her hair that bounce with each step. Myria might have laughed at her if she wasn't concerned with finding out more about her mother's past.

"Ah, Myria," Olympe says as she approaches, eyes focused on the wine barrels nearby. "Have you been enjoying yourself? Met the king yet? How was your introduction to Leor?"

"The meeting with Leor went well, and Geffrey just introduced me to the king and queen."

Olympe sips from her goblet. "Good. You will need their support, their *confidence* if Leor dares the inconceivable by selecting you for his bride. However, I doubt you will have issue securing King Uriel's good favor."

"What do you mean?"

Olympe scowls at her empty glass and sets it on the table. "Do you not know? King Uriel was engaged to your mother for a brief time. They were quite besotted."

Myria's eyes widen. "That's how he recognized my mother's pendant."

Olympe frowns, looking at the necklace in question. "Of course he did. He gave it to her."

Myria struggles to form words for a moment. "My mother was engaged to the king?"

Olympe nods, then looks around before leaning in close. "Oh, yes. Twenty-five years ago, she went through this very same ordeal; the Summer Courtship. She won."

"And she ran away because she didn't want to marry him?"

Olympe shrugs, and her tone becomes dismissive, as if such details are unimportant. "I am not entirely privy as to why she ran away. I know your grandmother thinks it was to marry your father but Callia was happy to be with the king. Something happened." Olympe fixes Myria with a stern expression. "Do not become distracted. Those details are all in the past. Focus on *now*; focus on Leor. Have you danced with him yet?"

Myria can barely think about dancing with the prince. "You don't think the king would feel insulted by my presence?" she asks. "I'm the daughter of the woman he picked to marry, and who ultimately chose someone else. Would I not remind him of that rejection?"

"I do not believe King Uriel feels that way. As I said, he was very fond of your mother. Now, I hope you are ready to dance with Leor. He has his eyes set on you." Olympe inclines her head toward someone behind Myria, a quick bob of her frame to acknowledge their superiority.

Myria spins to find Prince Leor standing there. She curtsies in kind and struggles with a breath suddenly caught in her chest. "Prince Leor. What do I owe the pleasure?"

Leor lets slip a hint of a grin, but stands resolute. "I was hoping you would grace me with the next dance."

His kind, warm eyes suppress any thoughts of her mother's history for the moment. Myria smiles back, her stomach fluttering. "I would be happy to do so." Then in a whisper, she adds, "But so you realize, I have never danced like this before." Her eyes flit to the center of the ballroom, where couples spin in graceful circles around each other.

Leor chuckles, offering his hand. "Worry not. Follow my lead."

Myria doesn't hesitate before placing her hand in his. "Let's hope I don't make you look like a fool."

His eyes never leave her face, even as they step in the sea of swirling dancers. His expression leaves her no room to doubt his words. "You could never."

The next song begins with a slow melody as Leor positions her hands. Her heart hammers as he takes the first step, and she tries to mimic his movements. Her eyes drift to the floor, trained on his feet as she steps with him.

Leor whispers, "Ignore your feet. Look at me"

She drags her gaze up to meet him before allowing herself to relax against his arm around her waist.

"This may be the only moment we have tonight," he says, drawing her through the slow circles. "Forgive me if that is so. Realize your mere presence at court delights me without end."

"What a relief," she says. "I wasn't sure if this would be a pleasant surprise."

"'Pleasant' feels to inadequate a description." He raises his arm, and she flows through an effortless twirl underneath before returning to his embrace. "I hope you never regret the decision to come here."

"Why would I regret coming here?"

"I understand, better than most, the burden court is. Doubtless you will receive a less than warm welcome from others, but do not let those sycophants scare you away."

Myria laughs. "I've tamed a minotaur. I don't scare easily."

His grin grows broad. "I am pleased to hear it." His his eyes trail down to her mouth.

Myria's feels a flush rise to her cheeks as memories of the previous night jump to her mind.

"Last night seems so long ago," Leor sighs.

"I couldn't agree more," she says, her breath coming in short gasps as her heart flutters.

He looks away, his shoulders tensing with that grim line again. "Last night was a dream but it cannot happen again. There is no room for Just Leor here, only Prince Leor."

Myria is suddenly seized with the desire to ease that tension, to make him smile for her again. "Who says that?" she asks, lowering her voice as an idea forms in her mind. "What if we were to sneak out tonight for a few minutes?"

His eyebrows lift in surprise. "What did you have in mind?"

"You look like you could use a moment as *Just Leor* again," she says. "As the one who knows the palace best, you can pick the spot and time. I will meet you there."

He grins, and seems to not need further convincing. "The gardens behind the palace. There are some trees past the hedges where it is rather private. An hour after the masquerade."

Her stomach churns at the prospect of their secret rendezvous. "I will be there," she promises again, making a mental note to have Geffrey give her directions.

The song draws to an end, and they immediately separate as Leor resumes his princely formality. "It was a pleasure dancing with you, Lady Myria. Once more, you look breathtaking this evening."

Myria cannot feel disappointed as he steps to his next partner. Despite his obligation to court all the suitors, she feels confident in his interest in her. Perhaps Geffrey is right; Leor craves something *real*. Myria gives a small victory spin, her dress twisting about her as she looks for Geffrey to share the good news. She makes her way to the wine table, thinking she would at least find Olympe. Instead, there looms an unexpected, yet familiar figure.

Emiri stands alone, wearing no mask and the plainest jacket of all the guests. He watches the room of dancers with a blank expression, taking drinks from his vessel. The rush from her dance with Leor emboldens her as Emiri's insulting comments return to her mind. *Dirty barmaid, eh?* She arranges a smirk and approaches him.

When he sees her, the bored line of his brow, the perpetual frown all do not seem to recognize her. "My lady," he acknowledges with a stiff nod. He takes another drink and looks away.

Myria is not discouraged. "That's all you have to say to me? '*My lady*?'" she repeats dryly. "I suppose it can be difficult to recognize a dirty barmaid dressed like this."

First, his brow furrows in confusion, then lifts in slow realization. His eyes soon follow suit, growing wide in recognition, then in horror. "Myria?" he manages after struggling for a moment. "What are you doing here?"

Myria maintains a forced cheerful tone as she cites his own words again, "I'm not here to *take advantage* of the prince, if that's what you're wondering."

She relishes in his stammering, in the sudden flush to his cheeks. More sharp words rise to the tip of her tongue, eager to be unsheathed against him.

Before he can muster anything more than a few strangled syllables, Eulalia's timely arrival interrupts their exchange. Her eyes dart between them as she approaches. "Apologies for my intrusion. I wanted to introduce Lady Myria to some of the other ladies of the court."

Myria turns away from Emiri, still beaming. "No need to apologize. Please, lead the way."

Eulalia takes Myria by the hand, a strangely familiar gesture, and weaves her way through the crowd. "Did I interrupt something important?" she asks in a low voice.

Once they are at a safe distance, Myria glances back to gauge Emiri's reaction. Geffrey speaks to him now, his mouth and hands moving about, appearing oblivious to Emiri's speechless gaping. Myria's tense shoulders slacken in genuine relief as she turns back to Eulalia. "Honestly, it was great timing on your part. I didn't want to linger there for long."

"If that is truly the case, I am glad I could be of assistance." Eulalia clears her throat "You have already had the distinct pleasure of meeting Duchess Cressida, so I thought perhaps you might appreciate an introduction to other suitors who will not prove as... intense."

"Or intimidating?"

Eulalia snorts, her hand quickly rising to cover her mouth and stifle the sound. She continues weaving through the ballroom. "The duchess did not seem to intimidate you."

"That's the key, Lady Eulalia. Even if she does get to you, you can't let her see that."

"Reasonable advice." When Eulalia halts their movement, Myria finds herself facing three other noble ladies. "Everyone, this is Lady Myria from House

Bramble. Myria, allow me to introduce you to Lady Brigid Rosenford, Lady Sabine Valenrence, and Lady Theodora Stirling."

Each woman inclines their head as they are named.

Brigid wears the ocean-blue dress Myria saw earlier, her black hair decorated with seashells. The theme matches what Myria has heard of House Rosenford's control of the long coasts and extensive waterways of Northwestern Avalion.

Sabine's dress is dark purple, almost burgundy, with grapevine designs embossed on the skirt in shining gold thread, emulating a vineyard or wine theme. Amethysts drape her dark skin and hair along gold chains to demonstrate the wealth of her family. Myria remembers from Geff's tutelage that House Valenrence is relatively new to their title. They quickly rose to prominence after successful business ventures in developing meads and exporting vintages, despite their small holdings centered around the town of Honeyridge. The sharp gaze of Sabine's eyes suggests her family's ambition.

The last lady, Theodora, wears a magnificent gown. The black skirt drapes and swirls in a swath of crow feathers while the bodice is sheathed in an array of silver scales, reminiscent of armor that shimmers and glows in the lantern light. Myria assumes the nature of her costume from the sword-shaped pin securing Theodora's platinum hair from her pale face. Geffrey offered little information on House Stirling, other than they are an old, respected family with traditional opinions steeped in exclusivity.

"Lady Myria," Theodora says, her lips pressed into a thin, expressionless line. Her gray eyes travel down the length of Myria's body. "You are certainly the big mystery tonight. No one expected House Bramble to submit a suitor at all. How are you related to Duke Bramble?" Her voice is calm and polite, but calculated. From her posture, to her expression, to her words, she seems careful to reveal nothing of her own thoughts.

"Geffrey is my cousin," she explains.

"Why haven't we seen you at court before?" Sabine asks.

Myria pauses, wondering how much she should reveal. Her existence as a barmaid isn't exactly secret. "My mother left court before I was born."

Recognition flashes over Theodora's face for an instant. "Callia Bramble is your mother."

Brigid and Sabine whisper to each other. Myria forces a smile, wondering how much everyone knows of her mother. "I am."

"How charming to have a commoner among us," Theodora notes. "Did your family run a farm? Were they miners?" Theodora sounds little better than bored. She looks away, finding something on the far wall to hold her interest.

"No," Myria said, her face aching from the forced smile. "I was… an innkeeper." Myria believes innkeeper sounds more dignified than *barmaid*.

"I bet you met many adventuring ruffians," Brigid says with a giggle.

"Did you have to scrub floors and serve meals?" Sabine asks.

Myria's blood rushes in her ears as the music swells in dynamic. "Yes, to both."

"While that sounds like hard work," Theodora notes with a condescending frown, "I suspect those skills will not serve you here. The Summer Courtship demands the best of us in many areas, and if you are lacking, the social season can prove unforgiving. It seems unwise that Duke Bramble would wager his house's reputation on such a prospect, even to offer charity for a penniless cousin."

The words are casual and emotionless, but Myria does not miss the insult. She inclines her head, rising to the challenge. "I've never shied away from hard work, and I have more skills to offer than you may think."

Theodora's expression changes. She offers a thin smile, but her eyes sharpen as if they could spear right through her. "I am delighted to hear. I have no doubt Geffrey keeps you informed on the happenings. You must know all about the tournament tomorrow."

This news disarms Myria, and she isn't sure how to recover. She struggles for a moment, then manages to say, "I look forward to meeting you there."

Theodora's placid façade returns. "It has been a pleasure meeting you, Lady Myria. While this courtship pits all of us against each other, there is no reason to forget our manners." She looks away, then adds, "Excuse me, I see an opening to dance with the prince."

Theodora brushes past, barely making a sound. Brigid and Sabine eagerly shadow her heels.

Alone with Eulalia, Myria takes a moment to breathe deeply. "Well, that was exhausting."

Eulalia chuckles. "The Stirlings are all quite imperious, haughty, steadfast patrons of tradition, and Lady Theodora is no exception. I believe she and Cressida will be the biggest contenders for the courtship. Cressida is the more direct of the two, but Theodora possesses more tact."

"What about you?" Myria asks, turning to the one lady she feels might be a kindred spirit. "You're just as beautiful, if not more so than them, *and* you seem much kinder. Prince Leor likes such tenderness."

"It takes much more than beauty and kindness to be queen. You have to be fierce, which is not a quality with which I am familiar. However, I appreciate the compliments." She sighs, reaching a finger under her mask to scratch her nose. "It is refreshing to meet someone so veritable at court."

"Veritable?" Myria repeats.

"Yes. You say nice things as everyone else does, but it sounds like you *mean* the things you say."

"Of course I do," Myria says, surprised. "To be honest, I'm a terrible liar."

"You handled Theodora well enough," Eulalia points out. "You kept your smile the entire time."

"Well, that's not lying," Myria admits. "It comes with experience as an innkeeper. When you work in the service of others, you have to learn how to control your temper, even when others are terrible to you."

"That makes sense. Worry not about Theodora's words. Your experience prepares you enough for court."

Myria laughs, a little too loudly as some nobles look their way at the noise. She covers her mouth. "Thank you."

They retreat to the banquet table, selecting a few pastries to settle their hungry stomachs. Eulalia suggests a few of her favorites, and Myria savors the fruit preserves, sugar icing, and flaky crusts.

"Have you danced with the prince yet?" Myria asks after a few bites.

Suddenly, Eulalia's eyes cut to the side. "Not yet. I know he is busy this evening."

Myria turns to spot Prince Leor across the room finishing up a dance with Theodora. Sabine and Brigid wait eagerly on the fringe of the crowd to claim their time. "Don't be ridiculous. The night is about us. He could never be too busy for you."

Eulalia follows her gaze to the dance floor, and her brightness dims. "Brigid and Sabine are waiting their turn."

Myria takes Eulalia's hand and gives it a gentle, reassuring squeeze. "You said that a future queen has to be fierce, so here's your chance to practice. Don't be afraid to assert yourself. Cressida and Theodora definitely wouldn't hesitate."

Eulalia takes a shaky breath as Myria weaves them through the spinning crowd as the music diminuendos to silence. Myria watches as Theodora holds onto Leor's hand and whispers in his ear. Leor laughs in response.

The scene gnaws at Myria's stomach, but she continues forward, reaching the prince before Sabine.

Leor's eyes light up as she approaches. "Lady Myria? I did not expect to see you again so soon." His gaze locks on her, trailing the length of her frame.

Myria cannot help the sly grin that comes to her face. The unease vanishes from her stomach as she clears her throat. "Your Majesty, I'm sure you've already met

Lady Eulalia." Myria steps to the side to bring her new friend forward. "I do not believe you have danced with her yet."

Leor seems surprised, but smiles warmly at Eulalia all the same. "How kind of Lady Myria to introduce us again. Lady Eulalia, it would be my pleasure if you would grace me with a dance."

Eulalia transforms. Her nervousness disappears as she curtsies to the prince. Her hands flutter to grip her skirts and her chin dips demurely towards the floor. "The honor is mine."

The music starts again. Eulalia mouths a word of gratitude to Myria over her shoulder before Leor sweeps her away. Sabine's sharp eyes flash at Myria, her mouth set in a stormy frown.

An unfamiliar chuckle tickles Myria's ear. "Very clever, Lady Myria. Not many would introduce their new friend to the prince, but I see its advantages."

Starting, Myria whirls around to see Theodora smirking just behind her. "Clever?" Myria repeats, smoothing over her startled reaction. "I was only kind."

"Then allow me to show you a kindness in turn. I assume many faces in court remain unfamiliar to you. Allow me to introduce you to my brother."

There is a strange, eager look in Theodora's eyes that Myria cannot quite explain. She merely nods.

The Stirling suitor leads her away from the center dance floor, nearing the royal dais where the king and queen watch the festivities. A few nobles speak to them in low, amiable voices. Theodora reaches one wearing a blue velvet jacket and black breeches, his ebony hair tied into a ponytail. With his back to them, he does not notice their approach.

"Dear brother, allow me to introduce you to the newest member of the court."

The man turns, and something in Myria's stomach plummets as she recognizes Aryn, the fourth friend of Leor's party that she served at the Morning Glory. His one memorable quality was his lousy temper and obvious distaste for commoners.

However, he does not seem to recognize her as he bows and kisses her hand. "Good evening, my lady. I am Lord Aryn Stirling of Elmground."

"Lord Stirling, the pleasure is mine," Myria manages in a tight voice. She drops into a quick curtsy, avoiding his gaze.

"Lady Myria is the suitor from House Bramble," Theodora explains.

"Lady Myria?" he repeats. "A beautiful name for a beautiful lady."

The compliment is as hollow as the many others she's heard repeated throughout the night, more of a formality than a true impression.

Her body stiffens as she observes him, but Aryn continues as if he does not notice. "And why have I not seen you at court before now?"

Myria wonders if he is polite or if he has a faulty memory. No doubt Aryn would inform his sister later about Leor's exploits at Talking Tree Forest. And no doubt Theodora would use that information to her advantage.

"A cousin who is stranger to the court," Theodora shares before Myria can answer. "Lady Myria has been a commoner most of her life."

Through the obscurity of his mask, Aryn's congenial expression never changes. "You could never tell by how stunning she looks tonight."

Myria nods and says, "Thank you, my lord."

Theodora hurries off to speak to someone else.

"It was nice to meet you, Lord Stirling," she says quickly, not wanting to be left alone with him. "I should probably find Geffrey."

"Lady Myria, I must offer my sincerest apologies," he says before she can escape. His voice is low, quiet enough where no one can hear him.

"For what?" she asks.

"When we met last night, I did not act like the gentleman I am supposed to be. The ambition you have shown tonight deserves more than my ill-temper."

Myria takes a moment to consider him. His face is smooth, showing none of the anger he expressed last night. "I appreciate that," she says slowly, wondering if he is sincere.

He leans to whisper in her ear, his hand gripping her shoulder like a vice. "You clean up well for a commoner, but a pretty dress is not enough. You will have to do more to prove yourself to me." The icy words and the fingers pressing painfully into her skin betray his true contempt.

Myria draws back, glaring. "Excuse me, Lord Stirling," she says through clenched teeth. "But I am confident I have nothing to prove to *you*."

She turns and marches away, forcing the glare from her face as his laughter floats behind her.

She finally finds Geffrey again.

"Myria," he beams. "I saw your dance with the prince, and everything looked…" He stops and frowns. "What is it? Why do you look angry?"

She sighs, hiding her face in her hands for a moment before letting them fall to her sides. "I had the displeasure of meeting Aryn again."

"Aryn?"

"Theodora introduced us, and when she left, he said I have 'to do more to prove myself to him.' I don't have anything to prove to him, do I?"

Geffrey shakes his head. "Do not permit his words to trouble you. The Stirling family has always been prejudiced against commoners. Think of something happier, like—*oh*!" He claps his hands together enthusiastically. "I held up my end of the deal. You have a magic teacher now."

Myria's irritation evaporates and her face relaxes with the news. "When can I start?"

"Tomorrow morning," Geffrey says. "Very early. Your first lesson is at dawn."

"That's no problem," Myria assures him. "I get up at dawn all the time—" It is Myria's turn to freeze as she remembers something. "Theodora mentioned a tournament tomorrow? What will I have to do for that?"

Geffrey waves off her concerns. "A popular summer event and nothing you need to worry about right now. Mother is taking care of all the details. Enjoy the rest of the night while it remains young."

"Wait, I almost forgot. I'm supposed to meet the prince."

"When?"

"Tonight. An hour after the masquerade ends." She beams with pride, eyebrows rising expectantly. "Aren't you proud? I secured alone time with the prince."

"This *is* great news. Mother would be impressed. Where are you meeting him?"

"In the palace gardens, by the tree line." She pauses. "You'll have to show me the way."

"Not to worry. Suitor Escort is not the worst job title I have held at court." He laughs. "You made a good impression on the king and queen, you met all the other suitors, and it looks like you continue to impress Leor. It seems like this has been a wonderful night for you."

Myria spends the rest of the masquerade by Eulalia's side, watching and learning as the more experienced woman speaks and dances with the other nobles. She seems well-versed in both areas, fluently navigating several topics and expertly shifting her body in time with the music. Eulalia takes some time to teach Myria a few steps in the corner of the room and promises to offer more lessons later. The masquerade attendees begin filtering out of the ballroom around midnight, and Myria bids goodnight to her new friend before seeking out Geffrey for her secret royal rendezvous.

4

MEETING

Under the light of the moon, the palace gardens are silent. The frivolities of the ball within the castle are muted, and Myria's footsteps across the stone pathways echo against the garden walls. Geffrey leads her to a bench in the far corner and instructs her to wait while he goes to hurry Prince Leor along.

"Don't be obvious about it," Myria calls after him. "We're sneaking. This is supposed to be secret."

Geffrey waves off her concerns before disappearing into the shadows.

The gardens are dark, most of the light coming from the moon or torchlight from the nearby palace. Myria removes her mask as she waits, wondering what she will say to Leor. Her nerves twist her stomach into knots as she wrings her hands in anticipation. She is not given long to dwell on these thoughts when a voice calls out to her.

"My lady?"

She rises to meet Prince Leor. Her mind struggles how to address him appropriately. "My prince," she decides after some hesitation, dropping into the customary curtsy.

Leor closes the gap between them. "You need not do that here. Right now, I am *Just Leor*."

The tension in her jaw fades and the corners of her mouth turn up seemingly of their own accord. "My apologies, *Just Leor*. Did you enjoy your evening?"

Leor combs a hand through his honey blond-hair and sighs, his shoulders sagging. "These events are always overwhelming."

"But you danced with many beautiful ladies tonight. Surely that was to your liking?"

"While there were indeed many fine ladies, only one caught my attention." Through the dim light of their surroundings, his amber eyes flash with characteristic intensity, that earnestness that makes Myria's breath catch.

The air between them feels suffocating, so Myria attempts some levity with a smirk. "I agree. Lady Eulalia is quite captivating."

He laughs, a deep rumbling that emanates from his chest. "It was very kind of you to introduce her."

"I wasn't sure if she would have the confidence to approach you on her own. I did not want her to get lost in the sea of Cressidas and Theodoras."

Leor nods and grimaces as if struck at the mention of the other suitors. "The other members of the court can be intimidating. I am relieved you recognize their nature. Ignoring it can be a hard lesson to learn the wrong way." Leor shakes his head as if to clear it, then holds his arm out to Myria. "Will you walk with me?"

Myria accepts Just Leor's elbow, demurely threading her arm through it.

He leads her through the maze of hedges beyond the palace lights, cloaking them where they are cloaked in complete darkness. Myria's mind floods with imagined objections from her grandmother; railing against the indecency of being alone with the prince in such a dark, secluded area. Myria does not mind; Leor has a comforting aura that makes her feel secure. She know she's safe with him.

"The palace and court take their toll," he says. "Even when I was young, I felt the weight of my station pressing down on me. As a child, I would sneak away with Emiri and we would chase each other around the garden."

Myria perks up at the name. "Emiri? You were childhood friends?"

Even in the moonlight, she can see the fondness in Leor's expression. "Yes, he is my dearest friend. He keeps me sane when the whole world wants to drive me crazy. Truly, he is the truest man I have known."

Myria frowns but looks away so he cannot detect her skepticism. "High praise for someone so gruff."

Leor chuckles. "Your reaction is unsurprising. Emiri is rough around the edges, but there is no better man than him. He has suffered much, but despite that, he remains the most loyal friend one could ever be blessed with. I trust him with my life."

Myria mulls over this assessment as they pass a row of herb garden beds, raised in stone planters. Their sharp fragrance fill Myria's nostrils. Emiri's words at the inn return to her mind—*dirty barmaid*—and a hot wave of indignation loosens her tongue enough to confide in Leor. "I heard him tell my cousin that he thinks I would take advantage of you."

Leor seems to consider her words for a moment, and Myria is relieved to find his eyebrows lifted in sympathy rather than drawn with suspicion. "Emiri has been given many reasons to distrust people and their intentions. That skepticism has kept him, me, and—I daresay—even my father alive."

Myria looks away, not missing the sudden sting in her chest at the thought of earning the suspicion of a man so nobly dedicated and protective of Leor. "It sounds like a blessing to be his friend. My only hope is that you understand I would never take advantage of you."

Her words crack Leor's smooth expression, revealing a hint of something more behind his royal mask.

"Myria..." he whispers.

"I know I was not born into this life and I do not understand the subtle social politics. It does not mean I seek to exploit knowing you. But..." Myria struggles between the need to play the court's games and her desire to be honest with Leor. The latter wins out. "But, it's true I struck a bargain with Geff to be here."

Leor's face is unreadable. "Tell me, Myria. Why are you here at court? Last night was remarkable, but I cannot imagine it is enough to want to marry me."

Guilt seizes her heart, feeling as if in the clutches of some beast. She wants to look away, but finds the intensity of his gaze locks her in place. "You're right," she concedes. "I don't know if I want to marry you, but my grandmother convinced me to come here—to live my life for myself for once. Maybe even figure out what it is *I* want. Geffrey offered to help her out with the inn, so I don't have to worry about taking care of her anymore."

Leor sighs through his nose and frowns. "An honest answer."

"I am sorry if that upsets you," she says, expecting at any moment to be ejected from the castle in shame.

"Why would that upset me?" he asks, arching an eyebrow. "That you had to be pried away as such shows how much empathy you have, and admirable dedication. I am touched that you would share that with me." He pauses. "You must care greatly for your grandmother."

She nods and pushes some stray hair behind her ear. "She is the only family I've known. I owe everything to her." Her chest pricks at the thought of her grandmother. While it's been less than a full day since their separation, Myria has never been parted from Grandma Iris for this long before. Without realizing it, a single tear leaks from the corner of her eye.

Leor, for all his pretense of maintaining a formal distance, reaches for her face. He pauses for a moment, his fingers close enough that Myria can feel the warmth emanating from them. Before he can pull back, Myria leans into his touch. Surprise flickers through Leor's face before his thumb brushes the tear away with a gentle swipe.

"I am sure she knows how devoted you are to her," he says.

Myria steps back, taking a deep breath to steady herself. Leor's hands return to his sides and his posture reassumes a rigid formality.

"I am sorry, Myria. I do not mean to be inappropriate. It's just so easy to be myself around you; to forget all the courtly rules."

Seeing him so suddenly shift from Just Leor to Prince Leor makes her regret stepping away. "I did not think it was inappropriate. I didn't want the *prince* to see me cry." She wipes the tears from her face with the back of her hand and musters a weak laugh. "It's not exactly the picture of an alluring suitor."

"On the contrary," he says as a grin peaks out through the royal façade. "I am touched that you feel comfortable being vulnerable around me. It shows how different you are from the rest of the ladies at court."

"And you're certainly not like anyone else I've met here. Or anywhere, for that matter." Heat blooms in Myria's face and chest again, and she cannot look away from Leor.

"Lady Myria, would you find it disagreeable if I wanted to kiss you again?"

Her hands tremble, but she smiles at him. "Only if you keep calling me *lady*."

This time his laugh is a low chuckle that vibrates in his throat. He closes the small gap between them once again, whispering against her lips, "My deepest apologies, Lady Myria."

His lips catch hers in a fervent kiss. His hands explore her body until one grips her neck and the other presses against her hip. In this breathless moment, her trembling hands grip the front of his shirt, wrinkling it as she pulls him closer.

Then the moment passes as they part. His breath blows warm and ragged across her face as soft laughter escapes his lips. "We should stop making a habit of this."

"Why?" she challenges.

He laughs again. "I don't know how many more private moments we can have like this, and I don't want to go without kissing someone as irresistible as you." He takes a deep breath, untangling his hands from her body. "Besides, I have no doubt the other ladies would find this as unfair treatment."

"If they find out," she says.

"If," he agrees. "But we should head back. I am sure Geffrey is waiting for you."

Myria is mortified to think of Geffrey as a chaperone waiting nearby. Leor offers a last smile for the evening and escorts her out of the garden. Her cousin waits near the palace doors, a respectable distance and out of earshot. Leor kisses the palm of her hand in a formal gesture turned intimate as it lasts longer than it should.

"I enjoyed our time together. Thank you for meeting me here, Myria. I shall see you at the tournament tomorrow. Best of luck."

Myria can only offer a wordless wave as she smiles wistfully at his retreating back. Her smile vanishes as soon as Geffrey approaches her.

"I sense great things for House Bramble. Leor looks happy, and you..." He narrows his eyes. "You *did* look happy. Why aren't you smiling anymore?"

Myria sighs, feeling exhausted in the wake of Leor's absence. "Theodora *and* Leor mentioned a tournament tomorrow. What is it? What am I going to have to do?"

Geffrey's eyes widen. "*Yes*, the tournament. It is a big summer event with jousting for all the knights and noblemen."

Myria arches a skeptical eyebrow. "Knights and noblemen?" she repeats, unconvinced. "What will I have to do at this tournament?"

Geffrey wrings his hands as his words spill out faster. "Yes, as Duke Bramble, I will have more to do tomorrow than you, but there is a small matter... No doubt it will be fine. You probably have some experience—"

"Just tell me."

He takes a deep breath. "Traditionally, the ladies of the court participate in a *pre-tournament* of various games, like archery and swordsmanship."

Myria buries her face in her hands. "Oh, is that all?"

"Yes," he says. "So, you are slated for a busy day tomorrow. First magic lesson at dawn with the court mage, and straight after, the pre-tournament. Then, you can relax and watch the joust. Mother has already arranged your tournament gear, but you can wear whatever you like to your magic lesson."

Geffrey drones on about the plans as they walk back to the Bramble suite, Myria acutely aware of how little sleep she would get that night. It takes some help from a chambermaid to release her from the masquerade dress, but soon she is in her nightgown and falls into her canopied bed in an exhausted heap. Her world goes black as soon as she shuts her eyes.

DAWN ARRIVES QUICKER THAN she would have expected as gray light pierces her eyelids. She pushes herself out of bed and dresses, electing to wear pants at Geffrey's recommendation. By the time her cousin arrives to collect her, she is taming her long hair into a loose braid.

"Good to see you awake," Geffrey says, using his fingers to flatten down his own unruly hair. "You will meet in the Mage's Tower for your first lesson. After an hour, I will retrieve you so that you may dress for the tournament."

"You haven't explained much about that," Myria points out, following Geffrey out of the room. "I'm not going to do well."

"Do not overwhelm yourself. Little is at stake for you compared to the actual event. Shoot some arrows at a target and then parry a wooden sword with another lady. You get points for every time you do well. The lady with the most points will give her favour to the prince for the joust. The whole affair is just ceremony.

"Even if you don't do well, your participation is what matters, and everyone will have forgotten it by the time the real joust." He puffs out his chest in a proud gesture, and Myria scoffs.

"The *real* joust?" she repeats.

"Well, yes. No offense, but no one expects the ladies to perform that well. The women's tournament is more theater than anything. A jest to warm up the crowd for the day's actual competition."

Myria narrows her eyes as her heart beats in her chest like a war drum. She's about to berate her cousin when he flashes an eager grin, spins, and waves for her to follow as he leaves the suite.

The corridors are quiet as Geff leads her to the opposite side of the palace, and Myria's voice echoes off the stone walls. "I can't tell if you're trying to make me feel better about the whole thing, or if you truly think yourself above women."

"Hey, the joust is *difficult*," he insists. "I have to wear a suit of armor more than half my weight. Then, I get battered by lances over and over. It leaves bruises for weeks."

"Sounds more exciting than dealing with the ladies at court."

"Maybe you will have your chance, then," he says. "In theory, the ladies of the court can participate in three events. The third is your own joust. However, since it is optional, and no lady has jousted in quite some time." He pauses, noticing a unique gleam in her eye. "I *do not* recommend it."

She punches his arm. "Just because you can't take a beating?"

Geffrey shakes his head, laughing off her words. He stops in front of a massive wooden door: The entrance to the Mage's Tower. The tower is a cylindrical structure jutting from the east wing. Myria hesitates before knocking, her knuckles hovering just inches from the door.

"Anything I should know before going in?" she asks.

"Relax. The other nobles have learned magic at some point. It will take some time before you master anything."

"It won't be odd that I am starting at such an older age? Don't most students begin as children?"

"Don't worry about it. The court mage knows all about our situation. I have arranged everything."

Before she can stall further, Geffrey raps on the door with a loud knock that punctures the castle's silence, pushes her through without waiting for a response, and closes the door behind her.

It slams shut with a loud echo and her eyes sweep the room, inspecting the Mage's Tower. She tugs her sleeves at her wrists, her plain outfit reminiscent of her station as a barmaid.

The entry chamber is large and round, with a fireplace next to a plush seating area. Bookcases line most of the walls, punctuated by tall, arched windows that provide a great view of the palace grounds. Opposite the fireplace is an opening to a large balcony that overlooks the gardens. Myria wanders closer to the balcony, admiring the height and view.

"Hello?" she calls out as she turns away from the balcony and scans a few of the titles on the bookcases. Unfamiliar runes inscribe their spines and covers.

"Myria?"

She spins around, noticing for the first time a winding staircase near the entrance. A figure descends the stairs, hovering above the last step—

Her breath catches in her throat. *Emiri?*

Myria frowns and folds her arms against her chest. A memory tugs at the fringes of her mind: Geffrey speaking to Emiri last night. "*You're* teaching me magic?"

He does not appear dissuaded as he steps closer. "Geffrey didn't tell you."

"He was probably afraid I would refuse to come."

"Would you have?" Emiri asks. The flicker of a smile suggests he is amused by her irritation.

"I don't know."

He moves past her and gestures toward the balcony. She follows him outside. His clothes consist of rough, worn leathers; quite unlike the clothes he wore the first time she met him. He stops at the stone railing, silent for a moment before responding. "Two nights ago, you asked me a question. I never got to answer it."

"What question is that?" she asks, struggling to remember it herself.

"You asked what a commoner like me was doing with nobles. Well," he turns and gestures up at the Mage's Tower, "this is the answer, more or less."

Myria backs against the railing, keeping a distance between them. "You're the court mage."

"Not quite. That was my father's job."

"Was?"

"He was killed in an assassination attempt against the king a few years ago."

Leor's tale about Emiri's skepticism keeping everyone alive returns to her. "I'm sorry for your loss."

Emiri seems to ignore her as he leans his elbows on the balcony railing and stares out over the garden. "The king never appointed an official replacement, but I've filled that role as best I can since his death. There you have it—why I'm your teacher." He flashes her a trite smile.

Myria senses he'd rather not be there at all. She leans one elbow against the railing. "That doesn't explain why you agreed to do this, only why Geffrey asked you."

"Why did I agree?" he repeats.

She scowls. "Surely you have better things to do than help out a *dirty barmaid*."

A flush of embarrassment colors his cheeks as he scratches the nape of his neck and looks away. "I didn't expect you to hear me say that. And I didn't expect to see you here at the palace."

"I tend to exceed expectations," Myria says with a smirk.

He looks at her finally, his expression unreadable. "I knew Geffrey was going to ask you to join the Summer Courtship. Persuading him to reconsider was my way of helping you."

"Strange way to help."

"I was doing you a favor, whether you realize it or not. You don't want to get involved in palace politics. This life demands much from someone, perhaps more than you'd be willing to give. I hate living here, surrounded by lies and betrayal. You saw it last night with every introduction: Duchess Nocturnus, Lady Stirling. Compared to them, I'm your best friend."

Myria considers him a moment, tilting her head. "So, you *don't* think I'm a dirty barmaid who is trying to take advantage of the prince?"

"To be honest, I don't know you well enough to make such a judgment. I only know what I can see for myself. You followed Geffrey to join the Summer Courtship, which tells me you want to be the queen like the other ladies."

Myria's cheeks flood with heat as her heart beats an angry rhythm. "I don't care about becoming queen, and Leor knows as much."

"So, what *is* your reason for being here?"

"To learn magic," she sighs, rubbing a hand over her face as she realizes dealing with Emiri is the only way to achieve her goals.

Emiri laughs. "I suppose we should get started then. That is, if you can accept having me as your teacher."

Unexpectedly, he juts out his hand in a peace offering. Myria considers it for a moment, her eyes tracing the calluses she first recognized. The reminder makes her reach for his hand, and they shake in arrangement.

"Good," he says as he releases her hand. "Lessons are every day, an hour at dawn. We have much to cover."

They linger on the balcony, and Emiri begins by explaining the foundations of magic. "Magic comes from the energy that surrounds us in the world, and as such, requires some kind of power source to perform spells. Most students practice in the morning, using sunlight to fuel their spells." Emiri sits down and motions for her to do the same. "Close your eyes and clear your thoughts. Feel the heat of the sun and use your mind to visualize the energy around us."

Myria feels the warmth around her like a glowing ball of light.

Emiri says, "Keep your eyes closed. Concentrate. Draw in the sun's warmth and picture an orb of light before you."

Myria focuses, but with her eyes closed, she is unsure if her efforts manifest into the orb she imagines.

"I already know some magic," she tells him, squeezing her eyes shut so she is not tempted to open them.

"What do you know already?" he asks, and the uninterested monotone in his voice tells Myria he is humoring her.

"Some healing spells. We would have a few mages visit the Morning Glory, and they taught me some things."

His tone shifts from disinterest to genuine curiosity. "What have you been able to heal?"

"Some bloody noses and a few split lips. Mostly injuries from bar fights."

His voice is tight, almost as though he doesn't want to sound impressed. "You were able to do that without any training?"

"Yes," she says, beaming with pride.

"Did you use anything with your spells? An energy source?"

"I always held a sprig of lavender. It would wither after the spell." For a moment, her mind recalls the image of the herb garden she keeps at the tavern, a small relic of her interest in healing. She pushes it aside and focuses again on her imagined orb.

Leather scrapes against stone as Emiri rises. Footsteps pad across the stone floor as he hurries back inside the tower. Myria struggles to keep her eyes closed, fighting temptation to see what he is doing.

Emiri's voice carries from a distance. "Lavender powered your spells. Plants are useful in a pinch, but they are not a reliable source of energy. They are finite in supply. Therefore, your sprigs would not last beyond the casting."

There is shuffling as he digs through something. Glass clinks together, books fall to the floor, and then his footsteps return in haste.

"Open your eyes," he instructs, his voice right next to her.

At first, the only thing she can see is a bright light that nearly blinds her. Perhaps the orb *had* materialized. She blinks several times before she makes out Emiri crouching, a rough, unpolished stone in his hands. It covers the palm of his hand with ease, reaching out with uneven, tetrahedral spears.

"Formally trained students of magic use a focusing crystal as their energy source. This is quartz, a very common utensil for mages. It doesn't have much energy stored at the moment, but try using this instead of a plant."

"How?" she asks as she takes the crystal and tests its weight. It is faintly warm to the touch and no heavier than a peach.

"To see the extent of your abilities, I want you to use a healing spell on me."

"But how? You're not even—*wait*!" Before she can stop him, Emiri pulls out a small copper knife and runs the tip of the blade down the center of his palm. A thin red line follows its trail. Myria pales at the sight of Emiri injuring himself.

"It's a small scratch," he points out. "Just use your healing spell."

Myria nods, gripping the crystal tightly as she pulls his hand closer. She focuses on the warmth emanating from the quartz, which feels different than the lavender sprigs she is used to. Still clutching the crystal, her finger traces the cut slowly and she feels the gentle itch of Emiri's skin repairing itself in her own hand.

When she pulls back, the cut has vanished. She loosens her grip on the quartz, and in her hand are small, pink indentations from its facets. Her fingertip has a small drop of Emiri's blood, the only remaining vestige of the injury.

Emiri inspects his palm closer, a faint smile on his face. "Impressive for a beginner. Even more impressive that you don't shy away from the sight of blood."

"I've seen a lot of blood in my life."

Emiri rises to his feet, and Myria does the same. "You can keep the quartz. You'll need it if you're going to keep practicing, especially as we get more advanced. When you go to bed, charge it with moonlight by your window. Make sure to put it away in the morning so the sunlight won't contaminate it."

"Sunlight can contaminate it?"

"Yes. Moonlight and sunlight power different types of spells, so you'll want to use different crystals for each. Moonlight powers healing spells, while sunlight has more varied applications."

"Should I have a second crystal for sunlight?"

Emiri chuckles at her enthusiasm. "I have plenty of crystals here charged with sunlight already. I'm giving this one to you since you seem to have a penchant for healing. Practice on your own, and tomorrow we'll start some conjuring. I'd like to continue further now, but—"

As if on cue, there is a knock at the door.

Emiri continues, "Right now, I believe you have a tournament to get to."

Geffrey pokes his head into the entry chamber, then calls out as he steps inside, "Everyone okay in here? Did we learn some magic this morning? Are we ready for the tournament?"

Myria frowns at her cousin. "Has it been an hour already?"

Geff claps his hands together. "Yes, and not a moment too soon. We've got many things on our schedule." He pauses and turns to Emiri. "Thank you for doing this. I know it can't be easy getting up at dawn again like when we were kids."

Emiri nods. "If you can handle *her*, I think I can handle getting up at dawn."

Myria scowls at the comment. "Is that supposed to insult me? Just when I thought we were making progress."

Emiri laughs nonetheless and flashes her a warm grin. She realizes he was likely being playful rather than insolent, so she resists feeling slighted by the remark.

Geffrey all but drags her out the door, already listing off everything they need to do, but she stops in the doorway and looks over her shoulder.

"Will you be at the tournament today?" she asks.

Emiri looks surprised and stutters for a moment before saying, "Leor invited me. He wants me to ride against him."

"Do you joust?" she asks in shock and steps back into the tower.

Geffrey calls out to her from the hall. "Myria, we have to go."

Emiri smirks. "Sometimes. Leor and I can be quite competitive."

Before she can say anything else, Geffrey grabs her by the arm, yanks her from the tower, and kicks the door closed behind them. "Come *on*," he urges.

They sprint through the palace to reach the Bramble suite. Once there, Olympe pushes her into the bedroom to get ready. Myria hides the focusing crystal under her pillow as her aunt lays out what she will be wearing. It is nothing as glamorous as the masquerade gown. The first layer of the outfit is a pair of thin leather pants and a simple cotton shirt. Fitted over this is a thin, flaxen-yellow padded gambeson—yellow for the colors of House Bramble—to provide some protection against minor blows. Olympe approves her current hairstyle, only weaving a black ribbon through the braid for added flair.

The final piece is her lady's favour, which Olympe holds out reverently, looking rather pleased with herself. "I had this made for you yesterday."

The favour is a long, pale yellow kerchief, thin enough to see through. As Myria examines it, she notices several personal touches. The edges are stitched with tree branch designs with thorns and clusters of red berries trimming them. Hawthorn branches, Myria realizes; an ode to her surname. In one corner of the kerchief, the initials *MH* are stitched in green thread.

"I love it," she whispers.

Olympe scoffs. "Of course you do, but resist becoming too attached. If we are lucky, you will give it to the prince today." With quick movements, she ties it around Myria's waist like a sash before pushing her out of the room.

Geffrey waits in the parlor wearing a matching yellow, padded arming doublet under a mail tunic.

"Is that the armor you will wear to the joust?" Myria asks.

"No," he laughs. "I wear this under a suit of plate."

"Enough dawdling," Olympe barks. "Shoo!"

They rush to the palace exit and across the courtyard. There, they climb into a carriage to take them to the tournament site—an empty field out of sight from the castle and open to the public.

"I hope you know I am not prepared for this in any way," Myria points out, her fingers feeling stiff and cold. She flexes them against her knees and runs them through the thin fabric of the favour tied at her waist.

"Don't worry," Geffrey says. "Just give it a good try. I expect little audience for the morn—" He falls silent as they crest a grassy knoll.

Myria's stomach turns sour and her heart leaps to her throat. The stands are filled with hundreds of spectators.

5

POINTS

As they draw closer to the tournament, Myria's senses are overwhelmed and she twists in every direction to take it all in. Performers fill the lists, the main sparring area for the joust. Dancers, fire-eaters, musicians, and acrobats all appeal to the morning crowd of peasants and nobles alike. A cacophony and cacosmia envelope the field as vendors peddle smoked meats and fresh bread around the stands. Colorful tents fill one side of the site. In the center of the stands, a vast pavilion covers a wooden balcony teeming with nobles overlooking the field. Tiered, wooden benches line the other side of the lists, crammed with sun-darkened faces of the provincial class.

Geffrey leads their wagon to the stables next to the armory. Myria suppresses the urge to throw up as she wobbles off the wagon, gripping the side with white fingers.

"Lady Myria!"

She slowly turns and is relieved to see Eulalia approaching her. Her friend is dressed similarly in a green, padded doublet. Her hair is divided into two small braids, tied with white ribbons.

Eulalia pauses as she looks over Myria. "Are you feeling well?"

Myria sways for a moment, gripping Eulalia's arm for support. "I have to confess. I am, in no uncertain terms, unprepared for this. I'm going to look like an idiot in front of all those people."

Eulalia pats the hand on her arm with a small smile. Myria reflexively loosens her grip as Eulalia reminds her, "You must not let them see you intimidated."

Myria frowns, recognizing her own words. "I told you that. You shouldn't use my own words against me."

Eulalia's laugh is drowned out by the roar of applause awarded to an acrobat landing a handstand on the lists. "Come. The first game is archery. Have you ever held a bow?" She leads Myria away from the stables toward a rack of bows. The official archery targets stand further down the field, and Myria can see the other ladies gathering near the range. Eulalia pushes a bow in her hands, and Myria tests the strength, pulling the string back a few times. If anything, she only has experience in archery. She used to hunt small game in Talking Tree Forest for dinners at the Morning Glory. She hopes the skill will translate today as she shoulders a quiver of new arrows. "We have two targets to hit," Eulalia explains as they walk toward the range. "A round target and a dummy. You have five turns with each target for a total of ten arrows. With the round target, you want to hit the center. With the dummy, the center is in the chest, but you get more points if you can hit the head."

Myria nods, processing the information. "That doesn't sound too difficult."

"Lady Myria, Lady Eulalia, how nice of you to join us," Theodora calls. Her gambeson is black, and her platinum hair is tied into an intricate bun, adorned with the same sword hairpin from the masquerade.

Myria takes a deep breath and forces the same composed smile to return Theodora's civility. The exchange does not go unnoticed by Cressida, wearing red, and the duchess crosses the distance to join them. Brigid stands nearby in blue, Sabine in purple.

Theodora greets them first. "While not much is expected of us these little games, some friendly honesty would not be misplaced. How many of you have practiced your archery lately?" She fixes each of them with a thinly-veiled smirk.

Cressida sneers at the question. "The Nocturnus family is *always* ready for combat. I have trained for this my entire life."

Theodora maintains her smirk. "You have trained your entire life for this specific moment? Let us hope you do well since you are not prepared to win the prince over otherwise."

Cressida frowns, folding her arms across her chest. "I am very prepared to win the prince."

Theodora turns her attention elsewhere. "What about you, Lady Eulalia? When was the last time you practiced your archery?"

Eulalia shrugs a single, modest shoulder, but a smile plays at her lips. "My parents insist on constant practice, but I would prefer to let my performance speak for itself."

A muscle feathers in Theodora's jaw, as if she is unsatisfied with Eulalia not taking her bait. The Stirling turns her gray eyes to Myria instead. "And you, Myria? How often does a common innkeeper use a bow? A sword?"

Myria does not miss the sharp edge in Theodora's words, likely designed to dismantle what little confidence she has. From the corner of her eye, she sees Cressida watching her closely. It is probably the first time the duchess has learned of her common roots. Myria forces her expression to remain placid as she attempts a lofty tone. "I don't want to brag, but usually when I am shooting, my targets are moving in a dimly-lit forest."

Nearby, Brigid and Sabine share a few giggles, and Eulalia grins with approval. The shine of Theodora's amusement wanes from her steely eyes, but she contrives a stiff smile. "We will see."

Three figures approach them, and Myria recognizes two of them as Queen Eloria and Aryn. The third is a middle-aged man with tanned skin and broad shoulders, introduced as the palace quartermaster, Jakobus, who will be judging the tournament. Queen Eloria welcomes them with a brief word before announcing the participating order. "I welcome all you distinguished ladies of court to the tournament, hosted by the benevolent House Stirling. The winner of this morning's competition shall be determined in the amount of points accumulated in each event. The victor will offer my son their lady's favour as a token of luck and love for his part in the joust. We will start in terms of rank with Duchess Nocturnus, followed by Lady Stirling, Lady Rosenford, Lady Valenrence, Lady Runewell, and finally Lady Hawthorne. I wish you all the best."

Jakobus explains the basic rules after Queen Eloria excuses herself to the royal. "The rules of this round are simple. Five points for the center. Two for the inner ring, and one point for the outer ring." Duchess Cressida is first at the round targets.

Myria whispers to Eulalia, "Is Theodora so confident because her brother is with the judge?"

Eulalia leans closer to answer. "Theodora's confidence stems from a family history of arrogance and ambition. This entire tournament is her family's social event, but that does not mean you should underestimate her skill. The Stirling's wealth comes from their iron mines and the weapons they produce. The whole family likewise trains in those weapons."

Myria offers a curt nod, swallowing past a dry lump in her throat.

Cressida's eyes skewer the target as she deftly draws back her bow. The arrow remains poised, the pale wood of the shaft a stark contrast against the rich colors of her hair and doublet. Myria thought the woman appeared lethal by her gaze alone, and now more so with a weapon in her hands. She stifles a shudder thinking of the duchess brandishing a sword.

With a reverberating *twang*, Cressida releases her arrow, and it finds its mark in the center of the target. The duchess indulges in a smirk before reaching for her next arrow. Behind her, Aryn praises the duchess's form, his tone rife with the sound of stiff obligation. The queen watches without a word, her face a composed mask of serenity. Myria forces her attention to return to Cressida, the remaining four arrows landing to circle the first. Jakobus hurries down the range to calculate the official point totals.

He returns shortly with the announcement. "Thirteen." One arrow in the center and four in the inner ring.

The number impresses Myria, but Cressida's face twitches, momentarily betraying an expression Myria can only name as dissatisfaction. Even Theodora reacts as if this bodes terribly for the duchess, practically skipping after the announcement to take her place as the second competitor to shoot.

"Surely it's not realistic to hit all five arrows in the center? There's not enough room," Myria whispers to Eulalia as Cressida stalks off to the next range.

"Maybe not *all* five arrows, but…" Her voice trails before posing a new idea. "What are the ladies of court if not ones expected to fail at unrealistic expectations? We all have impossibly high standards, even imposed by our own hand."

The impossibly high standards, however, seem to work in Theodora's favor. After smoothly drawing back her arm in near-rapid succession, her brother hurries off to return with a triumphant grin. "Sixteen." Jakobus, a step behind the younger man, nods in confirmation.

Myria does nothing to suppress the automatic eye roll. "Convenient that his sister scores the most points so far," she mutters to Eulalia.

The words are louder than she intends, as Sabine and Brigid turn to her with arched eyebrows. Even the queen's unflinching face shifts for a moment, recovering before anyone important can notice.

Brigid steps away for her turn, so it is Sabine who dares to ask, "Are you suggesting Lord Aryn would be dishonest?" The lilt in her voice hints that the mere thought is unlikely and offensive.

Eulalia clears her throat with a gentle cough, as if to remind Myria something to do about manners.

Myria does not heed Eulalia's message as she returns Sabine's skepticism, unsmiling. "With the throne of Avalion at stake? I think most people would risk some measure of dishonesty."

Sabine does not respond, looking away to focus on Brigid's performance, but Myria does not doubt the woman is forming her own opinion on the matter—either on Myria's bluntness of character or Aryn's propensity to cheat.

Brigid hits one arrow in the center. Myria notices her arm shaking with each subsequent shot. Two arrows reach the inner ring. However, her final two shots go a bit wide, landing in the outer ring. Jakobus reports her with a clipped tone, "Eleven points."

So far, the suitor with the least points. As Sabine takes up her position, Myria focuses her attention on Queen Eloria tucked away in the royal tent. While Brigid does little to hide her disappointment at the score, the queen continues her role by not reacting to any of the announcements. Myria marvels at the facade of indifference; a skill that Leor's future bride would have to practice *and* master.

Myria stretches on her toes and cranes her neck for a better look at the royal tent. It sits dead center of the stands, the occupants sheltered from the sun. King Uriel sits next to his wife, exuding the same statuesque, placid dignity he did at the dance. So much so, in fact, that he appears nearly bored by the contest. Leor sits at his father's side, also attempting to maintain a sense of regal detachment, though his excitement shows through his rapt attention and how his lips and brows flutter with every strike of an arrow. Myria cannot imagine how he would choose a bride that would willingly conceal all emotion, even for the sake of politics.

She turns away in time to see Sabine's first arrow hit the inner ring.

Soon, Aryn reports Sabine's score. "Twelve."

Nerves flutter in her chest as her turn draws near, but she shoves them down as Eulalia takes up her bow. The lady of House Runewell is the picture of grace and beauty, her olive skin brilliant in the sunlight. Her movements appear effortless with every arrow she picks up, draws, and sends sailing through the air.

The first two easily find their way in the center. Eulalia seems to permit herself a subtle smirk. The woman fires the remaining three with elegant ease; the trial proving none too challenging for her.

Jakobus's previous monotone makes way for a note of excitement. "Sixteen."

Tied with Theodora.

Eulalia bows to the onlookers, the humble gesture accompanied by a flourish of her arms which exudes well-earned confidence. House Runewell plays the courtly games well. Theodora watches from a distance, arms folded as she waits for the next round, porcelain skin pallid against the black gambeson. The stony expression refuses to yield anything brewing in her thoughts, but Myria thinks that obstinance is enough to suggest her annoyance.

Myria is shaken from her thoughts as Jakobus calls out her name. It's her turn.

She approaches with leaden footsteps, the bow she picks up is too shiny and too smooth compared to any she's held before. The arrow feels cumbersome, the arrowhead larger than any she's used to hunt. The pull of the bowstring is far heavier than her own. She calms her breath, slow and deliberate, and takes aim. She focuses on steadying her trembling hands. She lets out a long breath and looses the arrow with empty lungs in that moment of serenity, hoping it will be enough.

It is not. The first arrow fails to strike the target at all. Behind her, Aryn sounds all too pleased to criticize the height of her elbow. Gritting her teeth, Myria adjusts her arms as she prepares the next arrow.

She recovers when the second lands on the target, but it is too far away from the center to earn her five points. Two points at best.

Her ears ring faintly. Leor is watching from behind her. Leor is *watching* this embarrassing show—

A growl of frustration escapes her lips as she releases her third arrow much too soon. The drawstring snaps painfully against her cheek. The arrow arches into a wide path, missing the target once again.

Sharp fingernails prick the soft skin of her palm, and Myria forces herself to unclench her fist as she nocks a fourth arrow. *Calm. Aim. Steady. You'll embarrass yourself even more if you let yourself get too worked up.*

Her patience is rewarded when the arrow finally, *mercifully,* lands in the center. The fifth arrow joins it.

Her stomach twists when she sees Aryn make his way down the range to collect her arrows. He returns with the three arrows, his face limned with dark delight. "Nine points."

Jakobus palms his face in frustration at once again being subverted from his task, but he nods in agreement.

The revelation hits her like ice water and freezes her in place, stunned for a moment. Distantly, she is aware of Eulalia dragging her to the range of straw dummies.

Nine points. The *least* amount. She counts the arrows and points on her fingers. Three arrows with two in the center should have been *ten* points alone but—

"I hit the center twice, didn't I?" she hisses to Eulalia.

Her friend responds with a distracted shrug as Queen Eloria introduces the next round to the crowd around them, and Myria is forced to focus on her present surroundings.

The dummies are narrower and more difficult to hit.

Jakobus explains the scoring. "The center of the chest is worth five points, the inner and outer rings around it are worth two points and one, respectively. Headshots are worth ten."

Myria squints at the shapes in the distance, little more than a tiny corner of burlap.

As before, Cressida is first. She takes even longer to aim than the first round, precision now being even more crucial. She does not seem to breathe, holding absolutely still until...

The arrow lands in the chest.

This first mark seems to break Cressida's tension, but her refusal to look at anyone around her tells Myria she still is nervous. Her second arrow makes it into the chest as well.

Then, as if losing a breath, Cressida's arms shift, aiming higher, daring to attempt a headshot. The air buzzes around them when it is successful. Her final two arrows fly toward the chest once more, slightly lower than the first two. Jakobus awards her twenty-two points for the bout.

Theodora steps up next, her face the same placid mask as before. She does not take as long as Cressida to aim, and her first arrow lands in the chest. But as she readies her second arrow, she grins, her eyes flashing to the awaiting suitors. She winks before releasing the arrow.

After a loud thwack, the shaft wobbles before the center of the dummy's head.

Her last three shots come in rapid succession. She does not attempt a second headshot, aiming for the chest. But even Myria knows the center target is too small for all three of the arrows. Jakobus returns to proclaim, "Twenty-seven points."

Like the first round, Brigid starts strong, her first arrow landing in the chest. On the second attempt, Myria sees the arrow aiming higher; however, it misses the smaller target on the head, landing in the field behind. With shaking arms, Brigid focuses on the body of the dummy, each of her arrows spaced between each other. Ten points.

Sabine plays it safe, refusing to even attempt a headshot. Her first two arrows hit close to the center. The two after them fan out a bit wider. Hard determination lines her face as she releases her final arrow. It lands lower on the outer ring.

When it is Eulalia's turn, Myria recognizes the same air of dexterity as she takes her position. The drawstring yields easily to her proficient fingers, the wood glinting in the sunlight. Eulalia's first arrow catches in the dummy's head.

Myria wonders if she will attempt another headshot, but even with Eulalia's obvious talent, she does not risk it. She focuses lower, spraying the dummy with a variety of chest shots. When Jakobus returns, he nods with approval. "Twenty-six points." One point behind Theodora means one of Eulalia's arrows hit the outer ring.

Myria takes her spot as the last archer, rolling her shoulders to shake off her former embarrassment. If she can put aside that shame, even for a moment, perhaps she can perform better.

Becoming more familiar with the unfamiliar bow, she shoots once into the center of the chest. Her second shot misses, and a palpable groan rises from the crowd. She manages to land her next two shots on the dummy's chest, igniting a swell of confidence. With little to lose, she decides to take aim for the head in the hopes of making up points for the lost arrows.

Again, she focuses on her breathing. A gentle wind brushes her face, and she adjusts her aim for it. Her eyes lock on the dummy's head. Her shoulder burns from holding the bow drawn, and he hands tremble. *One more moment*, she thinks, but she knows she's out of time. With one final breath, she releases the bowstring.

The arrow flies out, spinning round and wobbling as it seems to soar in slow motion. Myria draws in a sharp breath and holds it as the arrow streaks out and veers in the breeze toward the target. It soars in from right to left, dead center on the dummy's head with mere feet to go, then soars right past it to sink into the bales of hay stacked behind the range.

Myria releases her breath in an angry grunt.

Aryn moves for the dummy, Jakobus hot on his heels, and she takes off after him to confirm the points herself. His sharp eyes look as though they would lance her through the chest if able, but he otherwise ignores her presence as she counts her pitiful achievements for herself. One arrow in the chest, two in the inner ring. Nine points. Even less than Brigid.

Aryn returns with Jakobus to confer again before announcing the current rankings. Theodora is in first place with forty-three points, Eulalia second at forty-two, and Cressida is third with thirty-five. Sabine has twenty-five, Brigid twenty-one.

And Myria—dead last with seventeen points. The disappointment and humiliation sag against her shoulders. At first, she doesn't move from the archery field. Eulalia hangs back with her while the others reconvene to the sword ring.

"You only missed four shots," she reassures. "There is still time to make up points."

"Archery was the only thing I had a chance in," Myria mourns. "I've never even held a sword."

"You cannot give in now," Eulalia urges. "Surrender is worse than defeat."

Myria sighs with a nod, conceding to Eulalia's point. She trudges back with as much dignity as she can spare.

Geffrey is there to meet them by the sparring ring. "So... They announced the, uh, rankings." A nervous edge crackles his voice.

Myria glares at him. "I'm aware of the rankings. I *told* you I was unprepared for this."

Theodora swoops between them, her face alight with glee. "I hope you are enjoying the festivities, Myria," she croons in a sweet voice. "The summer tournament is an event people travel far and wide to see. Our job is to give everyone the best show we can before the joust." She hides a demure laugh behind her hand.

Myria forces a bitter smile, discovering that her gloats are even more irritating now. "A simple 'good luck' would suffice, Lady Stirling."

In the distance, the judges call Brigid and Theodora to the sparring ring first. Theodora flits away, and Geffrey explains the rules. "You will have a dulled sword with a rounded tip, and your objective is simply to strike your opponent. Like so—" He mimes a few movements in the air with his arm. "You cannot strike your opponent in the face or on the head, or you will lose the match."

"Here, Myria. We have time until our own matches. Practice on me," Eulalia offers, tossing her a sword.

Myria grips the hilt. The weapon is heavy in her grasp. She swings it in the air a few times before taking a stance in front of Eulalia.

"Wrong," Geffrey hisses, nudging her heel with his toe. "Your feet must be shoulder-width apart. Stay on the balls of your feet, and you shall find movement much easier."

Myria groans and does as instructed before Eulalia beckons her to attack, holding up her own weapon. Myria charges and swings her weapon. Eulalia parries the blow and brings her own blade to counter on the backswing, whacking Myria in the side.

Myria jumps back, clutching herself. "Ouch!"

"You move too slowly," Eulalia critiques. "Practice increasing your speed. They will not give you a moment to catch your breath. Come at me again."

Myria tries again, and this time Eulalia spins out of the way before landing another strike on her other side. Myria turns, attempting to land a blow, but Eulalia parries once more.

"Maybe focus on defense?" Geffrey suggests. "If you parry or dodge every hit, at least your opponent cannot win points either."

"A start," Eulalia says. "But look for an opening. Let your opponent approach you, and only strike when they are vulnerable."

Myria takes a few more turns with Eulalia, focusing on defending herself and adapting to the rapid pace of strikes, but her arms strain against the unfamiliar weight of the weapon. Eulalia bests her with ease each time. Soon, Myria is panting and sweat dampens her forehead.

"How darling," sniffs a curt voice.

Myria straightens to see Cressida watching nearby, amusement stretching across the duchess's face. Myria grits her teeth. "Forgive my lack of experience."

Cressida snorts. "I did warn you not to get your hopes up."

Myria drops her sword to the ground and laces her fingers behind her neck to even her breathing. The crowd roars in the distance in response to Theodora's match. "This is just one event of the Summer Courtship."

"And these games symbolize your preparedness for battle, hailing back to ancient warrior queens that would join their armies in the war camps. However, I suspect victory is not within your reach today."

Myria bites back an insult by clenching and unclenching her jaw. Eventually she manages, "Duchess Cressida, perhaps you should use this time to study your true opponent instead of toying with the lady in last place. If you're lucky, maybe you will rise out of third."

Cressida chuckles. "I *am*. Lady Eulalia is my opponent, but I have also come to offer some friendly advice."

"Which is?"

"You may have less training and experience than the rest of the ladies at court. Where they are quicker and more practiced, you still have a small advantage. Your raw physical strength bests all of them, except me of course. Use it to intimidate in your matches, and they will hesitate against you."

Cressida's name is called to the sparring ring with Eulalia's, and the duchess turns to leave.

"Is she right?" Myria asks Eulalia, following her friend. "Could I use that to my advantage?"

Eulalia thinks on it for a moment, tapping her chin as Myria carries her friend's sparring weapon. "I suppose you could do that. I am not sure how effective it would be. My trainers have always taught me that speed is better than brute strength. You would need to be smart about it."

Eulalia enters the ring—a circular area marked off by a simple, single-rail fence festooned with streamers representing the colors of the competing houses. Jakobus officiates the match, declaring that the first one to earn five hits wins.

A piercing bell signals their start, and Myria is awed by what she sees. She can only think to describe it as a dance as Eulalia and Cressida slash, thrust, and parry with lightning speed. Eulalia hits Cressida first on the shoulder and then on the side in rapid succession. Dauntless, Cressida efficiently gets her first two blows in as well. Myria winces as the duchess's blade thumps into Eulalia's side. Her friend cries out in pain and stumbles back, clutching her ribs. Cressida is using her own strength against her opponent's tiny form.

For a moment, Eulalia is overwhelmed, and Cressida gets her third hit. Then Eulalia leverages the duchess's weight against her and responds with her third and fourth strikes. Cressida lunges forward, but the smaller woman dodges and spins to slash the passing duchess in the back to score her fifth and final strike. The bell clangs again, hailing the match's end.

Eulalia steps out, beaming with a victorious grin as the crowd cheers. Cressida's expression sours as she follows a pace behind.

Myria is next against Sabine, and the lady in purple hides any of her true thoughts behind a diplomatic smile. Myria meets her in the ring and the bell tolls.

Sabine charges before the echoes of the bell fade, and Myria unceremoniously jumps out of the way. The action elicits some laughter from the spectators. Sabine looks confused by the move, as if an inexperienced opponent running away from her was never part of her formal training. Sabine rushes her again and Myria parries the blow with all her might, sending Sabine's sword arm far to her side.

Myria's heart leaps as she recognizes the opening, but Sabine recovers, brings her blade around over her head, and hits Myria on the other side, winning the first point.

"Move quickly!" Eulalia shouts.

Sabine runs at her a third time, and Myria jumps to the side again, this time striking Sabine as her momentum carries her past. There are cheers from all around, Eulalia the loudest among them.

They continue this awkward dance as Myria dodges several of Sabine's blows. Sabine lands three more blows. But Myria matches each of them, keeping the score tied with four hits each.

The opponents step back, circling one another just out of reach. Fire rages across Myria's shoulders and back, and her arms tremble as she struggles to maintain her guard. Angry bruises throb on her flanks and back, each of Sabine's blows resonating despite the protection of her gambeson. Sabine flicks her blade out like a viper's tongue and steel rings out as Myria meets each test of her defense.

Sabine breaks the stalemate by raising her sword, stepping to the side, and bringing the blade around in a downward arc toward Myria's off-hand shoulder. Myria matches her foe's footwork, drops her guard, and narrowly ducks the slash. She steps forward and rises, bringing her own blade up in a smooth motion with all her might and catching Sabine in the belly. The noblewoman's breath catches in a gasp as she crumples over the blow and rolls over it, falling to the ground in a moaning heap.

The crowd leaps to their feet as roars and applause echo across the field.

Myria catches her own breath, then reaches a hand out to help her fallen opponent up.

Sabine smiles, taking her hand. "You fought well, Lady Myria."

"As did you, Lady Sabine," Myria says, pride swelling in her chest.

Out of the ring, Myria wipes the sweat and grime from her face with water from a nearby barrel. Eulalia and Geffrey rush over to congratulate her, the rapid succession of celebratory pats on the back sending fresh waves of pain coursing through her body. She waves them off and seeks out a seat to rest and catch her breath.

The next round of matches start, and Myria learns her next opponent is none other than Theodora. Myria takes some time to rest and nurse a waterskin while the subsequent match proceeds with Cressida against Brigid.

Theodora stretches on the other side of the armory tent, her brother standing next to her. Aryn gestures wildly as his lips move, concern writ plain in his expression. Suddenly, Aryn's eyes flicker up, connecting with Myria's. His face hardens and his brows draw together, lips no longer moving. Myria looks away, pretending to search for Geffrey. The sparring bell saves her the effort as the audience whoops at Cressida's victory. When the crowd simmers down, Jakobus announces the contenders for the next match—Theodora and Myria.

While Myria's arms and shoulders ache from the prior bout, she cannot escape the lingering suspicion that Aryn was speaking of *her*, knowing she would face his sister. Myria shakes the thought away as she turns to Theodora in the ring, brandishing her sword. The Stirling looks as though the warm morning has not created a single drop of sweat on her porcelain skin. Her hair and clothes remain immaculate. Myria glances down at the dirt coating her own boots and pants.

Theodora capitalizes on Myria's momentary distraction, striking Myria's shoulder with much more strength than Sabine ever used. Myria grimaces against the pain, backing away a few paces.

"Do not make this easy for me, Lady Myria," Theodora taunts in an airy voice.

She's goading. Don't listen, Myria growls to herself. All the same, blood pounds through her ears.

Myria charges Theodora this time, bringing her weapon down toward her opponent's shoulder. Theodora parries the blow, diverting the weight of Myria's attack away and sidestepping the charge. As Myria passes, Theodora swings her blade back in a slash across Myria's back.

Pain radiates from the blow as Myria stumbles under her own momentum, And the crowd erupts into cheers drowned out by the pounding her own pulse in her ears. She straightens her stance, bouncing on her toes, and locks her gaze with Theodora's icy eyes. Theodora smirks and charges at her once again.

Myria digs her toes into the ground and charges to meet Theodora head-on. She blocks the woman's sword with her own and shoves the Stirling woman back, sending her tumbling to the ground.

It takes Myria a moment for the pounding blood in her ears to calm before she can discern the sound that shatters the air: Laughter.

Waves of laughter rumble through the stands. For the first time, Theodora's confidence cracks, and her face reddens as she climbs to her feet.

If Theodora seemed overconfident before, her response to the laughter was unhinged. She flies at Myria, swinging her weapon in a flurry of wide slashes. Myria parries the blows as the contest for sport becomes a desperate need to defend herself from harm. Steel rings against steel as Theodora's sword crashes hers and reverberations ring through her aching hands and arms. Myria loses her balance and wavers as she retreats from the onslaught.

Without hesitation, Theodora takes advantage of the moment. She bats at Myria's sword with downward strikes, over and over, until her guard falls under the pressure. The Stirling then lands a slash across Myria's belly, follows up with a jab that forces the breath from her lungs and doubles her over. Theodora then brings her blade down against Myria's exposed back, sending her crumpling to the ground.

The bell rings out Theodora's victory, causing a new ripple of noise through the crowd that Myria cannot name, too concerned with the sharp stinging wracking her body. Dazed, Myria holds her head as it swims in the aftermath. Stars blot out her vision as she gasps for air and struggles to rise. Theodora approaches and yanks Myria to her feet, her sweet smile back in place while Myria cradles herself.

"You tried your best."

Myria stumbles outside of the ring, and Geffrey leads her back to the privacy of the armory. He urges her to sit down on a bench, and suddenly Olympe is standing before her, pushing a tankard of mead into her hands. The honeyed drink is refreshing as she drains the tankard between desperate, ragged gasps for air. But the alcohol does little to dull the pain of the beating.

"Are you okay?" he asks, his eyes nearly welling with concern.

All she can do is nod.

"You did well for your first sparring experience," Geffrey says, attempting a smile.

Myria prickles at the forced optimism, but it is the smile of her usually cynical aunt that soothes her annoyance—but only some. "What is it? Why are you so cheerful? I didn't win a single point against Theodora."

"No," Olympe agrees. "But you knocked her down and made her angry. That made the crowd laughed. Everyone wishes they had the chance to knock down a Stirling."

A pointed cough behind Olympe draws their attention to the opening of the armory tent, where Aryn Stirling stands. Myria's knuckles go white as she grips the mug even tighter. The sunlight silhouettes his figure like an ominous shadow, but even that does not hide the smirk that makes his eyes shine.

"House Stirling has always appreciated House Bramble's enthusiasm," he begins in a soft monotone. "However, I am here to inform Lady Myria that she has forfeited the rest of her sparring matches because of the excessive force she used against Lady Theodora. This, of course, means she does not have enough points to exceed beyond sixth and *last* place. We thank you for your participation at the tournament."

Aryn turns on his heel and disappears back to the sparring cages silently like a wraith. Myria grinds her teeth before chucking the wooden mug across the tent, where it clatters against a rack of dulled swords and sends them to the ground. "Excessive force against his sister? She nearly beat me to death!"

"It matters little," Olympe asserts. "The Stirlings host the tournament, so they make the rules here. We can afford one loss."

"*And* risk losing the day with Prince Leor to another suitor in a public show of favoritism," Geffrey grumbles under his breath as he stoops to replace the scattered swords.

Olympe shoots him an icy glare that immediately silences him when he returns to their side. "We can enjoy our small victories. You knocked Theodora to the ground. You rattled her. Why else would Aryn feel the need to remove you as a threat?"

Myria frowns back at her aunt. "She knocked me down as well."

"An unimportant detail," Olympe says. "A Stirling falling to the ground is a notable event. The best event."

"If you have finished congratulating each other for last place," interrupts a familiar, shrill voice. "I am here to offer you some redemption."

Duchess Cressida stands at the tent entrance. Her red doublet is crumpled, and her hair is erratic. Several dark strands escape her long, onyx braid. She frowns, clearly peeved.

"What redemption?" Myria asks.

"A third event is available to us—" she starts.

Myria perks up, remembering Geffrey's words from earlier. "The joust. Can we really do that?"

Olympe's eyes grow wide with panic. "*No.*"

Cressida turns her frown to Olympe. "Yes, she can. You need only a second volunteer to compete with you, and here I am here, at your service."

Olympe turns to Myria, pleading, all previous traces of amusement gone. "The joust is optional for a reason. People get hurt or *killed*—"

"And because of that, the event offers so many points that one could easily rise from last place," Cressida points out. "The other ladies lack the courage for it."

"You mean they lack foolishness," Olympe spits back. "No one has been foolish enough to take part in over twenty years."

The duchess angles her face, her pointed chin dipping as if to tempt Myria with an alluring gaze. "Imagine the glory this could give you, Myria. Positive attention for your bravery, not laughter and humiliation for your underwhelming performance."

"Why do *you* want to do this, Cressida?" Myria asks her, arching an eyebrow.

She scoffs. "I want to win. Right now, I need more points to rise out of third place."

"Why ask me to ride against you?"

Cressida pauses for a moment, frowning. "As I said, none of the others have the courage to take this on. From your performance in the sparring matches, I believe you do."

"And because you think I'm stupid enough to go through with it." Myria points out.

Cressida shrugs, but the frown shifts, curling with amusement. "If that makes you stupid, then I suppose I am stupid along with you."

Geffrey steps between them. "Myria, you cannot seriously consider this. The tournament is not worth that much. Right, Mother?"

But Olympe has suddenly fallen silent. Geffrey looks at her, confused.

"Go on, Lady Bramble," the duchess prods. "Inform Myria the names of the last two ladies who thought it worthwhile."

Olympe sighs and looks away, ashamed. "Your mother, Callia Bramble, rode against me over twenty years ago."

"Mother!" Geffrey gasps. "I did not realzie I descended from a jousting champion. Why have I been jousting for House Bramble all this time?"

Olympe glares at her son. "It was rash and idiotic, borne of misplaced pride and hot-blooded youth." She turns to Myria. "I broke your mother's nose, and she broke my arm. We were lucky we sustained injuries no more serious than that."

"What made you ride against each other?" Myria asks.

Olympe looks at her hands. Myria has to strain to hear Olympe's answer. "Because we thought it would be fun."

Myria rises to her feet and approaches Cressida, beaming. "I will joust against you."

6

FAVOUR

GEFFREY SPENDS THE NEXT hour explaining details of the joust to Myria while attendants hurry around them to prepare her equipment. A wave of excitement ripples through the stands as news of the lady's joust is announced, a spectacle not witnessed in over twenty years. Her gambeson is replaced with an arming doublet festooned with straps and buckles. A valet joins them—a skinny boy no older than sixteen, she thinks she hears Geffrey calling him Merek—and begins the arduous work of strapping the heavy steel armor on her—borrowed from the prime of Olympe's youth. As each piece is secured, she understands Geff's complaints about the weight.

The valet, Merek, fastens plates around her arms and legs with leather straps, leaving gaps at the joints covered with knee and elbow guards. He then squeezes a heavy cuirass closed around her torso. As he adds each piece, Myria finds it challenging to stand against their weight. The young man affixes a gorget around her neck, then buckles a grand guard over her left shoulder. Finally, he lowers a frog-mouth helm over her head and buckles it to the gorget.

"Myria," Eulalia's voice calls from nearby, but Myria cannot turn her head to see her.

"Geff, can you take this helmet off for now?" she asks as Eulalia enters her small field of vision through the slit.

"The helmet has to be secure so no wooden shards pierce your neck. Also, in case you fall from your horse, it diffuses the brunt of the impact so you do not break your neck," Geffrey informs her.

"I know, but we can put it back on later."

Geffrey begrudgingly complies, and suddenly the clean air outside the suit of armor chills her face.

"You are truly doing this?" Eulalia asks, her mouth agape in disbelief.

Myria smiles. "Of course. I wouldn't be putting this armor on for nothing."

"Is this because of Theodora? Or because you are in last place? You have nothing to prove."

Myria frowns. "I *do* have to prove something. I am the only common suitor the prince has."

Eulalia frowns. "You might have been raised common but you are anything but."

Myria's expression brightens and she casts a glance at Olympe. "I thank you, but that will not deter me. Besides, the joust sounds fun."

Geffrey sighs. "My mother has been trying for the better part of this past hour to convince her to set aside this notion. At this point, I think nothing will reach her."

"Geffrey, you get to joust at every tournament," Myria points out.

"Yes, and I dread each one. I told you how much I hate it."

"Myria," Eulalia tries again in a more patient voice. "Cressida is from House Nocturnus. The Stirling family may make weapons, but the Nocturnus nobles are all trained to fight with them from a very young age. She hails from a venerable lineage of ancient warriors. I have no doubt that she is formally properly trained for such a martial event."

"I don't expect to win, Eulalia," Myria laughs. "I have won nothing today. However, if Cressida has someone to joust against, then maybe Theodora won't get first place."

Eulalia appears baffled. "You joust to help Cressida win the tournament?"

"I am jousting because it seems fun," Myria repeats.

"Until you break your arm? Smash your face? Or worse?" Eulalia points out. "How can you impress Prince Leor if you end up bloodied and broken... or *dead*?"

"Simple," Myria says, continuing to beam at those around her to mask her impatience. "He will be inspired by my bravery and strength. I would have been a fierce warrior-queen that never backs down from a challenge."

An image flashes in Myria's mind of her as a regal queen, crowned and brandishing a mighty longsword at Leor's side with luxurious furs draped from their shoulders. She suppresses the chill that shudders down her spine by clearing her throat.

Eulalia, if not convinced, at the very least looks amused. "Can you even move in that?"

"Yes," Myria hisses. After an expectant silence, she bobs her elbow a bit as evidence. The effort demonstrates only a marginal amount of mobility, but Myria continues to plaster her smile as if this is normal. "Movement is unimportant compared to protection against a lance."

Eulalia exchanges a concerned glance with Geffrey, who merely shrugs, saying, "Her confidence is undeniable. But she's right: Jousting armor is designed more for protection than mobility."

Eulalia sighs and turns back to Myria. "The prince would not want you to risk your life for him."

"I'm not doing it for him."

"He would not want you to do it for anyone, not for Theodora or Cressida—"

"I'm doing it for myself." Myria does not want to argue with her new friend, but she cannot mask her irritation, exacerbated by the heavy suit of armor. "Besides, the prince isn't *here*."

Suddenly, the voice of a herald fills the small tent and interrupts their conversation. "Introducing His Royal Highness, Prince Leor of Avalion!"

Everyone in the armory spins around to acknowledge Leor's entrance with a bow. Myria struggles in the armor but manages a belated and awkward attempt at the gesture. Several guards, their apparent leader a severe woman with tanned skin and sharp features, flank the prince, and Emiri shadows behind them. The large number of visitors inside the armory makes Myria acutely aware of how every crevice of her body drips of sweat. She hopes the metal of the suit traps any unpleasant smells.

"Thank you all," Leor says. "I hope I am not interrupting." His doublet is similar to Geffrey's in style, only dark red and the mail pristine. Myria thinks he looks ready to command an army.

"You are certainly not interrupting," Geffrey assures him. "We were all wishing Myria the best of luck for the joust."

Myria suppresses the urge to roll her eyes at Geff's innocuous lie.

Leor hesitates. "I would like to do the same." His words hang in the air for a moment before he clarifies, "In private."

No further command is required on his part as Geff, Eulalia, and Olympe stream out of the armory. The guards keep their distance, filing outside to circle the tent with Emiri, who casts one last, furtive glance at them before following behind the others. The last to leave is the severe woman, who refuses them absolute privacy as she hovers at the entrance. At the very least, she turns her back to offer the illusion.

The woman looks so stern, Myria muses. *She must be the captain of Leor's guard?*

Myria is relieved she doesn't have to move anywhere yet, thinking it would be a strange sight with her shuffling around in the cumbersome suit of armor. She does not dare to glance down at herself to see what hulking shape the armor has turned her into. It cannot be a flattering look.

"Leor," she greets with a strained smile. "Based on our previous conversation, I had not expected any more private moments. At least, not for a while."

He avoids her gaze, scratching the nape of his neck. "I am sorry for this intrusion. The news of your joust with the duchess surprised me. I had to see it for myself."

Myria juts her chin up, playfully challenging. "Did you not think I would go through with it?"

"After the minotaur, I would be remiss to doubt your determination. However, I hope you might reconsider?" he poses, the question lifting with a note of anticipation.

Her bravado and excitement dim with a frown. "You don't want me to joust?"

He reaches for her hands, pausing only to ensure they don't have an audience. The guard continues her sentry without moving. "Only because I do not wish to see you harmed. I am sorry if that seems rather selfish of me." He squeezes her fingers gently through her gloves.

"Did you know my mother was one of the last ladies to joust?" she asks.

The information seems news to him. "Is that why you wish to compete so? To continue her legacy?"

"No. I wanted to joust before knowing about my mother."

Guilt stretches across Leor's face. "Do you joust because of me? I cannot stand the thought of you becoming harmed on my behalf."

Myria suffers a small smile. "If you think it so dangerous, perhaps you should abstain from jousting as well."

The suggestion makes him laugh. "A fair point. If I cannot dissuade you from the joust, then I wish you take the utmost care. It would pain me to see you injured."

"I appreciate your concern," she says, but the words are soft with insincerity. They are hollow things, a courtesy to calm *his* nerves. "I will do my best."

Leor's blue eyes burn into hers as he pulls her hands closer to him. "Please promise me you will be safe," he whispers in a husky voice that clenches her stomach and chills the back of her neck.

The intensity of his words leaves her little choice. "I promise."

He plants a kiss on the back of one of her gloves. "My thoughts are entirely with you today."

Through the swirling of her stomach, Myria manages a weak smile. "You should visit Duchess Cressida," she recommends. "So no one can accuse you of favoritism."

Leor smirks at the idea, nodding, before he turns and ducks out of the tent. His guard captain spares no backward glance as she falls into step behind her charge.

In his absence, Myria releases a sigh, wishing she had something to lean against as she sorts out the fervor and headiness of their exchange.

Geffrey returns with Merek, the reins of an armored steed in his hand, and waves for Myria to join them.

She takes a tentative step, then another, and is surprised to find walking in the armor is not as difficult as she had expected. While she thought the heaviness of the armor would drag her down at first, Myria now feels more comfortable with it. Perhaps she only needed some time to become accustomed to its weight? The arming doublet seems to hold most of the burden, and the weight is spread evenly, much more balanced than she would have thought.

As she exits the tent and joins them, Geff introduces the gray stallion as Stefan. Merek assists her with the arduous process of mounting the horse with the aid of some wooden steps. When she is finally secured in the saddle, Geffrey leads them toward the lists.

Myria blinks in the sunlight, shielding her eyes to look at her surroundings. The stands have increased in population, buzzing eagerly around the lists. Prince Leor has already disappeared with his retinue of guards. To her surprise, Emiri lingers, leaning against a railing nearby.

A small breeze chills some of the sweat against her face as she narrows her eyes at him. "Have you come to tell me how foolish I am, like everyone else? Convince me I shouldn't joust?"

Amusement lines his face. "Absolutely not. I'm excited to see it."

She cannot reply as Geff pulls them to the end of the field, where Olympe waits next to a rack of yellow and black lances. On the opposite end, Cressida emerges on horseback as well, decked out in elegant armor fit perfectly to her frame that gleams in the sunlight. Myria realizes, with a jealous clench in her chest, even the armor is flattering on the duchess. It is the last, unhindered view she has before Merek climbs atop a nearby platform and attaches the helmet once more to her gorget.

Myria's frantic heart hammers, and she imagines it's loud enough for her cuirass to echo the sound.

Merek struggles to pass her the first lance. Myria grabs hold of the weapon and lowers its until it settles on the lance rest protruding from the right side of her cuirass. She couches the rear of the lance below her arm, further supporting its weight, but it strains her arm to hold it steady as the tip wavers in the air before her.

Geffrey gives her some final advice while Merek checks all the straps. "Aim for her grand guard to earn points: an extra point if you break your lance striking it and five points if you unhorse her."

The crowd becomes restless and bombastic as the event is about to begin. Their shouts nearly drown out Geffrey's words.

He raises his voice to compensate. "You get four runs. If something happens, such as your horse stops or your lances do not hit, you have to do a rerun. And whatever you do—"

"Do *not* fall off your horse!" Olympe's voice cuts in suddenly.

"Hit the grand guard. Stay on the horse," Myria repeats, her own voice echoing inside her helm.

There is a new voice, a herald who addresses the crowd in a booming tenor as he introduces the joust and the two courageous ladies from court. Myria only half-hears his words as she keeps her gaze focused on Cressida at the other end of the lists. Her heart pounds in her chest and blood rushes through her ears, silencing everything. The helmet echoes her heavy panting back to her. Something new thrills through her veins like ice, and Myria cannot tell if it's fear or excitement. It makes her head swim.

A horn pierces the air and a flag drops. Myria presses her legs into Stefan's flanks, and he surges forward in a three-beat canter. Myria steadies her lance under her arm and aims for Cressida's grand guard as Stefan speeds to a full gallop, trying to avoid looking at the duchess's own lance as they meet each other.

An instant slows to a sedated moment. Myria senses rather than sees her lance connect with Cressida's guard, and the impact reverberates up her arm to her right shoulder.

Then her left shoulder is suddenly assaulted, and her body tenses automatically. The blow drives the air out of her chest as it jolts her entire being. It feels as though she is wearing no armor to absorb the force of the strike as it leaves her throbbing. At the sight of wooden shards flying, she squeezes her eyes shut. Stefan, well-trained and experienced, carries her to the other end of the field.

When the horse slows his pace, Myria pulls on the reins and realizes she has been holding her breath. She draws in a deep breath and notices the crowd is cheering wildly. She looks at the lance in her hands and is pleased to see it has shattered. She urges Stefan back across the field, passing by Cressida mid-way.

"Impressive, Hawthorne!" the duchess shouts. Her own lance is broken as well.

Myria can only bob her head in acknowledgment, not trusting herself with words and hoping Cressida can see the gesture through the slit in her own helmet.

She discards the broken lance for the new one offered to her, hearing rather than seeing the proud smile in her cousin's voice when he approaches. "Amazing! Both of you had broken lances. How do you feel? The first ride is always the roughest."

Myria takes a moment to assess her body. Her right hand stings as she grips the second lance, but it is nothing compared to the soreness on the left side of her body. She does not doubt bruises are already forming.

Still, the shock of the first impact is over, and though her body recoils at the new experience, she grins beneath her helmet. "Exhilarating."

She readies for the second run, feeling more confident and less timid. Knowing what to expect from the lance makes it easier to face it head-on. The words of the herald and the roaring of the crowd fade as she focuses on her task.

She braces herself on the second run, gripping the lance tighter, her knees clenched closer to Stefan. Cressida's lance hits her with more force the second time around, like a sharp stab in a bruised chest. Luckily, her lance makes purchase as well, resulting in a corresponding spray of splinters.

As per the rules of the game, the last two lances are wider, and Myria feels the weight strain against her tired arm as she takes up her third one. Undaunted, she grips the lance even tighter as she charges headlong toward Cressida, shouting through gritted teeth.

Her lance makes contact with Cressida's grand guard, but bounces off in one piece. Cressida's lance hits her like a stampede of cattle, obliterating every sensation as it shatters in splinters. It feels as though her armor warped itself at the force of impact, cutting through the doublet into her own skin, but Myria can't determine if the wetness she feels is sweat or blood.

She drops the lance before she rides back to the Bramble end of the field, struggling to breathe through a tight chest.

"Are you all right?" Geffrey shouts at her as she leans forward in her saddle.

Myria straightens and chooses not to tell him about the tightness in her chest, rolling her shoulders. "Yes, one more."

Geff's face is apprehensive as he holds out his arm in front of the squire with the fourth lance. "Take a moment to catch your breath."

But Myria is impatient, not wanting to lose the momentum she feels broiling in her veins. With an effort, she slows her breathing and growls at him, "I'm ready!"

Reluctantly, he allows the lance to pass over. The horses step up for the final run.

As Stefan charges, Myria can feel her grip on the lance go slack as it sags heavily against her. She desperately holds on, trying to aim for Cressida's grand guard, but it is too late. She cannot raise the lance in time as Cressida's red lance rushes toward her. A clash of metal rings out for an instant before her world goes black.

A glint of gold. A sweeping of silver.

Dark lips curling with malevolence. Laughter trickling like water.

A wet cough, bubbling—bubbling blood. Blood dripping—on her shoulder?

A sharp intake of breath brings her back. Stefan's gait has slowed to a walk, and Myria struggles to regain her bearings. The lance is no longer in her hand, and she feels blood rushing to her face.

But the rushing blood does not silence the crowd's deafening roars, which sound like they are shouting at her. Myria looks around, realizing the world is upside down, no helmet to keep it at bay either. She was nearly unhorsed. Only a chance strap tangles her legs in the saddle, her small savior keeping her from falling to the ground completely.

She reaches for a saddle strap to pull herself up, but the heavy armor proves too bulky, weighing her down as it pushes against her chest and stomach. She withdraws her hand, catching her breath as she continues dangling. The strap securing her leg starts slipping.

The crowd roars even louder at this, and Myria can make out a select few voices above the others.

"Get up!" Geffrey shouts.

"Pull yourself up!" Olympe screeches. "Do not *dare* fall off that horse!"

With a deep breath, Myria lunges, gritting her teeth past the burning pain in her chest and abdomen. She reaches for the pommel horn with her left hand and misses when a sharp pain causes her to snap her arm back. The movement loosens the strap around her leg even more. She feels herself falling from the horse.

She lunges again, this time gripping the pommel with her right hand, and *finally* pulls herself up with a shallow, rasping breath. The action is met with a thundering wave of applause from the spectators. She collapses forward against Stefan's neck as Geffrey crosses the field to meet her.

"What a show!"

"I don't understand," she says in between large gulps of air. "Cressida has more points than me. Why are they cheering?"

"Because you stayed on your horse," Geffrey says, leading Stefan's reins back. "Everyone loves a good underdog."

They pass Cressida on the field. With her helmet off, her victorious smirk is evident, but Myria doesn't detect any condescension. "Well done, Hawthorne," the duchess calls. "I am rather impressed. Perhaps I underestimated you."

"Congratulations," Myria says through a wince. "You definitely earned that win. I've never been hit so hard in my life."

Cressida's smirk evaporates into a frown. "You better get used to it. Others will hit harder in different ways, but it is useful to know you can take a beating." And with that, the duchess rides away.

"I can't tell if she's really impressed or merely insulting me," Myria confides to Geff.

"As a Nocturnus, it is *always* an insult," he responds with a laugh. "The tournament will take an intermission now, before they announce the winners. We should probably get you looked at."

"Good," she sighs. "I need to take this fucking armor off."

Once they are out of sight of the crowd, Myria unceremoniously dismounts—or rather *falls*—from the horse and onto the ground. Merek fumbles with clasps and straps of the armor, piece by piece, taking much too long for Myria's liking. Geff assists until they shed every piece of metal armor except the cuirass. They pause at those straps, their eyes going wide.

Myria looks down to see what has claimed their attention and—

"We must go," Olympe commands, grabbing Myria by the wrist and leading her away.

Instead of the armory, they enter a tent made of bright yellow canvas. At first, Myria thinks it is a tent for House Bramble, given its color and the fact that it's completely empty. But Olympe is quick to explain it's the healer's tent, which makes sense since it's filled with several cots.

"You are *extremely* lucky," she chastises after Myria sinks into one of the cots.

Geffrey nods. "Indeed," he agrees, without sounding as reproachful.

"I did well, though," Myria points out, still struggling to take an adequate breath even with most of the armor removed. "Geff, can you just take the cuirass off?" Her whole torso feels as though it's being compressed by the sharp angles of the steel.

Geffrey obeys, working at the straps.

Olympe frowns. "You may not be as lucky as we thought. Who knows what damage you—" But her aunt stops and visibly pales as Geffrey peels off the remaining armor.

Myria feels an immense weight gone as she can breathe easily again. She sighs in relief, but hesitates when she notices their frozen, grim expressions. "What is it?"

Olympe doesn't immediately answer. "I will fetch the healer," she announces in a weak voice before sprinting away. Geffrey rises to his feet, scouring around the tent for bandages.

Myria looks down at herself, confirming that the wetness she had felt earlier is indeed blood, and it has almost soaked the entire left side of her yellow doublet. The cuirass, lying on the ground before her, is buckled and cracked where the grand guard had rested over it. A jagged edge of the broken metal protrudes inwards. She pulls at the neck of the doublet, exposing a deep gash in her shoulder. She draws in a sharp breath as the wound throbs in the open air. Bruises cover her shoulder and chest. She tries moving her left arm and is met with a wave of sharp pain. Myria bites her lips, but fails to prevent a groan from escaping them.

"It looks worse than it is," she says to Geff, who kneels next to her with a cloth and a bowl of water. It's a line she has used many times when Morning Glory patrons saw her for bar fight injuries, but her cousin doesn't look convinced.

"This is serious," he points out. "If Cressida hit you another time, you might have lost your arm or punctured your lung."

She shrugs just her right shoulder. "I've seen worse."

Geff frowns as he cuts away pieces of the doublet to reveal the full extent of the injury. Then he sets to work, cleaning blood from around the opening. "Why are you not taking this seriously?"

"I *am*," Myria says with a huff. "Olympe is going to get a healer. Everything will be fine."

Geff continues his work, pressing a clean rag to the wound with enough pressure that makes Myria want to cry out. She bites her tongue to stop herself.

Eulalia suddenly appears, and her face turns grim as soon as she sees them. A wooden mug is in her hands. "I brought some water. Lady Olympe is still looking for help. Apparently, the healer has not yet arrived at the tournament. He did not expect any serious injuries until this afternoon."

Myria sips the mug, using her right hand as Eulalia inspects Geffrey's work. "Did Cressida get injured?" she asks.

"Only some superficial bruising." Eulalia tears her attention away from Geffrey's hands to look Myria in the eye as she attempts a smile. "You did great, like an experienced knight of the joust. My favorite part was when you climbed back up your horse."

Geffrey laughs. "An even more impressive feat considering *this* was under her armor."

"Should we tell the prince?" Eulalia asks with a sly smile. "I am sure he would be concerned for Myria's well-being."

Geffrey seems to consider the suggestion, but panic seizes Myria's chest.

"*No*," she hisses. "I don't want him to come in here and see me like this."

"Even if it would give you a private moment with him?" Eulalia asks, surprised.

Myria chews on her lip, imagining the prince looking over her torn, bloodstained clothes. Something about the image fills her with so much shame, the mere thought makes her cringe. "You could use this as your private moment," she suggests. "Tell him I need rest, and as my closest friend, you can keep him updated on how I am."

Eulalia seems to deliberate on the idea, her brow furrowing. "Are you sure?"

"Yes! Don't you want your chance to be alone with the prince?" Myria asks.

"Of course," Eulalia says with slow consideration. "Only, I never expected to have the chance to leave any sort of lasting impression on him."

Myria lies back against the cot, relieved and exhausted. "Of course you will. If we weren't friends, I would be looking for all sorts of ways to undermine you, because you're the most eligible suitor." She laughs weakly at this, and Eulalia gives her hand a gentle squeeze that makes Myria realize her fingers are going numb. "So now, Lady Eulalia, go forth and conquer your moment with the prince."

When Geffrey is the only one who remains, Myria feels safe enough to close her eyes and hears him chuckling. "You have managed to dismiss Eulalia *and* the chance of seeing Leor. You must really hate it when people see you in such a vulnerable state."

Myria frowns, keeping her eyes closed. "I do not *hate*—"

"How are you going to get rid of me?" he says.

Myria opens her eyes and rises to the challenge, pushing herself to sit up with some difficulty. "You could go help your mother find a healer."

His grin widens as he presses harder against her wound.

Myria involuntarily cries out in pain, then quickly covers her mouth. Geffrey's amusement turns to shame as he snaps his hand back.

"Apologies, I did not mean—"

"If you are quite finished torturing your cousin," Olympe's voice cuts in sharply. "I brought someone to help."

They look up to see Olympe approaching with Emiri hot on her heels. Myria straightens on the cot, despite the pain. "Why is *he* here?" she groans.

Emiri, apparently unperturbed by her acerbic tone, kneels next to her, amusement tugging at his smile. "Only because of your terrible jousting," he says while reaching into his pocket. He glances at the others in the tent. "I can take it from here. House Bramble should make an appearance outside to make a show of strength."

Geffrey hesitates, but Olympe manages to pull him along as Emiri produces a crystal, slightly larger than the one he gifted Myria earlier. He stares at it for a moment before it begins to glow with white light.

"I thought we put our enmity behind us," he remarks, peeling back the remaining pieces of her ripped doublet, exposing much of her arm, shoulder, collarbone, and... lower.

Myria winces as the fabric tugs against her skin, releasing a heavy sigh. She holds up the scraps of doublet with her good hand against the rest of her chest, but Emiri does a courteous job of keeping his expression clinical and focused on his task. "It's not easy for me to feel so helpless."

Emiri examines her injury, prodding gently around the edges. "So, Geffrey was right about how you don't like to be vulnerable."

"I am *not* vulnerable," she hisses, embarrassed he had heard that much of their conversation.

Emiri returns her indignant gaze with an even one. "This is pretty deep."

"So, heal it."

He chuckles at her impatience. "You know, when I showed you the healing crystals this morning, I did not anticipate using one on you so soon."

"Are you normally the palace healer?"

"Rarely. Only in emergencies." He holds the glowing crystal to the edge of her wound, and Myria feels a cooling sensation envelop the left side of her body, like cold water running over a fresh burn. "This is going to take a little while," Emiri explains. "As I said, it's deep."

Myria leans back against the cot, closing her eyes as the healing magic relaxes her. "I'm sorry to burden you with my *terrible jousting*." Her tone sharpens as she repeats his words.

"It was an entertaining show. Besides, Leor asked me to look after you."

Myria's eyes fly open. "He asked you that? Why?"

Emiri narrows his eyes. "Is it not obvious? He cares very much for you, despite only knowing you for a few days."

Heat rising to Myria's face and she looks down, focusing on the tetrahedral spears of the crystal pressed against her skin.

"You made a good impression on the people. I'm sure you have several adoring fans, even though you don't win."

"I didn't expect to win," Myria sighs. "I realize how very much out of my depth I am here. I know I cannot compare to the others. I've done nothing like this."

"You did well enough for someone with no experience. Hopefully, you will realize how dangerous court can be now." Emiri's tone is tight, his eyes focused on his healing work.

"How dangerous can it be after today? I survived the joust."

"There are more dangerous things than the joust. Why do you think the prince would ask me to look after you?"

"Maybe because you told him I am an untrustworthy, dirty barmaid that needs to be watched?"

Emiri smiles ruefully. "At this point, I don't think there's anything I can tell Leor that would warn him away from you."

"But *you* still think that?" she returns in a withering voice.

Emiri hesitates. "As previously mentioned, I don't know you well enough, but it is telling how you seem to value one criticism I made in private so much."

Myria frowns, turning her attention to the tent ceiling. "I think it was undeserved criticism. You could have just said you didn't trust me, but instead, you called me dirty."

"Myria." He says her name with an exhausted sigh.

"You didn't even apologize."

"For something I said when you were eavesdropping?" he asks with a look of disbelief, tilting his head at her. The action causes him to unwittingly move the crystal away, and the cool magic disappears, replaced with a sharp burst of pain.

She grimaces, drawing in a sharp breath through gritted teeth as she reaches for her injury with her right hand.

Realizing his mistake, Emiri swiftly replaces the crystal to its proper position, and the cooling magic resumes. "I'm sorry, then," he says. "For your pain, and the comment."

She forces her body to relax, and even manages a strained smirk. "Was that so difficult?"

"I didn't realize my words would bother you so much. You should be careful about being so open with your thoughts and emotions. Believe me when I say that someone like Cressida or Theodora would exploit that to their advantage."

Her smirk slips away. "Your words don't bother me so much," she insists, but the statement sounds hollow to her own ears. She changes the subject. "So, if you really care about my safety and are watching out for me as Leor asked, why didn't you try to stop me from jousting?"

"I'm sure you understood the danger enough. Why should I stop you from doing what you want? Besides, it's not every day that someone gets a chance to hit Duchess Cressida." His voice wraps bitterly around the name.

"You don't like her," Myria guesses.

"No, I don't," he says, words clipped. "She spent a lot of time in the palace when I grew up with Leor. She always chased him around like a shadow and was quick to remind everyone of my station. She would throw my food on the floor, yell and belittle me in front of the other nobles—including the king—and she would even go as far as push me around, knowing I could never hit her back."

"Why couldn't you?"

"Because I'm—" His tone peaks with exasperation before he stops himself. He sighs, regaining his composure, and tries again. "She's a noble, and I'm not. I would have been fettered in irons, or *worse*, if I ever laid a finger on her."

"I'm sorry I didn't hit her even harder, then."

"But like said, you can't show if any of that bothers you, because then they'll feed off that power they hold over you."

"Why don't you leave, if you hate palace life so much?" Myria asks.

Emiri heaves another sigh before answering. "Because of Leor," he says. "If I wasn't here, he would be surrounded by all these snakes with no one he can trust." It is a simple, believable answer; but from the hesitation in his words, Myria cannot shake the suspicion there's more to it than that.

Emiri takes a few minutes to finish healing her wound, and it leaves behind only a faint, itchy pink line. A dull ache still throbs through her shoulder and chest, and moving her arm brings fresh waves of pain, but it all pales compared to how it felt before Emiri's ministrations. Myria does her best to hold up the remaining scraps of her doublet, tying the shredded pieces together into a strap. Noticing the awkward angle, Emiri wordlessly helps her with the task.

"How are you feeling?" he asks, pocketing the quartz. "Can you feel your left hand? Move your fingers?"

Myria demonstrates her mobility by wiggling her left fingers in his face, relieved they no longer feel numb, even though she winces in the process of lifting her arm.

He nods in approval. "I know it still hurts, and you probably have a lot of bruising elsewhere on your body," he says slowly. His eyes briefly flit to the right hand she has clutched against her chest. "But here's another healing lesson for you today: It's better to put ice on it instead of meddling with it."

"Why?"

Emiri pulls out a second crystal. This one is yellow and smaller in appearance. "It is safest for healers, especially inexperienced ones, to treat only what they can see with magic. Otherwise, you might unintentionally cause more damage. And even for practiced healers, there are limits to what we can do."

"Are you saying you're inexperienced?"

He ignores her question. "Can you breathe without difficulty?"

Myria nods, watching how he uses the yellow crystal to conjure a small, white blanket covering a clean yellow cloth. After a belated moment, she realizes what it is. "Snow?"

A small surge of pride lifts the corner of his mouth into a half-smile. "It's cold as ice and much easier to manipulate against your body. The magic will make it last longer too."

He ties the cloth into a compress that he hands to her. Myria presses it against her collarbone, where she feels sorest.

"I know you've probably already heard this, but you got lucky today, Lady Hawthorne. Jousts don't always end so well. I would appreciate it if you made my job easier in the future."

Myria groans. "Call me 'Lady Hawthorne' again and I will make your job a nightmare."

She looks up as footsteps crunch through the grass outside, and Olympe appears in the tent; a yellow-gold, linen dress in her hands. She walks over to Myria and nods at Emiri's work. "Thank you for your help." Then she focuses on Myria. "I brought you something to change into. You should hurry. They will announce the winners right before the main joust."

Myria takes the new dress as Emiri rises to excuse himself and return to the prince. She waits for him to leave before she asks, "Do I even need to do this? I'm not going to win. The prince will accept someone else's favour."

Olympe fixes her with a stern look. "You are expected to make an appearance, nonetheless. Also, there is grace in shouldering defeat with dignity."

Her aunt helps her dress and tame the loosened strands of hair. She hands Myria her recovered favour, lost somewhere when she shed her armor, before ushering her out of the tent and into the bright afternoon sun. The other ladies of the court gather in front of the lists, and Myria hurries to join them.

Brigid notices her first, greeting her with an eager smile. "Lady Myria, it is wonderful to see you well after that exciting match with Duchess Nocturnus."

The duchess, hearing her name, joins the conversation. "Yes, Lady Hawthorne," she says with a tremendous smirk. "I am glad to see you moving around. You did well for a mere commoner."

Myria forces a smile, remembering what Emiri revealed to her about the duchess. "If only you could have knocked me off my horse, duchess, you would have won more points."

Her smirk vanishes into a sneer. "I did not need to unhorse you, but thank you. Without your help, I would not spend the day with the prince."

"Nothing is decided yet," interjects Theodora. Her hair and dress remain pristine as always. "Arrogance is not an attractive quality in any suitor."

Cressida smiles at the challenge. "We shall see, Lady Stirling."

Myria cranes her neck to look for Eulalia but does not see her around. Suddenly, the crowd cheers in a steady, revered uproar; a practiced crescendo of respect. They all turn to see the prince approaching on horseback, followed by Emiri and several guards led by their stern captain. Sitting in the saddle behind Leor is none other than Eulalia, a sight which elicits some complaints from the other suitors.

"How did *she* get to do that?" Theodora grumbles.

"It matters not, because I will spend the rest of the day with him," Cressida asserts.

"Clever," Sabine sighs.

Myria does not intervene in their bickering, studying the pale yellow kerchief with fine needlework in her hands instead. Her favour. At least she will get to keep it.

Prince Leor dismounts his steed and offers a hand to assist Eulalia down as well. She takes it with a demure smile and lands lightly on her feet before joining Myria. The prince climbs the steps to a wooden stage, facing the crowd.

"People of Avalion, my father, King Uriel, and I are pleased to offer this tournament for your entertainment. We are grateful for our distinguished hosts, House Stirling. Before we begin, I will now announce the morning results to see which lady's favour I shall bear with me in today's joust."

Queen Eloria arrives to hand over a small scroll. She turns to the suitors. "Duchess and ladies, I thank you for your participation. One of you will take the mantle as queen soon, which is no small task. I hope your experiences today somewhat prepare you for that feat."

Emiri joins the prince on the stage, carrying a small bag as Leor announces the winners.

"In third place, we have Lady Myria of House Bramble!"

Myria is stunned to hear her name as the crowd's uproarious applause meets the announcement. It takes a few gentle nudges from Eulalia before she realizes she's supposed to join the prince on stage. When she stands before them, Emiri pulls a bronze pendant from the bag and slips it around her neck. She nearly misses the small smirk on his face.

"Second place is Lady Theodora of House Stirling!"

When Theodora joins them on stage, she maintains a diplomatic smile, but Myria can see the woman's disappointment. Emiri hands her a silver pendant that she grips tightly in her white hands.

"And our champion for today is Duchess Cressida of House Nocturnus!"

The smug pride emanates from Cressida in palpable waves as she slowly, deliberately climbs the steps for her prize. At a glance, Myria can see Emiri rolling his eyes as Cressida pulls out her red kerchief for Prince Leor.

The prince smiles at the duchess, his amber eyes warm and embracing, as if he would have preferred no other champion than her. "Thank you for your favour, Duchess Nocturnus. I hope I can share your victories today." He holds onto the token as he personally bestows the gold pendant around her neck.

"The honor is all mine, my prince," Cressida says, her voice like sugar.

"The Nocturnus family would be proud of your accomplishments today," he says, kissing her hand.

Myria wants to look away from the courtly intimacy but stifles the urge.

Prince Leor turns to the two of them with an empathetic expression. "Lady Theodora, Lady Myria, I know it cannot be easy to be so close to victory, only to have it snatched from you. I hope you understand I am touched by all of your hard work today. Lady Theodora, as our second victor, perhaps you would find it acceptable to offer your favour to Sir Emiri as last year's champion."

What? Myria thinks. *How could Emiri be the champion? He's not a noble.* She watches Emiri at this suggestion, recognizing his abject disgust with the idea in his curling frown.

Theodora responds similarly. "But he's a *commoner*."

Her tone of unbridled horror is a mistake. The prince tenses at the unfiltered insult that targets his closest friend.

Theodora, realizing her error, attempts a hasty recover. "I mean, I *only* have affection to offer for you, my prince."

Silence lingers, stiff and uncomfortable, but Myria's eyes lock on Emiri. Although he did not seem to want any favour from Theodora, her revulsion seems to cut something deep in him, though he does well to hide it. The venom in *commoner* was undeniable, and Emiri turns away from the humiliation he's suffered his entire life in Leor's shadow.

"I will offer my favour to Sir Emiri," Myria says quickly, wanting to reach out and heal the hurt he's felt. "I'm not sure how lucky it will make him since I was in third place, but I would be honored for him to carry it," she says, glancing pointedly in Theodora's direction.

Prince Leor's stormy expression clears, revealing gratitude for Myria's gesture. He looks back at Emiri. "What do you think, friend? Will you accept this lady's favour?"

Emiri offers her an amused half-smile as he slowly reaches for her kerchief. He looks at it for a moment in his hands, as if not quite believing it is real, and then laughs as he winds it around his wrist. "I just hope I can stay on my horse as well as she did."

7

POLITICAL

THE REST OF THE afternoon passes in relative comfort compared to Myria's joust. All that is left for her is to enjoy the tournament's festivities, cheer at opportune moments, and wave as the participants ride by. Anyone walking past her—civilian and noble alike—cheers for *Lady Hawthorne* or *House Bramble*. Myria smiles and waves at them, eliciting additional cheers. Her head swims at the thought of having fans for simply taking a few hits with a lance, but she supposes men are honored at the tournament for lesser accomplishments.

Cressida's victory earns the duchess a spot in the royal pavilion. This leaves Myria and Eulalia able to sit and watch the lists without her renowned smugness. Olympe also promised to join them soon after acquiring a celebratory mug of mead.

It does not, however, save them from Theodora's condescension.

"You did your best," Theodora croons to Myria as she enters the suitor pavilion. "The barbarity of the event suited you well, Lady Hawthorne."

Myria is not given a chance to retort, as Eulalia intervenes on her behalf. Her friend leans across Myria to face Theodora, a sweet smile fixed on her face. "The silver medal suits your eyes well, Lady Stirling."

Theodora falters at Eulalia's sudden boldness, and even Myria looks her over to ensure her friend is indeed sitting next to her. The Stirling quickly recovers, pointing out, "Better than no accolades at all, Runewell."

"If you are quite finished pining after Duchess Nocturnus's victory, we would very much like to enjoy the tournament. Please, sit down, so we can have an unobstructed view of the lists."

At that, Theodora turns away with a flash of her black skirts and sits on the other side of the pavilion with Brigid and Sabine.

Myria nods with a gentle clap of her hands. "Well done, Lady Runewell. Where did that come from?"

Eulalia offers a sheepish smile before leaning back in her seat, her almond eyes bright and energetic. "She deserves it, you know. Treating Emiri that way on stage and clawing for the prince's attention while you were being healed. She acts so self-important, but she would not dare joust."

Myria tilts her head at Eulalia's tone. "What do you mean?"

Eulalia seems to consider her words, then a slow, mischievous smile stretches across her face. "When you sent me out of the healer's tent to... *protect our interests...*" She giggles at her word choice. "Theodora was there, doing the same. She kept insisting on how your joust was no meaningful accomplishment, so I challenged her."

Myria is stunned. "To a joust?"

Eulalia nods, her face reddening. "Yes. I know not if it was the heat of the moment or the inspiration of your efforts, but I wanted to joust her to prove her wrong."

"What happened?"

Eulalia shrugs. "She went silent. Then, her brother swooped in to whisk her away."

Myria feels something cold set her teeth on edge. "Aryn?" The name leaves a bitter taste on her tongue.

Eulalia nods. "He mentioned how she need not resort to such measures to prove herself."

Myria shifts in her wooden seat, gingerly adjusting herself, as any movement reminds her of her battered and bruised body. The snowpack Emiri made for her still chills against her skin, pressed against her shoulder now. "How was your time with Leor?" she asks, changing the subject.

A wistful smile stretches across Eulalia's face. "Prince Leor is the personification of courtly charm. He has a way of making you feel like you are the most important person in the room."

"I know exactly what you mean."

Gentlemen gather to the lists in brilliant, gleaming armor that reflects the sun to begin the official joust. The herald's opening speech about virtue and nobility reaffirms Myria's previous suspicions. Only the highborn are permitted to participate, making Myria wonder how Emiri can stand with the others—her favour secured on his wrist and fluttering in the breeze. Perhaps his father's status as the previous Court Mage distinguishes him enough. The other knights are a smattering of nobles, including a few dukes, several counts, and many minor lords Myria does not recognize. In fact, very few faces are familiar.

The knights of the tournament recite their customary pledge of loyalty to the king, who looks on from the safety of his pavilion. The joust begins with the lesser, ancillary nobles. Myria leans back in her chair, returning her attention to Eulalia.

"Do you think you would want to marry him? Prince Leor, I mean," she asks, suddenly serious.

Eulalia gives her a strange look. "What kind of question is that? Does my presence here suggest anything otherwise?"

"You wanted to get away from your parents, you said."

Eulalia blushes.

"And that's not a bad thing," Myria explains hastily. "I came to court for a different reason as well."

Confusion replaces Eulalia's blush. "Do *you* not want to marry Prince Leor? You two seem very close already."

This time, Myria looks away. "I don't know if I want to marry anyone I've only known for a few days."

Eulalia gives a small laugh, and it almost sounds bitter. "That is not so unusual in the life of the nobility. A lady might be arranged in a union without ever meeting her groom. Marriage is an act of politics or business. Alliances and connections. For all our wealth and privilege, sometimes the luxury we lack is the ability to choose for ourselves."

"That doesn't bother you?" Myria asks. She looks up to see her friend is no longer smiling.

"Honestly, it terrifies me." Her voice is grave, distant. "I do not imagine I will be lucky enough to win the prince's hand. However, for now, it is nice not to worry if my parents are arranging a marriage for me without my knowledge. I could marry someone who would take pleasure in torturing me, someone who is a monster."

Myria reaches for her hand. "Would your parents truly do such a thing?"

Eulalia gently squeezes her hand back. "Would they know if they had? The court is so full of liars and deceivers, any eligible lord could charm my parents to get my dowry."

Myria's thoughts rush to her mother. Grandmother Iris always told her Callia left the court to pursue a marriage she wanted. Perhaps it was because she wanted to avoid marrying someone else. Her mother had been selected for the king, after all. "If you married Leor, would that be so bad?"

Eulalia regains her soft smile. "I would not mind marrying Leor, but that wedding is more than the prince. He comes with the whole kingdom."

"Would you not want to be future Queen of Avalion?" Myria nudges her playfully.

"I find *that* the most intimidating part."

"If you were queen, you could outlaw arranged marriages."

"If only," Eulalia sighs, then laughs, and says nothing else of the suggestion.

After the lesser nobles finish with the field, the main jousting event has five matches, featuring representatives from each noble house. The first two at the lists are from Houses Rosenford and Valenrence. Eulalia identifies the contenders as Lord Sigurd, Brigid's brother, and Duke Cirrus, Sabine's father. After their four runs, Sigurd proves victorious. Myria cannot help but be impressed with Rosenford's agility as he easily overcomes the aging duke.

The second match is between Geffrey and Aryn. However, Myria's resounding cheers and the tight grip on her chair do not win her cousin any favors. Geffrey's lance rarely finds its mark, and Aryn Stirling is declared the winner. Myria's hands come together for polite, unenthused applause, and she is careful to avoid eye contact with Theodora.

The banners of Houses Nocturnus and Runewell are raised for the third match. Eulalia excitedly points out her cousin, Count Alanis, riding against Cressida's cousin, Lord Godric. Both seem equally matched, unable to break their lances on each other. But on the final run, Godric's lance fails to make contact with the count's grand guard, earning Alanis enough points to be the victor.

This continues for hours as man and beast play at war, charging one another for the entertainment of the masses, the favor of the crown, and glory. Despite the shade the suitor's pavilion provides, the afternoon heat is stifling. Myria would like nothing more than to shed her uncomfortable dress and exchange it for something more practical. The snowpack makes its way across her neck to relieve her flushed skin.

Finally, the tournament draws near its end. The next match is between the two finalists with the highest points, Sigurd and Aryn, for the right to challenge the current champion. Brigid cheers for her brother while Theodora watches in rapt silence. In the first three runs, both knights break lances. Myria leans on the edge of her seat, ignoring the sting in her shoulder as her cheers for Sigurd join Brigid's.

The horn echoes, and the knights charge for each other.

At the last moment, Aryn's lance lands too high and shatters against Sigurd's helmet, a clear violation of the rules. Sigurd is thrown back, unhorsed, and falls to the ground in a cloud of dirt and a crash of buckling armor. The air escapes the field in a collective gasp. The dust clears. Absolute silence descends as every eye trains on Sigurd's unmoving form.

A shriek rings out as Brigid rushes out to her brother. Without thinking, Myria bolts after her.

"Where are you going?" Eulalia calls after her, but Myria is already too far to answer.

When they reach him, Sigurd remains still. Brigid's hands flutter uselessly in the air above him as she wails in unintelligible syllables.

"Brigid," Myria directs in an even voice as she crouches next to the prone Lord Rosenford. She removes his helmet to reveal a tangle of sandy blonde hair. "Stay calm. Talk to your brother like he can hear you. Keep saying his name."

Brigid nods, reaches for her brother's hand, and does as instructed.

Myria unbuckles and removes Sigurd's grand guard and gorget next, then makes quick work of the cuirass straps and removes the breastplate. She is relieved to see his chest rising and falling in a steady pace and looks back at his face. His eyes remain closed, and Myria taps out an anxious rhythm on his cheek, calling his name.

No response. Brigid's breathing hitches as her voice nears hysterics.

Myria thinks of something she's never done before. A traveling mage showed her a trick for waking up patrons who had been knocked out during bar fights. He described the process as *plucking* at a person's consciousness to wake them up.

Without wasting another moment, Myria presses two fingers to Sigurd's temple, closes her eyes, and concentrates. Unable to see anything, she uses her own energy like a mental eye to search for his consciousness. It is there, glowing dimly before her mind's eye, lying dormant and shrinking. She reaches out for it with her own mind, like a hand, and gently *plucks*.

A gasp. Her eyes fly open in time to see Sigurd shoot straight up. He looks about with wild, frenzied eyes, uttering his confusion in a series of monosyllabic questions.

"Where?" His head jerks about before his eyes finally land on Myria. "Who?"

With a cry of relief, Brigid throws her arms around her brother's neck. Myria smiles at her handiwork, but a new exhaustion tugs at her limbs. A surge of onlookers intervene—an assortment of courtiers and guards in blue Rosenford livery. Someone pulls her to her feet, and she turns to see Eulalia with a bewildered expression.

The crowd parts for an ancient man with hunched-over shoulders. He hobbles his way to Sigurd, throwing a disapproving frown in Myria's direction that sets apart the deep wrinkles of skin hanging from his face.

Eulalia whispers, barely hiding her giggle. "I believe you upstaged the healer."

Myria watches the frail man as he pries Brigid away from his patient. "He's a healer? He looks ancient."

More knights swarm the area, carefully lifting Sigurd onto a stretcher that has suddenly materialized between them. The Rosenford lord is carried away from the field, Brigid shadowing closely behind.

A new voice draws the crowd's attention, and Myria turns to see Aryn dismounted in his perfect, polished armor. He has eyes only for Prince Leor—stalking toward them like an angry lion of Avalion's sigil. Myria's never seen the prince in such a way. His blazing eyes do not match the kind, charming prince she has known.

"Your Majesty, I wish to formally apologize for the joust's turn of events," Aryn begins in a voice much too lofty for the circumstances. "My grip on the lance failed me and resulted in a near tragedy. To pay for my transgressions, I would like to concede defeat and declare Lord Sigurd as the winner of the match."

Everyone turns to Leor. His mouth is a hard line as he considers Aryn's words. Myria can tell the prince is unhappy as his amber eyes flicker between each expectant face as if his thoughts are racing. She understands his dilemma. What recourse is there for him? Everyone knows the dangers of the joust. It would be impossible to determine if Aryn intentionally harmed Sigurd; the implications of such are far more dangerous than the prince not accepting Aryn's apology.

Then Leor flashes a smile, and it is genuine enough to melt the tension. "Very well," he decides. "Since Lord Sigurd is currently indisposed, you will ride in his stead for House Rosenford in the final rounds."

Aryn's smooth face cracks with a grimace. "You mean..." He trails off, eyes moving beyond the prince.

Emiri appears at Leor's shoulder, uncharacteristic amusement crinkling his eyes. He grins with pure delight as he approaches Aryn and claps him on the shoulder. "Looks like you're riding against me, Stirling."

Aryn does nothing to conceal his disgust. "I anticipate the moment," he grumbles through clenched teeth. Before the crowd disperses, Emiri spares a single, curious glance in Myria's direction. But the moment passes, and Eulalia pulls her back to their seats.

Olympe is there, having finally returned from her quest for mead. She cradles the mug close to her chest. "It is unusual to have this much excitement for a tournament," she says by way of greeting as Myria sits next to her. Eulalia takes her former place on Myria's right side.

Geffrey appears, sliding into a seat behind them. Despite his previous battering against Aryn, he looks no worse for wear. "I doubt you have stayed sober for this long in years past."

When Olympe doesn't argue, Myria dares to ask, "Why is Emiri jousting in the final rounds?"

Geff's is the first response, accompanied by scoff. "Do you not know? He is the reigning champion from last year. I am fine, by the way. Only took a few hits from Sir Stirling himself. *Before* Sigurd, I might add."

Myria rolls her eyes. "I'm glad you weren't more seriously injured. However, tell me how exactly Emiri is able to joust? He doesn't belong to one of the noble families."

Geffrey blinks at the question and frowns at her concern. "Emiri has always taken part in the joust."

"Can anyone joust, then?" Myria prods. "Not just nobles?"

A slow blink from Geffrey suggests his confusion. "Emiri is noble enough. He has always been at court."

Olympe issues a soft groan before explaining, "My son is so eloquently explaining that Emiri is part of the prince's inner circle. He is not noble, but that does not mean we let the common rabble take up the lance. Emiri jousts only because Leor allows it—and moreso, because Leor *wants* it."

Geff nods. "One year, he even rode in the prince's stead when Leor injured his leg in a hunting accident."

Olympe leans closer to Myria, as if to block out the unhelpfulness of Geff's details. "It is not a popular decision at court. Leor has earned himself a few vocal opponents because of it."

The snow compress burns against its spot on her collarbone. "Like Aryn Stirling?"

The single, curt nod from her aunt is all the confirmation she needs.

Emiri and Aryn's arrival on the field is hailed by a surge of cheers all around. Myria's gaze sweeps either end of the lists. Although Aryn's black armor appears menacing, Emiri handles his steed with indescribable familiarity. They stare at each other across the lists as their horses and lances are prepared.

"Have they ever faced each other in combat?" Eulalia asks, leaning forward in her seat in anticipation.

Geffrey looks at her sideways, smirking. "No, Aryn has always found a reason to not ride against Emiri. He says competing against a commoner is below him."

"And it *is*," interjects a shrill voice on the other side of the pavilion. Myria glances at Theodora, having almost forgotten her presence. Aryn's sister keeps her eyes trained on the field as if she's not eavesdropping on their conversation.

Geffrey is not discouraged. He continues in a louder voice, "But I believe the true reason is because Aryn is afraid of him."

Theodora gives a disgusted scoff. "That would-be mage would do well to remember he would have nothing without the generosity of the prince."

Myria recalls Theodora's reaction on the stage. Her aversion was apparent at the mere suggestion of offering Emiri her favour, but how deep does it run? *How much did she hold back in front of Leor?*

A retort easily rises to Myria's lips, and she does nothing to suppress it. "Emiri *is* a mage. He lives in the Mage's Tower, doesn't he?"

Theodora does not turn to look at her. "Another act of charity from the royal family. Perhaps it will reach its limits when there are far superior mages to occupy the tower than that court mage pretender."

Myria wonders who she can mean, realizing she has not seen *any* noble perform magic in any capacity. Only Emiri.

A horn bellows and the two armored men gallop toward each other until they meet with a sickening crash. Myria involuntarily jumps at the noise, but forces her eyes open to see both lances are broken. Emiri and Aryn return to their respective sides without acknowledging the other, gearing up for the second ride.

The following two runs end in the same fashion, with lances breaking on both sides, but Aryn leans more and more to the side with a presumably sore shoulder. Emiri appears unaffected, always picking up the next lance as if it weighs no more than a needle.

"Is he even human?" Eulalia marvels, echoing Myria's thoughts. "He acts as if he rides through a spring field, as if Lord Stirling's lance is no more than a drooping tree branch."

"Such is Emiri for you," Geff chuckles, propping his feet up on Brigid's empty chair. "I used to practice with him. Trust me, he hits like a bull. He is champion for a reason. Solid muscle, that one."

Myria smirks at her cousin. "If he's so good and you practice with him, how come your jousting skills fare no better?"

Geffrey scowls. "I said I *used* to practice with him. I stopped after he dislocated my shoulder last year."

Emiri charges for the final run, barreling toward Aryn. The Stirling's posture sways and dips forward. Emiri's lance catches him in the center of the grand guard, throwing him entirely off his horse.

Aryn lands with a heavy thud on his backside, and the crowd drowns out every sound and thought in the ensuing, thunderous applause. The reaction is a considerable difference from Sigurd's unhorsing.

Unlike Sigurd, Aryn is conscious and alert, his hands fumbling around in angry, jerking movements. From the corner of her eye, Myria sees Theodora leave the tent, quick and soundless like a wraith. Her exit does not even draw Sabine's notice in the seat next to her. However, Theodora does not go to her brother as Brigid. Instead, the Stirling slips through the crowd and disappears, her face red and hard.

Emiri does not revel in his victory, ignoring the fallen knight as he rides away and exits the field. Instead, Prince Leor reaches Aryn on the field, surrounded by a retinue of attendants who help Lord Stirling on his feet before he ambles away.

Geffrey turns a smirk to Theodora's empty seat and falters. "Oh, she's gone. Pity. She cannot even indulge us the satisfaction of winning."

"Perhaps she has gone to check on her brother?" Eulalia suggests, her tone as soft as the almond eyes that search for the missing suitor.

Myria watches the crowd, recognizing no platinum head of hair making its way to Aryn. "I don't think so."

Several minutes pass as everyone prepares for the next match between the prince and Emiri. The crowd waits with charged anticipation, buzzing with hushed murmurs that surge through the stands.

Suddenly, a herald steps forward to an audience that immediately falls silent. "Introducing Sir Emiri and His Royal Highness, Prince Leor of Avalion."

Their horses stride out on the field and the crowd cheers for the combatants. Prince Leor, his helmet still off, raises a hand to acknowledge the spectators. His armor gleams brilliantly in the afternoon sun, a swath of vibrant crimson adorning the cuirass. Cressida's red favour is tied around his wrist, fluttering in the breeze. On the other end of the field, Emiri waits like a silent sentry, his dark helmet obscuring his face and any expression he might have.

"Who do you think will win this one?" Myria asks.

Geffrey's answer is automatic. "The prince, definitely."

Eulalia nods in agreement.

"How are you so certain?" Myria asks.

Sabine takes a seat closer to their group. "The prince *always* wins."

"Does he joust often?"

Geffrey shakes his head. "For his safety, Prince Leor is usually limited to one match."

"I can't imagine he is safer if that match is against the joust's champion," Myria muses. The vigil guard captain keeps close watch on Leor's side of the field, the sunlight passing across her armor in flashes, betraying her anxiousness as she shifts her weight from one leg to the other in constant motion.

Prince Leor's helmet is secured, and the first run begins at the traditional horn. Myria leans forward in her chair in anticipation, pressing the snowpack against her shoulder. Both lances connect against their opponent, shattering into a spray of wooden shards. The men recover in the wave of cheers that follows them back to their ends of the field.

The second run ends much like the first, with lances breaking. Leor and Emiri never waver atop their horses. Emiri's strength shows in the way Leor recoils in his saddle, and the prince's stamina reveals itself in how he quickly recovers and reaches for his next lance. By the third run, Myria cannot deny she finds something mesmerizing in the relentless and fearless way they meet the next hit. The echoes of her own joust flare against her shoulder with each crashing lance and battered grand guard. The chanting of the crowd favors the prince, and it seems to fuel the contenders' energy for the final run.

Myria leans even further from her seat to watch, chewing on her bottom lip. Her hand is cold from the snowpack she holds against her skin. Even though her chest still aches from bruises, she does not move or shift into a more comfortable position. Her own yellow favour serves as a stark contrast to Emiri's dull armor, and he absently tightens it around his arm as the eyes of his helmet train ahead of him. At three runs, the points are tied.

They charge at the last horn. With the beating of the hooves against packed dirt, Myria catches the slightest change in Emiri's otherwise consistent posture. The tension in his shoulders slackens minutely, the lance not reaching the necessary level. It misses—

Leor's heavy lance hits.

Emiri lurches in the saddle while the prince remains untouched.

The crowd erupts in a tumultuous wave, deafening every sound to the point of near-silence. The ear-splitting noise drowns out any would-be distraction as Myria watches Leor and Emiri round the lists and meet each other in the center of the field to shake on the joust's conclusion. Emiri's helmet nods stiffly before he disappears to the stables.

As Prince Leor addresses his people with words of humility and generosity, Myria glances at the others in confusion, but they are all cheering. Her eyes lose focus on their wide smiles and red, clapping hands as she realizes the significance of Emiri's *deliberate* actions. They would never cheer this loud, this hard, for him. A commoner, a court mage pretender.

Silent understanding dawns on Myria: A prince should not lose his joust.

Before she is given time to consider this, a familiar face approaches their tent, expertly weaving her way through the dispersing crowd. When Brigid stands in front of them, she averts her shy gaze, but the small smile suggests her brother is doing well. "My brother, Lord Sigurd, is faring well after his match. I wanted to personally offer my gratitude for your assistance, Lady Myria."

Myria returns her smile. "I didn't do much. I am glad his condition has improved."

Brigid lifts her eyes to meet Myria's, but the expectant line of her shoulders does not soften. "Sigurd is asking for you. He wants to see the person who saved him."

Myria blinks. "Me? I wouldn't say I *saved* him..." She trails off uncertainly, looking to Eulalia, who merely shrugs.

"He remembers your face," Brigid persists, all previous shyness replaced with insistence. "Even if you do not believe you saved him, he would still like the opportunity to thank you for your kindness. No one else rushed out to that field to aid him the way you did."

Myria casts a searching glance at her cousin, who also shrugs. She clears her throat and rises to her feet. "Very well, I will meet your brother."

The response earns a relieved sigh from Brigid, which makes Myria cautious. Should there be a reason for Myria to reject? She can't imagine the harm in visiting a knight who has just fallen off his horse. She knows nothing about Sigurd Rosenford, but her previous encounters with other nobles makes her wary; especially if they are anything like Aryn Stirling. Geffrey must sense some of her trepidation, because he announces his desire to accompany them to the healer's tent.

As they walk through the maze of canvas and mud, trailing behind Brigid, Myria asks her cousin in a low voice, "What do you know about Lord Sigurd?"

"Lord Rosenford and his sister do not come to court often," he answers, folding her hand in the crook of his elbow. "But he seems decent enough from the few interactions I have had with him. Other than that, they mostly keep to themselves, which might account for Lady Brigid's shyness."

Myria ducks into the yellow canvas tent behind Brigid. The ancient healer stands a few cots away, tending to a particularly fussy and swearing Aryn Stirling. Fortunately, Brigid ventures to a bed on the opposite side of the tent, where Lord Sigurd sits, fully alert. The sandy, freckled face immediately fixes his bright, blue eyes on Myria.

"Brother," Brigid introduces, "this is Lady Myria from House Bramble. She is competing in the Summer Courtship with me." A bitterness turns Brigid's last sentence, but her sharp eyes are focused on her brother instead of Myria.

Myria is not given time to wonder at her tone as Sigurd jumps to his feet. He wears leather pants similar to Geffrey's, but a dirty white undershirt has replaced what would have been a matching doublet. The neckline is loose, exposing bruises that mirror the ones on Myria's shoulder and collarbone.

"Lady Myria, it is an *honor*," he gushes in a deep, earnest voice, taking her hands into his own. His open, pale face and blonde hair are impossibly bright, and the warmth in his hands makes her feel as though she is standing before the sun. Pure, unadulterated light and heat. She cannot help but smile as she squints at him, unable to determine the reason behind his brightness. She senses nothing about him his contrived.

"Lord Sigurd," she greets. The warmth from his hands is fiery enough to bring a blush to her cheeks. She feels as though the gesture is too intimate, but to pull away would be impolite. "I am pleased to see you are doing well."

Sigurd draws her hands even closer and brushes his lips across her knuckles. The closeness of the contact, the flare of sunlight, burns her face even redder. "And *you* are the reason I am doing so well," he states in a voice that mirrors the intensity of his azure gaze. "I wanted to personally thank you for your intervention on the field. Without you, I do not know if I would be awake."

Brigid attempts to remind her brother of appropriate behavior by gripping his shoulder, and Sigurd releases her hands. Myria maintains a polite smile while something in her chest wilts at the attention. "I assure you, Lord Sigurd, I did nothing as amazing as you claim."

"But you are wrong, Lady Myria," he continues. He starts to take a step closer, but Brigid's hand tethers him, reminding him of his overexuberance. He bounces on the balls of his feet instead. "I was knocked from my horse, and everything went black. Then I saw you, not just on the field. You were in my *mind*, like a bright star, beckoning me to wake up. I wanted to stay asleep, but your face urged me not to. You woke me, and when I opened my eyes, you were there. It is because of you that I am awake—and I daresay, alive."

Sigurd is nearly breathless with gratitude, and Brigid's eyes seem to apologize for her brother's excitement. Myria's mind races with Sigurd's perspective, and Emiri's words ring in her head.

It is safest for healers to treat only what they can see with magic. Otherwise, you might unintentionally cause more damage.

She wonders if by reaching into Sigurd's mind to wake him, she unintentionally caused more damage by altering his memories... or something else? Something worse? Her stomach turns, and she hopes Sigurd is not affected another way because of her meddling.

"I am glad I could help you," she manages after a speechless moment.

"I would have never imagined another noblewoman rushing to me when I am injured on the field, let alone one who is a complete stranger. Your compassion cannot be overstated, Lady Myria. I would offer you my hand in marriage—"

Brigid hisses, narrowing her eyes at him.

"—*if* you were not already trying to win the prince's hand."

Myria's head swims at the suggestion. Her cousin takes a step closer to Sigurd, and his presence at her side puts her at ease. Geffrey clears his throat. "Lord Rosenford, House Bramble is happy to accept new allies. Perhaps we can think of a different way to show your gratitude?"

Sigurd nods as Brigid pushes him back on the bed. "Of course, Duke Bramble."

Geffrey smiles, but it is different from his usual expression of light humor. This Geffrey is the scheming courtier. "We should let you rest now."

Myria's legs feel numb as Geff steers them outside, but she waits until there is some distance between them and the healer's tent before she turns to her cousin. "What just happened?"

Geffrey chuckles, patting the hand she has tightened around his arm. "That, my dear Myria, is you making a new friend at court."

"He wants to *marry* me?" she asks, still shocked. Her mind wanders to the conversation she had with Eulalia.

Geffrey stops by the stables, turning to face her so that he can study her reaction. "And if you were not competing for Leor's hand, what would you say to that proposal?"

She throws her hands in the air, exasperated. "I don't even know him."

"He might stay at court a while, during the social season. You should use the opportunity to acquaint yourself better."

Myria closes her mouth, realizing it is agape, as she pieces together Geffrey's suggestion with his previous words. "Because he is now an ally."

He nods. "Exactly. Brigid is, as well. You might have an unwanted admirer because of your actions, but you should be careful not to offend him." He pauses. "Although, from what I have heard of Rosenfords, you would find him preferable to Aryn."

Myria concedes his point with a nod. "Not that Aryn would propose marriage to me. So, what do we do now that the tournament is over?"

Geffrey grins. "What better way to celebrate a tournament than by drinking with friends?"

"Is this another competition?"

"Nothing like your other social engagements. Most ladies of the court do not mingle with us for a celebratory drink, which would afford you a unique opportunity if you found a moment with Leor. Come tonight to the mead hall. Make an appearance and create new friendships. Win a drinking game or two. I suspect, as a former innkeeper and barmaid, you would have a distinct advantage. We use this time to unwind, relax, and brag about our jousting accomplishments. No harm in reminding them of *yours*."

Myria snorts. "My accomplishment of placing third?"

"That you had the courage to even make the attempt is remarkable. And at least you stayed on your horse—Aryn Stirling could not even manage that."

Another snort. "Let's go drink, then."

8

TOASTS

NEWS OF PRINCE LEOR'S evening celebration spreads through the Ilona Palace with ripples of anticipation. As an informal event, Geffrey explains the king and queen would not be in attendance; only the prince, discerning knights, and other tournament contenders. However, to not risk offending the noble families, the invitation often extends to the highest-ranking members of each house. What would be an intimate affair quickly turns into a sizeable party of prominent individuals.

Olympe has a dress selected for Myria by the time they return to the palace, reminding her that any social gathering is an opportunity to capture the prince's attention. With the promise of celebratory alcohol, Olympe's attendance is no surprise, and her dress matches Myria's: A black and crimson ensemble that makes up for its simple design with its flattering shape.

"We should extend the invitation to your friend, Lady Runewell," Olympe suggests as she tightens the dress's corset until Myria is appropriately breathless. "Something tells me she would appreciate the company of friends rather than being alone in her room tonight."

"Wine is the only guarantee of Mother's attendance for any courtly event," Geffrey explains with a tight smile.

"Clove wine is a royal specialty, and it would be simply *irresponsible* if I missed the chance to imbibe," Olympe defends without looking up. "I hear it is all the better when surrounded by friends." She scoffs at her own words.

Before Olympe can prod Myria out the door, Geffrey holds her back and whispers, "I know my mother is not your responsibility, but I would be forever grateful if you kept her under close watch."

"You speak as though she isn't a grown woman capable of conducting herself at a social event."

Geffrey sighs. "I know how she is and I worry about her. Her drinking can become rather overzealous, especially when surrounded by others."

Myria nods before he heads off to the mead hall on his own. Olympe leads Myria to the Runewell rooms. A lady's maid answers the door and lets them inside at Eulalia's instruction. When they enter, Eulalia lounges on a settee in a green robe, her brown hair hanging loose and damp across her shoulders.

"Get dressed," Myria says with a grin. "You're coming with us to Leor's celebration in the mead hall."

Eulalia's brows raise and her mouth gapes open for a moment before she responds. "I could not impose. My cousin already makes his appearance. The party is for the dukes and duchesses, and the knights who competed in the joust." She cocks her head to the side, apparently considering Myria's own inclusion in the festivities. "And the ladies who did likewise, it appears."

"Nonsense," Olympe says. "Nearly all the palace is abuzz about the gathering."

"But—" Eulalia starts, but Myria cuts her off.

"But nothing. If nothing else, you will be my guest. And it's another chance for you to steal some time with Leor."

"When you put it that way..." Eulalia says as she rises from her seat and disappears behind a changing screen in the corner, accompanied by her maid. She reappears moments later in a simple yet flattering ebon-black gown.

The three walk together arm-in-arm to the mead hall, laughing along the way as they reminisce over some of the other suitor's more unfortunate exploits during the tournament.

They arrive to find tables and benches lining the hall, while luxurious furs adorn the walls like tapestries. Torches fashioned from animal horns illuminate the long room in flickering light, casting irregular shadows. The dark, smoky atmosphere reminds Myria of the relaxed air of the Morning Glory. The dull cadence of multiple conversations fills the hall, setting Myria at ease as no one seems to notice their entrance.

Olympe navigates her way to an empty table in the corner, and Myria follows with Eulalia in tow. Geffrey stands among the center crowd of noblemen flanking the prince, and Myria realizes few women are in attendance.

"What shall your poison be?" Olympe asks, eyeing the barrels nearby. Eulalia and Myria take a seat opposite of each other.

Eulalia follows her gaze and hides her wringing hands under the table. "Wine will do."

Olympe gives a dramatic eye roll. "What sort of wine?"

Myria intervenes. "How about mead for both of us?"

Eulalia nods at the suggestion, and Olympe saunters away. She returns after a minute with a tray of several drinks and takes a seat next to Eulalia, who takes a test sip of the mead before a smile spreads across her face. For herself, Olympe holds two glasses, one for each hand. She tilts her head back, quickly draining the contents of one cup, and slams it back on the table. Eulalia jumps at the sudden sound.

Myria gapes at her aunt. "Did you find your clove wine?"

Olympe smirks and prepares to do the same with her second goblet.

Remembering Geffrey's words, Myria reaches across the table, covering the cup with her palm and dragging it away from her. "Maybe we should take it slow?"

Olympe scowls.

Eulalia clears her throat. "Perhaps a drinking game? Do you know any, Myria?"

"A few. At the Morning Glory, we used to play Fables and Legends, Save the King, Dragon Tail, or Court the Maiden." Myria pauses, her face twisting as she considers how most of those games would not be suitable for court.

But Eulalia seems to brighten at the suggestions. "Let us try the first one. Fables and Legends was it? How do we play?"

Myria suppresses the urge to sigh with relief when Eulalia chooses the safest game, but she narrows her eyes at Olympe.

The scowl does not entirely disappear. "Fine, I shall play along too."

Myria returns the goblet. "Fables and Legends is pretty simple. We take turns by stating two things about ourselves, one truth and one lie. The others try to determine which one is the truth. If you guess it correctly, the liar drinks. If not, then you drink."

"I will go first," Olympe volunteers, straightening in her seat. She clears her throat. "One, I am the mother of a duke. Two, I am descended from common blood."

Myria frowns. "The first statement is obviously the truth."

"Correct!" she exclaims. "Now, I drink." As promised, she drags her wine back across the table and takes a deep draught.

Eulalia looks puzzled. "I am not sure if I understand the point of this game."

"The point of this game is to make the lie sound like truth or the truth sound like an outlandish lie. Make it convincing, something that isn't so obvious. Unlike Olympe, you'll want to avoid getting drunk since the loser is the one who drinks."

Eulalia nods.

Myria groans. "I'll go now." She drums her fingers on the table, thinking. A slow smile spreads across her face. "One, I've had a nobleman entertain the idea of marriage to me *today*. Two, a fisherman once proposed to marry me in exchange for my grandmother's inn."

Understanding flashes across Eulalia's face. "Oh, I see. Both statements should seem unlikely."

Myria smirks. "So, which one is the lie?"

Eulalia strokes her chin in thought. "I would say your first statement is false since we are competing to marry the prince."

Myria turns her smirk to her aunt. "And what do you think?"

"I would have to agree with your friend."

The smirk widens, flashing teeth. "And in this case, you would both take a drink since my first statement is actually true."

Eulalia's eyes widen as Olympe takes another greedy gulp of wine without question. "You got a marriage offer today? When? From the prince?" Something minute tightens in her eyes, and Myria is almost too afraid to name it as jealousy.

"No, of course not," Myria denies in a voice that sounds too loud for her ears. She then lowers her voice. "There was no outright proposal. A certain Lord Sigurd was so grateful for me helping him, he merely mentioned thanking me with a marriage proposal." The levity she previously imagined at the topic weighs like lead in her stomach as she's reminded of the intensity of Sigurd's affection.

Eulalia giggles, and her eyes snap to the center of the room. Myria follows her gaze to see Prince Leor surrounded by several nobles. However, Sigurd stands out among them as he suddenly makes eye contact with her.

Myria looks away, heat rising in her face. "Don't look at him," she hisses.

Eulalia does as instructed, but Olympe does nothing of the sort, her eyes locked on Sigurd. She nods, lips pursed. "Were you not trying for the prince, Sigurd would be a suitable match. Geffrey would approve. He has the right physicality."

"*Olympe*," Myria issues through clenched teeth. She lifts a hand to shield her face from an approaching figure.

Her aunt continues, undeterred. "We are about to find out if he can make for stimulating conversation, as well."

Myria's voice is a low growl. "I swear—"

"Lady Myria, I did not expect to see you tonight."

Myria's stomach plummets when she hears the undeniable voice next to her. She forces a smile and looks up at him. "Good evening, Lord Sigurd," she greets in a weak voice.

His face is dazzling even in the dim hall, scrubbed clean of any tournament grime. He has tamed his wiry copper beard into a pointed braid, but a sling ties up his right arm, perhaps a vestige from falling off his horse. His smile is polite and reserved compared to the unbridled openness from the healer's tent. "Might I join your table, ladies?"

Courtesy prevents Myria from rejecting the request, so Eulalia speaks up in her stead. "Certainly, my lord. Lady Myria was teaching us how to play Fables and Legends."

Lord Sigurd eases himself on the bench next to Myria. Olympe does nothing to hide the amusement on her face, but Eulalia at least strives for an expression of apologetic pity.

"Whose turn is it now?" Sigurd asks, surprising Myria by maintaining a respectable distance between them. He seems to avoid making eye contact with her as well, instead training them on the wood grain of the rough table.

"My turn, I believe," Eulalia says, clearing her throat. Her face scrunches as she thinks for a moment. "Okay. First, I was once engaged to a foreign lord. Second, my father tried sending me away to live in a temple when I was a child."

"I'm going to say the first one is the lie," Myria says after a moment's consideration. Olympe nods in agreement.

Eulalia flashes a triumphant grin. "Well, you would be wrong. I was engaged to a foreign lord, but it was actually my *mother* that tried sending me away."

Myria frowns as Olympe takes an eager drink. "Neither of those circumstances sound particularly pleasant."

Eulalia shrugs as she stares into her cup. "I never met the lord, but it was an arrangement my parents tried securing for me when I was a child. And my mother believed if I lived at the temple, I would have access to an unparalleled education. But the temple was very far away, so my father refused to entertain the idea." Her soft, brown eyes meet Myria's, and she grins. "It's your turn to drink now."

Myria obliges.

"Would you care to take a turn, Lord Sigurd?" Eulalia offers the silent man next to them.

Sigurd considers the offer. "I did not bring a drink with me to play." He looks across the room where a barkeep serves alcohol and then glances down at his arm in the sling. Thick eyebrows draw together as if in silent calculation.

Myria rises to her feet. "I'll get you something, Lord Sigurd. Do you have a preference?"

"Ale is fine. Thank you, Lady Myria."

Myria weaves through the crowd, again reminded of the Morning Glory. She almost smiles at the coincidence of playing barmaid to Sigurd before shaking her head to clear her thoughts.

"Lady Myria?"

She whirls around at her name, Sigurd's frothy mug of ale swishing in her hands. She keeps it from spilling as she notices Leor in front of her.

She inclines her head with a smile. "Prince Leor, you did well at the tournament today."

A smile graces the prince's face, but it does not quite reach his eyes. "I should offer *you* the same compliment."

Myria rolls her eyes. "At least you won your joust."

"Are you going to formally introduce us yet?" asks a female voice next to Leor. "You denied me the pleasure at the joust." It surprises Myria to see it belongs to the guard shadowing Leor at the tournament. The woman wears beautiful plate armor, an Avalion lion painted on her cape and a sword sheathed at her waist.

Leor turns to introduce her. "Ah, yes. Lady Myria, this is my Captain of the Guard, Rozenna. Captain Rozenna, this is Lady Myria."

Captain Rozenna regards Myria with what looks like a critical eye. Her dark hair is secured in a tight braid that showcases sharp cheekbones. She folds her arms across her chest. "So, you must be the prince's new security concern."

Myria struggles to maintain her smile as she looks between them in confusion. "I'm sorry, security concern?" she repeats.

"Yes, the unknown variable at court with no established background. You are fond of luring our prince here to secret adventures." Here, Rozenna turns a critical eye to Leor. "Adventures that our beloved prince knows may lead him away from the watchful gaze of the guard. Such actions can be dangerous."

"I apologize. I did not intend to endanger the prince," Myria says.

Leor beams, as if unashamed of his crimes. The reminder of their private moments only seems to amuse him as he continues flashing that royal smile. "I shan't apologize for roaming the grounds of my home."

Rozenna's smile is thin. "Of course, Your Majesty. If you will excuse me, it was a pleasure meeting you, Lady Myria."

Myria nods, but based on Rozenna's icy tone, suspects it is not a pleasure at all. The captain excuses herself all the same, disappearing among the crowd.

"Please do not mind her abrasive demeanor," Leor says, stepping closer. "Her job is to protect the royal family, and the job can cost anyone their good humor. It is good to see you tonight."

"Likewise," Myria agrees, smiling. The flickering torchlight make Leor's honey-colored hair appear darker in the hall.

"Where are you sitting? I should like to join you."

Myria leads Prince Leor to their table, and the eyes of Olympe, Eulalia, and Sigurd widen in shock at her new guest. "I believe you are all familiar with Prince Leor?" Myria asks, unable to hide the smugness in her voice as she sinks into her seat.

Lord Sigurd hastily rises to his feet for the prince, but lets out a pained groan as his injured arm catches the edge of the table. Myria pulls him back to his seat with his other elbow.

Eulalia flutters her eyelashes at Leor, and Myria tilts her head, recognizing the courtly flirt for what it is. "It is kind of you to join us, Your Majesty. We were just playing a game."

Leor takes a moment to reply, his amber eyes on Sigurd. He takes the seat on Myria's other side, asking, "What game is this?"

"Fables and Legends," Myria answers, scooting the mug of ale to Sigurd. "It's Lord Rosenford's turn."

"I trust that this will make for better entertainment than Duke Bramble's dancing," Leor says with a chuckle.

At this, everyone turns to see Geffrey dancing on the center table as others chant around him. Olympe's face drains of color as she stares at her son, then she climbs to her feet. "Nope, not enough wine for this," she mutters before disappearing.

Myria turns back to Sigurd with some difficulty, attempting to banish the horrifying images from her mind. "Lord Sigurd?" she prompts.

Sigurd contemplates for a moment. "One, I once became shipwrecked and stranded on driftwood for days after a terrible storm. And two..." Here, Sigurd pauses, meeting Myria's eyes with an intensity that causes the hair on the back of her neck to prickle. "I made an absolute fool of myself today."

Myria tilts her head at the second statement, deciphering some hidden message. *Is this an apology for his behavior in the healer's tent?* When he says nothing, as if waiting for her response, she smiles at him.

"Lord Sigurd, you did not make a fool of yourself today, so your first statement must be the truth," she informs him.

Leor and Eulalia murmur in agreement. Sigurd looks stunned. "You are very gracious, Lady Myria, but you already know—"

She speaks over him to save him from embarrassment. "We already know you behaved honorably at the joust today, Lord Rosenford. It is not your fault Lord Aryn slackened his grip on the lance to make you fall from your horse. Since we easily detected your falsehood, it is your turn to drink." She pushes the mug closer to him for emphasis.

A moment of consideration passes. Sigurd shares a look of relief before obliging her.

"Prince Leor," Eulalia addresses. "Would you like to continue the game, or should Myria teach us a new one?"

Before Leor can answer, a new and unwelcome voice interjects. "It is unsurprising to discover a barmaid familiar with an abundance of drinking games." Aryn appears in a dark tunic, fingers curled around a large horn of ale.

"However, one should not forget that such pastimes are not becoming of a lady, much less a potential queen of Avalion."

Myria's face flushes at his presence, reddening in anger rather than embarrassment. She struggles to keep her tone even. "I find drinking games a great way to strengthen the bonds of a community, Lord Stirling. A perspective unable to understand the value is too narrow-minded to serve their kingdom properly."

Aryn smiles, as if her response both amuses and impresses him, but the condescension remains in his tone. "Your Majesty, I would like to propose something a bit more dignified than a drinking game. How about a *sumbel*?" He gestures toward the horn in his hand.

Prince Leor nods at the idea and climbs on the table. "A sumbel!" he announces to the hall. The cadence of conversations pauses, and all the men shout in excitement. Even Geffrey stops dancing.

Myria glances between Eulalia and Sigurd at the unfamiliar term. Neither seem to share her confusion. When she looks back at Aryn, his malicious smirk is on her, perhaps relishing in her discomfort. The noblemen in the room gather in a tight circle around the prince and their table. They pack too tightly for her to escape. Even Eulalia is lost from her sight as others press close. Her throat goes dry.

However, Sigurd whispers in her ear, his reassuring words like a drop of water in a barren desert. "A sumbel is simply a long series of toasts. Everyone takes turns in a rule of three. The first toast is for a winner, the second toast is for a loser, and the third toast is for royalty."

Before Myria can thank him for the information, Aryn climbs on their table. His foot knocks into her mead, spilling the drink on her dress. No one seems to notice as she tries to wipe herself dry and scowls at the offending lord.

"I would like to make the first toast," Aryn says, calling the room to silence. He raises his mug and fixes his sharp eyes on someone Myria cannot see. "Our revelry tonight would be remiss if we did not celebrate the only victor who matters. I drink to Sir Emiri, who is *not* a knight, who is *not* of noble blood, but yet, somehow, still surprises us all with his powerful capabilities and enduring friendships. For Sir Emiri!"

The room erupts in a chorus of cheers as Aryn takes a swig from the horn, but Myria can only scowl at the thinly-veiled insults. She cannot see Leor's face with his back to her, but his displeasure is apparent in the tense line of his shoulders.

Aryn's eyes fall on her next, and he holds out a hand. "I call upon Lady Myria to make the next toast."

Her mouth falls open in surprise. Her mind races as every eye falls upon her. She attempts to get to her feet, but a deft movement from Aryn's hand roughly yanks her onto the table before he pushes the horn into her hands.

At first, her finger traces the smooth curve of the horn, idly wondering what beast it came from. She is unable to speak or think as the hall of expectant faces watches her and the soaked front of her dress. Is this what Aryn wanted to do? Humiliate her?

Her eyes finally stop on Sigurd, closest to her feet, and she remembers his words long enough to find her own. Winner, loser, royalty. She clears her throat and raises the horn. "And I would like to raise a toast for Lord Sigurd. Although he fought valiantly in the tournament, we should recognize that his loss only came as a result of Aryn's poor jousting skills. To Lord Sigurd, who can only lose when someone fights in his stead!"

The cheers for her toast are louder than they were for Aryn's, accompanied by boisterous laughter. She catches a glimpse of Aryn's displeased expression before turning to see Sigurd's appreciative smile. He raises his cup and drinks as she does.

She passes the mug to Sigurd, helping him to keep his balance as he climbs on the table before she steps down. Safe on the ground, she allows herself a steady breath as Sigurd says, "I would like to propose a toast to Prince Leor for hosting such a riveting and spectacular tournament."

Sigurd hands the mug to Leor. The prince pauses, his eyes sweeping the dim room before a smile stretches across his face. He locks eyes with someone in the crowd and begins his toast, raising his arm that still has the red favour tied around his wrist.

"Let us not forget the brave Duchess Cressida in our celebrations, who was one of the first ladies to joust in *years*. Her victory is a lesson to us all on tenacity and strength."

Myria cranes her neck to see Cressida standing at the fringe of the crowd. A tight smile graces her lips as she raises her glass in acknowledgment of Leor's words. As everyone takes a drink, Myria slips through the crowd and makes her way to the duchess.

"I didn't realize you were here," Myria greets with a smile, surprising herself with her own authenticity. "I would have invited you to our table."

Cressida spares her a brief glance before returning her attention to the crowd in front of them. "I am here due to social obligation as the head of my house, not to play silly games. I am not surprised to see you. Does the wine call to you like Dowager Duchess Bramble, or just as a barmaid?"

Myria's eyes widen at the remark, reminded of Aryn's snide comment.

Cressida smirks, a vicious flash of brilliant teeth. "Oh, yes. Word has been traveling fast about the extent of your common heritage. Lord Aryn has made sure of that. The novel lady taking the court by storm is truly an innkeeper. Then, the innkeeper is actually a barmaid. I would not be surprised if soon, the barmaid turns to prostitute—anything to ruin your chances at court."

Myria's eyes flit to Aryn, still standing next to Leor, as her face drains of color. She struggles to keep her voice even as she responds. "You know, Duchess Cressida, there is no reason we cannot be friends."

"I think otherwise," Cressida disagrees. Myria turns to see the vicious teeth sheathed for now, replaced by a stony mask. "There is every reason we cannot be friends. We come from vastly different worlds. You would never understand the nuanced complexities of my station, and as such, you should not even be here trying to win the prince's hand. He will never choose you for his queen, and if he did, he would be making the biggest mistake of his life."

Myria recalls everything Emiri told her about Cressida. At that moment, she can understand his contempt for the duchess. Taking a sip of her mead, Myria scrutinizes Cressida's face and seeks any stray thought that might pass through her expression. "Would it be a mistake just because he didn't pick you?"

"While not picking me would be a mistake itself, selecting *you* over any of the other suitors is an ill-advised decision—a slap to the face of this entire kingdom. Imagining you as queen makes me taste bile."

The insults do not hold the bite Cressida intends. Myria conceals a grin by taking another sip. "Please, my dear duchess, do not hide your true feelings from me. I think honesty best serves us both."

Cressida glares down at her from the rim of her goblet. "You may think yourself cheeky, but it will not be enough to rule the country."

"Out of curiosity, if the choice was between Lady Theodora or me, who would you rather see on the throne?"

Cressida's glare shifts to Aryn, and something imperceptible hardens her face even more as she lowers her goblet. "The Nocturnus and Stirling families have been at odds for years. Usually, I do not have the patience for such rivalries; however, Theodora as queen would be a mistake of its own kind. One can hardly prefer the better mistake, the Queen of Fools or the Queen of Evil." Cressida pauses as if waiting for Myria's reaction, and then clarifies, "You would be the Queen of Fools in this scenario."

Myria frowns, but it is not for the reason Cressida expects. "You think Theodora would be an evil queen?"

"Of course, you are surprised. You are a youth when it comes to courtly politics." A servant passes by, and Cressida sets her empty goblet on his tray. "Keep up your naïve hope that there is good in everyone, and you shall only prove me right in that you are the Queen of Fools."

Myria turns her gaze to study elsewhere. "Thank you for your counsel, Duchess Cressida."

Cressida scoffs before walking away. By now, Leor holds up the sumbel horn for a second time, now refilled with ale, and looks across the faces in the crowd. His eyes briefly meet Myria's, and she can see the hint of an intrigued smile before he looks somewhere else. "Sir Emiri, would you care to give the next toast?"

The crowd parts as they turn to the man in question, standing next to Captain Rozenna. Emiri looks surprised at the attention, but his face remains impassive as he climbs onto the table next to his friend. He takes the horn and raises it with a hand still bearing Myria's favor tied around the wrist.

"A toast to someone defeated is next, correct?" Emiri scans the crowd until he spots her. "A toast to Lady Hawthorne, who—despite her defeat—inspired many with her resiliency on horseback."

Myria's face burns at the cheers his toast brings, and she raises her goblet in response.

The mug continues to pass to various lords and nobles in the room until the toasts eventually die down. Myria looks for Olympe, having not seen her since their drinking game, and finds her outside on a nearby balcony. As she joins her aunt, the crisp night air washes over her sweat-beaded face.

"Olympe?" Myria calls. She places a reassuring hand on her aunt's shoulder just as Olympe doubles over the balcony railing, gripping her stomach.

Olympe waves her off. "I am fine, just too much clove wine." She makes an awful retching sound, and Myria is quick to hold back her hair. She does not want to think if there are any unfortunate passersby below.

"Maybe we should get Geffrey to help you back to the room?"

Olympe straightens, her expression so severe one would not think she just vomited her guts over the railing onto the grounds below. "You will not get Geffrey. You will, however, find me some water."

Myria complies for the moment, hurrying back inside. She approaches the barkeep with her request, and while she waits, overhears familiar voices drawing near.

"...it's a rather *public* statement..."

"I assure you, Captain..."

Emiri and Captain Rozenna fall silent as soon as Myria turns around, Olympe's water in hand. Myria looks between them as the sudden, suspicious silence drags for a tense moment.

"Sir Emiri, Captain," Myria says with a nod to cut through the thick air between them.

Rozenna's mouth twitches into a half-smirk. "Lady Myria," she returns. "You've already met Emiri."

"Yes, we have met," Emiri says before Myria can respond. He shifts his arm, catching Myria's eye, as he appears to hide something behind him.

"Enjoying the celebrations?" Myria asks, returning her attention to their faces.

Rozenna shifts her weight, leaning against Emiri's arm. "Emiri here is not one for parties, but he manages for the sake of the prince." Rozenna leans further, but Myria can tell her action is deliberate, the guard captain too keen and alert to be drunk.

Both of Emiri's hands reach out automatically to steady Rozenna before she can lean too far and lose her balance. In doing so, Myria notices his right hand clutching the yellow favour no longer tied around his wrist. Her favour.

Rozenna continues, keeping a grip on his forearm. "He often finds the company of nobles lacking."

It takes another moment of staring at her kerchief for Myria to realize they had just been speaking about *her*. The thought makes her feel uneasy, but she meets Rozenna's smirk with a wide smile. "He is fortunate, then, that you are here to save him from such company. Please excuse me, I must return to my aunt."

Rozenna waves her off without a second glance. Emiri hesitates, inclining his head at her meaningfully. "I will see you at dawn, Lady Myria."

She remembers her scheduled magic lessons and turns her smile to him. It feels much more genuine this time. "Of course. Good evening, *Sir* Emiri." She laughs at the imposed title.

Outside, Olympe accepts the water goblet and drinks, heedless of liquid dribbling down her face and dress. After draining the goblet, she slams it on the railing and buries her face in her hands.

"We should probably retire for the evening," Myria suggests. "It is rather late."

Mercifully, Olympe does not protest. Myria retrieves Eulalia, and her aunt accepts their arms as they escort her back to the Bramble suite. They help her undress for the night and make her comfortable in her bed. Soon, the sound of her heavy snores fill the room.

Eulalia closes the door behind them with a giggle. "She seems to have enjoyed herself."

Myria nods in agreement, but her mind is elsewhere. "Eulalia, would you consider yourself knowledgeable in the realm of courtly flirtations?"

Eulalia arches a beautiful eyebrow at the subject change. "I may be knowledgeable in the customs and practices, but I doubt if I would consider myself *experienced*. I am not here at court often."

"If we give our favour to a knight, like at the joust, what happens to it? Do they keep it?"

Eulalia considers the question for a silent moment. Her bright eyes seem to penetrate Myria, as if they can read her inner thoughts. She finally answers, "Typically, the favour is offered back to the lady in question. Many consider it rude for the knight to keep it, unless you are betrothed to him. Unless it is a favour of love; a token of the affection shared between them. Both a secret and public declaration of their attraction." Her friend pauses, offering a sly, intrigued smile.

Myria frowns. "Why are you looking at me like that?"

"Whatever happened to your favour, Lady Myria?"

Myria's stomach clenches, not in the same way Olympe's did earlier. Her mind scrambles for an explanation. "Oh, it—"

Suddenly, the door to the Bramble suite bangs open and Geffrey appears, his eyes red and his hair a ruffled mess. He pauses when he notices the two of them standing there. "Lady Eulalia, Myria. I did not mean to interrupt."

Eulalia curtsies, but her eyes never stray from Myria's face. "It is no trouble, Duke Bramble. I was just returning to my room for the night." Her eyes pierce Myria before she disappears, and Myria knows she will not escape her questions later.

Myria bids Geffrey goodnight before taking refuge in her own room to reflect on the day's eventful nature. She thinks of Sigurd's interest in marriage and Cressida's words on the Stirlings. However, as she sets her new crystal on the window ledge to absorb the moonlight, her mind lingers on Rozenna leaning on Emiri and the favour he held in his hand.

9

HISTORY

At dawn the next morning, Myria wanders the halls of the palace as she makes her way to the Mage's Tower alone to allow Geffrey to sleep in after his long night. Several questions weigh on her mind, chiefly about Rozenna, Emiri, and their conversation the previous night. But Myria does not want to bring up the conversation with Emiri at the risk of shattering their tentative peace. *Would answers about Rozenna's disapproval of Emiri's 'public statement,' and everything that might entail, be worth a tense magic lessons?* She wants to avoid another 'dirty barmaid' incident.

Myria finds the massive wooden door to the tower without problem but hesitates before knocking. Her fingers spin her moon crystal in agitated circles, a wave of doubt sickening her stomach. A quick breath steels her, and she raps on the door with white knuckles.

The response is instantaneous. "Come in."

Emiri's voice does not fill her with the relief she hopes for, but Myria quickly does as bid.

He waits by the balcony. After a quick glance of his expression, she determines he does not seem annoyed, impatient, or reluctant about their lesson. An uncharacteristic timidity keeps her tethered to the spot.

She closes the door and searches for a greeting that will ease the tension she feels in her fingers, shoulders, and jaw. "What are we doing today?"

"I thought I might leave the decision to you," he says. He eyes her form lingering by the door but continues. "I've told you we have sun and moon crystals which satisfy different purposes. Because you are already familiar with healing magic, I can do more to strengthen your knowledge of moon magic. Or I can teach you something new with sun magic. The choice is yours."

Myria considers his suggestions, finding herself lost in newfound indecisiveness. Her eyes trail the shape of the hearth on the opposite side of the room, lost in thought. A painting of a sword hanging above it captures her attention. The background is a body of water, and a pale hand reaches from the water's surface to grasp the sword hilt.

"Is there something on your mind?" Emiri's voice interrupts her reverie.

She blinks to see him stepping closer. Her toes curl in her boots and her grip tightens on the crystal. The questions linger just beyond her lips. What was the public statement Rozenna referred to last evening? Why did she disapprove? And the favour...

Myria's throat swells as she searches for a different topic to distract herself. Her instinctive step back to put more distance between them results in her back pressing against the wall. Emiri seems to notice her retreat and freezes in his tracks.

She clears her throat and forces a placid smile. "I was curious about *you*, actually," she begins. "You said yesterday that you're not the court mage."

"That is correct."

"Was no one ever appointed after your father passed?"

A grim smile twists his features. "No. King Uriel has not seen it as a pressing issue."

"Why?"

He pauses, an idle thumb scratching his chin. "A difficult question. I am not the king, but I suspect that committing to the appointment would create some resistance among the peerage."

Theodora's words echo in her mind. *Court mage pretender.* "You're the only one I've seen perform magic. Is there even another person suitable for the job?"

His chuckle is dry and humorless. "No. I was around when my father taught them, the lords and dukes and duchesses. The ones who were willing to learn from him, anyway. The older generation—your aunt, for one—couldn't learn; they couldn't manage a single spell."

The information surprises Myria. "Why not?"

"My father speculated it was because they were too closed off. They grew up valuing material things, not appreciating nature. Magic comes from the world around us, and to harness it, you need to be receptive to its energies. Their children were easier to teach by fostering those values at an early age. But they were still terrible, using magic as little more than parlor tricks—still victims to their parents' influence."

"I haven't even seen a parlor trick from Geffrey."

Emiri's eyes crinkle and he looks past Myria's shoulder, as if lost in some memory. "Geffrey is bad at magic too. Few of them practice anymore, because it requires more than they're willing to give."

"Which is?"

"Hard work. Dedication. A bit of ourselves devoted to the spells which we can never get back. It's hard to pinpoint *one* reason. Magic may be reserved for the nobility, but even among them, it isn't for everyone."

"But I'm not a child, and I've been able to use magic,"

Emiri examines her from head to toe and back again, the severity of which makes Myria flush. "You're right. Maybe because you weren't raised as one of them. You've had to work hard in your life and you're more perceptive to your surroundings. Perhaps a stronger will..." He trails off.

Myria clears her throat. "How could you and your dad learn magic if you weren't nobles?"

He considers the question through narrowed eyes before turning his gaze on the painting that caught her attention before. "It is true that only nobles may learn magic here in Avalion. However, Avalion is not the only land, and it certainly doesn't hold all the magic in the world."

Myria's mouth falls open as she realizes his meaning. "You're not from Avalion."

He offers a wry smile, eyes moving to the painting. "No, my birth home is a place to the north called Caliburn."

"What made you come to Avalion?"

For a long moment, Emiri doesn't answer. When he responds, his voice sounds distant. "I don't blame your curiosity, Lady Hawthorne. However, the answer is a long, complicated history full of military conquest and pain. I would prefer not to recite it this morning."

Myria's face burns, ashamed. "I'm sorry. I did not intend to revive painful memories."

Emiri shakes his head, as if to clear it, before meeting her eyes once more. She can see the vestiges of his past receding from his eyes as he forces a smile that does not match the hard planes of his face. "So, do you want to learn something new or practice what you know?"

"Something new," she decides, pocketing her moon crystal.

She follows him outside to the balcony, where the sun gilds the sky in a fiery glow that softens Emiri's face.

He begins, "The moon is the celestial body of change. Just as the moon changes shape throughout the month, it also affects the tides. Conversely, the sun is the celestial body of creation. It fuels life, warmth, and harvest. When none of them are present, such as during a lunar or solar eclipse, the world is then cast in darkness. This is the magic of destruction."

"Change, creation, and destruction," Myria repeats.

"As I said yesterday, moon magic is the primary source for healing magic. Healing is the intentional manipulation and change of the human body. You may change the position of flesh or bone, but you are not adding anything new for consideration. Healing is just a small facet of moon magic."

"And sun magic?" she prompts.

"The possibilities are almost limitless. Weaker mages may only be able to conjure images, but more capable ones can summon corporeal objects."

He gestures behind her, and Myria turns to see a large standing mirror on the balcony. In the reflection, she can see in sharp detail her scuffed leather pants, the erratic strands of hair escaping her braid, and the oppressive bags below her eyes. She averts her gaze from the mirror, the reflection a stark contrast to the glittering nobility that surrounds her within these walls. "What's the mirror for?" she asks.

Emiri hands her an empty goblet. "Focus on the reflection of this cup. You can feel how it's empty, but you're going to conjure water in it by first focusing on changing its image in the reflection."

"Don't I need a sun crystal?"

In the mirror, she sees Emiri grin. "That would be the easiest method." He does not move to offer her a crystal.

"You *don't* want me to start something new using the easiest method?" she asks.

"What's the point of learning something new if you don't understand it fully? What energy would the sun crystal give you that you don't already have?"

She ponders his words for a moment, eyes drifting to the horizon. "You want me to use the energy from the sunrise."

She looks back to the mirror, and he nods over her shoulder. "It will be more difficult, of course, without the concentrated energy source, but you'll be better off for it. Absorb the energy from your surroundings, become in tune with the environment, and the magic you harness from the natural source will be stronger. The crystals should be reserved for when the sun or moon aren't available to you."

Myria focuses on the water goblet in the mirror. Emiri takes a step back so that he is no longer in view.

"Imagine the cup filling with water, and what that looks like in the mirror. Then, we'll focus on the real thing and what it would feel like. How heavy would the cup feel in your hands, how warm or cold, and how full it should be."

A knock at the door interrupts her concentration. She turns to glance back inside the Mage's Tower.

Emiri releases an impatient sigh behind her. "One moment," he mutters. "Keep concentrating."

He walks away to answer the door, which hides the visitor from view as Emiri steps into the corridor to talk to them.

Myria frowns, returning her attention to the goblet in her hands. She ignores the mirror altogether and focuses on the heat from the morning sun, her eyes locked on the cup in her hands. Several minutes pass, her only movement the slow, even rise and fall of her chest as she breathes. A faint ringing in her ears occupies her senses, and the strain forces her to blink. Suddenly, the chalice is full of water. The room tilts for a moment before righting itself.

A proud smile stretches across her face as she turns around to see Emiri returning. He eyes her expression warily before his eyes fall to the goblet she holds up for his inspection.

"You did it," he remarks, his voice mute with what sounds like disbelief and surprise. He takes the goblet, tests its weight, then suddenly tosses the contents over the railing. "Do it again."

Her smile dissolves into a frown. "You don't think I did it right the first time?"

"I have no doubt, but consistency is always a valuable quality in a mage."

Scowling, Myria snatches the goblet back and refocuses her concentration. Her jaw clenches until the familiar ringing returns to her ears. A moment later, she presents her second goblet of water.

Emiri does a poor job of concealing his surprise. "You didn't even use the mirror." He gingerly sips the water before emptying the cup over the railing like the first. An idea forms in his eyes, a new determination settling across his face. He hands the goblet back with a new demand. "Make the water *cold* this time."

Her smirk is short-lived. "How?"

"The same way you made the water the first two times. Think about it, conceptualize it."

Myria drums her fingers against the rim of the goblet as she focuses her energy a third time. The ringing in her ears makes her feel lightheaded, but she grits through the discomfort as water materializes once again in the vessel. She can feel the chill through the metal.

He does not compliment her progress, but his astonishment is apparent in the wide regard of his eyes. The lesson continues, and he gives her a series of tasks with the water goblet, each more complex than the last. With every accomplishment, he dumps the water over the balcony before requiring a new achievement. He asks for boiling water, dyed water, frozen water. The ice gives her some difficulty. Emiri guides her to imagine something solid instead of liquid, to trace the precise shape and size with her mind. Then she executes it easily enough.

The persistent ringing slowly swells in volume with each task, but Myria uses it to help her focus. A dull pain throbs in the back of her head. "What's next?" she asks.

Emiri narrows his eyes. "You want to do *more*?" He holds up a hand to shield his eyes as he analyzes the sun's position.

Myria can tell the agreed-upon hour has passed, but she does not want to lose her momentum. "Unless you have other plans?"

He shakes his head, though she can see the hint of a smile in his features. "Does your magic not take a toll on your body? It can be rather draining for new students."

She shrugs. "I can feel a little of that, but it is nothing I can't handle."

He considers her for a moment. "Would you not rather use this time to break your fast with the other nobles? Increase your chances with the prince?"

Images of the other nobles—the scorn on Cressida's and Arryn's faces, Theodora's condescension, even Eulalia's pity—flash through her mind. The thought of seeing them again so soon makes her stomach plummet. "I think I will manage without them."

Emiri studies her in silence, and the air between them charges with an inexplicable intensity. But when he shakes his head, the moment passes. "Your progress has been rather impressive. I've never known any students of magic to master the things you have so quickly."

Myria does not suppress the proud smirk that rises to her face. "How many students have you taught?"

"You're my first formal student, but I used to assist my father when he taught the other nobles." His eyes lose focus on some distant memories.

Her smirk fades as she watches his expression shift. "You learned everything from him?"

He nods. "He was exceptionally talented and had great patience for the tempers of noble children. He protected me as much as he could when *my* temper got the best of me."

"You had a temper?" Myria asks, amused by the thought.

He arches an eyebrow, and his voice takes on a dark edge. "Is that so difficult to believe? The likes of Duchess Cressida enjoy throwing their weight and power around to hurt those they see below them. I didn't understand how this was the way of things. I... struggled to accept it."

"I have no doubt of Cressida's entitlement. However, it's hard to imagine you with a temper. You're always standing in the prince's shadow like nothing in the world can bother you. When Theodora insulted you at the tournament yesterday, Leor seemed more upset by her words than you did."

Emiri offers a wry smile. "It didn't come easily. My cool exterior comes from years of being put in my place. Besides, I would have to value Theodora's, or any Stirling's opinion, for it to bother me. I'm not concerned by the thoughts of snakes."

Myria hesitates at his words, strongly reminded of the advice she gave Eulalia at the masquerade.

"If we're going to continue the lesson, you should at least take a break and eat. Come, I'm sure the kitchens will have something."

They leave the Mage's Tower, and Emiri leads her through private corridors in the palace she has never seen before. Soon, Myria smells the sweet scent of baking bread before Emiri ducks through the low kitchen doorway. She stays close behind him, eyeing the bustling servants toiling at breakfast preparations without a second glance at them. The excessive noise overwhelms Myria; the banging of pots, the clattering of plates and cutlery, and the shouts of servants calling back and forth to each other.

"Hattie!" Emiri yells over the din in a voice much more jovial than Myria's ever heard from him. She peers around to see a woman with strong hands and silver hair jump at the sound before she turns a stern gaze on Emiri.

"What are you doing in my kitchen?" she scolds, though there is a teasing edge to her voice. "Don't you know I'm busy? I've got an entire palace of nobles to feed, and they're very particular about their food."

Emiri chuckles and steps closer to the woman. "We won't trouble you for long. We were looking for breakfast as well."

"*We?*" Hattie repeats with suspicious curiosity.

Emiri side steps, presenting Myria. "This is Lady Myria Hawthorne. Myria, this is Hattie, the head cook of the palace." Myria cringes at the formal address, suppressing the urge to punch him in the ribs.

"*Lady?*" Hattie repeats again, her eyes roaming over the humble leather pants Myria chose to wear this morning. "She doesn't look like any lady I have seen."

Hattie's words sound more intrigued than critical, but Myria still cannot help the blush that rises to her cheeks. She greets with a polite curtsy, "It's nice to meet you."

Hattie laughs as she glances sideways at Emiri. "Definitely not like any noble I've ever seen." She reaches for Myria's hand and takes it within her warm grasp. "It's a pleasure to meet you as well, *Lady* Myria."

"Just Myria is fine." As she says this, she stifles a giggle as thoughts of 'Just Leor' pop into her head.

With Hattie's permission, Emiri pilfers a fresh loaf of bread and a plate laden with slices of salted ham before they slip back to the Mage's Tower. Myria is relieved they do not encounter anyone on the way back.

They eat on the balcony, their legs hanging in the air through the stone railing and a comfortable silence lingering between them. Myria tears into her half of the bread, pairing it with the ham. She savors the tender meat before chewing.

"I think Hattie's cooking would put my grandmother's to shame," she remarks. Her eyes wander over the outline of the palace gardens, lost in thought as she wonders how Grandma Iris is faring.

"You miss her?" Emiri asks.

A sharp prick constricting her throat confirms his words. She swallows past the lump and merely nods.

"Will you tell me about her?" he asks.

At first, Myria does not trust herself with words. She steals a glance at Emiri through her eyelashes. His face, open and curious, stuns her. His gaze, earnest and burning, steals her breath.

Myria turns away, clearing her throat. "Really, she's the only family I've ever had. I don't remember my parents. After they died, she was the only one there for me. She took care of me and taught me everything I know. I helped her run the Morning Glory. Of course, I was not without a penchant for mischief." A faint smile flutters to her lips as she remembers the many scoldings Grandma Iris gave her.

Emiri chuckles beside her. The sound isn't dry, like before. "You, a troublemaker? I wish I could say I was surprised."

"Why?" she asks, mustering the confidence to look back at him.

"From the few days I've known you, you refuse to take 'no' for an answer. You don't let the Stirlings—or even Cressida—intimidate you." He snarls the names, but his tone relaxes as he continues. "And despite what I told you about healing only what you can see, you did not hesitate to wake up Lord Sigurd by another means." He inclines his face pointedly.

Her mouth hangs open in a guilty expression. "I... I'm certain I don't know what you're talking about," she lies after fumbling for a moment.

The corner of his mouth twitches into a ghost of a smile. "I think you know exactly what I'm talking about, Myria Hawthorne. After all, Sigurd never stopped singing your praises after you saved him."

She turns away, face burning. "I was just trying to help."

"While noble of you, you should practice restraint as a mage. Your actions could have been met with more dire consequences. The mind is a complicated enigma for even the most celebrated of healers."

"I'll be more careful in the future," Myria says, though the words sound false to her own ears. Emiri laughs at her promise, and she knows they must sound the same to him.

He returns to their original subject. "How did your grandmother react to you leaving for Ilona?"

Myria looks down at the ground below them. Their height, along with a creeping sense of guilt, gives her stomach a sinking feeling. "She was the one to encourage me to take Geff's offer. Not that she wants me to marry Leor; she just feels guilty about depriving me of a life outside the inn. I helped her run it, and it was our livelihood. We've struggled for a while lately. I can see how it takes its toll on her. She isn't that old, but the work ages her so much." Myria breaks off as the plummeting feeling in her stomach grows. She keeps her face trained on her lap, pressing her forehead against the railing of the balcony.

"Do you regret coming here, then?"

"I probably wouldn't have even agreed to leave with Geff if he didn't promise to help her with finances and ease some of her burdens." She takes a shaky breath, relaxing the tense muscles of her shoulders.

"You didn't answer my question," Emiri points out after a moment, but his tone remains soft. "Do you regret coming here to Ilona. To the palace?"

"I don't think I have a simple answer for you," she counters with a fresh surge of confidence strengthening her voice. "Coming to the palace has given me many new experiences I would have never known. I've made some friends, met my aunt, and learned magic. I wouldn't regret that, but the other parts of palace life—the politics, the catty nobles, *Aryn*—" she growls out the name, "I could do without. I've been so busy with tournaments, dances, and social obligations that I haven't even had time to write to her like I promised."

They fall back into contemplative silence, and soon they clean the plate of all ham and bread. Emiri wipes his hand on his pants before climbing to his feet, a new energy invigorating his movements.

"For your next lesson, I was going to have you continue to practice summoning, but I've got another idea."

She tilts her head up to look at him, shielding her eyes from the rising sun.

"Instead, I'm thinking telekinesis. It's a more advanced form of magic, but one of the more useful ones. After your performance earlier, I'm interested to see if you can handle it." He holds a hand out to her.

Myria stares at it for one slow heartbeat. Her gaze lands the callouses she noticed the first night she met him. When she reaches for the outstretched hand, it envelops hers in his warm, secure grip as he pulls Myria to her feet in a smooth motion.

Once on her feet, she withdraws her hand before it can linger to relish the feeling. Emiri returns inside to retrieve a few items. Myria clutches her hand close to her chest, turning back to the grounds below to hide her suddenly flushed cheeks.

Soon, he rejoins her on the balcony with parchment, quills, and ink in hand. He explains his intent as if he had been unaffected by the moment their hands touched. "Once you get the basics of telekinesis, you can practice by moving the quill to write a letter to your grandmother. The exercise will be good for your precision, like fine motor skills."

His thoughtfulness surprises her, and she smiles in kind. "Thank you, Emiri," she issues in a soft whisper. Then, clearing her throat, she asks in a stronger voice, "So what do I need to do?"

Emiri sets the items aside, holding only the feathered quill in his hands. "Telekinesis is not like summoning or healing, where it requires a specific type of energy. Any energy source will work, whether it's from celestial sources or the environment. For now, perhaps you should just continue using the sun to power your magic. The key is to focus on a specific object, and direct where you want it to go by using your imagination. It can be challenging for mages to master if they do not know how to focus their energy. Not enough will fail to lift the object in question, and too much will send it flying across the room.

"Of course, different objects require different levels of energy. The heavier it is, the more demanding. Moving multiple objects is advanced for any mage, and there are certain limits that almost no mage can overcome."

"Such as?"

"Sometimes, telekinesis is limited to how much your body can physically carry. You are also limited to the object's distance from you. It is nearly impossible to move what you cannot see."

"Can you do any of those things?" Myria asks. "The difficult parts of telekinesis?"

"Only a few times, and never consistently. The largest object I was able to move was a tree, but I'm not sure if that counts since I didn't truly lift it, only redirected its path when it was falling."

"Could your father do those things?"

A small smile graces Emiri's features. "My father was a very powerful mage, indeed. I daresay he was more talented than I, though he had his own limits."

"Do you know *anyone* who could accomplish those feats?"

Emiri crosses his arms. "Do you want to practice, or not?"

With an indolent huff, Myria sets to work, focusing on the quill Emiri places on the balcony's banister in front of her. Her mind searches for the familiar hum of energy. Her brow furrows, and she grimaces as sweat beads across the back of her neck.

Several minutes pass without progress.

"It's okay if you don't get it right away," Emiri says. "It's a very advanced skill—"

"I can do it," Myria growls through clenched teeth.

"I'll still let you write the letter, whether or not you move the quill," Emiri insists, but there is humor in his voice.

A small ball of pain blooms behind Myria's right eye. The previously faint ringing buzzes much louder than before, but it yields no headway. "Just shut up and let me concentrate."

Emiri emits a soft laugh. "You know, there is only one mage rumored to accomplish everything you asked about."

Although it disrupts her concentration, Myria does not silence him—her curiosity besting her as she listens.

It is signal enough for Emiri to continue, and his boots click on the balcony as he paces behind her. "One mage, mythical in nature. A Caliburn legend. They called her the Lady of the Sea."

He pauses, as if tempting her to ask questions. Myria does not give him the satisfaction as she remains quiet, her eyes drilled on the quill.

"The Lady of the Sea is a title given to a woman thought to be the protector of Caliburn. Once she passed from this life, her descendants would inherit her powers. It was her job was to maintain peace in the land, and her unbelievable feats of magic would humble any foe."

Myria loses focus as she imagines the exceptional abilities of the Lady of the Sea. Emiri names a few for her, painting the visions behind her eyes.

"Supposedly, she could move mountains..."

A cloaked woman stands on the precipice of a snowy mountain range. A blizzard whips her cloak and hair about her in erratic streaks. Once she raises her arms, the thunderous crack of shattering stone reverberates throughout the vale, and the mountain peak crumbles.

"...command the seas..."

A roiling storm beats down on an ocean. A lone figure floats, as if riding on a tidal wave that could overcome any ship. Her eyes glow bright blue with the lightning that strikes around her. Darkness obscures the rest of her face.

"...face entire armies..."

She stands alone on a battlefield, her outstretched hand commanding a murder of crows as it speeds toward the enemy.

"...and some say she can see through time, glancing into the past or peering into the future."

Myria blinks, suddenly aware of Emiri standing right next to her, studying her reaction. She narrows her eyes at him. "And you're telling me the Lady of the Sea is a real person?"

Emiri shrugs one shoulder, leaning on the railing. "If she is real, many suspect her bloodline died out a long time ago. None have seen a Lady of the Sea in centuries. More of a legend than anything, an inspiration to all scholars of magic. Remember the painting of a sword you were staring at earlier?"

Myria glances over her shoulder at the painting above the hearth.

"My father painted it. Supposedly, it came to him in a vision. He thinks the hand and the sword belong to the Lady of the Sea."

"A vision of the past or the future?" she asks.

"It is not a scene from our history he is familiar with, so he always thought it was yet to come."

"So your father believed in her, and your trust in his faith outweighs your own," Myria guesses.

He chuckles. "I'm not entirely sure my father *believed*, but he couldn't shake the vision. Few mages have them."

"Did he have any other visions?" Myria asks, turning back to him.

"Just one he shared with me," Emiri says, and the grim line of his jaw tells her it was not a pleasant vision.

She decides not to press further, instead changing the subject as she studies the painting. "Is there something significant about the sword?" The only notable feature of the weapon is the ruby-inlaid hilt.

"He never told me if he thought so." Emiri sighs. "My guess? If the Lady of the Sea were ever real, my father's vision was likely something of the past. She doesn't exist in the present. I imagine the sword is a symbolic relic. I can't think she would have any need for a weapon if the legends about her power were true."

Myria presses the heel of her palms into her eyes, attempting to squash away the pain behind them.

Emiri raises his eyebrows in concern. "The magic. It's bothering your head."

"I'm fine," she says, dropping her hands to her sides.

Emiri seems unconvinced. "Just as you were fine at the joust? If you want to do your best as a mage, we have to be honest with each other. It would not do well if we pushed you past your limits."

Myria sighs, and it releases some of the tension in her shoulders. "I just want to try one more time."

Emiri nods for her to proceed.

She takes a moment to breathe deeply, attempting to clear her mind of any distracting thoughts. Still, the images of the Lady of the Sea's feats return to her.

The mountain cracking, the glowing eyes, and the swarm of black feathers are all so vivid to her. Myria cannot help but aspire to reach even a fraction of that power. She wants to be that fierce.

She closes her eyes to banish the visions. She imagines the small, feathered quill lying in front of her. She reaches out to the image with her mind and visualizes it floating.

She wills for her thoughts to be real, then opens her eyes.

And before her, the quill floats precisely at eye level.

Smirking, she focuses on making the quill float in a circle around Emiri. His eyes follow the quill in stunned silence.

"You did that with your eyes closed," he gasps.

"You sound surprised," she says with a coy smirk.

She urges the quill further and it floats about like a butterfly, first outside on the balcony, and then inside the Tower. She soon understands Emiri's warnings of limitations. The farther the quill is from her, the more energy it drains from her.

It floats around the room one last time before settling back to its place on the railing.

Suddenly, the door slams open and strikes the wall with a resounding crash, breaking her hold on the quill. It tumbles from her mental grasp, falling to the ground below.

She leans over the railing to reach for it, but it is already too far away.

"There... you are... Myria." Geffrey pants, each syllable coming at significant effort. "You are going... to be... late."

Myria whirls around on him, her sudden exhaustion and the drain of the magic increasing her irritation. "Late?" she repeats shrilly. "To *what*?"

Not fully recovered from apparently racing to the Tower, Geffrey doubles over and holds onto a stitch in his side. "The queen's... lunch."

"Lunch? What are you talking about?"

Emiri steps forward and helps Geffrey onto a seat near the hearth, explaining for him. "The queen sometimes hosts a meal to welcome the ladies of the court at the beginning of the social season. Your attendance must be expected, as the featured lady of House Bramble."

"Thank you, Emiri," Geffrey sighs, throwing his head back as he wipes his sweaty brow.

Myria bites the inside of her cheek to stay her temper. "Why didn't you tell me this earlier? Like... *yesterday*?"

Geffrey does not answer, still recovering.

Myria groans, burying her face in her hands to calm herself. The thought of the impending social engagement twists her stomach with dread. The visages of the smug Theodora, the critical Cressida, and the stony, enigmatic Queen Eloria paint little confidence of a pleasant afternoon. She considers declining the event altogether, at the risk of her reputation. However, when she finally lowers her hands, her eyes fall on the parchment and inkwell presented earlier by Emiri. They remind Myria of her grandmother and her deal with Geffrey; to help him at court in exchange for saving the Morning Glory.

She releases another sigh, resolve hardening her face. She turns an apologetic expression to Emiri. "I'm sorry for dropping your quill."

For a moment, Emiri says nothing. He returns to the balcony's edge and peers below at the tiny quill. "I assure you, it is of no consequence."

With a sudden wave of his hand, it levitates upwards until it hovers between them. Emiri's fingers remain pointed up, keeping the quill suspended. He inclines his head toward her, and understanding his signal, she plucks it from the air.

Myria gapes at his abilities. "How did you do that?"

"I'm no Lady of the Sea," he says with a husky chuckle. "But I do have many years of experience in my favor. Go on, keep it and the remainder of the supplies. Write that letter to your grandmother."

The heaviness in her limbs eases with his generosity. "That's truly kind of you. I'm sure I couldn't repay you for all the gifts you've given me."

Emiri smirks, and there is a unique, playful glint in his eyes that makes the rest of the room feel insignificant. "Perhaps I will keep the one thing you've given me in exchange for now. It seems to have given me good luck so far."

Myria tilts her head in confusion as she ponders his meaning. He absently scratches his right arm, and the action reminds her of the favour tied there the previous day. The thought of it, coupled with the implication of Eulalia's words, flushes her cheeks with a sudden hesitation. Before she is given time to consider his words or challenge his smugness, a recovered Geffrey all but drags her out of the Mage's Tower.

IO

STRENGTH

When they return to the Bramble suite, Olympe has a massive, formal dress waiting for Myria. The heavy black folds of fabric flare out from the wide skirt, and the ridiculously long bell sleeves reach past her hands. Gold embroidery curls around the bodice, and the stiff boning works in tandem with the corset to make breathing nearly impossible. In the mirror, Myria cedes that while it looks lovely on her frame, she feels utterly stifled on the inside.

"If you can breathe, you are not wearing it correctly," Olympe says, seeming to read Myria's thoughts from her expression in the mirror. Her aunt works with deft fingers on her hair, braiding the small front pieces into a small crown as the rest remain loose and curled. "To remind a woman that her place is to be silent and suffocated."

Myria steals a glance at her aunt's attire in the mirror, noticing she also wears a formal black dress. The elder's dress appears more restricting, denser with additional layers and a front gold panel. Myria's shoulders and collarbone are at least free from fabric, a style for younger ladies of court, according to Olympe.

"Do you really think that's a woman's place?" Myria asks.

Olympe scowls as she continues working. "Whether I believe it is irrelevant. It is the world we must contend with."

Myria shifts her weight to one leg as the edge of the corset digs into her hip. "Are you coming with me to the queen's lunch?"

Olympe offers the first hint of a smile Myria has seen from her so far that day. "It would not become of me to leave you to the wolves on your own. You have handled yourself well so far, but an afternoon of *ladies* can be trying for anyone." She sticks out her tongue, pretending to gag, and Myria giggles at the sight.

"Is that why you avoid as many social events as you can?"

Olympe laughs, a high-pitched tinkling sound without humor. "Darling, I am sure by summer's end you can answer that question for yourself."

"Can you tell me what to expect today? I've never even spoken to the queen. Even at the masquerade, it was just a passing greeting."

"Today, you will know her more intimately. I know not what she has planned, but your safest path is to be humble, respectful. Do not look her in the eye unless she speaks to you directly. The queen favors polite ladies at court, but she is *not* a fan of fake flatteries. She prefers honesty over compliments. I hope I need not stress the importance of winning her favor today. She is the mother of the prince you are trying to marry; it will be *her* position you take. The Queen of Avalion."

Satisfied with her efforts, Olympe leads the way through the east wing. But instead of passing the Mage's Tower, they veer in a different direction up the staircase. Here, the halls indicate a passing from the elegance of the palace at large to the opulence of the royal abode. Paintings of faraway landscapes adorn the walls, and their footsteps echo against the polished tile that gleams with their reflections. Myria is not given a chance to study those landscapes, a horizon of mountain peaks, rolling hills streaked with rivers, and enormous trees of an ancient forest. Her aunt stops before a pair of doors and fusses over some of Myria's flyaway hairs.

"Is this the royal dining room?" Myria asks, turning her head to admire the elaborately carved doors.

Olympe scoffs as she jerks Myria's head around and tucks the stray hairs back. "No. This is the Queen's dining room."

Hearing this, Myria's eyes are drawn back to the doors with renewed curiosity. *Her own dining room?*

A nearby page opens the doors, revealing a long table laden with silver dishes and cutlery. Several ladies are already seated, including the five other suitors. Myria catches Eulalia's eyes for a moment before she realizes Queen Eloria also waits at the head of the table, her face a smooth, unreadable mask. She wears a deep crimson dress sewn with rubies, and her honey hair is down, making her appear significantly younger. The crown sitting on her head is the same one from the masquerade. The sapphire and diamond jewels sparkle in the midday light streaming in through the tall windows on either side of the room.

Servants in white jackets float about the table to clear platters of half-eaten finger foods. Myria watches with the vain hope that this means they missed most of the luncheon.

Olympe breaks the silence as she sweeps into a low curtsy that Myria hurriedly follows. "Forgive our tardiness, Your Majesty," her aunt says in a demure voice. "The seamstress was late with our order and put our whole schedule behind. At least the dress was worth the wait. Do you not agree Lady Hawthorne looks lovely, Your Majesty?"

As Myria straightens under renewed scrutiny, a clipped snort echoes across the room before a small cough covers it. Theodora, sitting at the queen's left-hand side, does nothing to conceal her smirk when Myria meets her gaze.

Queen Eloria does not acknowledge the sound. She offers a courteous smile at the two of them, waving her hand to two empty seats on her right side. "I agree. All is forgiven, Lady Olympe, Lady Myria. Please, have a seat. I am eager to begin."

By the time the servants have cleared the room, Myria follows her aunt to the gestured seats, noticing a name card specifies that the chair closest to the queen is for her. Brigid, offering a friendly smile, is at the queen's immediate right hand. Eulalia sits directly across, between Theodora and Cressida. The former glows from her position, while the latter appears wholly annoyed.

"Thank you for joining us, Lady Myria," the queen says. Her voice is low, like Olympe's, but resonates with authority. "Lady Rosenford was eager for your company, and I look forward to meeting you properly myself."

A sharp jab in the ribs from her aunt prompts Myria to answer. "Thank you, Your Majesty. I look forward to it as well."

Queen Eloria snaps her fingers twice, and servants file into the room to deliver another round of plates to each guest, a deep dish of pink soup topped with a whole shrimp still in the shell and sprigs of parsley. "Creamed shrimp soup," she announces.

At Myria's confused expression, Olympe explains under her breath that this is only the second course out of seven. An herbal aroma faintly reminiscent of the sea rises from the bowl. Before diving in, Myria has the sense to wait for everyone else as the queen lifts her glass of wine.

The queen toasts, "I thought I would pay homage to my original family with this meal—the Rosenfords, the original fishermen of the kingdom. While Lady Brigid here does not share a direct familial bloodline with me, I am still proud to see such beauty represent our house."

Myria raises her glass with the others. The queen takes the first bite, and the other ladies follow suit. For several minutes, the loudest noise in the room remains the clattering of cutlery. A stark contrast in how the men conducted themselves the night before with noise and drink, the silence fills with expectant tension. The ladies all exchange glances between them, while the queen does not acknowledge anyone's discomfort.

Myria attempts to focus on the unfamiliar dish, which is surprisingly delicious. While salty, the soup and roasted shrimp also offer flavors of smoke and white wine, and the texture is creamy. She forces herself to keep pace and not slurp, her spoon keeping time with the others. Her inexperience with gourmet dishes only shows when she does a messy job of peeling the shrimp. The shell breaks off into numerous small pieces, unlike the single one removed by Olympe's deft fingers.

As the servants return to clear this round of dishes, Myria glances around to see if any of the ladies have noticed her messy handiwork. Thankfully, their eyes are glued to the queen, still silent and tense, as if waiting for permission to shatter it.

The third course is salad, but Myria hardly glances as the vibrant and colorful leaves as she studies the uncomfortable expressions of each luncheon guest. However, the pungent odor of vinaigrette drags her attention to her plate, where she inspects the unfamiliar, pale yellow cream dolloped atop red and purple garden greens. She waits for Olympe to take a bite first before spearing a small helping of greens and cream onto her fork. The taste is not as off-putting as suspected, a nice balance between the sour, vinegar-drenched greens and the familiar sweetness of honey in the cream.

Probably why it's yellow, Myria assumes. She is impressed with the combination, almost to the point of voicing such compliments. But a glance at the queen, the uncomfortable line of Eulalia's shoulders, the stiff movements of Cressida all keep her in check.

Is this a test? If so, would it be best to speak or stay silent?

The queen announces the next item on the menu, "Chilled scallop with caramelized onions." By the time the appetizer is placed before her, Myria struggles not to release a pent-up sigh. But when she glances down at her plate, even this dish gives her pause. The scallop is a small, white medallion covered in a latticework of browned onion slices, much like a small food tower. A closer look proves that the scallop sits on a small slice of lemon without the rind, the source behind the fresh scent of citrus. Myria balances the small stack on her fork before making quick work of it and popping the entire thing in her mouth.

The curious looks of Cressida, Brigid, Eulalia, and a smirk from Theodora are the first clues of her mistake. The bright, overpowering cleanse of the lemon is the next. The sour rush eclipses the faint, buttery chunk of scallop and onions, and a lip muscle quivers as her tongue recoils. Too late to turn back now or risk spitting it back up, Myria forces it all down in a painful swallow, glancing to see if the queen picked up her faux pas.

Queen Eloria's head tilts, and although her expression is unreadable, Myria senses the action did not go unnoticed.

Olympe leans to whisper, "You eat the lemon last."

"A little late for that," Myria hisses back, a little too loud. Her voice makes Eulalia flinch. Cressida frowns, deepening her scowl of general annoyance. Theodora looks as though she wants to laugh. Still, no one disrupts the gods-awful silence.

By the time the main course arrives, Myria's embarrassment turns to impatience. She looks once at the grilled swordfish lying on a bed of sauteed vegetables before turning her attention to every person seated at the table. While everyone still appears uneasy with the silence, Myria feels emboldened and takes a sip of the course's mild, red wine to clear her throat. Her gaze connects with Eulalia.

Eulalia seems to understand her thoughts, and her friend's eyes grow wide as she shakes her head with fervor. Myria does not heed the warning. She turns to the queen and asks, "How did you enjoy the tournament yesterday, Your Majesty?"

Her words silence the room, cutlery included. Myria feels every eye boring into her with the same shock she saw from Eulalia, but Myria does not feel intimidated. *At least being bold will leave a lasting impression on the queen, especially if everyone thinks I'm going to bumble it up. Bold is better than nothing.* She forces herself to remain calm while tasting a bit of the smokey fish.

Queen Eloria tilts her head and considers the question for a long moment. "It was very entertaining," comes the diplomatic reply at last. "I was quite partial to your joust with Duchess Cressida. You both performed with excellence."

"Thank you, Your Majesty." Myria glances at Cressida, who smiles thinly at sharing the compliment, nodding toward the queen. Eloria's response encourages Myria further. "Did you ever joust?"

The queen chuckles, dabbing at her mouth with a cloth napkin. "Certainly not. I never had the same physical grit or tenacity that our very own Lady Olympe possesses."

Olympe shoots Myria a quick glare that seems to command her not to start conversations with the queen that mention her aunt again. Myria ignores it while she finishes her fish and vegetables.

Across the table, Eulalia sets aside her fork to address the queen as well. "What was your best event?"

Eloria reflects while servants busy with supplying yet another course, warm goat cheese on toasted bread and topped with raspberry jam. "I believe archery was my best. Of course, after I married, I continued honing my skills with both the blade and the bow."

Theodora nods as if the queen's words are the most sensible ones she's ever heard. She leans forward, closer to the queen. "Did you give King Uriel your favour during the tournament of his Summer Courtship?"

Myria, pleased that someone else is maintaining conversation, takes a slow bite into the sour cheese, intrigued how the cold, red drizzle of the jams balances it with sweetness.

Eloria's eyes tighten at the memory, and she sets her napkin aside. "No, I did not win the tournament that year. That honor was bestowed upon none other than the esteemed—"

"Lady Callia Bramble," Olympe interjects. It surprises Myria to see a soft smirk on her aunt's face as she swirls her wine glass's contents, this one a sparkling mead from Honeyridge to accompany the cheese.

"Yes, the mother of our very own Lady Hawthorne." Queen Eloria clears her throat as if attempting to soften her stiff tone. "At the very least, I would emphasize that the tournament's results should not discourage you. While Duchess Cressida's victory certainly gives her an edge for the rest of the summer, it does not discount the rest of you in the running."

Myria thinks she hears the slightest faint sniff from Cressida as she takes a sip of her mead.

Sabine, further down the table, has to crane and stretch her neck to see the queen past everyone else. "How did you secure King Uriel's hand in marriage?"

Eloria grins, the expression neither polite nor regal as her piercing gaze sweeps across the room. She does not answer at first, gesturing to a cart as the servants bring in the final course. Myria cranes her neck to see a spread of miniature white cakes, three tiers each circled with servings of mixed berry chutney.

Eloria says, "Allow me to introduce the dessert first."

Myria understands before the queen explains, recalling the one time she has ever seen a white cake in Everhaven.

"The whole point of the summer is to prepare for a wedding. Unfortunately, there can only be one royal bride. Why not gift each of you an opportunity to taste a royal wedding cake? Consider it a reminder of what is at stake."

A servant pours fresh glasses of sweet, red wine for this course from a crystal decanter. The white frosting of the cake is whipped, delicate, and swirled in elegant patterns. Myria marvels at the artistry, identifying tiny rosebuds in her serving. Impressed, Myria dares to ask, "Hattie made all of this?"

Eloria's eyes glaze over with brief confusion, triumphant smirk gone. "Excuse me?"

Myria thinks back to her morning trip to the kitchens with Emiri. "Hattie, your chef?"

"Oh." The queen waves her hand in the air as if to dismiss the unimportant detail to her like a foul odor. "I suppose; she does have a full staff."

Myria suppresses the urge to roll her eyes as she samples the cake and chutney.

Queen Eloria does not take cake for herself, instead waiting for everyone to taste theirs before she proceeds to answer Sabine's earlier question. "How did I win King Uriel's heart? Of course, you all want to know the secret to winning over my son. I would offer this advice: do not underestimate yourselves, and *definitely* do not underestimate anyone else at this table."

The queen's gaze falls to Myria last, the sardonic smile all but wiped away. Her attention is unwavering, challenging, and Myria does not understand until after the queen returns her attention to lunch.

Eloria not King Uriel's first choice? From everything Myria can gather, he may have chosen her mother to be his queen.

When the meal finishes, attendants return to clear away the plates, and Queen Eloria straightens in her seat, addressing the table. "One of you will be queen of Avalion, which will make Ilona your home. For the rest of the afternoon, we will tour the streets, giving you the chance to familiarize yourself with the people and city. As queen, you must make appearances before your subjects to establish the presence of your reign. Meanwhile, I will have a private conversation with each of you to discuss what I think would be your strength and weakness as a queen."

"*All* of us?" Theodora asks in a dubious voice.

Eloria gives a curt nod. "Yes. I do not want to presume who my son will select. It only benefits Avalion if the future queen recognizes her own shortcomings and takes an active effort to overcome them. Some of you, I have known for many years. Others, I have only known for a few days. However, I believe I have something of value to offer each of you."

The queen then leads a procession to the front drive, where several carriages wait to whisk them away. The first is the smallest but most opulent, a carriage designed for the queen and only able to accommodate a few guests. A canopied roof and curtains keep the sun off its passengers. There are additional carriages behind the first for the rest of them, bigger and less extravagant, with nothing to shield them from the sunlight but modest white canvas. Drivers are dressed and ready with the horses, and four guards take positions on horseback around the train while a score remain on foot with halberds.

Eloria turns to them. "We will first make our way to the hospitals in town, then the orphanages. A queen's greatest weapon is the ability to appear compassionate and generous. Being seen tending to the most vulnerable in our society is one of the simplest ways to gain favor with your people."

Several of the ladies murmur and nod in acknowledgment, but the cold and calculating way that Queen Eloria explains the necessity of benevolence makes Myria's stomach turn. She never thought of helping people as a matter of politics.

"Duchess Nocturnus, I should enjoy the opportunity to have you as the first guest in my carriage," the queen bids as a footman helps her climb inside.

Cressida does not waste another moment, marching away. Meanwhile, Olympe pulls Myria by the arm to claim the carriage directly behind the queen's, and Myria drags Eulalia along.

Theodora scowls, noticing their actions. She attempts to follow them into the carriage. "Excuse me, I think someone of a *reputable* family should follow behind the queen's wagon."

Myria hovers on the steps, blocking her path. "Of course, Lady Stirling. That is why I invited Lady Eulalia to join us. I'd ask you as well, but unfortunately, this carriage is already full."

Theodora's lip curls even higher. "There are four seats and only three of you."

In a louder voice, Myria replies, "Yes, you're absolutely right. However, I also promised a seat for *Lady Brigid.*"

Brigid stops in her tracks upon hearing her name and makes her way to Myria, a dazed smile on her face. Eulalia stifles a giggle behind her.

"Lady Rosenford?" Theodora scoffs in disbelief. "I was here first."

Myria inhales a sharp breath. "Very true, Lady Stirling. However, I'm sure Her Majesty appreciates your sacrifice of letting someone of her own house ride in the first carriage."

Theodora's face flushes deep with indignation, but she says nothing else and stalks off to the second carriage. Myria then eases herself in a seat, welcoming Brigid to their group.

"That was very kind of you, Lady Myria," Brigid says as their procession rumbles down the paved road.

"It was the least I could do after you saved us a seat at the queen's table," Myria says with a shrug. "I didn't realize you were related to Her Majesty."

Brigid looks at her hands. "Queen Eloria was indeed from House Rosenford; however, we are a distant relation that I cannot quite describe to you. Her mother married into our family after she was born."

"So, she's a bastard?" Olympe's voice is blunt.

Brigid's face reddens, and her head snaps around to see if anyone heard Olympe's words. "No, not a *bastard*," she whispers. "Her father died when she was a child. Her mother remarried."

Olympe shrugs as if the distinction matters very little to her. Their wagon suddenly jostles on something in the path, and Myria leans out to watch the tall wheels creak over uneven stones.

Myria turns her attention back inside the carriage when Eulalia says, "You competed in the Summer Courtship with Queen Eloria, did you not?"

Olympe arches an eyebrow. "That was a long time ago, before my family arranged for me to marry Caspian."

Eulalia leans forward, closer to Olympe. "But that means you were there. How *did* Eloria become queen?"

Olympe looks away. "It is difficult to say. I remember little of her accomplishments that summer. She was quite forgettable, but to her credit, there was only *one* frontrunner. Your mother, Myria. No one else seemed to capture Uriel's attention like she did. I quickly gave up on even trying, using the summer to avoid social events and get drunk."

"So, you have changed little through the years." Myria remembers the sight of her aunt retching over the balcony, and a chill teases the base of her neck as she recalls how the habit has devolved into a problem.

Olympe doesn't hide her amusement, but something darker flickers across her face. "Everyone was so certain Callia Bramble was going to be the next queen. The noble families used the time to secure other marriages for their eligible daughters, myself included. Eloria was different. She did not have any suitors, claiming piety and virtue even if it was a lost cause."

"Is that it, then?" Eulalia asks. "Was Eloria the only lady of the court not engaged? Because of her, erm... *status*?" She glances at Brigid, who does not seem to take offense with the words.

"Excellent theory, Lady Runewell," Olympe says. "However, I doubt such is the case. As king, Uriel could have ended any engagement to get his pick of a wife, but something happened. When Callia left, Eloria captured his attention first."

"Surely that is not a bad thing," Brigid offers in a tentative voice. "Queen Eloria has been good for Avalion."

"She has definitely played her role well enough," Olympe agrees.

"But what happened to Myria's mother?" Eulalia presses. "Why did she give up being the queen?"

"My grandmother always told me my mother left court so she could marry my father. However, the longer I'm here at court, the more I doubt that's the full story," Myria says, looking at her hands. She peeks at her aunt through her eyelashes.

Discomfort lines Olympe's features as she shifts in her seat, but her aunt says nothing else. Myria recalls her first night at the palace. At the masquerade, Olympe hinted at the same suspicion, but was unwilling to divulge more. *Ask her later, in private.*

The queen's retinue makes several stops in the city, including the sick houses and orphanages as promised. With each stop, the queen steps out of her carriage and signals for an attendant to hand over a small purse of coins to the master of each establishment before reciting a few polished and rehearsed words to the small crowd following them through the city. The speeches are very much identical at each stop, but that does not discourage the citizens who have heard them already, apparently determined to follow them the entire way.

The ceremony of it all makes Myria uncomfortable. She does not smile or wave at the queen's indication, her face remaining like stone as the patrons clap at the appropriate intervals. The charity is not genuine, only political, and the disgusted sneers from Cressida and Theodora show their true thoughts. *What marvelous queens they would make.*

Eulalia, as if sensing Myria's discomfort, places a gentle hand on Myria's arm. "Even if it is for the wrong reasons, the donations still help," she says in a soft voice as they climb back into their carriage.

Myria's expression twists as she grapples with the logic. "Only because it's convenient. What if it were not so? What if the crown and the royal family were struggling financially? The people of Avalion would struggle more. Do you think they would open the palace doors to help them then?"

"What would you do differently?" Eulalia asks.

Myria ponders for a moment. "If I were queen, I wouldn't use my charity as a lesson to noble ladies on how to improve their public image. I would make it a lesson on serving your own people since that's *definitely* a weakness for many self-serving nobles."

"What does the intention matter if the result is the same?" Olympe points out. The procession continues through the streets. More and more observers join the crowd following them, keeping their distance with the guards on horses.

Brigid eagerly speaks up in Myria's stead. "Because that intention will not always produce the same result. Just as Lady Myria suggested, if it came between themselves and their people, who do you think a noble would choose? Queen Eloria is giving small purses to each place we stop at, but do you not agree she is capable of offering more?"

Olympe looks Brigid over anew, as if seeing her for the first time. "I would never imagine Lady Brigid Rosenford would so brazenly criticize the queen."

Brigid's cheeks flush. "I am not... I do not mean..."

Olympe leans back in her seat, sprawling her legs out in an unladylike manner. The gold panel of her skirt glints in the afternoon sun. "Oh, it is not a criticism. I am rather impressed; I heard the Rosenfords were all soft-spoken flowers."

"But she's right," Myria says. "Empty gestures often mean little when it matters most."

Eulalia shifts in her seat. "I suppose that makes it even more important Prince Leor chooses the right bride. It is not just for his sake, but for the entire kingdom."

A soft smile cracks Brigid's face. "Prince Leor seems to conduct himself admirably. I think he would be an excellent judge of character. He would do well to choose any of the three of us."

"As long as it is *not* Cressida or Theodora," Eulalia agrees with a groan.

Myria cranes her neck for a better view of the queen's carriage, her attention on the queen's current guest. "What about Lady Sabine? I know little about her."

Brigid follows her gaze. "I have spoken with her on a few occasions. Her family, House Valenrence, is a rather recent noble house. Their duchy is small. Her father, Duke Cirrus, reached nobility status after he amassed lands and wealth because of his keen business sense and political connections. He started off as a minor lord in the court, a count from House Bramble, I think."

Olympe confirms this. "He negotiated the Honeyridge lands between my husband and Duke Mathias Runewell—your father, Eulalia. They were agreeable enough. After that, he needed majority approval from the other duchies to approve his new title. Can you guess which house voted against it? There was only one."

"The Stirlings?" Myria growls the name.

Olympe shakes her head. "No, the Stirlings were one of their first allies. Caspian thought perhaps that Theobald loaned Cirrus the money for the land acquisition. House Nocturnus, actually. Duchess Cressida was just a teenager. Everyone thought it was strange that a fresh duchess, a teenager, would be quick to rebuke potential allies at court."

Myria finally catches a glimpse of Sabine, enjoying her private time in the queen's carriage. Emiri mentioned how horrible Cressida treated him just for being a commoner as kids. Her prejudice must run deep. "So, this must all be new to Sabine as well?"

"Not entirely. As a count's daughter, she was familiar with a life of privilege. Once her father became a duke, that simply improved her situation."

By the time they near the end of their city tour, Queen Eloria has spoken to most of the ladies. After Duchess Cressida, she entertained Theodora, Eulalia, Brigid, then Sabine. Myria is last; summoned when the queen takes a brief respite by a magnificent fountain in front of Ilona's Temple of the Sun.

Myria hangs back when she sees Eloria kneeling by the fountain's edge. The queen drags her fingers across the surface, her lips moving fast in silent prayer. She touches her wet fingertips to her brow for a still moment, her eyes squeezed shut before she straightens and turns to Myria.

"Lady Hawthorne," she bids with a warm smile, holding out her hand. "Please join me inside the Temple."

Myria hesitates before reaching out, using her other hand to gather a fistful of her skirts to prevent herself from tripping. The queen's fingers are deft and her grasp firm around Myria's own as she leads her through the wide open doors. To Myria's surprise, only a single guard accompanies them inside.

The Temple of the Sun is a single magnificent structure that seems to demand silence from each patron despite only holding two other people—a priest and a patron. Their footsteps echo against the lustrous stone floor, and large stained-glass windows filter sunlight in a myriad of colors from their massive heights on the walls. Queen Eloria steps reverently down the middle aisle, stopping before the central altar, its basin filled with crystal clear water. Sunlight, clear and pure, bathes the altar—focused there by a clear glass dome dominating the center of the temple above them.

"The Temple is my favorite place to visit," the queen whispers to Myria in such a way that her voice does not echo to everyone else. "Tell me, Lady Myria, what has been your experience with temples?"

The reverent silence makes the blood rushing through Myria's ears all the louder. She struggles to recall Everhaven's temple, a structure she only visited twice in her life. Once at birth, too young to remember, and once as a child when her parents died. Grandma Iris always muttered about the uselessness of temples and priests, their grubby fingers always reaching for coins people could not spare. Myria spares the queen from the trained response of her grandmother. "Truthfully, Your Majesty, I have little experience with temples." Despite Myria's attempt at a whisper, she does not prevent her words from echoing.

"You had other, more demanding responsibilities?" Eloria predicts.

"Yes, Your Majesty. I worked every day in my grandmother's inn, so we might survive."

Queen Eloria takes a nearby golden goblet, its rim encrusted with diamonds, and dips it into the water. She sips from it before offering it to Myria. After a single, encouraging nod, Myria mimes the queen, taking a small sip of the water, which is warm from the sunlight streaming down on it from above.

Eloria replaces the goblet on its pedestal before drawing Myria back to sit at the nearest bench. "Yes, I have learned that religion is yet another privileged boon granted to the aristocracy. I had hoped every person of Avalion might find comfort and familiarity in these sacred halls, but I am not blind."

The queen motions toward her guard, who makes quick work of clearing the room of its priest and worshipper. He closes the open doors with a resonating bang that echoes for several moments. Myria realizes she is alone with the queen.

"I understand how alienated you must feel at court right now. Since this is the first time we have spoken, you probably think I have nothing to offer you in terms of advice. How can I give counsel to someone I have never met before?"

Myria says nothing, waiting for her to continue.

"The truth is, Lady Myria, we are not so unlike each other. You may have heard rumors of my upbringing already."

Myria does not want to confirm such rumors, but the queen gazes at her so expectantly she cannot avoid answering. "Yes, Your Majesty. I have heard... *rumors.*"

Queen Eloria turns away, focusing on a grand painting behind the altar. It depicts several supplicants paying homage to a silhouetted figure floating in midair, engulphed by the brilliant orb of the sun. "I was born into a common family. My father was a soldier in the king's army, and my mother was a seamstress. My father died when I was only six years old, and then my mother had the good fortune to remarry my stepfather, a minor lord in House Rosenford. I never imagined I would end up as *Queen* Eloria of Avalion." She sighs, a weary sound, almost as if forgetting Myria is there next to her.

"Queen Eloria, Your Majesty, why did you bring me here alone?"

"My mother used to drag me to the temple as a child to pray for my father when he was away at war, begging for his safe return. I have always found solace in the quiet peace. I visit here often. I hope it will give you the same peace of mind as we speak, so that you might better reflect on what I have to say." Eloria turns her attention from the painting and locks Myria's eyes with her own. "My son is quite taken with you."

Myria's mouth goes dry and she attempts to lick her lips as she prompts the queen to continue. "About my strength and weakness, Your Majesty? What are they?"

Eloria turns a grim smile to her. "Your strength is that you already have much strength, both in spirit and in your physical drive—a tenacity the other ladies of the court will never understand. One that comes with your hard upbringing. I understand it well."

"And my weakness?" Myria asks in a voice distant to her own ears.

"Your weakness will prove difficult for you to conquer. You are at a distinct disadvantage, and it is *not* because of your common upbringing. Manners, politics, diplomacy; these are all skills you can master the longer you are at court. Your weakness is borne out of your heritage. I saw much of this same trait in your mother, and I have seen it beset you in our few days together already."

"So, what is this trait?"

"It is hard to form it into a single, precise word. But as I told the other ladies, most often your weakness derives from an imbalance of your strength. Your greatest strength and weakness both is your passion."

A confused silence drags between them as Myria puzzles this out. "How is passion a weakness?"

"Of course, passion is not necessarily a bad thing, but too much of anything is dangerous. Your spirit is strong, and your passion will not allow you to avoid doing what you believe is right. In cases of injustice, this is an invaluable quality to have. It makes you incorruptible. But this... *lack of restraint* is not always desirable in a queen. Displaying your emotions for all to see makes you an easy target for your foes and proves that you are easy to manipulate."

"How can I be easy to manipulate if you just said it makes me incorruptible?"

The queen turns to Myria, again fixing her with her stern visage. "Because smarter courtiers can use that to their advantage to discredit you or hold you hostage against your morality, especially if you make rash decisions. They already have. Take the tournament into consideration. You performed admirably, with a lot of heart and honor. Yet, Aryn Stirling easily removed you from the sparring matches because of your match with his sister."

"*Excessive force,*" Myria repeats, remembering Aryn's decision at the tournament. "I did nothing Theodora didn't already do."

"And do you believe that matters when Aryn serves as host or judge? Luckily for you, Duchess Cressida was there to convince you to risk everything for her own advantage."

"Our mutual advantage," Myria hisses, forgetting her manners in front of the queen. Something in the back of her mind insists that this is proof enough of the queen's words on Myria's lack of restraint, but Myria pushes the niggling thought away. She knows she has done nothing wrong.

"It seems to me as if the duchess had the better advantage, but at least you were there on stage to see my son accept her favour."

Myria's teeth clench. "It was better than Theodora's favour."

"Never underestimate a Stirling," Eloria warns in a thick voice that almost sounds threatening. "You gave them even more fuel to use against you yesterday when you intervened for that common mage."

Myria blinks, stunned momentarily before a familiar heat rises to her face. She does little to tame her anger, because at that moment she doesn't care if it only proves the queen's point. "Theodora disrespected Emiri," she snarls.

A small smirk curves one side of Eloria's mouth as she angles her face at Myria's reaction. "Yes, I know his name, the son of our former court mage and the closest friend of my son. Do not think me so indifferent to the common folk, Lady Myria. I used to be one of them."

Myria does a better job of smoothing over her features to respond calmly. "I think you have become too comfortable in your station. You *are* indifferent to us 'common folk'. You don't know the name of the chef who works hard on your seven-course lunch. You recognize how Emiri is disrespected, refusing to use his name yourself, yet you do nothing to change it. Your only contribution is continuing this cycle, flaunting your wealth when it best suits you. You care only about your image as a charitable queen. This whole day has been a show to stroke your ego and remind people who is in charge. You don't really care about the people in those streets."

Queen Eloria's smile turns wry. "And *there* is that strength and passion, working in tandem. You do not fear standing up to your queen. Yet, you are also foolish enough to indicate how the politics of our world upset you. I would recommend not showing your hand so easily to everyone else at court. You could very well endanger the people you care so much about."

Myria doesn't respond, turning away to consider her words as she chews on her bottom lip.

"My son is a uniquely compassionate soul. He is firm in his morality, much like you, but is more equipped to mask such emotions."

"I agree, Your Majesty," Myria says, allowing her tone to soften at the thought of Leor.

"Because of this, I hope to only tell you this once..." Queen Eloria's voice, fond when describing her son, suddenly adopts a sharper edge. It forces Myria to look at her.

Queen Eloria rises to her feet, and in deference, Myria follows suit and gathers her skirts in preparation to leave.

But Queen Eloria remains rooted where she stands, a thunderous expression darkening her face, her eyes like lightning. "Lady Myria Hawthorne, like your mother, I do not think you will be a good queen for this kingdom. I especially think you will not be a suitable match for my son. Your wild emotions shall only prove dangerous, and so I strongly recommend you consider withdrawing from the Summer Courtship."

Myria is unprepared for such a declaration, the queen's hostility disarming her. "Your Majesty—"

"And if you will not do what is best for your kingdom, then maybe you have the empathy to do it for my son."

"I don't understand—"

"You will not survive in this world; not like I have. Your mother knew she could not, that she could never be the queen Uriel needed, so she left. I suggest you do the same before you break my son's heart." Her voice drops to a whisper. "Like Callia Bramble broke my husband's."

Myria's throat pricks, and she struggles to form the words to defend herself. "I would *never* break Leor's heart. I would be a good queen. I would serve the people of Avalion." Her protests sound hollow to her own ears.

Queen Eloria's smile vanishes, all humor gone. "I suggest using your strength now to leave the court while you can. There may be a time when you are no longer strong enough to do so."

The queen turns, marching toward the doors. Myria finds she has no strength in her legs to carry her forward. Her knees shake as Eloria's words weigh on her heart.

Queen Eloria spares a glance over her shoulder. "Take a moment to collect yourself if you must. My procession will leave soon."

The doors of the temple close with the same resonating bang as before, but the echoes ring much more ominously as Myria grips a nearby stone column for support.

II

APPEARANCE

AT QUEEN ELORIA'S SUGGESTION, Myria takes a few moments to collect herself. She smooths over her facial features and straightens her posture. Finally, her legs find some strength—perhaps the inner strength Eloria recognized—and she rejoins the queen's retinue. She holds her head high, shoulders straight, and musters a carefree, natural smile. The others turn as she exits the temple alone. But Myria does not let their critical gazes fracture her smile. She strides to her carriage with her aunt and friends, settling in her seat and pretending to be a paragon of dignity and confidence.

As the procession sets out to return to the palace, Brigid and Eulalia discuss their time with the queen, recounting much different experiences.

"She inspires such confidence," Brigid gushes. "She makes me feel as though I can accomplish *anything*."

"And she is quite perceptive," Eulalia agrees. "She described me as if she has known me my entire life."

They continue sharing what the queen said about their attributes. Eulalia's grace and Brigid's generosity are their strengths, with insecurity and timidity as their weaknesses, respectively. When the white noise of their conversation halts, as if in anticipation of her response to some question, Myria turns to meet their expectant faces.

"What did the queen say of your attributes, Lady Myria?" Brigid asks, perhaps repeating herself.

Her mind returns to the tense exchange in the temple, and Myria clears her throat to answer. "She said my strength and weakness were the same. Strength of spirit and body, but my passion paves the way for lack of restraint."

The others nod and mutter on about the queen's insightfulness, but Myria does not rejoin the conversation. Instead, her eyes are drawn to the faces of the people they pass. Faces of grime, resignation, and weary determination. A baker's expression mirrors a mother's. A beggar with a sharp-nose mercenary.

Even children, their faces round with youth, hold the same hollowness as they find some entertainment in makeshift dice and runestones as they predict each other's fortunes. Each drawn face denotes some level of struggle, a life hardened by the misfortune of their birth. The faraway glaze of their eyes suggests but a dim hope for a better life. Nothing like the privilege she suddenly finds herself surrounded with.

The quiet focus of someone prickles the back of her neck. When Myria glances up, she meets Olympe's calculating eyes, her mouth pressed into a thin line. Myria summons her previous smile, but it feels weak in front of her aunt. Myria suspects it would be difficult to hide her feelings from someone who has suffered herself with the courtly life of deception and gilded lies.

Mercifully, Olympe does not draw attention to Myria's gloom, only tightening her eyes in suspicion. The carriage continues its return trip to the palace without interruption as Brigid and Eulalia continue singing the queen's praises. When they arrive at the castle once more, Myria descends the carriage steps, hardly registering Queen Eloria's parting words of wisdom to the surrounding entourage. Myria ducks away before anyone notices her absence, and the queen's voice recedes before disappearing entirely once she enters the palace.

But someone catches her just as she reaches the staircase. "Lady Myria," Eulalia calls from behind. "Will I see you at dinner tonight?"

Myria pauses for a moment, her face fixed forward, hand frozen on the banister. The same dread she felt in the Mage's Tower fills her stomach again. She imagines an unpleasant evening surrounded by the nobility, even with the calming presence of her friend. She turns slowly, steeling her chest for an unfavorable answer.

But Olympe is suddenly there at her elbow, placing a firm hand on her back, and answers in her stead. "House Bramble will have a private supper tonight, Lady Runewell. We have much to do to prepare Myria for the rest of the social season."

The relief Myria feels makes it easier to turn and offer an apologetic smile to her friend. They wait for Eulalia's slow nod of understanding, and Olympe whisks Myria away to the seclusion of the Bramble suite.

In the safety of her bedroom, Myria wastes no time in ripping at the ribbons and straps of her gown, wanting to be freed from the accursed corset. Her fingers are clumsy and unable to reach the intricate laces. Suddenly, she feels Olympe's deft fingers making quick work of them for her.

"So, what is it?" her aunt asks. Her flat tone provides no room for argument. "What did the queen say to you?"

Myria swallows past a thick lump in her throat and grits her teeth through the shame pricking her chest. "Queen Eloria wants me to leave the court."

Olympe's unlacing efforts stall as this news surprises even her. "Why?"

Myria takes a liberating gasp as the corset releases before grabbing the pants and shirt she wore that morning. "She thinks I will break her son's heart. Apparently, my mother did the same to her husband."

Once dressed, Myria turns to face her aunt, but a new conflict brews in Olympe's scowling face. Her aunt leaves her bedchamber, and Myria follows her to the common room.

"She thinks you will do what Callia did," Olympe says as she reaches for a decanter of wine on the table. "She thinks you will run away." Before she can pick up the decanter, Myria snatches it from her grasp.

"Well? Did my mother run away? You said we could discuss her decision to leave the court in private. Here we are—in *private*." Myria holds the decanter to her chest as a bargaining chip for the truth, but she cannot help the bitterness coating her words as she accosts her aunt.

Olympe sighs, sinking into a chair. "Very well. You of all people deserve to know."

Myria takes the seat across from her, leaning forward. "Deserve to know what?"

Olympe's mouth works itself into a taut line as she looks at her hands for the right words. "I will tell you everything I know, Myria, but I fear it will not nearly be enough. I know not the entire story myself."

Myria allows her tone to soften. "Something is better than nothing."

Olympe nods, a new certainty setting a firm line to her shoulders as her eyes lock on Myria's. "Twenty-five years ago, I entered the Summer Courtship to bid for Prince Uriel's hand in marriage, just like your mother. Much like you are doing now. What I said earlier was true; Callia Bramble was Uriel's favorite from the start. Everyone knew he would pick her as his bride, but we still had to go through the social season. It made us less concerned with the events. Callia and I..."

Olympe pauses, her voice dipping low as she struggles to compose herself. Her eyes turn to the window, and she gazes through it as if seeking a glimpse of a long-forgotten past.

"Even though the nature of the season tried to pit us against each other, Callia and I became close. We were the best of friends. I think it was one reason my father arranged the marriage with your uncle, Caspian. We got along so well. You are very much like her, you know. Queen Eloria may want to say your passion is your weakness, but your mother's passion was her strength. Callia was simply unafraid of anything and anyone. She never backed down from a challenge. And she was *smart*. If she found herself in trouble, she could always talk herself out of it."

Myria reaches out for her aunt's hand, but a strange new acidity stings her chest: envy of her aunt's familiarity with the mother she never knew.

Olympe turns back, meeting Myria's eyes and giving her hand a gentle squeeze before continuing. "At the last event, the Eventide Ball, Prince Uriel announced his decision. Callia Bramble would be the next queen of Avalion. He gave her *that* amulet"—Olympe nods toward the pendant hanging from Myria's neck—"as a token of his commitment. A sign of the betrothal."

"And then what happened?"

Olympe sighs. "She left. You say your grandmother believes it was to marry someone she loved, but I *know* that is not true. It cannot be. Your mother loved Uriel. On the night of the Eventide Ball, she visited my room and we talked for hours about our new engagements. She had so many ideas for the kingdom, and she was eager for me to be by her side the entire time. They summoned her to Ilona the next morning. We assumed it was for the royal confirmation to legitimize the engagement. We did not learn until that evening, she disappeared from Ilona."

"Disappeared?" Myria repeats.

Olympe's eyes burn, and her voice drops to a fierce whisper as she leans closer to Myria. "She never said goodbye to us—her family, or me. Duke Theobald later informed us she abandoned her position at court, and that Uriel had chosen a new bride—Eloria."

"Do you think Eloria had something to do with her disappearance?"

Olympe shakes her head and shrugs. "I have often speculated that myself. The Brambles and I never stopped seeking answers. We sent out search parties. We thought the worst. But then I received a letter from Callia almost a year later, after I married and became pregnant with Geff. After Prince Leor had been born. It said little, but she told me she was living a private life in Everhaven. She didn't want me to say anything to her brother, my husband, but I knew something frightened her. I tried writing to her several times, but she would not respond for several years, not until she felt she had anything worthy to tell us."

A small smile lifts the corner of Olympe's mouth, and Myria swears she sees tears pooling in her aunt's eyes.

Myria realizes her meaning within a heartbeat. "My birth."

Olympe nods. "This time, she addressed the letter to your uncle and me. She wanted us to know that she had an heir. When Caspian discovered this news, he tracked her down to try and convince her to return home. He was angry with me when he found out I had hidden her whereabouts from him. We found her in that grimy old inn of your grandmother's, and the two of them yelled at each other for what seemed like hours."

She chuckles at the memory, but her face quickly darkens. "No matter what we said, Callia refused to leave. Shortly after that day, both your mother and father succumbed to sickness, leaving you an orphan in the care of your grandmother at the inn."

Myria studies the calluses on her hands from working in that inn as she struggles to piece together her past. She tries desperately to picture her mother's face, picking out fragments of hazy memories and descriptions from other people.

"Your uncle and I tried to persuade Iris to release you into our custody many times. We felt as though you were family, that you belonged with us. One year, we even brought a law cleric to grant us legal guardianship, but Iris possessed your mother's will. In her own hand, Callia stated her desire for you to grow up outside the life of the court. After that, there was no other recourse. At your grandmother's request, we stopped visiting."

Myria looks up at her aunt. "Do you think she wanted that for me because of what made her run away?"

Olympe leans back in her chair and sighs as her shoulders sag. "I think it is likely. I just wish I knew *what* those reasons were. I do not think she left to marry your father. She did not even meet him until years after she ran away. However, I am afraid the extent of my knowledge ends there; I wish I could give you more information."

Myria shakes her head and returns the decanter to the table. "You've offered enough."

Olympe does not even reach for it. Her eyes fixate on its shape, her face drawn with misery.

Myria turns to squint at the sinking sun through the wavy window panes. She presses her palm to the glass, feeling the warmth of its rays. Suddenly inspired, she closes her eyes and focuses on the sun's energy, imagining two wine goblets and visualizing the minute details of their shape and design. When she hears her aunt gasp in surprise, she opens her eyes to see her success.

Olympe pours wine into the newly conjured glasses for both of them. Myria savors the acrid flavor as it spreads across her tongue and warms her insides. The spicy aftertaste offers a firm note of clove, and Myria realizes this is a bottle of Olympe's favorite wine, pilfered from the previous night.

Her aunt raises her glass. "I detest sweet wines."

"I can taste that," Myria says, running the edge of her tongue across the roof of her mouth.

Olympe takes another sip. "If you still thirst for answers, I imagine your grandmother knows more than she told you. It might be worthwhile to prod her for more information."

Reminded of the writing supplies Emiri gave her that morning, Myria takes her wine glass and retreats into her bedroom. She smooths out the parchment and hesitates, quill in hand, for several minutes as she contemplates what to write. Much has passed in her few days in Ilona, so much so that she wonders if her grandmother could grasp all the changes she faced. With a frustrated sigh, she drops the quill and rubs her face in agitated circles.

She is not sure how to begin to explain all the unpleasantness, things like dealing with Theodora and Aryn. But the court has redeemable qualities, such as Eulalia and her magic lessons with Emiri. Myria leans back, staring at the ceiling as she recalls the positive aspects of court. The list grows longer than she expected. So, newly inspired, Myria picks up the quill again.

Grandma Iris,

I am sorry it has taken me so long to write. Court has demanded much of my time, just as I am sure the inn demands much of yours. How is the Morning Glory? Has Geffrey made good on his promise? I hope you are not overworking yourself.

I wanted to tell you about all the wonderful things I have found at court.

The first is getting to know my family. Geffrey and my aunt, Olympe, have been wonderful to me. I think you would like them if you got to know them.

The first friend I made at court is a lady named Eulalia. She is shy but kind, the kindest noble I have met here. She makes me feel welcome. I made another friend, Lady Brigid, when I saved her brother at the tournament. Speaking of the tournament, I actually took part in a joust! It was one of the most exciting things I have ever done.

The prince is as gracious as ever. He will rule the kingdom well, I believe.

And of course, there are my magic lessons. I have been progressing rather quickly, according to my teacher, Emiri—

Myria hesitates, the tip of the quill hovering after Emiri's name as she struggles to describe him. The mage. The prince's best friend. Champion of the Tournament. The knight who possesses her favour—

A fiery blush warms her cheeks as a dark circle of ink drips from the quill. It dries to the parchment before she can wipe it off. She continues below the inkblot.

Emiri is a friend. He is cynical about the nobility and reminds me of you.

It is not adequate, but she continues, thinking of everything Olympe told her.

There are many here who remember my mother. I hate to think of her as a stranger to me while others knew her better. Is there anything else you can tell me about her? What was she like when she left the court? How did she meet my father? Why did she leave court?

Myria draws her hand back and looks at her hastily scrawled words, imagining Grandma Iris scolding her penmanship. The thought brings a smile to her lips. Despite the burning curiosity she has about her mother, Myria ends her questioning there, almost too afraid to know what the truth contains. Perhaps she should have heeded Grandma Iris's warnings more seriously. Perhaps there is a real danger for her at court. Is Queen Eloria the source of that danger? Or is the queen trying to protect her?

Heaving a forlorn sigh, Myria signs her name.

I miss you very much and think about you every day. Write soon.

Love,

Myria

She melts yellow wax with a candle on the table, pressing the Bramble seal on the letter. Returning to the common room, she finds Olympe still there, reclining against the daybed. The bottle of wine next to her is nearly empty.

"How can I send a letter to my grandmother?" Myria asks.

"Find Geffrey. He can dispatch a Bramble rider for you."

"Where is he?"

"Probably still at dinner," Olympe says, waving her hand. "However, the decision to neglect valuable face time with the prince was probably a poor one for you. I have a servant bringing us some food."

Myria's eyes flit to the doorway. "Should I wait for him?"

"Go to the stables yourself if you are so impatient. The Bramble riders wear our house colors."

Myria gives in to the urgency of the moment, slipping silently through the palace corridors as she navigates out of the west wing. Thinking back to that afternoon, she crosses the center stairwell to the east wing, retracing her steps from earlier. Myria has never seen the palace stables, but she imagines they cannot be far from where they began the queen's procession that afternoon. All she needs to do is find a door that leads outside.

Several doors line the halls, most of them closed with nothing but silence behind them. One door stands ajar, and Myria carefully peeks to see another dining hall. The scene inside shows the vestiges of a royal dinner wrapping up. Discarded plates remain on the table with food scraps, wine goblets emptied to the dregs, and many nobles standing up to leave while offering a few words to bid goodnight to the other guests.

Myria glimpses Eulalia curtsying to Prince Leor, a faint redness rising to her face as he brushes a kiss against her knuckles. Myria smiles to herself before recognizing Queen Eloria nearby. She retreats from the doorway. Holding her breath, she presses herself flat against the wall and waits for several agonizing minutes while the dining room clears out before proceeding down the hall.

Further on, another door stands partially open, offering Myria a sliver of darkness to squint through. With no windows inside, the light from the hall provides the only illumination in the shadowy room. She can barely discern the outline of a round table when someone calls out to her.

"What do we have here?"

Myria spins around, pulling the door shut behind her with an echoing bang. Standing before her is none other than Aryn Stirling, his face arranged into an expression of dark humor. Her own face settles into a glare almost by instinct. She says nothing to him and merely continues her path with angry strides. The footsteps behind suggest he follows her.

"There is a rumor circling around that you left court, abandoning it like your mother," he recounts to her in a velvet voice, easily keeping pace.

"I can assure you, Lord Stirling," she all bust hisses through clenched teeth. "Your rumor is unfounded."

"And yet here you are, skulking about the palace in the rags of a peasant."

Myria glances down at her attire, realizing how her stained shirt and scuffed leather pants are in stark contrast to Aryn's glossy jerkin.

She stops in her steps, turning to him with a thin smile. "Indeed. Here I am in the Ilona Palace and not abandoning court."

There is a flicker behind the sheen of his eyes, and she can see the impatience in his forced humor. He still suffers a courtly smile. "Then what are you doing, *Lady* Hawthorne, meandering through the hall and dressed for the country's muddy fields?"

Myria stifles an urge to lash out at him, remembering the Queen's words about her lack of restraint. Her weak smile wavers into a grimace. "Not that it's any of your business, Aryn, but I am looking for the stables." She banishes any notion that he might help her locate them.

He arches a thick eyebrow at her boldness. "Please, my name is Lord Aryn or Lord Stirling to you. I recognized your charade of a title and likewise expect the same respect."

Impatience expands from his eyes to his tone, and she bites down on a sardonic laugh. "I didn't realize that my words meant anything to you, *Lord* Stirling. I was always under the impression you cared little for my opinion."

His nostrils flare as he exhales sharply. He does not appear as impressed with her humor as his own smile sours, and he steps closer to her. She takes a step back, feeling the wall press against her back. He leans closer still and asks, "And what business, pray tell, do you have at the stables?"

Myria's heart hammers in her throat at their proximity as she resists the urge to break eye contact with him and search for the quickest escape. She maintains her glare at this trespass of her personal space, hoping he does not notice the trembling of her hands. Aryn Stirling is but one man, but there is an undeniable, calculated threat barely masked by his icy demeanor. "As I said," she replies in a low, controlled voice, "It's none of your concern." She grips the letter closer to her chest.

His eyes do not miss the movement of her hand. Without warning, he rips the letter from her grip.

"Hey," she gasps, reaching to grab it back.

But keeping his eyes on the letter, he uses his free hand to knock away hers, pinning her arm to the wall. She struggles beneath his firm grip, her breath catching as the position strains against her bruises from the joust.

"The Morning Glory in Everhaven?" he reads. "That wretched tavern you call home? I suppose you must feel homesick; the palace is nothing like the squalor of your pigpen."

Myria attempts to shove her weight against Aryn with little success. "Let go of me," she growls.

Aryn does not heed her words as he eyes the wax seal. "If I were to open this, what would I find? Ambitious plans to increase your political power? Intimate details of how best to infiltrate the palace? Perhaps a desire to rob the royal treasury?"

"How about a solid kick to the groin?" suggests an angry new voice behind them.

It is enough to distract Aryn, and his grip on her arm loosens. She does not spare a glance at their guest before stomping on Aryn's instep. He reels back in pain, releasing her. Myria snatches the letter and stumbles away from her attacker.

She looks up to see who has joined them at that opportune moment, and her eyes instantly meet Emiri, the owner of the groin-kick suggestion. He flanks Prince Leor along with Captain Rozenna.

Myria dips her head with the customary obeisance for the prince, her eyes trained to the floor. Her mind races through the last few moments, wondering if her assault on Aryn would be a condemnable offense, despite its apparent justification. Braving a meek glance at Leor through her eyelashes, she sees his expression is hard, but he is focused on Aryn.

"Care to explain yourself, Lord Aryn?" Leor asks in a thick voice.

Aryn grunts as he straightens himself before the prince, but he squares his shoulders as if he is innocent in the altercation. "Your Majesty, this is a mere misunderstanding. I am investigating our Lady Myria here. She was absent from dinner, and now she roams the corridors dressed in *that*. After all, you just saw her attack me."

An angry retort rises to her lips, but Myria practices self-restraint, biting her tongue and glaring at the wall instead.

The prince responds with a strain, his voice struggling to remain even. "Lord Stirling, it seems as if we have different understandings of the words 'investigate' and 'attack.'"

Despite the undeniable anger in Leor's voice, Aryn remains calm, composed, and almost condescending. "I meant no disrespect, my prince. If only we can clarify our misunderstandings in private—"

"On the contrary, Lord Stirling," Leor interrupts, his voice rising. "If you wish to remain with the court this summer, I suggest you return to your quarters at once."

A tense pause endures as Aryn does not respond at first, stunned as he analyzes Leor.

"You are dismissed, Lord Stirling," Leor growls.

Aryn lowers his head with another bow before spinning on his heel and marching down the hall. It isn't until he disappears entirely from sight before Leor's shoulders relax with a sigh. Following the prince's suit, Emiri and Rozenna ease their stances.

Leor manages a dry chuckle and turns to Myria. He no longer seems angry, only concerned, and the raw energy of his compassion pierces through Myria like a blade. "I am not sure what you did to Aryn Stirling, Lady Myria, but you have definitely captured his attention—and quite possibly his enmity." He attempts a light tone, but Myria does not miss the bitterness behind it.

Emiri, however, does not mask his own acidity, glowering at his hands. "Myria only exists, and that is an affront to any Stirling. You remember how he treated her at the Morning Glory."

Captain Rozenna stays silent, glancing sideways at Emiri.

"Are you well, Lady Myria?" Leor asks, taking a step closer. His hand twitches toward her before he forces it down to his side.

Myria rubs the bruises around her shoulder. "I am fine. I was trying to find my way to the stables." Glancing at her hands, she notices her carefully prepared letter is riddled with creases, courtesy of Aryn.

"I would be happy to escort you, if you find the arrangement acceptable," Leor offers.

Myria's eyes flicker between the prince and his companions. "I couldn't impose. You are clearly engaged with another matter."

"I welcome any opportunity for your company." With a quick gesture, Leor signals something to Rozenna.

Rozenna works to keep her face neutral as the corner of her mouth curls in amusement. "I encourage you not to leave the palace, Your Majesty. Otherwise, I will command a company of troops to track you down, and your father will not allow you to leave again until we make for Dawnmourne." With that, she steps away, motioning for Emiri to follow her.

For a full heartbeat, Emiri acknowledges nothing around him. His eyes remain on Myria, and hers on him, unaware of anything else. Eventually, he tears his gaze from her as he permits Rozenna to lead him away by the arm.

Myria clears her throat, shaking her head to clear it of the moment, and turns to the prince. "You are far too kind to me."

Leor gives her a wry smile before offering his arm. She takes it with tentative fingers. After a tense silence, he says, "I missed you at dinner, Lady Hawthorne."

"I am sure there were others to make up for my absence," she teases, feeling a bit more relaxed. "Duchess Cressida or Lady Theodora would make fine conversation partners."

His laugh, genuine and full-bodied, surprises her. "But none of them could match your wit, however."

Her smile turns flippant. "I am sorry to deprive you of my wit, then. It was not my intent when I retired with my aunt this evening."

His humor vanishes, and she feels his attention on her once again. "Are you feeling well? I know you must have lingering injuries from your joust."

She smiles to reassure him. "Because of Emiri, my injuries are healing nicely. I should thank you for asking him to watch over me."

Leor blushes, and Myria giggles at the sight. He stammers out a quick explanation. "I hope that was not too forward of me, Lady Myria."

She waves off his concerns. "I find it charming."

"A newcomer to court is an easy target for the vultures."

"Especially if that newcomer is a commoner," she adds grimly. She tugs at the hem of her shirt, recalling Aryn's remarks. "I apologize my current appearance does not suit your royal company."

His hand covers the hand she has on his arm with sudden warmth. His fingers ghost against her palm as he takes it into a comforting grip. "There is no need for you to apologize." His voice is firm, and then his mouth turns up to a fond smile as he passes an appraising eye over her outfit. "I remember you wearing that when we first met. I find it as flattering as any fine gown."

"If only the rest of the court shared your sentiments, Your Majesty."

A passing thought darkens Leor's expression, and he hesitates before voicing his concerns. "I hope nothing has overwhelmed you here."

"What do you mean?"

"This evening, my mother suggested the idea that you might have left court."

Myria's grip reflexively tightens on his arm, and her entire body tenses as she recalls Eloria's wish to see her leave, repeated in Aryn's talk of rumors. It is not surprising to think the queen would use her absence at dinner to confirm her desire. She forces a smile to comfort Leor. "I assure you the rumor is unfounded. I have absolutely no intention to leave." She doesn't add, *Not when the Morning Glory depends on it. Or my magic lessons.*

His arm relaxes beneath her grip. "I am relieved. It would be a tragic day if you left court."

"Then, I will do my best to prevent such a tragedy."

He finally leads her through a door that takes them outside, depositing them in an arched breezeway. Across the yard is an out-building dotted with several gated stables. Myria eagerly skips toward them, identifying the glossy mane of Jadis—the mare Geffrey gifted her—even from a distance. Leor laughs as he follows behind her.

After greeting Jadis, Myria searches for a Bramble rider and finds Merek, her valet from the tournament. "Merek! I hope you are well."

The boy meets her greeting warmly. "I am, my lady. Thank you."

"I have a letter that needs to be taken to the Morning Glory inn. Might you see it there?"

Merek tips his hat. "You have my word. It will be delivered this night, and I will return with any reply in the morn."

"Thank you," Myria says, clasping the boy's arm as he takes the letter. Then he disappears to prepare for the journey.

When she returns to Leor, she discovers her cousin Geffrey has appeared to engage the prince in polite conversation. They laugh as she approaches.

"What are you doing here, Geffrey?" she asks.

"Mother said you were trying to find the stables, so I thought to make sure you did not get lost. It seems you were rather fortunate that His Majesty was there to help."

When Geffrey turns to smirk at her, his expression dissolves entirely. His wide eyes scan the length of her attire in what Myria can only deduce as horror. Myria arches an amused eyebrow as he stifles a theatrical gag.

"If only you had time to dress appropriately," he mourns.

Leor intervenes with a chuckle. "I think it is appropriate enough. A refreshing change to see her express herself so freely."

"You are such a benevolent prince, Your Majesty," Geff says, attempting to rein in his disgust as his eyes linger on her scuffed pants.

"I appreciate the kind words, Duke Bramble. However, since you are here, perhaps you could escort your cousin back to your suite? I fear I must take my leave."

Geff nods. "Of course."

Leor turns to Myria one last time, his face warm and inviting. The rest of her surroundings fade away at the strength of his gaze. "I wait until next we meet." He brings her hand to his mouth and brushes his lips against her knuckles. Then, slowly, he releases her, turns a mischievous grin to Jadis, and pats the horse's neck. "Perhaps soon, you will have the opportunity to ride her again."

Myria's smile at his brightness is automatic. "Good night, Your Majesty."

She waits until Geffrey takes her back to their rooms before turning her full attention onto her cousin. Olympe and her clove wine are nowhere to be seen, and Myria assumes that both are hiding behind her aunt's locked bedroom door.

"I need to know what the next social event is," she insists. "I can't keep getting surprised."

"I agree," Geff says, sinking into a cushioned chair. "You should be prepared. And you should never skip royal dinners." He angles an accusatory glance in her direction.

She folds her arms across her chest. "I'm allowed to have one night off."

Geff shakes his head, yielding no agreement. "It creates an opportunity for rumors to be spread about you."

"About me leaving court? I've heard about that already. The queen wants me gone, and she's not making a secret of it."

"The queen wants you gone?"

Myria nods. "She told me so herself on our public outing. She thinks I'm going to break Leor's heart, so she wants me to leave before I do."

Geff frowns and shakes his head. "Well, the prince must be quite taken with you if he finds you so entrancing while wearing *that*." He gestures at her attire. "But we should still get to work if we are going to make you queen."

Myria sighs, lowering herself into a seat across from Geffrey. "Are you sure I should even be queen? Some think I shouldn't even be here. Cressida, Aryn..." Her voice trails off into an apprehensive groan at the last name.

"I think all of Avalion would benefit from you as queen. Your perspective is one most nobles would never understand. You would fight for what is right. And, despite your inexperience, you have already shown a knack for politics. A few days into the summer, and you already secured alliances with Houses Runewell and Rosenford."

Myria narrows her eyes. "Do you really think that, or is that your ambition speaking? Besides, what good are two alliances if the queen and other nobles are working against me?"

"I have faith in you. Your spirit reminds me of my father. He dedicated his life to serving Avalion. However, it is not really my opinion that matters. Ultimately, the choice belongs to Prince Leor, and I have always believed the prince to be an excellent judge of character."

"So we should trust in the prince's judgment?" she asks with a thin smile.

"And in my training," Geff points out with a wide grin. "Now, the tournament surprised you, but the next events will be great opportunities to show everyone you are a force to be reckoned with."

"And those events are?"

"Each noble house hosts a social event during the summer. The palace opens the season with the masquerade ball. The tournament is the product of House Stirling. In the next few weeks, we will tour around the kingdom to the homes of the other noble families. House Bramble will host the closing ceremonies; the Eventide Ball, we call it. That will be your home advantage, so to speak."

"And what about the other houses and their events?"

Hesitating, Geff chews on his lips before he blows out a sharp breath. "House Nocturnus will host the next event. The entire court will travel to Dawnmourne later this week. Truthfully, it will be a disadvantage for us."

Myria leans back in her chair, her lips puckering. "And an advantage for Cressida."

Geffrey nods. "She has never been one to shy away from exploiting situations in her favor."

"What can I expect in Dawnmourne?" she asks warily.

"Cold, snow, and a *lot* of ice."

12

PEARL

THE FOLLOWING WEEK ESTABLISHES a set routine for Myria. Her mornings are with Emiri, delving further into honing her skills with telekinesis and healing. It's exhausting work but rewarding. Then, Geoffery tutors her on etiquette. In the afternoons, she spends time with the ladies of court, usually with Eulalia, walking the gardens, practicing dances, and catching up on the latest gossip.

The routine finally ends when the day of their departure arrives. Geffrey wakes Myria early, and she prepares herself for the long, impending ride, lamenting the disruption to her magic studies. Olympe has a riding outfit arranged for her, a simple green and black ensemble with loose sleeves, a velvet cape, and ties in the front. It is undoubtedly one of the more comfortable dresses she's been gifted, but Myria knows by now not to be optimistic with the impending tightening of the corset.

The morning brightens with the arrival of Grandma Iris's letter. Myria asks Olympe to read it to her as she grips the bedpost with white, anticipating fingers. A servant prepares the dreaded corset.

"I thought your grandmother was illiterate. Her handwriting is atrocious."

Myria grits her teeth as the first line of laces are secured. "You could wear the corset while I read it instead," she quips back.

Olympe's chuckle is brief. "Do they still bother you? I imagine you would have grown used to them by now."

"Besides, Grandma Iris has better handwriting than I do." Two more laces.

Olympe pauses at this with a small, muted gasp, as if this information concerns her. "We will have to tell Geffrey to add penmanship to your studies."

"The letter?" Myria reminds her firmly, toes curling against the floorboards as the next laces cinch her waist.

Olympe clears her throat.

"Dear Myria. First off, girl, I know I taught your letters better than that. Hold your pen with purpose and you won't get inkblots on the paper." Olympe pauses to scoff at Myria.

"Told you," Myria says, glaring back.

With a huff, her aunt continues. "The Morning Glory goes on as it does, with or without you here. Your cousin has made good on his promise. We now have two strapping young lads and a strong woman to help cook, clean, and run the errands. I hardly lift a finger anymore.

"I am glad you are making friends but remember to keep them at arm's length. You've always been a good judge of character, but those court vipers are masters of hiding their true nature. Be safe." Again, Olympe pauses, this time offering an arched eyebrow and an expression somewhere between bemused and offended.

Myria shrugs, only to be jerked back upright by the tightening of more laces.

With a roll of her eyes, Olympe finishes reading the letter. "I wish I had more to offer than the vague warnings of your mother. She didn't speak much of her life before coming to Everhaven, other than what I have already offered you. I got the impression she was trying to escape those memories. Perhaps you could ask those who knew her at court. They would have more information than I.

"Be well, my sunflower. Love, Iris."

"Thank you," Myria says with a deep sigh as the servant ties off the last pair of laces, both in relief at the end of the violent tugging and at the words of the letter.

Olympe lays the letter down on a nearby table. "I assume you are satisfied your grandmother is being well cared for."

Myria, muffled through layers of fabric as the serving girl drops the heavy dress over her head, says, "Yes, very much so." As the garment falls onto her shoulders and her head is exposed, she smiles at Olympe. "Thank you."

"Very well," Olympe says with a sigh bordering on disinterest. "I'll leave you to it, then. I'm sure your cousin will wish to instruct you more on what to expect from our journey. And I have my own affairs to set in order."

With Myria properly attired and her aunt departed, servants mill about the suite, hauling luggage to the stables to pack and prepare the carriages. Geffrey appears with them, as predicted, and uses the opportune moment to trace the path of the Summer Courtship on a curling map of Avalion. He begins at the center, the Ilona capital. "The social season follows a traditional path counterclockwise that corresponds to the order of families hosting the events," he explains.

He moves his finger in a straight line up the map. "First, we go north into Nocturnus lands to Dawnmourne Keep at the mercy of Duchess Cressida.

She typically enjoys subjecting the court to unseasonal winter games." Geffrey shudders, presumably at some memory.

"A game I will have to take part in," Myria says. "Shouldn't I know what it is?"

"I would love nothing more than to inform you of the plans of Duchess Nocturnus, but she enjoys maintaining an element of surprise." His finger trails at a downward curve left, resting above a small cape jutting into the sea. "This is the Rosenford duchy. After Dawnmourne, the court will travel to Goldeport. The Rosenfords prefer the comforting heritage of their sea-faring ancestors, so expect something with water or a boat."

Myria smiles to herself. "Geffrey, you are an absolute *fountain* of information."

He smirks. "A Bramble is nothing if not helpful. After playing guests to Lord Sigurd, Lady Brigid, and their father Duke Aelric, we will arrive at Kinggrove, the forest of the Runewells. There, Duke Mathias will host the annual Wild Weald Hunt."

"A hunt?" Myria repeats, thinking of Eulalia's gentle demeanor. "That doesn't sound so distressing."

Geffrey's finger points to a small circle of land surrounded almost entirely by a river between Runewell and Bramble lands. "This is Honeyridge, the domain of House Valenrence. Duke Cirrus is rather new to the social circuit, so I am not entirely sure what to expect there either, but after *that...*"

Geff's voice hitches in excitement, pointing to his home of Fairthorne. However, Myria's eyes pin to the city annotated below that. *Everhaven.* Her home.

"...The Eventide Ball," her cousin says, breaking through her reverie. "Hosted by yours truly, it will be the event at which Prince Leor announces his bride."

Myria sways on her feet as a faint buzzing fills her ears. "And that's at the end of the summer?" she asks.

He nods. "Precisely. I have no doubt of your success. You have captured his attention, ensnaring him will be of no difficulty for you."

"*Ensnare?*" she repeats, something icy washing over her body. "I don't intend to trick Leor into anything."

He waves off her concerns. "Of course, nothing as conniving as that. However, you know that Cressida and Theodora would not hesitate to hatch some diabolical plots. We should be ready ourselves for anything."

"Then I suppose we all should trust the prince's judgment on such an important matter."

He pats her arm. "And remind him of his better options. Now, you have already made friends with the suitors of House Runewell and Rosenford—"

"Eulalia and Brigid," Myria points out flatly. "They do have names."

"And their friendships are important for alliances. You have half the court in your favor, but consider your rivals."

"Cressida and Theodora," she sighs.

"Yes, *exactly*. Your disgust is a natural reaction to their unpleasantness. Still, there is one more lady you have yet to recruit," Geff points out, arching his eyebrows.

"You mean Lady Sabine?"

"The Valenrence family is so young in court, so I am sure she feels as much the outsider as you do. Befriend her. Cressida and Theodora likely only see her as a pawn that is easily manipulated."

"And is that how I should conduct myself?" Myria asks, her voice distant, eyes staring at the wall in front of her. "Manipulate her into one of my pawns as well?"

Geff draws back, seemingly offended. "Of course not. Myria, I may be savvy in the ways of diplomacy and politics, but it does not mean I think people only have value in how they benefit me. I am not so selfish."

"But you're still saying we should befriend her for a selfish reason, to help *us* at court. I befriended Eulalia and Brigid naturally, not for personal gain."

He nods, conceding to her point. "Then you should decide how best to approach her *naturally*. Politics aside, I think she could use a genuine friend. She definitely has not found one in House Nocturnus."

Myria releases another sigh, her shoulders tensing as she directs a withering gaze at her cousin. "And what about Aryn? For the sake of politics, should I attempt a friendship with him?"

He shrinks from her steely eyes. "I recommend avoiding him altogether."

"And what if I can't?" she presses. "Every repulsive encounter we've had was not the result of me searching for his company."

Geffrey's expression turns sympathetic. "I know. There is no straightforward solution. The Stirlings are a rather established family."

"Yet, do you not think it strange that they are the *only* noble house not to host the court at their own home? Instead, they get the tournament in Ilona?"

Geffrey offers a disinterested, noncommittal shrug. "The Stirlings have always been private when it comes to Elmground."

A messenger arrives to inform them everything is ready for the journey. Geffrey retrieves his mother, and the three of them make their way through the palace to the front entrance, where horses, wagons, and carriages all wait for their dignified riders. Myria takes a moment to drink in the bustling sight of the people gathered. It is a far grander assembly than the queen's retinue earlier that week, outfitted with more armored guards and liveried attendants than Myria has seen in one place. The rich assortment of colors drowns out the white paved stone beneath their feet.

Geffrey leads them to the Bramble section of the winding line, the second noble family behind the royal entourage, just behind House Nocturnus. Olympe immediately takes refuge in the covered wagon while Myria smiles at Jadis, saddled and ready for the ride. Geff disappears in the swath of nobles, just as Myria recognizes a Bramble valet approaching her.

"Are you sure you would not be more comfortable riding in the carriage with Lady Olympe?" Merek asks. He is the same boy who delivered the letter to Grandma Iris.

"I prefer the fresh air today, Merek," she answers as the summer warmth beats through her thick dress. A walk in the palace gardens does not compare to an invigorating ride through the kingdom. "Thank you."

Merek helps her into the saddle with a steady hand before bowing away and disappearing into the flurry of people rushing around them. Myria cranes her neck to look behind her, noticing the banners for House Stirling just behind them and House Runewell beyond that.

"Good news!" Geffrey exclaims, reappearing suddenly and throwing his hands in the air. He climbs into the seat next to the carriage driver, much to the driver's surprise as he makes room for the duke. "I have just heard that Aryn Stirling will not be joining the court to Dawnmourne Keep."

Myria's chest feels lighter with the information. She breathes more comfortably, and the sun's morning rays appear blinding now. "Is there a reason for his absence?" she asks, unable to help the trepidation waiting behind her relief.

"I only know that he will remain at the Ilona Palace with Duke Theobald for the time being. I do not expect it to be a permanent arrangement, but even a small reprieve is a welcome one."

When the procession of the entire court finally sets off, Myria cannot deny the extra energy with which she grips the reins of Jadis. The court keeps a steady pace as it exits the city and treks through the countryside. Though their speed is sluggish, the procession stretching out of sight fascinates Myria. It makes her feel like an essential link in an influential chain. Many faces hurry to greet them or jump out of their way; men, women, and children alike. Myria catches them bowing reverently to the royal banners, rising just in time as House Bramble passes, their eyes widening. Myria wonders how much she looks like a distinguished noble in the beautiful riding habit and a net of pearls pinning up her hair. It feels out-of-place, extravagant, and gaudy against the backdrop of the muddy country road. Pushing aside these feelings of inadequacy welling up inside her, she smiles warmly at those she passes, waving to them.

Although they return her smiles and waves, it does nothing to assuage a growing pit in her stomach as she peers into the lean, dirty faces. She does not deserve the privilege given her, not when so many of these hollow eyes struggle so much.

Farm after farm. Hovel after hovel. Myria stops smiling, stops waving, haunted by the same guilt she felt riding through the capital with the queen. She has nothing to offer—

Her hand flutters to her hair, fingertips brushing against the smooth pearls. Idea forming, she rips it off, her long locks of hair tumbling past her shoulders in a very unladylike fashion.

She tears one pearl off at a time from the hair net, stopping to offer it to each individual she passes. Their faces are shocked, and Myria continues with the court procession before anyone can respond to her. Geffrey, who must see what she is doing from his position, says nothing of this charitable behavior. Therefore, she assumes he approves of her actions.

After an hour into their journey, only one pearl remains, and the procession halts for a brief reprieve. The land is mostly featureless, save for the single slice of road through the grain fields, notched by mile posts that measure out the barren countryside. Myria dismounts and takes the waterskin Geff offers her, which she returns as the rhythmic canter of riders approaches them.

"I think we've found our source," muses a voice from behind. Myria recognizes it as Emiri's before she turns to see him and Rozenna behind her.

"Your source?" Myria repeats.

Captain Rozenna scowls, her gaze piercing through Myria with either contempt or apathy. "Are you sure she fits the description?" she asks in a monotone.

Emiri smirks, thoroughly amused as he looks Myria up and down. "'A beautiful, noble maiden giving away treasures?' Have you seen *any* noble lady outside their carriage?"

Rozenna shrugs a single shoulder. "Beauty is rather subjective, I've found."

Myria frowns, her face growing hot with a flare of annoyance. Geffrey intervenes before she can say anything. "Is there anything you need, Captain?" he asks, placing a tethering hand on Myria's shoulder.

Myria attempts composure. "Besides talking about me as if I'm not here," she manages through clenched teeth.

Captain Rozenna's smile is thin. "At the end of the convoy, we've had several reports from the peasants about a noble lady handing out pearls. If this is you, Lady Hawthorne, I must ask that you stop at once."

Myria squares her shoulders as she meets the captain's challenge, despite the warning flex of Geff's fingers. "Why?"

The thin smile melts away into unabashed scorn. Rozenna urges her horse a few steps closer, hovering above Myria. "My concern is the safety of the royal family. If stories of your charity spread throughout the countryside, we risk the people swarming the caravan. The potential ramifications are *not* worth the risk, Lady Hawthorne. I must confiscate any remaining pearls and return them to you upon our destination."

The single remaining pearl presses sharply into Myria's palm as she clenches her fist. "There are none," she lies. "I just gave the last one away."

Rozenna studies her, her sharp face cut into firm angles of suspicion.

Myria crosses her arms in defiance. "Shall I turn out my pockets for you, Captain?"

Rozenna smiles without humor. "That won't be necessary, Lady Hawthorne. Duke Bramble." She briefly inclines her head toward Geffrey before spurring her horse away in a furious gallop to the front of the caravan.

Emiri remains, observing Myria, the hint of his amused smile still on his lips. "You shouldn't be so difficult," he says. "Roze is just doing her job."

Myria does not suppress the urge to roll her eyes. "I didn't realize helping someone other than myself would mean I am difficult. And *Roze* doesn't have to act like a—"

"*Myria!*" Geffrey hisses, cutting her off at the opportune moment. His countless reprimands of her swearing from their etiquette lessons run through her mind.

She grunts in frustration, folding her arms across her chest. "I wasn't going to swear, but it would be justified if I were."

Emiri chuckles as he steps off his horse. "Not everyone is out to get you, Lady Myria."

Myria turns away from him, reaching for Jadis's pommel. She grits her teeth, biting down on a retort. She does not want to quarrel with Emiri, but her experiences at court suggest otherwise. Aryn. Cressida. Theodora. The queen. Who is Rozenna except another name to that list of enemies? "It doesn't matter anymore," she says with an impatient sigh. "And I thought I asked you not to call me that at the joust."

Suddenly, Emiri stands right next to her, offering a hand to help her in the saddle. She hesitates with the illicit pearl in her grasp, before slowly accepting his assistance. His smirk deepens as he feels the gem in her hand, and he leans close to whisper in her ear. "For what it's worth, I thought it was impressive and *very* unlike a noble."

Except for registering how his breath tickles across her skin, she does not have time to react before he effortlessly lifts her up into the saddle. She blinks as he slips the pearl from her grasp and steps back.

"I never imagined Lady Myria Hawthorne would ever be left speechless," he muses with a smirk.

The tips of her ears burn in indignation. "I am not... You don't..." But she remains at a loss for a proper retort. She juts her chin away instead, deciding to ignore him altogether as he shares a chuckle with her cousin.

They continue for most of the day. The riding proves a new strain on her legs, but she is too proud to give up the saddle for the comforts of her aunt's carriage. While Myria could handle the soreness from riding the first day of the journey, unfortunately, it would continue for another four days. By the third, she is absolutely miserable enough to ride inside the carriage with Olympe. The presence of roadside inns is not even a welcome sight, since they have to stop and camp in fields to accommodate the entire court, the size of a small army. Myria is not averse to camping, but the time it takes to set up camp often meant hearing the endless stream of complaints from unsatisfied nobles.

Nightfall on the fourth day sees them to the base of the mountains for their final night of camping. By noon on the fifth day, their path inclines steeply into the mountain. As they gain elevation, the wind picks up and the temperature plummets. Around midafternoon, Myria clutches the velvet cape of her dress, drawing it closer around her shoulders. The wind swirls tiny dustings of snow that sting her cheeks and nose red.

The royal procession climbs on, navigating tight hairpin curves that wind up the mountain face. Glancing up, Myria can make out the looming shadow of Dawnmourne Keep's formidable towers. She shivers as another sharp gale bears against the mountain.

An hour before dusk, the sinking sun casts an orange glow on the blanket of snow on either side of the road, and Myria's ears have popped for the third time with the increasing height. Jadis trudges over the frozen ground with numb repetition, rounding the last curve before the castle comes into full, dominating view.

It is an ancient structure of gray stone, perched into a draw carved into the mountainside. Myria's jaw goes slack as she gapes at the enormous construction. Geffrey jumps to the ground, the snow crunching beneath his feet as he stretches out his sore limbs.

"Magnificient, is it not?" he asks. Myria notices Duchess Cressida claiming the entire royal family's attention by the front entrance as she welcomes them inside, Leor clasped to her side. Merek leads Jadis toward the stables, and dour-looking servants rush forward to take care of the rest of the horses, carriages, and luggage as other noble families disembark, shouting clipped orders for their rooms and comfort.

"I did not realize it would be this cold in the summer," Myria says. She hunches her shoulders, hiding her hands in her cape, and draws her hood over her ears.

"The perks of living in the mountains," Geffrey says, his breath clouding in his face. "Most of the castle actually tunnels *inside* the mountain. House Nocturnus is fabled to be the protectors of old, guarding the northern border of Avalion as its stalwart sentry. I have also heard the castle cuts all the way to the other side of the mountain, where one can see the North Sea, but I have not seen this for myself."

"The ocean is on the other side of these mountains?" Myria asks. "I've never seen it."

"It is unlikely you will see it here, but you shall have the opportunity when we stay with House Rosenford."

A stony-faced servant wearing the crimson and black colors of House Nocturnus leads Myria and her family inside the dark castle to their rooms. She is intrigued by the stark contrast between Dawnmourne Keep and the palace. While Ilona is bright and vivacious, the mountain castle proves more austere, almost dismal. Here, wealth is measured by strength of pragmatism rather than colorful, resplendent luxury. Even inside, the shadowy halls do not afford them protection from the frigid temperatures, and so Myria is grateful to see a crackling fireplace once they reach her room. Geffrey sets off to locate their trunks, while Myria huddles near the mantle, thawing her stiff fingers. A quick survey shows sparse furnishings, a posted bed laden with animal furs, and a faded red rug that partially covers the worn, wooden floorboards.

Olympe does not retire to her own room just yet, pacing behind Myria as she shares insight on what to expect that evening. "Cressida will do everything she can to eclipse the other suitors, especially you. This means you might not see the prince as often as you like, but it is still imperative to leave a good impression."

"Who will be watching for my good impression?" Myria asks, annoyed. She desires nothing other than to climb into bed to give her sore legs some reprieve, briefly considering the practice of her healing magic. But to do so, she would need her moon crystal, which is stowed away in the luggage her cousin is looking for.

"Alliances are the most important at court. I am sure Geffrey has already explained to you the benefits of befriending Lady Sabine—"

"Yes, *manipulating* her. Geffrey explained that well enough," Myria grumbles, rolling her eyes.

"Call it what you like," Olympe brushes off. "If acknowledging your ulterior motives makes you feel better by owning up to what you will do, then so be it. However, my pearl of wisdom for you—do not make unnecessary enemies."

A familiar pride floods Myria's face with heat, and suddenly she stands to face her aunt, forsaking the warmth of the hearth. "I will not manipulate anyone, and I do not make unnecessary enemies."

Olympe arches a disbelieving eyebrow. "You've seemed to have done a fair job of it with several others. Aryn—"

"Hated me from the start."

"Theodora?"

"Hates everyone, like her brother."

"The queen?"

"Is probably jealous of my mother."

"Captain Rozenna?" Olympe counters with a sly smile, clearly already informed of their previous confrontation.

Myria hesitates at this one. "I don't think we're enemies. Yet."

Olympe sighs, taking a seat on the bed. "Since you will not see much of Leor tonight, use the extra time to your advantage. Make some friends."

Before Myria can respond, the door bangs open and Geffrey drags her chest of dresses into the room. It scrapes loudly against the floor, leaving marks in the wood planks that he ignores. "Was something said about seducing the prince?" he asks, popping the lid open.

Olympe rises to her feet to dig through the trunk. Myria retreats to a washbasin of fresh, warm water set into the hearth of the fireplace, splashing her face.

"This is the one!" Geffrey exclaims, shaking out a dress for her to see.

It is a beautiful gray gown trimmed with white fur on the sleeves and neckline. Silver ribbon outlines the elbows and waist, and metallic, delicate patterns criss-cross the bust and corset's boning. A few slits in the skirt reveal a layer of ivory silk beneath.

"It's beautiful," Myria agrees. "But what's the point? You both said I won't see Prince Leor tonight."

Olympe impatiently shoves the dress into Myria's arms. "Because we are *Brambles*. Because we do not shrink when the trial proves tough. We exploit every opportunity to grant us victory."

The uncharacteristic pride in her aunt's voice momentarily pulls Myria from her dejected mood. She straightens her back, nodding at such sensible inspiration, and prepares herself to represent the Bramble name.

THE GREAT HALL OF Dawnmourne Keep stretches to an immense length, lined with rows of tables and benches. A single long table stands perpendicular to the rest at the head of the hall. This table features King Uriel, Queen Eloria, Prince Leor, and Duchess Cressida. As Myria enters the room, Nocturnus pages lead guests to their assigned seats for the evening. The higher lords and ladies of the court are seated closest to the head table.

Across the room, Eulalia sits close to the royal family, surrounded by Theodora, Brigid, Sigurd, and Eulalia's cousin Alanis. A page leads the Bramble family directly on the other side, equally close to the head table.

Myria prepares to sit down when the servant stops her. "I am sorry, Lady Hawthorne. These seats are only for Duke and Dowager Duchess Bramble. If you follow me, I will take you to your seat."

She nods, feeling a faint wave of embarrassment ring in her ears. Olympe turns a stern gaze to the page. "This is most unusual. Lady Myria is a part of the Bramble family, and should sit with us."

"My apologies, Lady Bramble," the page says, earnestly ducking his face. "I regret to inform you that this seat is already assigned to Lord Godric."

Indignation flashes through her aunt's face, so Myria intervenes, arming herself with Olympe's previous words. "It's fine, Olympe. I am sure Duchess Cressida has her reasons for the seating arrangement. I will make the most of what I'm given tonight." She turns to the page with a gracious, courtly smile in place. "Please, take me to my seat."

Her seat, as the whims of Duchess Cressida would have it, is the farthest one from the head table, practically invisible to the royal family. Myria would laugh if it wasn't so clearly insulting. However, sitting next to her is none other than Lady Sabine, craning her neck to see the rest of the court's prominent members.

"Lady Myria," Sabine greets with a thin smile that hardly conceals her frustration. "It seems Duchess Cressida perceives us as similar status." A lilting note in her voice threatens to crack, and Myria's shoulders deflate with pity.

"I am sorry that she feels the need to insult you."

Sabine waves a dark hand, turning her attention to an empty plate in front of her. "I am used to such offenses. Many did not receive my family's ascension to nobility with much hospitality."

"That doesn't make it any easier," Myria points out. "You definitely shouldn't be back here with me. I'm just a peasant girl in a fancy dress. You've at least learned etiquette and dancing like a real noble." The self-deprecation comes easy, and it may cheer up Sabine.

Sabine chuckles at the remark. "No matter how this evening turns out for us, we should not allow it to discourage our efforts. Queen Eloria says that she was the unlikely candidate for King Uriel's hand in marriage. Perhaps the same can happen to *us*."

Myria does not miss the way Sabine's lips curve over the last word, a reluctance to consider herself as an equal to Myria. Despite this, Myria forces the same gracious smile that makes her face ache and her insides clench with tension. She attempts polite, friendly conversation with Sabine. However, there is still an edge to Lady Valenrence's words that do not sound genuine.

Eventually, when the hall is filled, King Uriel stands up to deliver a quick welcome speech. He thanks Cressida for her gracious hospitality before Myria's attention wanes completely. The king's voice is a distant drone of formal niceties and supplications.

Servers stream into the hall, delivering dishes. Naturally, Myria's comes last. The process takes longer than she thinks is necessary, leaving her stomach growling by the time a servant places a bowl of cold stew in front of her. Platters of breads and cheeses fill the tables between the guests before the servants fade into the shadows. Altogether, it's a paltry presentation compared to the queen's luncheon. But in the biting cold, a bowl of warm stew would be more than welcome. If it *were* still warm.

"Enjoying your evening?" asks a sardonic voice. Myria looks up as Emiri lowers himself into the bench in front of Myria and Sabine. While his question attempts civility, an agitated scowl mars his features. He places a bottle of mead on the table. The cork is missing.

She smirks at him, stirring her stew. "I would have expected you to be sitting next to Prince Leor."

He scoffs, glancing at the head table. "I've been invited to Nocturnus events before, so I know how her seating chart works. My place is always at the bottom of her food chain." He takes a generous swig of the bottle's contents. "So, as recompense for my time, I helped myself to her cellars."

Myria hides a snort behind a hand, ignoring Sabine's disdainful visage. "At least your experience has prepared you."

"The company isn't always bad either," he admits. "Any enemy of Nocturnus must be a friend of mine." Emiri offers her the bottle, and Myria does not hesitate to partake. A sweet, herbal, and rich currant flavor warms her from the inside.

When she returns it, Emiri surprisingly offers the bottle to Sabine. The lady looks at it, her hands glued to her lap as she considers the offer for a long moment. Slowly, she reaches for it. "And what has made you such an enemy of Duchess Cressida?" Sabine asks before taking a polite sip.

"The moment of my birth marked us as rivals," he says with a breathy chuckle. "Suffice it to say, Duchess Nocturnus doesn't deserve the pleasure of having any friends."

Before returning the bottle to him, Sabine takes another draught, a small smile curling her lips. "My family exported this mead several years ago. There was only a small batch to increase its demand."

Emiri tips the neck of the bottle toward her in a toast. "If I am to deprive Cressida Nocturnus of anything, let it be her most expensive mead."

Sabine giggles. From a glance, Myria can see her shoulders relaxing much more in Emiri's presence than being alone with Myria. Perhaps Emiri is better at talking to nobles, or maybe the alcohol worked in his favor. She shrugs internally, appreciative that Sabine is finally enjoying herself rather than being tortured with stiff propriety.

Duchess Cressida rises, and the room falls silent at her imposing height above the tables. "Now that you have enjoyed the hospitality of Dawnmourne Keep, I believe it is time to make merry with pointless courtly frivolities. Shall we have a dance?"

Servants clear the tables with practiced efficiency and the nobles stand as music fills the hall with a lively tempo. Myria looks mournfully at her half-finished stew before reluctantly standing as well.

The nobles divide into partners, and Sabine eagerly turns to Emiri. "Would you care to dance with me?"

The unexpected request sends a strange shock wave through Myria. She grips the table and keeps her face neutral while watching Emiri closely for his reaction.

To her amusement, Emiri looks just as stunned. "Apologies, Lady Sabine. I am not much of a dancer, and I was just heading back to my room."

Sabine hides her disappointment well and takes the rejection in stride. "Dancing is not a complicated activity. If ever you are interested, I would be happy to teach you."

The relaxed demeanor Emiri maintained earlier vanishes. He nods stiffly at her suggestion, offering nothing else in the way of words.

A sharp note of laughter interjects as Captain Rozenna approaches them, looping her arm through Emiri's. "Don't take it personally, Lady Valenrence," she says with a leaden smile. "Emiri simply doesn't dance. He has never danced in his life."

Curiously, Captain Rozenna's eyes turn to Myria, unreadable with their message. Myria lifts her chin in challenge, allowing the corner of her mouth to curl into a tiny smirk, and dares to ask the question weighing on her mind. "How long have you known Sir Emiri in all of his non-dancing ways?"

Rozenna laughs at the title. "*Sir* Emiri and I trained together as soldiers before he decided he enjoyed the life of being Prince Leor's pet."

Emiri forces a mirthless smile as Rozenna jokes at his expense. "While that is certainly not the worst thing someone has said about me, I must leave you all to this charming event." He shrugs himself away from Rozenna, straightening his tunic.

Sabine bids him farewell, and Captain Rozenna follows her to circle the room's perimeter, maintaining a keen watch over Leor. Myria takes a moment to watch the prince as he sweeps Cressida across the dance floor. Eulalia and Theodora eye them from a distance. Geffrey converses with Sigurd while Brigid dances with Alanis.

Fingers tug at Myria's elbow. She turns to see Emiri still there, standing quite close, his previously strained expression gone. Now, it is alight with humor.

"Feel free to enjoy this party for as long as you want, but—"

"Are you telling me what to do now?" she asks coyly. "You're starting to sound like Geffrey and my aunt."

Emiri smirks, continuing with his statement as if she hadn't interrupted him. "If you want to continue your lessons here in Nocturnus, you should also think about retiring early. Tomorrow's lesson begins an hour before dawn."

Mischief glints in his eye as he catches onto her meaning. He holds out his palm, revealing the pearl he stole. When she reaches for it, he closes his fingers around her hand and his eyes darken with an unreadable look. "More pearls await you tomorrow morning, an hour before dawn, Lady Myria."

She frowns and jerks her hand away. "I await what will happen to you if you keep calling me that."

"I'll meet you in the corridor outside your room."

He offers a single, mocking bow before turning on his heel and slipping out of the great hall. Myria casts one furtive glance back at the crowd as Cressida claims a second dance with the prince. The other ladies watch helplessly, Sabine now joining them.

Geoffrey's eyes meet hers from near the others, nodding his head toward them as if urging her to join the preening flock.

Myria escapes her cousin's gaze and retires early for the evening.

13

VULNERABLE

MYRIA SPENDS MOST OF the night tossing and turning in the fur blankets of her bed. *An hour before dawn*, Emiri said. Did Castle Dawnmourne have wakemen to announce the hours of the night? How would she wake on time? The plaguing questions keep her mind restless, unable to find reprieve, especially with icy drafts seeping through her room. Acknowledging that sleep will continue to elude her, Myria wraps herself in furs and searches through her trunks for a warm pair of pants. Disappointment greets her when she discovers none.

She releases a defeated sigh and instead looks for a suitable dress for the upcoming lesson, warm but casual. Anything but formal. Myria shudders when her hands find a thin layer of transparent silk, and she prays Olympe did not commission it for a glacial Nocturnus ball. Eventually, she settles for a thick, olive-green outfit with wooden buttons, a hood, and matching coat. Once she slips it over her head, she smooths down the skirt with tense fingers and examines herself in the mirror. The fabric clings to her frame with a flattering shape, but her hair remains a wild disarray of tangles. An attempt to tame them does not work in her favor, so she leaves it down—loose and unruly.

To wait down the hours, Myria perches herself on a chair by the fireplace, relishing its warmth as she draws her knees to her chest, pressing her cheek against an arm wrapped around her legs. Her window's view upon the black landscape offers no revelations about the outside world. It merely rattles in the swift mountain winds. Her mind replays every moment of the day, especially the discomfort of climbing the mountain path.

Her eyelids droop, lulled by the sanctuary of the flames crackling before her, as the moments from the journey blend in a seamless conglomeration. Emiri on his horse, Rozenna on hers, Sabine sitting alone, then Rozenna again, then Emiri with a pearl and smirk.

A sharp knock cuts across the images, startling her from the reverie. The fireplace is nothing but cold embers. Myria jumps to her feet, her eyes desperately trying to focus as she steadies herself with groggy limbs. She quickly rubs the sleep from her eyes, grabs her moon crystal from the windowsill, and hurries to answer the door.

Emiri leans against the doorframe, seeming to appraise her appearance. Something about it must please him, as he offers a faint smile. "Good, you're dressed for the weather."

With a jerk of his head, he indicates for her to follow him and turns on his heel. She struggles to catch up to him. "Is there a reason I had to get up so early?" she asks, schooling her breathlessness as she keeps pace.

"Would I ask you to get up at this hour without a good reason?" he asks, casting a sideways glance at her.

She frowns, unimpressed with the carefree attitude he exudes this early. "You have made me perform some ridiculous tasks for your own entertainment." She cringes, remembering an incident a few days ago involving telekinesis and paint.

Emiri maintains a mask of indifference, but his voice betrays his own amusement. "If you're referring to the paint incident—"

"I am," she interrupts, voice tart.

"I told you it was an accident. Plus, I've already apologized."

"It's fascinating how your apology didn't remove the stains from my *favorite* shirt."

He bites down on a laugh, covering it with a cough. "You should bring it to the next lesson, and I'll show you how to fix it."

Myria notices their path does not lead them outside through the front entrance. Emiri instead expertly weaves her deeper into the castle's depths. There are no windows or guards. No torches. Emiri instructs her to summon a ball of light.

"All I have is my moon crystal," she says, showing it to him.

He looks at her pointedly. "The moon has light."

Suppressing an impatient sigh, she closes her eyes and, gripping the crystal with both hands, focuses on the hum of the space around them to clear her mind. The moon energy in her hand feels different from the sunlight she's familiar with at dawn. It is reserved and cool, reflecting the space around them, as opposed to fiery, unbridled power.

She frowns, struggling to conjure the image in her mind. Her instinct is to summon a spark of fire, but the energy in her hand refuses, leaving an acrid stench of smoke hovering around them.

"This isn't sun energy," interjects Emiri's patient voice. "You will not be able to conjure the same sort of constructs. Imagine the soft glow of moonlight. Nothing tangible, just an incandescent glow."

His hands cover hers, warm and inviting. Suddenly, in her mind, she sees a small, shimmering orb twinkling like a star. There is a sudden rush of energy as it sucks in the surrounding air. Myria opens her eyes and gasps. An orb of light floats in front of her.

Emiri withdraws his hand, brushing them on his pants.

"What was that?" Myria asks. The moon orb drifts about serenely, casting silvery light on the dank walls. Her voice echoes back with a slight, vibrating timbre. The back of her mind senses that they are now standing in a vacant part of the castle.

He attempts a demure smile, avoiding her gaze. "Moonlight differs from sunlight. The moon reflects the sun. Therefore, it can't create anything on its own. It has to borrow energy, so I was lending you some of mine."

Myria nods toward the orb. "And you made that?"

He shakes his head. "*You* did." His voice is thick. He clears his throat, resuming his haste to rush her along. "And now you get to use your telekinesis to bring it with us. Light does no good to us in this darkness if it stays behind."

She stretches her mental awareness to the orb, struggling at first to grasp its ethereal form. It resists her grasp, like water through the fingers. Instead, she waits, beckoning it closer with a mental summons. The orb heeds her call, subtly connecting to her energy, and soon she is able to push it ahead gently with a mental lead. Emiri nods in approval, and they continue down their path.

After striding along for several minutes, Myria struggles to maintain her focus on the orb. The thinning air winds her, and each breath is like a shard of ice. There is no warmth in this part of the castle. "Where are we going?"

Emiri stops, and Myria catches herself before bumping into him. A large metal door blocks their path, with a metal bar locking it into place. The thick layer of dust on the door's surface suggests it has not been opened for some time.

He turns to her with a barely concealed smirk. "We are where we need to be. We have to get through that door, so tell me how we should open it."

"Is this your lesson for me?"

"Not quite. The lesson happens on the other side of this door. This is practice, so you are more comfortable using magic to solve problems."

"By opening secret magical doors?"

Emiri narrows his eyes. "Is it magical? You've been practicing enough that your senses should detect magic when you encounter it."

She reaches out with her mind, but can determine nothing extraordinary about the door. "It's not magical."

"Correct. So, how do you open it?"

Myria steps up, running her fingers on the edge of the bar. Her fingertips are coated gray with the accumulated grime. A tiny draft of frigid air sways a few hairs around her face. She turns to Emiri in surprise. "This leads outside."

There is an impressed glint in his eye as he gives her a single nod. "Observant."

"We could lift the bar securing the door in place," she suggests.

"Try it."

She releases her mental hold over the orb and senses Emiri maintaining its light behind her. Before using any magic, she tests the strength of the bar by lifting it with her hands. It is undoubtedly sturdy, but her movements cause the metal to shift in place with a loud, resounding scrape. Myria jumps back as the noise rings around them, followed by the sound of rust sprinkling the floor.

"Very practical," he praises. "Testing its weight with your physical strength before your magical strength." Emiri offers nothing else in the way of guidance.

She attempts to use telekinesis on the bar to lift it from its place. The effort of attempting to move the immense weight causes sweat to bead across her brow. Eventually, she manages to raise the bar high enough to clear the door's brackets. She pulls it away from the door, but her concentration falters. She panics, and her mind recoils. The bar drops with a thunderous bang, chipping the smooth stone floor.

"The bar has been removed," Emiri says. "Try opening it now."

A sinking feeling gnaws her stomach at his words, suggesting the task is far from complete. She reaches out to turn the latch, and the door does not budge. She sighs in frustration, her mind racing, too proud to ask for assistance.

"You better hurry, or we will miss our window of opportunity," Emiri prods behind her.

She frowns, several complaints regarding his teaching skills running through her mind before she pushes them away to concentrate on the riddle before her. The only energy she has available is the moon crystal in her hands, severely limiting her options, since she does not think Emiri will lend her a sun crystal for the exercise.

Recalling his earlier suggestion, she reaches out with her mind to determine what's on the other side of the door. Closing her eyes in concentration, she amplifies her senses with the moon crystal. The biting gales of the mountaintop greet her, battering her mind's eye against the door. The door's other side has an identical latch, encased entirely in ice.

"The door is frozen shut," she realizes aloud, eyelids flying open.

"Now that you know what blocks you, how will you overcome this obstacle?"

"Helpful as always," Myria mumbles in a low voice. She presses her palm against the cold metal of the door, feeling the wind reverberate through its frame. "I could melt the ice on the door," she muses aloud. "But that wouldn't guarantee that the door isn't just *stuck*. It obviously hasn't been used in years. Or I could use the wind as a battering ram, but the door might open in the opposite direction."

Emiri doesn't respond to her calculations, remaining silent as she sorts out her choices on her own.

She decides to melt the ice using the moon crystal as a conduit for change. Closing her eyes once more, she focuses on changing the solid ice into liquid once more. The dripping water painstakingly drains her crystal of its energy.

But it takes too long, and there isn't enough energy to fuel her magic. She feels the crystal deplete, extinguishing the energy inside it completely. The moon orb behind her fades into nothing as a result, shrouding them in darkness.

She hears Emiri take a step closer, and sees the empathetic lines on his face even though her eyes are closed. In a rush of exhaustion, hopelessness, and frustration, she slams her fist holding the empty crystal into the door. Blistering pain erupts on her knuckles, and white light explodes across her vision, blinding her to everything else.

Suddenly, a wave of heat consumes her whole body. It burns her face, scorches her arms, and suffocates any scream that might rise to her lips.

Then it is gone, dissipating like a whisper on a breeze. Myria is slumped on the cold floor, sagging against the icy metal door. Lightheaded, she finds Emiri's face, grave and concerned, inches from hers.

"What happened?" she asks, struggling to draw an even breath. She feels no remnant of the fire that had felt so real moments before.

He does not immediately answer, his eyes boring into hers as if trying to see something hidden inside her. He tears his eyes away and picks up the emptied moon crystal, which she must have dropped, to examine it.

"Emiri?" Her voice sounds hoarse and shaky.

The sound of it must be enough to turn his examination back to her. "How are you feeling?" he asks, the lingering gaze piercing through her core in a way that makes her feel small and exposed.

She braces her voice with iron determination. "Tell me what happened."

There is no question in her tone, no room for debate. Emiri seems to struggle to form a response. "I don't—I *think* there was a backfire from the crystal, where it took energy from you. It is unwise to deplete them like you just did."

Myria squints at him. He doesn't seem convinced by his own explanation, but she does not push the matter. A wave of nausea makes her head swim. Squeezing her temples, she waits for the moment to pass. When it does, Emiri helps her to her feet and they turn to the door. Large scorch marks blacken the surface around the handle, and it effortlessly swings open with a gentle push.

"At least your method was effective," he notes under his breath with a quiet laugh.

The darkness of the hour reveals little of their surroundings. While Myria can hear the roar of ocean waves crashing against the cliffside below them, the gray sky affords almost nothing of illumination. Squinting, she can just make out the whitecaps of sea foam. Her breath fogs the air in front of her face, nearly masking Emiri from sight as he makes his way up the frozen path.

"Why did you bring me here?" she shouts over the wind and the waves, struggling to follow him. Her hair whips about her face, further obstructing her vision.

Emiri stops to pull himself up on an outcropping, giving himself a vantage point that overlooks the sea. He motions for her to hurry. "You've practiced summoning, telekinesis, and healing. This is a prime opportunity to introduce you to a new form of magic."

As she reaches for him, her foot catches a patch of ice. Her arms flail about for balance. Before she can fall, Emiri reaches down in a fluid motion to grab her, pulling her onto the ledge. The glacial snow and blustering wind numb her extremities, but the closeness of Emiri's body provides a welcoming warmth, something she feels where their shoulders touch, in the pit of her belly, and then suddenly at the back of her neck when she decides not to pull herself away.

"What is this form of magic?" she asks, clearing her throat to keep her voice impassive.

He does not meet her eyes, his attention trained on the northern horizon. "Illusion. I've heard this skill will prove useful to you later in the summer."

Myria groans, burying her face in her hands. "I'm going to have to use magic in the Summer Courtship?"

Emiri scoffs, feigning offense. "I thought you enjoyed learning magic."

Myria lifts her face. "I do enjoy the magic. I don't enjoy the court, the ladies, and the insipid, passive-aggressive comments about everything."

"It is interesting where your path has led you, then. As someone who loathes the noble lifestyle, you are rather gifted in that arena."

"Gifted," she repeats in a biting tone. "Yes, that's why I was assigned to sit at the back table last night."

He shrugs. "Cressida put you there because you intimidate her."

She laughs. "You must jest, sir," she insists with a cynical scowl.

Emiri cocks his head and squints, his eyes boring into hers.

Myria falls silent as she puzzles how Duchess Cressida could possibly find her intimidating. She reflects on every miserable encounter, and recalls only instances where Cressida had the advantage.

Emiri does not offer the courtesy of explaining, instead resuming his search of the horizon. "Illusion magic is different from summoning. Illusions are not tangible. Rather, they are intended to fool one's senses, any of the senses. It's all about tricking someone into thinking the illusion is real. The more believable it is, the more powerful it becomes. With that in mind, what type of illusions do you think are the most powerful ones?"

She considers the question. "Mundane or ordinary objects. Things people wouldn't have to take a second glance at. Like something as simple as adding another scratch into the countertop at the Morning Glory. There are so many of them, an additional one wouldn't be suspicious."

"Precisely, but illusions aren't just visual deceptions. As I mentioned, the best ones trick multiple senses, even one's tactile sense. In your example, the illusion of a scratch at your grandmother's inn could also be *felt* by one of her patrons."

"Then what separates illusions from the real thing?"

"Illusions end once their source is gone or when the caster ends the spell. They leave nothing behind and require less energy than summong magic. They are also powered by moonlight."

"I've already used up my moon crystal for today."

"You needn't worry about that right now. Successful illusions, especially larger ones, can be paired with a secondary, mundane one. The mundane powers the larger illusion in a symbiotic relationship, feeding a loop of energy and plausibility."

"Does that mean an illusion could power itself perpetually? Without the need for moon magic or a mage?"

A half-smile flickers across Emiri's face. "In theory, yes, but it's never been implemented successfully. Something always wanes: the energy source, the mage, or the illusion. However, I've brought you here to witness one of the most powerful illusions at work in the kingdom, and what happens when it falters."

By now, the sky is a dull, slate gray with the sun just below the horizon. A faint orange glow slowly brightens the east, casting soft, pink light on the nearby clouds. "Is the sunrise an illusion?" she asks.

Emiri points to the seascape horizon that has fully captured his attention. "Keep watching, *there*," he instructs.

His knuckles are strained white with anticipation as he leans forward, his torso hanging dangerously over the cliffside. Myria pulls back his elbow, securing him on the precipice, and stares at the ocean where he indicated.

The moment the fiery golden sun peeks over the eastern horizon, the ocean waters reflect a metallic sheen in a cascading wave. In that instant, the water blinds her like a mirror in the sun. The reflections shimmer around something new in the distance. Myria strains her eyes, focusing until she can just make out the distinct shape of land—an island.

It sits serenely in its place on the ocean, very far away. Several heartbeats pass as the ascending sun illuminates it further, bringing it into sharper relief.

Just as quickly, another ripple of the water's metallic sheen swallows the island in a brief flash of light and it dissolves out of sight.

Stunned by the spectacle, Myria looks to Emiri for an explanation, her mouth agape. But Emiri's eyes are fixed ahead. A small smile which seems full of fondness and sadness lifts his features. The red light of dawn casts a warm, fiery color on his face, but Myria is sure his eyes are red for a different reason.

Her hand, still on his elbow, rubs a gentle, soothing pattern on his arm. "Emiri?" she whispers.

His arm tenses beneath her touch, so she releases him. He is quick to scrub at his face. When he speaks, his voice is composed. "Tell me what you saw," he directs, ever remaining the teacher.

Myria wants to sigh at his deflection, to know more about what has gotten him so worked up, but she refrains from doing so, granting him space. "There was an island on the northern horizon." She frowns, a distant memory persisting at the back of her mind, slowly resurfacing. Her mind races through the facts set before her, especially Emiri's sudden yet brief display of vulnerability upon the sight of an island.

The pieces suddenly snap together, and she gasps. "It's Caliburn, your home."

He turns to face her. "You do pay attention."

Her brow creases in confusion with this newfound mystery. "But why is there an illusion over it?"

"You're capable and cunning. Why would an entire island try to hide its existence?"

Something deep inside her chest crumbles when she remembers something Emiri said the morning he taught her summoning.

I don't blame your curiosity, Lady Hawthorne, but it is a long, complicated history full of military conquest and pain.

"To protect itself," she realizes as the air escapes her lungs. The pain Emiri tries to hide in his eyes is so grossly evident that it radiates from him in waves. "From Avalion?"

Emiri turns away and does not answer.

"Do you still have any family there?" she asks.

Emiri clears his throat, and his voice remains as steady as ever. "The presence of the illusion suggests that I do. It is difficult not to be hopeful. Seeing it for a few moments each morning when the court visits Dawnmourne is the only moment of reprieve for me."

"When was the last time you were there?"

The question makes his voice hollow. "Not since I was a boy. Over twenty years ago."

"Why haven't you returned?" Her voice lowers to a soft whisper, and she almost regrets her question.

Emiri examines his hands and sighs. "I wish I could give you a simple answer, Lady Hawthorne." His voice thickens. "But there is none. The Avalion court has a way of trapping people, something I'm sure you will see for yourself before the summer ends."

A thick silence lingers between them, but Myria patiently waits as the tense line of his shoulders loosens. Eventually, his body's tight angles completely relax, and he drags a hand through his dark hair.

"Thank you for bringing me here, Emiri."

He turns to face her, repositioning himself on the ledge and turning away from the sea, and she's glad to see a carefree smirk playing on his lips once more. "I'm glad you appreciate it. You're the only one I've brought here."

She arches a skeptical eyebrow. "You haven't shown this to anyone else? Not even to Captain Rozenna?"

Emiri rolls his eyes and jumps down from the ledge, back onto the path. "We might have grown up together, trained together as guards, but it does not mean she's privy to every aspect of my life."

Myria laughs at his annoyance. "Are you sure the captain would agree to that?"

He shakes his head, decidedly ignoring the question, and holds his hand out for her.

She looks down at him in alarm. "Are you not going to teach me an illusion spell?" she asks.

He chuckles. "While I applaud your enthusiasm, I would rather not push you after the incident with the door. Overextending yourself with magic can be harmful and dangerous."

She reluctantly takes the proffered hand, stepping onto the path next to him. She brushes snow from her dress' skirts, feeling uncomfortable wetness as some of it melts and soaks into the fabric.

As they make their way back inside, Emiri reaches into a small bag hanging from his shoulder and produces a parcel wrapped in thick paper. He unwraps it, revealing a sizable portion of a heavy, dense cake. Emiri picks up one piece for himself, devouring half of it in a single bite before handing the rest to her.

"Dawnmourne is also known for its sweet desserts," he explains past a mouthful of cake.

Myria takes a bite as they continue back toward her quarters, savoring the taste of walnut flour with hints of cherry and apple. "It's rather *sweet* of you to bring me food a second time."

Emiri narrows his eyes at her pun. "I wasn't planning to share, but you should probably eat after you almost passed out."

Myria wipes the last of the crumbs from her face with the back of her hand. "What sort of illusion magic will I have to use for the court?"

"I haven't yet heard."

She is unable to puzzle through the mystery as Emiri stops before her door, reaching for the latch. Before he can swing it open, she shoves her weight against the frame, blocking the path. He eyes her curiously.

"I understand you're on strict orders from Leor to watch over me," she says, crossing her arms. "But you should know that I am quite capable of opening doors for myself." A teasing smile plays at her lips.

Emiri smirks at her boldness, and he leans closer to her ear. "You definitely proved it earlier when you fainted."

His breath tickles her earlobe, and her smile dismantles as she struggles to concentrate. "I did *not* faint."

Emiri draws back briefly, his pointed gaze silencing her. Myria becomes acutely aware of the proximity of their faces, the curve of his mouth, the strange magnetism that makes her lean closer—

The moment is broken when Emiri takes an immediate step back, straightening his shirt and looking away. He coughs, refusing to meet her eyes. "Good luck today, Lady Hawthorne. I hear Cressida is preparing some sort of race for the suitors. The prince would prefer you not to make any reckless decisions. He cares very much for your safety." With that, Emiri offers a quick bow before disappearing down the hall.

Myria blinks in the aftermath, and her sluggish mind sorts through her thoughts as she takes cover in her room, retreating to the bed, and hiding her face in the fur blankets. *The prince cares very much for your safety.*

14

MEMORIES

SOMETIME LATER—PERHAPS MINUTES, PERHAPS hours—there is a knock at Myria's door and Olympe is suddenly at her bedside, dragging her out from the covers. Her aunt critically eyes Myria's crumpled dress before retrieving a new one, an ocher wool gown trimmed in black fur. Geffrey slides through the doorway just as she's finished putting it on.

"Oh, Myria. Thank goodness you're ready. The court is gathering outside for Duchess Cressida's event."

They hurry through the dark corridors, and Myria wonders what sort of race Cressida could have planned. They are soon outside the keep, approaching the nearby edge of the thick pine forest and a frozen river. A wooden platform sits empty, as if awaiting the duchess' grand appearance. Eulalia sidles up next to Myria with a dazzling smile just as they join a crowd of nobles decked out in warm furs, wool, and leather.

"How was your night?" Eulalia asks. "I am sorry you had to sit in the back. I tried looking for you after dinner."

Myria returns her enthusiastic smile, banishing all confusion centering on Emiri. "I retired earlier in the evening. It was clear there was no point in staying..." Myria freezes when her words make Eulalia frown.

"You could have stayed with me," she points out.

Myria sighs. "You're right. I didn't mean that. I was tired and didn't want to give Cressida the satisfaction of seeing me upset. It was a long ride to Dawnmourne, after all."

Eulalia nods in understanding. "She probably would not have noticed you there, honestly. She refused to let the prince dance with anyone." Her whisper hitches to a conspiratorial snort.

"A bit desperate?" Myria giggles.

"Yes, we were all saying the same." Eulalia's voice climbs to a higher pitch of enthusiasm, causing someone in front of them to turn around. She lowers her voice, covering her mouth as she continues whispering. "But some good news for you—I heard Aryn did not arrive in Dawnmourne."

"That's what Geffrey told me. Good riddance."

"Without her brother, Theodora has been more tolerable, if you can believe it."

Myria cranes her neck to look for the telltale splash of platinum blonde hair but is unsuccessful. "Perhaps there is hope for her yet." Her tone remains unconvinced.

"I know you have been even more suspicious of her since Cressida called her evil, but you have to remember your source. Cressida considers everyone an enemy. She was the only one who voted against House Valenrence's ascension. It benefits her if the rest of the suitors are leery of each other. Besides, she called you a fool, and she was clearly mistaken then."

Myria permits a small smile at that comforting thought. "Perhaps Cressida is the evil fool instead."

Eulalia struggles to bite down on her laughter just as the whispering crowd around them falls silent.

Duchess Cressida leads a small entourage through the crowd, which readily parts for her, and steps up to the raised wooden platform. Standing above everyone else, she is adorned in her house colors with a brilliant, scarlet silk dress that reflects the sun with a blinding light, contrasting deeply against her pale skin and black hair. Several others join her on the platform, including Prince Leor and several armored guards, one carrying an ornate cedar box.

The duchess regards the crowd gathered before her with unsmiling eyes, holding herself high with a severe austerity. "As your host, I would like to welcome each of you to the illustrious Dawnmourne Keep. The Nocturnus people have always been a formidable strain. We never back down from any challenge, as our words suggest: To be valiant is to stand." She pauses as a flicker of a menacing smile creeps across her lips. "Therefore, for the Nocturnus event, I would like to invite all of you..." Her eyes sweep the crowd, and land on Myria, who stares back. "...to prove yourself likewise as fearless, dauntless, and indomitable."

She motions to some servants out of sight, and two wooden sleighs—pulled by majestic black horses with thick, muscled flanks and steaming breath—pull into view behind her on the frozen river. The crowd of nobles titter.

"Welcome to the Summer Sleigh Races," Cressida booms, flashing her gleaming teeth in that sinister smile.

Sigurd bravely steps forward to be the voice of reason. "You cannot really intend for us to ride on the ice." His protest slices through the cold air. "The river only has a thin layer of ice in the summer, which will melt and crack even more beneath the runners."

Cressida waves away his concerns, the smile disappearing with an expression of annoyance. "This should serve no problem for those with a true Nocturnus spirit, but no matter. I have a solution for those of you too timid to brave the summer ice."

Another signal from the duchess summons the guard holding the cedar box. He steps forward, presenting its contents to his mistress. Cressida reaches in, eyes shining with something akin to avarice. She reverently pulls out a polished stone, too smooth and too round to be natural, about the size of her hand. Its blue surface swirls with ethereal white mist. Although Myria does not recognize it, others around her do, if their awed gasps and low murmuring are any indication. However, a different noise rises above the rest—a sharp, ungracious hiss. When Myria looks for the source, she finds Emiri's face. His features are set in hard, angry lines like she's never seen before, not even from Aryn or Theodora.

But Myria cannot keep her eyes on him. As Cressida grips the strange stone, the air around them thrums with unnatural energy. Myria feels it pulsing in her veins. A sudden cold blast of winter rolls off the stone in unforgiving waves, bringing new ice and frost to their surroundings. Despite the fresh biting she feels in her bones, Myria weaves herself through the crowd, drawing close to the frozen riverbank. The currents rushing beneath the crust of ice halt their pace, and deep, reverberating cracks sound as the river freezes anew into a road of black glass, then rimes with a top layer of frost.

Snow flurries drift in bizarre ripples. Myria almost tastes a foreign hunger in the hum of energy, a desire to freeze anything left exposed to the unforgiving air. She squints through the snow blindness to recognize the hazy duchess standing proudly on her stage. Perhaps she would continue to stand while the others around her freeze.

Mercifully, the aberrant blizzard ends, allowing all to inspect the new, safer path for her sleighs. Cressida returns the stone to its chest before descending from the stage with a slow step, as if disappointed by her guests' desire for security. "There you have it," she announces in a bored tone. "A frozen, winter path for your riding pleasure. However, should anyone dare attempt the more exciting adventure, we can have a race on a spring river."

Cressida's voice and eyes alight with new excitement. Though Myria is peering down the vast length of their racetrack, she senses Cressida's words directed at her.

"There is a prize, of course," the duchess offers to the crowd off-handedly. "After all, I must find some means to entertain the lot of you. The family who wins the Summer Sleigh Races earns themselves a private dinner with the royal family—or just one of its members," she stipulates with a note of intrigue.

Speculation arises throughout the gathered nobles as they imagine the best use of such a prize. The obvious, most discussed answer involves a suitor enjoying a special evening alone with the prince. Many families can be heard strategizing how best to accomplish such a feat.

Myria's eyes remain on the sealed cedar chest in the arms of the Nocturnus guard. She wonders if Cressida can provide a spring river the same way she summoned a winter river through a mysterious, magical stone designed to conjure bright flowers and warm sunshine. It is the first time she has seen a noble at court perform magic, discovering it to be more impressive than she might have imagined. She recalls the hunger of the winter's wind. It gnaws on her belly, wanting to be closer to these seasonal expressions of power. She wants to see the stones for herself, and what colors they might possess. She imagines the sensations of touching their smooth surface, the weight in her hands.

A voice silences the quiet strategies buzzing around. "I will race on the spring river."

Myria looks around to glimpse the volunteer. However, it isn't until Cressida smirks at her wolfishly that she realizes the voice is her own.

The declaration is met with astonished silence and dumbstruck faces. Myria swallows past her own shock as they stare at her in disbelief, the horrified Olympe, the nervous Geffrey, apprehensive Eulalia, and, chief of all, the distressed shadows on Emiri's face.

EVERYTHING IS DARK AND numb, and that nothingness obliterates Myria's memory and awareness while stealing the breath from her lungs with sharp relief. She reaches out through the void, searching for respite, and an odd thought occurs to her.

Even a spring river in Dawnmourne is cold as ice.

Then the memories return in a rushing flood.

In perhaps a foolish moment of misplaced pride, she agreed to Cressida's challenge for a race on a spring river. The disapproval from those around her was tangible, but Myria remained steadfast in ignoring their concerned or critical faces as she waited through the agonizing minutes. During this time, other members of the court performed their best on the safety of the winter river. As if understanding Myria would not be dissuaded, Olympe pulled her to a secluded clearing in the forest with Merek and a Nocturnus groom to teach her the rudimentary skills for steering the sleigh on ice.

Others came to visit during that time. Geoffrey with his incessant pacing and Eulalia with her concerned eyes. Prince Leor did not come, but Geoffrey assured Myria she was on the prince's mind, and he wished her well in the upcoming race.

At first, Emiri also did not come. She wondered if he knew what singular motivation drove her to this action—if he recognized the inexplicable hunger she felt to see Cressida's magic stones in action. She tried to forget the unease she saw on his face, but that memory burns into her eyes even now, etched into her mind.

It is the same distress that follows her to this moment, floating in a soundless abyss. Utter bewilderment drowns her senses as she struggles to recall the recklessness that pursued her here. When the moment of her race arrives, all of Myria's rudimentary training is forgotten as Cressida reveals the second stone from the revered cedar chest. This one is soft pink, the color of spring blossoms. The duchess's fingers tighten around the relic. Warmth floods the clearing and patches of bright green grass shoot through the thinning layer of snow. The river loses its frosty appearance, thawing into transparency. Currents ripple beneath the glassy ice. Myria knew in the back of her mind this was an unnatural spring, especially for Dawnmourne, where thick blankets of snow are typical of the summer landscape.

But even this information did not discourage Myria from her path. As the sleighs were brought to them, she focused on the magical stone in Cressida's hands. She thought nothing of the duchess's smug expression or of the danger ahead. There was only an insatiable desire to hold the stone, to keep it for herself. This singular urge eclipsed every other effort and motion as she drove her sleigh over the ice. No awareness of anything else, not the biting wind that whipped her hair about her face or the dangerous, reverberating cracks below. Only the sudden icy plunge into freezing sharpness and subsequent numbness dulls her senses, returning her to this moment of clarity.

If she does not do something soon, she will either drown or freeze to death.

Her heartbeat thrums in her ears, a dull, sluggish tempo that signals the precious moments slipping from her grasp. Turning her face to the surface, the rippling promise of sunlight greets her from above the dark depths. She focuses her sluggish mind on the light, willing it to energize her limbs as the current buffets tirelessly against her.

Warmth pools at her fingertips, the magic making them twitch in anticipation. She imagines a lifeline, the end secured somewhere on land, perhaps around a tree trunk. As if on command, she *senses* rather than sees the sun's energy materialize into a tangible object, a rope, stitching together from the power that fades from her fingers. The anchor around the tree forms before the end of the rope descends to her at a crawling pace.

Myria turns to reach for it, but something catches her eyes through the dimness. A pale figure wrapped in scarlet silk floats nearby, eyes closed and dark hair splayed across her face. Duchess Cressida.

Myria cannot recall the moment they fell through the ice, but she springs into action without hesitation. Her lungs burn without air and her throat pricks, desperate to take a breath. Choking with a sudden burst of bubbles, Myria redirects her magic toward Cressida. The rope wraps itself around the duchess's torso and under her arms. With a frantic wave of her hand, Myria uses her remaining dregs of energy to pull Cressida out of the water with the lifeline.

Black spots erupt across her vision as water floods her mouth and nose. She clutches her neck with one hand and claws with the other for the surface she cannot reach. Instinct urges her to use magic to save herself, but there is no cohesiveness to her thoughts. Only confusion and cold darkness prevail as she succumbs to her heavy eyelids.

Blinding light suddenly fills her vision, obliterating all pain and panic. She shields her eyes and realizes she is no longer drowning. As her vision adjusts to the light, she finds herself standing in a long corridor with uneven stone flags and arched windows. The steady stream of afternoon light illuminates the figure of a woman whose back is turned to Myria.

You thought you were safe.

The mature voice suggests a shrill malevolence that stiffens Myria's chest and makes the fine hairs on her arms rise.

Nowhere is safe for you.

Myria does not move, but the woman's back draws closer, bringing into detail white-blonde hair tied back from her face and cascading down her back in elegant curls. The mysterious woman turns slightly, revealing a dark pigment on the soft curve of her lips.

Did you think you could hide from me, Callia?

Myria gasps at the sound of her mother's name. Suddenly, the vision vanishes in the same flourish of blinding light with which it arrived. With a heavy pounding on her chest, her gasp turns into choking, and Myria turns over to cough up icy water from her lungs.

She braces herself on an arm as she regains her bearings. Secure on dry ground, she shivers uncontrollably beneath her soaked dress. Someone drapes a fur blanket over her shoulders. As the image of the white-blonde woman fades from her mind, Myria realizes someone has pulled her from the river. She looks up to find the dark, reassuring eyes of Emiri staring back into hers.

Warmth flushes throughout her body, as if ignited by the intense fire in his piercing gaze.

His eyes never leave hers, even when he's spurred into urgent action once more. He cups his hands over his mouth and releases a deep, steady breath. Vapor steams the air, curling between them. Emiri places his palms to the sides of her face and heat floods from his hands into her, traveling from her head down her body in radiant waves. She shudders despite herself, a shiver not born of the icy chill, as the intensity of the moment makes every detail of his face stand out.

He pulls his hands away and Myria draws in a deep breath to calm herself. She notices water dripping from Emiri's hair and clothes and realizes *he* must have jumped in the water after her.

They sit in silence for several moments until the surrounding noise breaks the spell that holds them in place. Nobles move about in uncertain panic that mirrors the general cacophony of noise around the riverbank. Myria cranes her neck to see the crowd swarming a single figure some distance away. The ancient healer from the palace weaves his way through, quickly disappearing behind others. Myria's ponders all this for a moment before realizing they are surrounding Cressida.

"You saved her," Emiri whispers, a hint of surprise in his voice.

Her shoulders tense, though his tone holds nothing of the sharp disapproval she would have expected from him. "It was the right thing to do."

Emiri does not argue. "You used the few moments of consciousness and what little magic you had left to save her. I don't know if she would have done the same."

"Are you saying I shouldn't have?" Myria asks, unable to stifle the note of bitterness as she glances at him.

Emiri leans back, studying her. His voice is even quieter than before. "You could have died."

Despite the softness of his words, she does not miss their severity. Something about that quickens her pulse. She offers him a teasing smirk. "Not with you diving in after me. It appears I should be more grateful to you for always watching out for me."

The sudden flush of pink that rises to his cheeks pleases her, and a desire to see him squirm under such attention fills her. Once again, their faces linger close to one another.

A renewed boldness seizes her. She leans closer, bridging the gap between them even more. Her eyes narrow and her lips pulled back in a smug grin. "You know, it *is* natural to be worried about someone. You shouldn't be ashamed to be concerned with my safety."

She feels a rare moment of power over him, and she expects his face to harden defensively and deny any such claims of concern. However, he surpasses all expectations, merely staring in wide-eyed shock, lips working into flustered, unintelligible syllables as he flounders for a response.

She isn't sure what to make of such a reaction until he returns an immodest smirk. "You already know my concern is that Prince Leor charged me to look after you."

Before she has time to consider these words, Emiri quickly pushes himself to his feet, offering a hand to help her up as well. When she takes it, there is a sudden charge that jolts her skin at the touch, and she barely registers the strength of his arm that steadies her as a she remembers the fleeting interaction they shared before the race that nearly sent her to a watery grave. How much he had protested it.

"It was stupid." Myria just notices how tightly she holds onto Emiri's arm for support.

He looks down at her curiously, not withdrawing from her grip.

"Yes," he agrees.

Chewing her bottom lip, Myria considers the inexplicable effect Cressida's stones had over her and the mysterious vision of the woman speaking to her mother. She can't help but wonder what they could mean. Was the white-blonde woman the key to learning more about her mother's experience at court? And how could she explain the insatiable *desire* to glimpse the magic stones? Would Emiri even have any insight?

"Myria! There you are!"

Suddenly, a new force pulls her away from Emiri, and Myria finds herself surrounded by the tangled mess of her aunt's hair. Geff hovers nearby, his face lined with grim lines as his mother chokes whatever life Emiri revived from Myria.

"We thought... When you fell..." Olympe straightens, checking herself as she resumes a more sober countenance. "That race was ill-advised."

Myria releases a heavy sigh. "I know. I am not sure what came over me." Her eyes dart to the side with the simple lie, and they land on Emiri, who studies her with his own narrowed.

Her aunt and cousin attempt to usher her back to the palace, circumventing the concerned crowd around Cressida, when the prince intervenes, halting their surreptitious escape. The three of them greet him with a demure bow. As Myria forces a courtly smile, the exhaustion of her near-drowning tugs at her limbs. Emiri's warmth already fades, leaving her shivering beneath the fur blanket.

Prince Leor does not shy from bold, improper contact as he closes the distance between them to hold Myria's hands in his own. His face is drawn. "Lady Myria, I am so pleased to see you safe. My heart stopped when I saw you fall through the ice."

Myria barely remembers the moment herself. "Luckily, everyone is safe," she manages. "Even Duchess Cressida."

"Thanks to you," a new voice says, crisp and curt, unlike Leor's.

Myria turns to see the duchess herself approaching. Her face is as smooth as stone, but there is something foreign about how she holds herself and regards Myria. The crowd stands just behind her, watching the exchange with rapt interest.

Myria finds it challenging to meet Cressida's probing glare and looks away. "It was nothing," she dismisses.

Cressida gives a hot sniff. "A lie, Lady Myria. You saved my life. While I recognize the Summer Courtship puts us at odds with each other, setting us as rivals, I still must embody the values of my family name. In House Nocturnus, we pride our honor. Saving my life, at the risk of your own, is a debt I cannot easily repay." Cressida's nose crinkles as if the admission fills her with disgust, but her shrewd eyes warn against any interruption.

"Duchess Cressida, I do not require or want any sort of repayment—"

A sharp jab to her ribs silences her. Myria does not look at Geff, but she quickly understands his thoughts. House Nocturnus would be a powerful ally.

Cressida waves her hand to some servants, ignoring Myria's concerns. "I will hear no refusals. Tonight, you are the guest of honor. You shall dine with me privately, and we can discuss the finer points of our alliance." Several attendants swarm forward to lift Myria onto a litter that seemed to materialize out of nowhere.

Upon hearing such news, Geffrey hastily dips into a gracious bow. "We are honored by your generosity, Duchess Cressida."

Cressida's mouth quirks into an amused smirk much more fitting to her character. "I look forward to our mutually beneficial relationship as well, Duke Bramble. However, make no mistake, even though you are the head of the house, the terms of our alliance rest on Myria's shoulders."

BACK INSIDE DAWNMOURNE KEEP, Myria warms herself before the fireplace in her room. Nocturnus servants swirl around her in a buzz of activity, preparing a custom gown for the night's dinner; the first of many promised gifts from Duchess Cressida. Myria sits, lost in the hearth's flames, as Geffrey coaches her on alliance terms.

"With the backing of House Nocturnus, we will be one of the strongest families in the kingdom, but only if the terms are to our liking."

Myria's energy wanes as she struggles to pay attention to his words. "What if it's all a trick? Don't you think Cressida would be capable of betraying us?"

"Despite all of Cressida's shortcomings, the Nocturnus family is renowned for their loyalty. Besides, I do not think she would make such a public proclamation of our alliance if she wanted to turn on us."

"Then why does she want to see me alone? Why is it up to me to navigate the political schemes? She knows I am the most unqualified of our house to do so."

Geff grumbles under his breath, his impatience showing through. "Then it would do well for you to pay attention to what I am telling you. House Bramble offers much in terms of our wheat and food stores, which would benefit the Nocturnus people most. However, we desperately need something she has."

"Which is?"

Geffrey eyes flicker to the surrounding servants, then leans to whisper in Myria's ear. "Money."

Myria scrutinizes her cousin. "If that's so, then how are you able to afford to travel around the kingdom, purchasing new dresses for me, and helping my grandmother's inn?" Her voice hitches involuntarily at the last question.

Geffrey shushes her. "We have money to last us the year, but our treasury is quickly depleting. My mother blames it on..."

He hesitates, checking himself, and does not continue. Myria frowns, her irritation increasing. "Go on. It can't be my fault you're no longer rich? Your money problems started much earlier than when I joined the court."

"That is true. It was your mother, actually. When she was engaged to the king, House Bramble offered quite a large dowry, assuming the marriage would give us access to the royal coffers in return. However, when your mother left court, events transpired in an unexpected fashion."

"Olympe never mentioned that before," Myria says, glaring at her hands as her brows knit in confusion. "Do you think my mother stole that money when she ran away?"

"I have no discerning opinion on the matter, Myria," Geffrey sighs. "This occurred before I was even born. There is only the aftermath now. My mother always believed Callia would have never *stolen*—"

"Well, she didn't," Myria hisses, rising to her feet. She ignores the wave of dizziness as she stares at her cousin. "We lived in complete poverty. There was no way she had a stash of treasure hiding at the Morning Glory."

"Of course," Geffrey blurts. "I never meant to imply that. Try to understand how destitute it has left—"

"Oh, yes. How *destitute*." Myria's words are venom. "I cannot imagine the suffering you went through as a child. Forgive me if I have some difficulty in pitying you. I did not realize touring the countryside and dining at the palace was the same as when my grandmother couldn't afford our next meal!"

Geffrey shrinks back, her outburst loud enough to give the Nocturnus servants pause. She turns away from them all, looking back into the fire as she pulls the furs tightly around her shoulders.

Geffrey attempts a soft tone. "Myria, I—"

"Don't worry. I'll negotiate favorable terms for House Bramble. Please, just leave me alone now."

In the corner of her eye, Geffrey nods and signals to everyone else to file out of the room. He is the last to leave, closing the door behind him. Finally alone, Myria's thoughts focus on replaying the vision of the white blonde woman in her head, grasping at the finer details slipping from her memory. Black tiles. Silver threading on a green dress. Those dark, dark lips. With a new facet to the mystery of her mother revealed, she wonders if the woman had any hand in the missing Bramble dowry.

15

HONOR

MYRIA SLEEPS THE REST of the afternoon away without dreams to torment her. In a matter of hours, the door to her room opens again, and she wakens to Olympe barging in, followed by two maids. As Myria blinks at her visitors, her aunt takes one sweeping look around the room before issuing instructions to the servants behind her. They bring warm water and lay a new dress across the bed.

"Geffrey told me about your disagreement," Olympe says, running her hand across the fabric of Cressida's gifted gown.

Myria stands to inspect the vibrant scarlet silk. While undoubtedly beautiful, something in her stomach falls at the sight of the gossamer material and plunging neckline, quite unlike any other gown she has worn. She says nothing to her aunt.

Olympe continues. "I understand your frustration, but I ask you not to hold anything against him. After Caspian passed away, Geffrey had to assume the role as head of the house and the burden of its responsibilities."

"Should I hold it against you then?" Myria asks, the bitterness coating her tongue. "Since you seem to think my mother stole her own dowry?"

Olympe stares back as if silently assessing her, but Myria does not turn to meet her gaze. Her aunt's voice is composed. "If it makes you feel better, blame me. I do not think your mother stole the dowry, but I believe it is somehow involved with her mysterious disappearance. However, right now, we can do nothing about the past. You have a task ahead of you."

Myria crosses her arms as she glares at the revealing dress. "Do I have to wear this?"

"It would be a sign of good faith to our hostess. The red represents her house colors."

"But it's so..." Myria struggles for the right word. "Immodest."

Olympe snorts, her mouth curling ruefully. "It cannot be considered inappropriate if deemed worthy by the duchess."

As the maids help her bathe and dress, Myria realizes the neckline is even more revealing than she thought, dipping dangerously close to her midriff and requiring special boning hidden in the layers of the dress to keep it in place. Her aunt eyes the dress, but says nothing of the scandalous cut. Myria's hair remains loose and long, adorned only with a few matching ruby hairpins near her temples.

As the preparations complete, a Nocturnus steward arrives to escort her to Duchess Cressida's private chambers.

Myria glances to her aunt once more.

Olympe offers her a final, encouraging nod. "Trust your instincts with the duchess."

Despite whistling winds buffeting and rattling the windows of Dawnmourne Keep, the corridors prove temperate and sconces cast warm torchlight on their path. They encounter no one else in the halls, and Myria wonders if this is an intentional design. The steward leads her through the more luxurious parts of the keep, furnished with rich tapestries and regal paintings of Nocturnus nobles. In one, Myria sees a ship, a galleon, traversing stormy waters, and the details of the image give her pause until the steward beckons her to keep up.

At last, they stop at a set of double doors flanked by guards. The scene seems to Myria more like the entrance to a king's private quarters than a duchess's. The steward's sharp knock elicits Cressida's command, "Enter."

Myria steps into the deliciously warm room, the first of what she assumes is a sprawling suite. A dining area spreads before her. The crackling fire on the left wall and tall black candles on a small round table illicit flickering shadows throughout the room. Cressida stands across the chamber, her back to Myria as she gazes out a massive set of windows. On the right wall, a mahogany portal leads to what Myria imagines are private sleeping quarters.

Cressida turns, and Myria recognizes her golden gown as a show of respect for the House Bramble colors. She breathes a little easier, thinking Cressida is sincere in her offer of an alliance.

The duchess nods approvingly at Myria's appearance. "The dress is flattering on you. Please, have a seat." She gestures at the table, set for two in the intimate setting.

Myria perches on the edge of the closest seat, and Cressida sits across from her. A server appears to set a first course of soup and fill their goblets. Slivers of onion and mushroom float in a dark broth, which is earthy and rich. Myria recognizes the dark wine paired with it as the same brand Emiri stole the night before.

Cressida does not eat, merely watching Myria as she takes a few tentative sips of her soup. After a few minutes, Myria sets aside her spoon to return the duchess's hawklike glare. "Should we get right to business?" Myria asks.

Cressida smiles, and it is the most genuine expression Myria has seen from her. "Straight to the point, then? As you wish, Lady Myria." She waves to the servant, who disappears through a hidden staff door. Only her steward remains with them, just out of sight.

"Forgive me, Duchess, but I must ask. Are you earnest in this desire to form an alliance with me and House Bramble?"

Cressida leans back in her chair and twirls a strand of her black hair, still not touching her food or wine. "Your misgivings are understandable, considering our previous encounters. Nevertheless, take comfort in that I honor the reputation of my house."

"Why would you ask to meet with me?" Myria asks, arching a suspicious eyebrow. "Why not my cousin? He's the head of our house. He understands its needs and has more experience in the political arena, something you've frequently enjoyed reminding me I lack."

Cressida's next smile shows teeth, taking on a predatory edge. "Do not worry. I am already well aware of the state of House Bramble's financial affairs. I can do my part to assist Duke Bramble with his gold problem if we confirm our alliance. However, I asked to see you because you are the one who saved my life. I would like to know what *you* want without the whispered words of your cousin next to you. Besides, the Summer Courtship already makes us rivals; this meeting offers an opportunity to rise above that with a demonstration of unity."

Myria narrows her eyes as she takes another generous sip of the wine. "If you intend to help our family financially, then I am not sure what else I can ask for."

Cressida sighs impatiently and stops twirling her hair. "There are many things I can do for you. May I call you Myria?"

Myria nods.

"*Myria,*" Cressida savors the sound on her tongue for a moment before continuing. "A while ago, you asked me a question, and I never gave you a proper answer."

"Please remind me," Myria says, leaning back as well. Her tense shoulders do not relax.

"After the joust, I called you a Fool Queen and Lady Theodora the Evil Queen. You asked what would be worse for our kingdom. The truth is, the Fool Queen is no better than the Evil Queen, because a fool is easily manipulated."

Myria suffers a thin smile. "You still think I am a fool."

Cressida does not hesitate. "Quite so, but perhaps not as big a fool as I thought. You lack only experience and training, something I can help you with as a sign of our burgeoning friendship."

"I fail to see how you are so willing to help me when we are competing for the same thing."

Cressida's lips press into a thin line. "The throne of Avalion." The duchess stands and slowly paces the length of the room. "In that regard, I would like to offer a compromise. I still stand by my previous assertation that you are not the best choice for our country, yet I cannot force you out of this courtship—as much as I would like to." The shadows across her face accentuate the austere line of a cynical smile.

"It sounds like we are at an impasse."

"Not quite. I would like to offer you an alternative, the opportunity of an advantageous match for your station. My cousin, Lord Godric."

Despite not drinking any wine at that moment, Myria feels herself choke. "Lord Godric? I hardly know him, much less *love* him."

Cressida stops pacing, pinching the bridge of her nose. "No offense, Myria, but this is an area where you are a fool. In the court of nobility, *marriage* and *love* are two separate matters, the latter of which has no place in our politics."

For a moment, Myria remembers the conversation with Eulalia at the joust. *Marriage is an act of politics or business for us. Alliances and connections. For all our wealth and privilege, sometimes the luxury we lack is the ability to choose for ourselves.*

She attempts to compose herself, but her racing heart makes it difficult for her to maintain focus. "Of course, but even for an arranged marriage, you can hardly expect me to marry someone I have never even met."

"You could use the rest of the social season to acquaint yourself with Godric," Cressida points out.

A plethora of thoughts barrage Myria's mind, and she struggles to voice her concerns. "Does Godric even know you are bartering off his marriage bed tonight?"

Cressida shrugs. "He understands his marriage is mine to arrange since I am the head of our house."

"What if I don't like him? What if I end up *hating* him?" Myria's eyes grow wide as dire possibilities paint themselves in her mind.

Cressida chuckles at her panic. "Then make life miserable for him. The marriage would be a political one, not an affair of the heart. You can marry someone without liking them, but if the prince is the source of your reservations..." Here, Cressida hesitates.

"What do you mean?"

The duchess clears her throat and presses forward with her offer. "If you gave up your claim to wed the prince, and if *I* were to become the queen of Avalion,

I would understand how driven to emotions the two of you are. I have seen the way he looks at you. One would have to be blind to miss it. My offer is this: You marry my cousin and I permit you to carry on your romance with Prince Leor, including whatever intimacies that may entail."

Stunned, Myria's face drains of all color despite the suddenly overbearing warmth rising through her neck, threatening to suffocate her. "Duchess Cressida, I don't... I don't think..."

"You do not have to decide right now. I understand this is no small proposition. You would also require Duke Bramble's approval."

The mention of her cousin reminds Myria of her present course, the entire reason she is in the Summer Courtship. "I am not sure I could consent to this, even if I wanted to. I agreed with Geffrey to represent House Bramble. In exchange, he supports my grandmother."

Cressida purses her lips, waving her hand as if this is no concern. "Duke Bramble seeks the throne because of his financial distress, which I could relieve. In addition, I would support your grandmother. She would want for nothing."

Myria chews on her lip. "This show of generosity cannot be overstated, Duchess Cressida." She cannot deny the duchess's magnanimity, even if she is hesitant to trust the woman. While Myria shudders at the thought of marrying for political gain, she understands the offer may be a sincere kindness from Cressida. Still, Grandma Iris's words ring in her ears. *Do not marry someone you don't want to.*

Possibly sensing Myria's reluctance, Cressida tries a different tactic. "I understand my offer demands much from you. As you take time to consider it, know I can help in other ways. I have access to a wealth of resources. Our friendship means I am at your service."

"I only have to forfeit my claim in the Summer Courtship?" she asks.

The firelight lends a devilish temper to Cressida's grin. "As I said, take your time to decide. If there is nothing else you desire, I have a final, parting gift for you."

Myria feels as though she is striking a deal with a demon, sacrificing her own happiness for the sake of her family and this alliance. It turns her stomach with guilt as she recalls how much scorn Emiri has for the duchess in how she has treated him.

"Wait," Myria says. "While I consult with my family, there is something else you could do as a show of good faith."

Cressida arches an eyebrow, intrigued. "Please, go on."

"You should do right by Emiri. Treat him better. He's not a servant you can shove at the end of the dining table."

Myria braces for whatever reaction Cressida might have to the request, but is surprised when the duchess smiles. The expression seems one of amusement, bordering on malevolence. "You want me to play nice with Emiri? I take it he has told you about our history."

Myria nods, a determined frown set on her features. "You've treated him horribly since you were children."

Cressida trills a high-pitched laugh. "Is that what he said? Oh my, what a gracious lie for my sake."

Myria feels her shoulders falling. "A lie?"

"Oh, yes, my dear Myria. The truth is actually a much more sordid affair." Cressida turns to her steward, hidden in the shadows, and commands with a firm voice, "Bring him here. I do not care if he sleeps. Lady Hawthorne's surprise will have to wait for now."

The steward nods before striding out of the room.

The duchess turns back to Myria, sinking into her chair once more. Cressida finally takes a long draft of her wine, and when she sets the glass down, her lips are stained dark as if by blood. "As a symbol of our new friendship, I can offer you the truth, however damning it may be."

The minutes pass. Myria's face and neck flush with a stifling heat that has nothing to do with the flames crackling in the hearth and all to do with the Nocturnus duchess's unsettling smirk. With no other recourse, she sips the rare currant wine in a thin attempt to settle her nerves, but it does nothing except exacerbate the warmth spreading throughout her body. Cressida's eyes watch her as if anticipating any reaction from Myria to use for her own advantage.

As they wait for the steward's return, Myria trains her attention elsewhere, schooling the panic that bubbles in her chest. She tries to understand it; the most likely answer she can imagine is worrying about Emiri seeing her with Cressida. Or worse: he lied to her. She wonders why he would lie, but her mind fails her in this respect.

Too soon, a knock at the duchess's chambers ends the agonizing wait. As Cressida bids the visitor enter, Myria keeps her face forward, her back to the door.

Cressida does not rise to greet him, which is telling enough of her thoughts without the wolfish grin that stretches her face. "Ah, dearest Emiri. How lovely of you to join us."

Slow, heavy footsteps echo in the chamber, and when Cressida's grin falters, Myria hides a smile, knowing Emiri isn't bowing for her.

The agitated voice confirms his identity. "If only I shared your opinion of loveliness. Your steward offered me no choice in the matter as I was quite forcibly escorted from my room."

Cressida's mouth twitches, but this time, Myria cannot determine if it's from annoyance or humor. "Please, do not hide your true feelings on my account. We are among *friends*." Her sharp eyes flicker to Myria's face on the last word, lilting in a way that makes Myria's stomach plummet.

Emiri seems to miss Cressida's tone shift, and his voice rises in anger. "Of course, I should not be surprised a Nocturnus feels at ease forcing their will upon anyone—"

His rebuke stalls suddenly. Myria knows why when she turns to see him standing next to her, mouth agape at her presence. Her lips tighten into a thin line that she is sure looks nothing akin to a smile.

"Lady Myria," he says in a strangled voice, belatedly bowing to her.

"Emiri," she replies, voice also strained to a near growl. The honorific remains unwelcome, even in this circumstance.

Cressida studies them for a moment, leaning back in her chair as she considers the pair through steepled fingers. The predatory grin returns as she motions to her steward. "Set the table for a third guest. Sir Emiri, I insist you dine with us."

Myria casts an anxious look in the duchess's direction. Emiri's expression hardens with his apparent preference to do no such thing. "My lady," he says through a clenched jaw. "I would never ask you to trouble yourself."

Cressida shrugs a single shoulder. "The pleasure is all mine. After all, Lady Myria is the one who insists I act more inclusive toward you."

Emiri's head snaps to Myria with an accusing motion, but his eyebrows knit together in concern. Myria turns away, feigning interest in the craftsmanship of her wine goblet.

Once his place is set, Emiri sinks into the third chair placed between them. He does not touch his serving of braised goat, instead shifting his eyes between the two women. Occasionally, Myria peeks from beneath her eyelashes to see Cressida watching her and Emiri glaring at his food.

None of them speak for several long minutes. Cressida takes a long draught of wine and sets her goblet on the table with a heavy thud. "Really, Emiri, I would expect you to be much friendlier."

"And when did I ever offer that impression?" he asks. The anger he restrains is every bit as palpable to Myria as her own head swimming and the bitterness coating her tongue.

Cressida chuckles. "When you lied to our friend, Lady Myria, you told her you hated me because I was mean to you as a little girl."

"I..." Emiri's jaw works shut as he struggles to search for the right thing to say. "It wasn't a *lie*," he manages at length, and his voice lifts strangely on the last word.

The strain in his voice almost sounds like guilt, and Myria casts a puzzled expression on Emiri. Still, no matter how much she studies his face, he keeps it half-hidden from her, trained on the servings of food before him. His hair falls over his face, further concealing him.

As if delighting in the visible tension, Cressida claps her hands together. "Come now, Emiri. You know as well as I that hiding a portion of the truth is as good as any lie one could fabricate. I assumed since you decided to withhold the most unsavory bits of truth from Lady Myria, you must have done so for my benefit."

His hands clench into fists, and his knuckles strain white. His voice is low and dark, matching the smoke curling from the hearth as he responds. "The time hasn't been right."

"What better opportunity to clear the air than this?" Cressida asks, and her brightness makes Myria suspicious of her intent.

"Why do you care?" Emiri all but growls.

Cressida sighs, rising from her seat to pace the room. "Lady Myria and I are in the process of forging a new alliance, the terms of which are still mutable. Lady Myria desires I alter my behavior toward you. As a potential ally, I want to make sure she is fully informed. It is hardly my fault you have only shared partial truths with her, thus making her ill-equipped to properly negotiate her terms of our arrangement."

Heat flashes through Myria at Cressida's comment, and she squares her shoulders as she speaks up. "I don't need to know your full history for you to treat someone with basic respect."

Cressida halts to regard her with folded arms. "Then consider this a token of good faith. Perhaps you should take the full history of House Nocturnus before forming an alliance with us."

"Then tell me yourself. Why bring Emiri into this, if not to torture him further?"

The duchess's shrug this time is careless and indifferent. "It is not my story to tell."

"It's fine," Emiri says. "I don't mind sharing it with you, especially if it'll warn you away from any dealings with a Nocturnus."

Myria focuses on Emiri, observing his expression. His hands push back the curtain of dark hair, revealing flushed cheeks as he fixes her with an unrelenting, impenetrable gaze.

"You already know I come from a place called Caliburn," he begins, "a single island in the sea north of here. It was my home for the first six years of my life, until..." His eyes cut toward Cressida, glinting dangerously, and his voice darkens to a pitch Myria's never heard from him. "*Her* family came along."

The hiss makes Myria want to cringe and fold away into herself. Cressida, the target of all his contempt, doesn't so much as flinch.

"Caliburn was a peaceful settlement full of mages, witches, and wizards. Sorcerers, all of us. We studied magic by connecting with nature. We lived in clay hovels compared to the glittering palaces and stony fortresses of Avalion, but it was enough for us. It was not enough for others. The Nocturnus family once lived honorably by swearing to protect the borders of both Avalion and Caliburn. We didn't have an army..."

Emiri's voice falters for a moment, and he fixes his eyes on the hearth, swiping gruffly at his nose.

"We shared some of our magical knowledge with the Nocturnus family in exchange for protection from invaders. Sea-roving bandits learned to leave us alone against the might and valor of the Nocturnus navy. We thought we were safe, but then we were *betrayed*."

Myria's throat pricks. "By whom?" But she knows the answer.

"None other than Cressida's father himself, Duke Hestor Nocturnus. He led an assault against us alongside Duke Theobald and his majesty, the king."

"King Uriel?" Myria asks in a whisper.

"Power-hungry, greedy for magic of their own—"

"Careful, Emiri," Cressida says, standing by the window. "Your words stray too close to treason."

He ignores her, words dripping with tight rage. "My father would have shared it with them peacefully, as he did in the end, to save us. Yet, I can still smell the smoke, still see the fires and the blood—all unnecessary. My father called for peace, even during battle, trying to negotiate to save us. Eventually, King Uriel *graciously* afforded him an audience and accepted my father's terms. The attack on Caliburn would end, and in exchange, my father would leave to serve Avalion's court in all matters of magic, including teaching the nobility our skills. King Uriel even confiscated all Caliburn's magical relics and kept me as a palace ward to ensure my father's loyalty. My father never saw my mother again because he died protecting the king."

Cressida sniffs. "You neglected to mention, Emiri, that your father was not wholly innocent. Ambrose Magnus killed his own share of victims, including my father."

Emiri is suddenly on his feet, knocking the chair over as his fist connects with the table, sending all the dishes clattering and causing Myria to jump. "In self-defense, in a war which Duke Hestor *started*."

Cressida does not appear affected by the sudden outburst, keeping her back to the room as her eyes remain on the landscape outside the windows. "I suppose I cannot expect you to understand the political complexities my father was involved in."

Emiri snarls, spittle flying from his lips as his voice rises even further. "I suppose the infamous honor of House Nocturnus is also too complex for you or your father."

Cressida whirls around, and her face like ice and stone as she glares at Emiri. "That is all, Emiri Magnus. Leave."

Emiri does not argue with the command, giving the fallen chair a kick as he storms out. Myria watches for a moment as her mind reels with all she has learned. The pain in Emiri's rage is undeniable, like an open, festering wound that Cressida enjoys poking. The heavy door slams behind him, and Myria reaches a hand out before glancing uncertainly at Cressida.

Surprisingly, the duchess's face softens. "I will not pretend to excuse the actions of my father. I was as young as Emiri at the time, and had no way of understanding his reasons. I do, however, know the Battle of Caliburn made me an orphan, and I became a ward of King Uriel as well. Hence, my behavior toward young Emiri was born of a child's grief for her father." Cressida turns back to the window, adding without turning back to Myria, "Go to your friend. We can resume our negotiations tomorrow."

Myria hurries out of the room without a second thought. She finds Emiri after the turn of the first corridor, pressing his forehead to the cool glass of a tall, arched window, struggling to control his breathing. He straightens when he sees her approaching, watching her movements with guarded eyes.

Myria stops, leaving several feet of space between them, wringing her cold fingers. "I don't even know what to say."

Emiri glances out the window, as if he could trace the indeterminable lines of the mountains through the darkness. "I apologize for losing my temper in there."

"I should be the one apologizing. If it weren't for me, you wouldn't have been dragged into that."

He offers a wry smile, still not meeting her gaze. "The Nocturnus duchess delights in torturing those she sees as inferior. I would be mindful of that in whatever alliance you decide to form."

Myria senses a rift between herself and Emiri, a gaping void she knows not how to bridge. Perhaps it is only the fresh reopening of old wounds that makes him so distant, but Myria cannot stave off the guilt that washes over her. "You *know* I don't care about Cressida Nocturnus or some silly alliance, don't you?"

He finally meets her eyes but says nothing, waiting for her to continue.

She stumbles over her words. "I'm not in there eating dinner with her because I want to be. I'm not here with the court to make myself queen by the end of the summer. I'm here because of my grandmother..." She trails off, unable to make sense of her thoughts, and looks down at her wringing hands.

"And to learn magic," he points out.

She looks up again to see a teasing, half-smile brightening up his features. "Yes," she nods. "I have to be in there. This is my deal with Geffrey."

He regards her for a silent, solemn moment, and Myria's shoulders tense as she waits for whatever judgment he gives. When he finally speaks, his voice is low like a soft curse, his words thick with their message. "Myria, you will have to make a choice. You say you don't want these things, that they are for your cousin or for your house, but that does not deny where you are. You very well may be the next Queen of Avalion."

"Only if Leor picks me. I am the least likely choice," she insists.

Emiri scoffs without meeting her eyes. "You are the most likely of choices. He cares for you very deeply. He uses the summer to justify your place as his queen." Emiri hesitates, turning his head further away to stare out the window at the inky black night. "And I do not think it would be the wrong choice for Avalion."

The wintry corridor of Dawnmourne Keep seems to sweep through her, almost freezing her into place as she sorts through Emiri's meaning. "What are you saying?"

"You would be the best queen for us, but only if you choose it. You cannot continue shifting the responsibility to what Geff wants. *You* have to want it, or the choice will be made for you. The day passes and the court goes on whether or not you're with it. Events will transpire in spite of anyone's indecision."

Myria hesitates. "Leor knows what I want." But her words sound hollow to her own ears.

Emiri echoes her doubt with a dark chuckle. "Yet here you are, all the same, competing for his hand with the others. Decide what you want, Myria," he repeats. "Before the choice is taken from you."

She wraps her arms around herself, warding off the chill that emanates from her own chest. She cannot blame Emiri's bitterness, not when there is truth in his words. "I hope you will forgive me," she says in a soft voice. "It was not my intent that you relive those painful memories."

"I do not regret it," Emiri says, finally turning back to her, a glimmer of his former self in his expression. "It is good that you know, that you are aware."

Suddenly, Emiri's eyes catch something over her shoulder, and he pushes himself away from the window, straightening his posture. Myria turns to see none other than Prince Leor approaching them. She dips into a quick curtsy as Emiri similarly sinks into a bow next to her.

"Please, that is not necessary. We are friends," he says in his warm-honey voice.

Myria can't help but smile at the characteristic humility he has shown since their meeting at the Morning Glory. "To what do we owe the pleasure of seeing you tonight?" she asks.

"Sleeplessness," Leor admits. A sudden flame flickers in his bright amber eyes as he notices the cut of her dress. His eyes wander down her frame for a moment until, realizing what he is doing, a fierce blush blooms across his cheeks as he looks at the floor. "You look lovely this evening, Lady Myria."

Myria tucks a loose strand of hair behind her ear, smiling demurely up at him. "Thank you, Your Majesty. I was about to return to my chambers."

"I can escort you," he volunteers, offering an arm.

Myria's eyes cut to Emiri as she reaches for the outstretched arm. Her fingers graze the soft sleeve of Leor's velvet tunic. But Emiri, whose face is smooth, his eyes dark and unreadable, captures her attention. His previous warning echoes in her head. Her stomach twists at the thought of taking Leor's arm and how it feels like accepting the games of court over what she really wants.

Emiri inclines his head, offering few words. "Your lesson is at dawn tomorrow. I shall meet you outside." Then, he bids good night to the prince before stiffly taking his leave. Myria watches him go, the same unsatisfied longing seeding in her stomach. Despite his cautious smiles and severe reassurances, she feels no closer to bridging the rift grown between them.

"Did I interrupt something?" Leor asks.

As Myria glances up at him, his brow creases with worry. A sudden flash of ice spikes through her at the implication of his words. Her explanation spills from her lips in a torrent. "No, we were just—Emiri was just leaving. Cressida upset him, so I wanted to check on him."

It is evident from Leor's patient expression he is concerned for his friend, not assuming anything scandalous. "Yes, the two of them have never gotten along. Do you know their history?"

"Yes, I just learned of it this evening. It was why Emiri was there in the first place, so Duchess Cressida could inform me of all the unpleasant details."

"It's not a pretty story," he agrees. "Definitely one of the darker chapters of my father's reign as king. I wish I could explain his actions, but I was only a baby at the time."

Myria considers how a king attacking a defenseless village to steal magic paints the qualities of a tyrant. However, she does not voice this, and her thoughts turn to her mother probably having been lucky to escape the royal life before becoming complicit in the king's misdeeds.

Leor continues as he leads her down the corridor, "Despite their animosity, I also grew up with the duchess, and it has given me more insight into her character, even if she treated me better than Emiri."

"So, what insights do you have of the duchess?" Myria asks.

"She has a rough exterior in the sense that she often comes across as cold or abrasive. Perhaps this is her mountainous upbringing bleeding through, but she is as much a victim in this life as any of us are. She lost her parents and knew none of her family as she grew up in the palace. Emiri, at the very least, had his father in this strange world. She learned early lessons about the vicious nature of court. She understands her duties, so she plays her role well. As the female head of her house, she often must appear strong. I do not begrudge her for it. Underneath it all, I know she has a good heart."

Myria does not doubt this. She has seen glimmers of this heart at court—a warning about the Stirlings and gratitude for saving her life. Even so, Myria struggles to accept the treatment and abuse Emiri has known his entire life. Cressida might have lost her parents, but Emiri lost his homeland. Cressida might have been forced into role as duchess at a young age, but Emiri had his entire heritage stolen to see it paraded as trinkets for the wealthy.

She is aware of Leor watching her reaction, so she dons a smile. "I think it is important to remember everyone is capable of feeling and inflicting pain. We should be mindful and empathetic."

She returns his smile, only letting it slip when he turns away just as they reach the doors to Myria's room. Emiri's words press against her thoughts, and not for the first time that night, guilt burrows its way through her stomach. He was right; she needs to make a choice before it's made for her. "When you have a moment, I wish to speak with you."

The urgency in her voice demands his attention so strongly that his head snaps to her in an instant. "I am yours, Lady Myria." The hoarse whisper sends a shiver down her spine, and she forgets her thoughts entirely as she stares at his earnest face. So open and comforting, like a prince. Like a genuinely benevolent king. And at that moment, with the way he looks at her, she does not doubt Emiri's belief that Leor cares for her very deeply. The shining respect and affection are so evident in his eyes, making her belly swirl and her head spin. Her tongue stalls.

They are too close, the air too charged. Like with Emiri that very morning. But Emiri stepped away, made his escape.

Words flee her. So takes her own escape, stepping back with a hand grounded against the door. The only words she can conjure are, "Good night, Your Majesty."

16

SELF-AWARENESS

THE NEXT MORNING, MYRIA changes into her green dress and furs to meet Emiri in the agreed-upon spot outside Dawnmourne Keep—the small, tucked away mountain precipice with swirling snow above raging seas. Pulling the fur-lined cloak tighter around her shoulders, she strains her eyes against the predawn darkness and finds Emiri already waiting.

She knows he is not there early for her. His eyes remain on the horizon for the flash of light that signals his home. She hesitates, now knowing his past—the separation from his family and the brutalization of his home. Instead of approaching him, she watches from the door for several minutes as the emerging sun illuminates the gray sky and highlights the metallic sheen of the ocean's surface. The rippling effect flashes against the skyline, offering a brief glimpse of his homeland, Caliburn.

He lingers, unmoving, for a few moments after, and Myria does not have the heart to shatter his peace. When he finally moves, he does not appear surprised to see her.

A realization occurs to her. "When I asked you yesterday why you don't leave the court to see them, it's because you cannot. Correct? You are a ward of King Uriel. You're basically a prisoner here until he says otherwise."

Emiri's looks at his hands, a humorless smile lining his face. "Yes." He turns away from the rising sun, his expression replaced by a mask of indifference. "Let us begin your lesson."

Myria does not miss the careful space Emiri keeps between them as he paces around her. Something in her chest wilts, but she tries to remain focused on his words and the lesson, her eyes on the ground.

"For some, illusion is the easiest skill for a mage to master. For others, it remains the most difficult. I suspect it will prove difficult for you since you performed the other forms of magic so naturally." Emiri carves a wide arc around her, the snow crunching beneath his boots, which leave packed, muddy ice in their wake.

She nods. "Should I approach this differently from conjuring? I'm still confused about how illusions are different."

"The illusion should be inherently tied to your magic. Once the connection to your magic ends, so will the illusion. Start with something small, maybe a peach. And use only your moon crystal."

The mention of the fruit reminds her of the midnight glen with the minotaur. Brief images flash through her mind—holding onto Emiri's hand, the minotaur kneeling before the prince, kissing Leor. She shakes her head to clear these intrusive thoughts, hoping Emiri does not notice how her cheeks flush suddenly. Her grip tightens around her newly recharged moon crystal and she concentrates on her assigned task.

A small orb shimmers to life in her hand, taking on the warm colors of a peach. The energy from the crystal feels as though it wavers beneath her mental hold, as if her connection is fragile. The fingers on her outstretched hands reflexively twitch around the ghostly image, causing it to evaporate entirely.

She releases an impatient breath, rolling her shoulders in slow circles.

"An impressive first try," Emiri says.

She braves a glance, recognizing he has drawn no closer to inspect her work, and frowns. She wants to ask him how he can see from so far away, but stifles the urge. "The moon's energy feels different," she complains instead. "Even when I use it for healing, it's not like this. It's like trying to hold on to water running through my fingers."

Emiri considers this, running his foot back and forth on the hard packed trail his path has created. "Perhaps you're trying to use it like sunlight by making something tangible. Creating illusions should be very much like lying, an attempt to trick or deceive the senses."

Myria scoffs. "I see. The nobles must be quite talented at casting illusions."

She refocuses, trying to apply his advice. Her mind weaves through the vast memories of all the peaches she's touched in her life, their fuzzy texture and sweet aroma. Spinning them together, the glimmering light takes form, fusing, and the new peach sits on her palm. She smiles, turning it in her hands before tossing it to Emiri for appraisal.

He regards it with wide eyes for a brief moment before his expression smooths over with indifference. "Not bad," he says, returning the fruit with another toss. "Perhaps you are more like your noble peers than you think."

Emiri attempts a half-smile, but the bitterness in his voice is unmistakable. She stumbles when she catches the peach, juggling it and the moon crystal until she regains her balance. When she straightens, her breath clouds the air before her in short puffs as a new heat surges to warm her face. She schools this new swell of emotion behind a thin mask. "What now?"

At first, she thinks her voice might be too low for him to hear over the blistering winds. Then, after a long moment of silence, he replies. "Hold the illusion as long as you can. Feel the drain of the energy so you can understand what it takes to create and maintain the illusion."

They test the illusion's extent, slicing open the peach and tasting it with a few bites. The sugary juices taste authentic as Myria tears into the soft flesh with her teeth. However, when she swallows the fruit, nothing substantial hits her belly.

"An effect of the illusion," Emiri explains at her confused look. "While it deceives your senses, it cannot truly provide sustenance."

The energy of sustaining the illusion ebbs away slowly, and she feels the slightest pull, like an ache, at the back of her head. Usually, her magic pains the space behind her right eye, so she supposes the new feeling is an effect of moon magic for illusions. A nod from Emiri permits her to end the illusion altogether. She takes a small respite, lowering herself to the ground as her head swims in the aftermath. Emiri regards her while he leans against a wall of stone coated in ice.

She cannot discern the stray thoughts that linger behind his sharp eyes, so she avoids his gaze, tracing the shape of the crystal in her hand as it buzzes with cooling energy. "Do you remember yesterday..." she trails off, thinking through the number of incidents that occurred the day before. Viewing Caliburn from a distance. Drowning. Proposing a new alliance with House Nocturnus.

Emiri issues a soft snort. "What about yesterday?"

"Duchess Cressida had these stones..." she pauses again, struggling, and watches him for any reaction. A ghost of the inexplicable hunger she felt yesterday gnaws at the edge of her mind. She is almost too afraid to revisit the thought, anxious she will lose herself again with that obsession.

"The Perennial Stones," Emiri answers, his voice tightening. "One of many relics stolen from Caliburn. She has four of them in her box, one for each season of the year. To a lesser mage, they can be used to mimic the weather patterns of their season, like what Cressida did yesterday."

Myria draws her knees closer to her chest, wrapping her arms around them as if to keep herself together. Her curiosity controls the words on her tongue, but her fear clenches her entire body, like a tightly coiled spring. "And what about stronger mages?"

Emiri's visage softens, although Myria does not miss how he keeps his eyes on the ground. "A limited imagination uses them to change the weather. The stones were created as a means to embody the very powers of nature. Imagine how powerful one could be by harnessing a drought or commanding a blizzard at a mere whim."

Myria focuses on her knees as she deliberates on revealing the truth to him. "Has anyone ever... felt a connection to a magical relic?"

This finally seems to stir him from his withdrawn demeanor. His weight shifts against the snow, as if he dared a step closer. "A connection?" he repeats.

She does not look up, only catching his movement from the corner of her eye. "Or perhaps a magical relic holds an effect over someone?"

The minute that drags in contemplative silence suggests the experience she describes is unusual or unnatural. She chews on her lip, still unable to meet Emiri's eyes. The sharpest memory she can recall from yesterday is floating in a frozen abyss. The moments building up to that icy plunge are hazy to her, almost watching herself through a glass window.

She does not break the stillness, unable to further describe the events to Emiri. She presses her left cheek to her knees, turning her face away from his ruminating eye.

Finally, he breaks the silence with cautious footsteps that crunch the snow before he crouches next to her. His voice is low and thick, a close, reverberating sound that settles the anxiety flipping her stomach. "What happened yesterday?"

When she blinks, she realizes her eyes burn with unshed tears. Shame for alienating him last night with those painful memories. Embarrassment for risking herself on the ice. She keeps her face turned away as she uses her sleeve to wipe at the tears surreptitiously. Her voice mirrors his in pitch, an attempt to sound calm. "Something happened to me when Cressida pulled out those stones. I... changed."

"Changed how?" he asks.

"I became consumed with the stones; I wanted to see them up close. And it was all I could think about and why I agreed to her race. I was like a different person, like someone was controlling my thoughts."

Myria lifts her face despite her stinging eyes as she recalls another memory.

"What is it?" Emiri asks, noticing her distraction.

She turns to him, heedless of the wet streaks that leak from the corners of her eyes. "There's something else. When I fell into the river, I passed out. Everything went dark and numb, and then I saw a vision."

More hesitation stalls her words as she bites her lower lip. Was it even real? Was it a hallucination induced from drowning? A dream?

Emiri's brows knit together, appearing invested in her experience. "Tell me," he coaxes.

"There was a woman I've never seen before. She had white hair, but she wasn't *old*, probably as old as my aunt. She mentioned my mother."

His head tilts. "Do you remember exactly what she said?"

Myria shakes her head. "Something about my mother not being safe. I didn't understand it. It felt... ominous."

More silence stretches on, and she can almost see the thoughts whirring behind Emiri's dark eyes. Crouched next to her, so close, she realizes it would take such a slight effort to reach out and stroke his cheek. The mere thought of doing just that—that gripping *urge*—stuns her, muddling her already confused thoughts. Myria averts her eyes to the ground, stuffing her hands in her armpits to restrain them.

When she finally braves a glance at him, they lock gazes. "I—I have never heard of this happening. I'm sorry I cannot answer more questions, but I will do what I can to find out more." His voice darkens with fierce determination, charging the air between them.

Myria cannot look away from him this time, transfixed by his piercing eyes. She is reminded of another, similarly spellbinding moment from only the previous day. How short-lived it had been when Emiri seemed to realize their magnetism. She does not want to move, afraid it will draw his attention to their proximity. She surprises herself by wanting to prolong it, a new haziness clouding her thoughts.

In a swift movement, Emiri stands and turns on his heel, retreating as he did before. It stings something in Myria's chest, and she tightens her arms around herself as to keep the discomfort at bay.

"For now, we should continue practicing your illusion magic with the remaining hour that we have." There is a new urgency in his voice that gives her pause as she pushes herself off the ground.

"Why the rush?"

He gives her an odd look, with the barest hint of an amused smirk. "Your cousin really doesn't keep you informed of your schedule."

She rolls her eyes, her irritation replacing any previous desire to touch his face. "Well, by all means, don't keep me in the dark."

"The court will leave Dawnmourne soon. Before that happens, the duchess has a morning activity planned for the nobles."

"What sort of morning activity?" Myria asks, her stomach acquiring a new sinking sensation.

Emiri shakes his head. "I wish I could say, but the duchess enjoys keeping the court in suspense. In any regards," he dismisses any further discussion of Cressida with an angry gesture, "back to work. I want you to practice something larger. Change our surroundings to make it appear we are somewhere else."

Myria's eyes grow wide in shock and a new kind of sickness twists in her gut. "Isn't that a sudden leap from a peach?"

"I only know that you'll need to learn illusion for an upcoming challenge for the Summer Courtship. I know nothing of the specific details planned. Therefore, we need to cover a variety of approaches."

"*Who* is planning those details, then?"

"House Valenrence."

Myria thinks back to the map Geffrey showed her. The court would visit the lands of Valenrence near the end of the Summer Courtship, just before the Eventide Ball. Perhaps if she continued befriending Sabine, the lady would reveal the challenge her house is planning.

"I want you to make this area look like it's spring," he calls to her over a high-pitched wind that whips through them, breaking her train of thought.

She frowns, unable to stop herself from pointing out, "Would that even change anything? It's summer now, and it looks like it's just in the middle of winter. Dawnmourne doesn't really have expressive seasons."

She does not miss his agitated eye roll. "Then *make* it look like a normal spring. That's the point of an illusion."

Her eyes trace the bleak surroundings of snow and icy rocks. Warmth from the sun hardly reaches them through the thick fog of cloud and snow blindness. The whistling winds and the roaring ocean waves drown out any potential for other noises. If she were to create an illusion of that scale, she would need to focus an enormous amount of energy. Her stomach clenches with uncertainty. "I could do that if I had a Perennial Stone," she muses aloud.

He folds his arms across his chest. "You don't have a Perennial Stone."

"But Cressida does."

"A Perennial Stone wouldn't create an illusion. A moon crystal creates illusions, and that's what you have. Make use of it."

She glances at it in her hand. "I don't think it has enough energy."

"It does."

"For this whole mountaintop?" she asks in disbelief, waving her arms around the expansive space.

"It doesn't have to be the whole mountaintop. Start small, with the grass or something."

"Well, for the illusion to work, you said it has to be believable, which means silencing the winds and making the sun shine."

Emiri studies her for a moment, his eyes narrowing. "Why are you avoiding this?"

For some reason, the observation bothers her more than anything else he's said, and an angry, defensive heat rises to her face. "I'm not avoiding anything."

But he seems already convinced and leans back on his leg, as if to puzzle this mystery out. "You've never backed down from a challenge before. In fact, you're usually fearless to a fault, pushing yourself past your limits. What are you afraid of now?"

She glares as her jaw sets with gritted teeth. "I am not afraid." Her hands clench into fists, her left one tightening around the moon crystal, which feels like it absorbs the heat of her anger. She takes a deep breath to calm herself. "It's not ridiculous of me to want to be cautious after yesterday when that—that explosion happened after using the crystal's energy."

Her explanation does not convince him, but Emiri retrieves a bag left by the door, tossing it to the ground in front of her. A few of the contents spill out onto the snow—more moon crystals. "If you're afraid of running out of energy, I brought more crystals. Use as much as you need."

Myria is shocked to discover this newfound solution does not assuage her nerves. She stares at the bag of crystals with her heart hammering and her knees locked into place.

"Well?" Emiri says, as if expecting to call her bluff.

"I..." but she has no words or explanations for him. She is afraid to admit she doesn't quite know what has her paralyzed.

"Be honest with yourself, Myria. You're afraid of something."

And because it is easier to be angry than afraid, she resumes her scowl from before. "I'm *not*." The crystal in her hand flares with heat again. This time, a small wave of flame ignites before her. It disappears almost immediately, but not before Myria recoils in astonishment, dropping her crystal to the snow with the others.

Emiri does not miss the phenomenon, and his head tilts.

"I didn't mean to do that," Myria says quickly.

But Emiri does not appear angry with her. "What do you think just happened?" he asks, gauging her reaction. Another teaching moment.

Her mind considers the possibilities, recalling how she used the moon energy. "A fire illusion? The moon crystal reacting to my emotions?"

Emiri neither confirms nor denies her theory as he runs a hand through his hair. "I remember a time, a conversation, some time ago. You don't like it when people see you in a state of vulnerability."

She knows exactly the conversation he is referring to—when he healed her injuries after the joust. Figuring it useless to challenge his words, she glares at the ground instead, hating how factual he sounds—like he knows so much about her.

"It is acceptable, and expected, to be vulnerable sometimes. What is not acceptable is not recognizing these moments for what they are. Tell me, why are you so afraid?"

She considers his question, unsure of the answer herself. She cannot imagine herself performing the illusion successfully. Still, it would not be the first time she was unsuccessful in their lessons. What would be different now?

Then, yesterday's events flood through her mind, and she realizes *precisely* why she is afraid. But admitting such fears to Emiri makes her even more afraid. Her lips clamp shut as she vigorously shakes her head in refusal.

Emiri's shoulders fall in disappointment. "I cannot teach you if you are not truthful with yourself, Myria." He turns away, and when he steps closer to the metal door leading back into Dawnmourne Keep, she realizes he intends to leave.

This strikes her worse than anything else he's said or done that morning. Panic seizes her chest, bubbling in her throat. "Wait! I'm sorry. I—I can't..."

But her faltering words do not stop him. She anxiously looks around for a solution to keep him there, and her eyes fall on his discarded bag of moon crystals. The solution bursts into her mind so clearly that she does not hesitate. With a new resolve, she picks up the fallen bag and squeezes her eyes closed.

With a sudden *snap*, her eyes fly open again.

Emiri freezes in his tracks, his foot hovering over a bed of soft, green grass. By the time he turns around to face her again, the entire peak is covered in the summery green blanket with not a single snowflake in sight. The sun shines brilliantly on them. Pink and blue wildflowers bloom to life in dense patches. The air is quiet, with no trace of blustering winds.

His expression is rendered utterly dumbfounded and filled with, Myria realizes with smugness, amazement. A thick sheen of sweat covers her brow as she holds the illusion in place.

"You..." But no words rise to his lips. The only explanation is the apparent truth.

"I can be honest with myself," she says, panting slightly. The panic, the fear, has disappeared, replaced by a new self-awareness. Her hand shakes as she grips the bag. "But that doesn't mean I have to share every secret with you."

He crosses the distance between them in three loping strides, threading the strap of the bag from her grasp. The illusion still holds, and his eyes dart to her heaving chest with concern. "Let go," he whispers.

She does. The snow, the ice, and the winds all return. Myria's legs crumple beneath her in exhaustion. Emiri catches her before she hits the ground. The last thing she sees before her eyes flutter close is a foreign expression she has never seen before on his face.

Fear.

When she blinks, there are two faces.

First, Emiri hovers above her.

Then it's a new face, not quite so familiar and shrouded in darkness. She struggles to focus on it.

Emiri is talking to someone. His voice is raised, but Myria cannot make out his words.

The other face replaces Emiri's. They whisper. As their lips move, their dark color reminds Myria of another vision. She strains against the exhaustion that keeps her limbs in place, trying to focus on this new face.

She feels herself moving in Emiri's arms, and when her head falls back against a pillow, it turns, allowing her a glimpse of her aunt and cousin. Their faces are twisted in alarm and anger. Myria frowns, wanting them to calm down, but she does not have the energy to speak. Her eyes flutter close, this time her mind drifting to oblivion.

Eventually, muffled voices pull her awake. Myria opens her eyes to a room cloaked in shadows, and she is unsure where she is or how she got there. She strains to find something familiar to determine where she is when the previous voices sharpen into focus.

"It seems unlikely," a man hisses, dripping with venom.

"It would be unwise not to investigate," a composed female replies.

Myria's eyes persist against the darkness, and two dim figures sharpen into view. The woman's white hair stands out in the dark—white hair like in Myria's first vision. She holds her breath, listening intently.

The man is obviously not pleased with the woman's judgment. He huffs, stalking around the room in angry paces. He does not, however, argue with her further.

This elicits a soft chuckle from her. "We must all play our part, whether we like it or not."

"I think we would be better served without wasting our time on fruitless endeavors."

The woman turns around to face the man, then her eyes seem to lock onto Myria's. Her mouth parts into a slow, deliberate, and sinister smile. "I think we are closer to our goals than we realize."

Myria's heart leaps into her throat as she scrambles away from the woman, throwing her arms in the air. Someone grabs onto them, wrestling them to her sides.

17

BARGAIN

"Myria, it's me!"

Myria stops struggling as she recognizes Geffrey in front of her. Olympe hovers nearby, the same concern twisting her features.

"I..." Myria struggles to gain her bearings, chest heaving until she realizes she's back in her room at Dawnmourne Keep. She swallows past a dry lump in her throat. "Where is Emiri?"

Geffrey exchanges a glance with Olympe, who nods at him in return. "He brought you here after your lesson. He said you overextended yourself with a spell."

Myria blinks as she recalls the illusion she cast and how quickly it had drained all her energy, despite not maintaining it for very long. And for what? To keep Emiri from walking away? But she knows the truth runs deeper than that. Her face flushes scarlet. "It was a mistake," she blurts out. "I was trying to show off."

"What were you thinking?" Olympe asks, voice rising. "Magic is dangerous."

Geffrey raises a skeptical eyebrow, as if to agree with his mother, and Myria wonders how much Emiri told them. She was not showing off; she just had an overwhelming desire to prove herself, and pushed her limits more than she should have. She wanted to prove herself worthy of Emiri's time and attention despite associating with the barbarians that destroyed his home.

"It's fine," she says, trying to brush off their concern and escape their scrutinizing gazes.

Olympe is not easily dissuaded. "Perhaps we should reconsider this arrangement with Emiri if he cannot keep you safe."

The suggestion ignites a surge of panic that tightens Myria's throat. She forces her words out with a dry tongue. "Emiri's not to blame. The fault is all mine. I was reckless. Surely, he told you that much. Where is he now?"

"It matters little now," Olympe says. "Emiri was required elsewhere. The duchess is preparing her final event for the court before we leave."

"And before that," Geffrey says, "we need to talk about this alliance with House Nocturnus."

Dinner with Cressida feels so long ago to Myria. Navigating politics, the bargaining, it's all *exhausting* and the mattress beckons her to sag deeper into its embrace. But—as Emiri pointed out last night—she needs to make a decision before it is made for her. Perhaps this is just her chance for that. "Duchess Cressida is very open to an alliance, and she seems willing to offer nearly anything to our house to make that happen."

"Yes, but what does she require in return?" Geffrey asks.

"Isn't it obvious? She wants me to drop out of the Summer Courtship. She wants a better chance of marrying the prince."

Geff's expression hardens, like a storm darkening his features. He growls out his decision. "Absolutely not."

Myria is taken aback. "You haven't even heard her terms."

Geffrey steps back, smoothing out his tunic. His shoulders assume a sharp line that contrasts everything she has known of her cousin. "It matters not. You will stay in the Summer Courtship."

Myria swings her legs over the mattress, stands, and steps toward him. She senses the small window of chance she has closing. "Why is that so important?" she demands. "She's willing to give you as much money as you want—"

"Nothing can compare to sacrificing our chance at a royal marriage," Geffrey says.

"Is that all you care about?" Myria asks, shocked. She reaches out a hand toward him.

He catches it roughly before she can touch him, and the grip is tight, painful. He turns, a new shadow flickering across his face. The lighthearted cousin she has known is replaced by a steadfast, commanding duke. "We will stay the course. You will continue courting the prince. We do not need the Nocturnus alliance."

She pries her hand from his grasp, and he strides out of the room, slamming the heavy wooden door behind him. In his absence, Myria turns her wide eyes on her aunt, who appears just as stunned. "Why does he act this way?"

Olympe frowns, smoothing out nonexistent creases in her skirt. "Being head of the house takes its toll. It did the same to his father. I am sure Geffrey has his reasons."

"Don't defend his atrocious behavior."

Olympe sighs in defeat. "I do not mean to say he acted appropriately, but he has a lot on his mind. Perhaps you will have better luck talking to him later." She holds up a new dress for Myria, made of crushed red and black velvet, lined with ermine fur at the collar and sleeves. "Another gift from the duchess."

Myria runs her fingers down the luxurious fabric. "What are we doing this morning?"

Olympe attempts a bright smile that misses its mark. "Ice skating."

Myria pales. "I don't know how to ice skate."

Olympe sets to work on securing Myria in the new dress and the many restricting layers that accompany it. "Perhaps the prince would be willing to teach you," she suggests.

Myria does not respond to the idea, her stomach giving an anxious flip. "Should we not accept an alliance with Cressida? Would that not be best for House Bramble?"

Myria feels her aunt's fingers hesitating on the laces. "The decision is not mine to make. My opinion is irrelevant."

"But I'm asking for your thoughts."

Olympe sighs. "I have been a part of the court my entire life. There was a time when I would have jumped for any chance of excitement or risk. Now, I am inclined to favor the safest bet. Objectively speaking, the likelihood of a marriage with Prince Leor is small. An alliance with House Nocturnus is more present, more *real*. It would be the more secure option to explore."

"You should talk some sense into him," Myria says.

Olympe barks a humorless laugh. "He stopped listening to me a long time ago. You have a better chance than I. Besides, as much as I crave safety, it is not in me to deny you a chance with Leor."

Myria does not respond. Her eyes lose focus as she stares out the frost-covered window at the bleak mountain landscape beyond.

Her aunt steps back from her work. "What troubles you? You seem quite melancholy this morning"

"I passed out during my magic lesson, then woke up to *this*," Myria says, waving a hand around the room in agitation and at the door Geoff just slammed in a thin attempt at humor. She picks up a piece of dried fruit from a nearby bowl, her stomach growling in gratitude.

Olympe tilts her head. "Do you not want to marry the prince?"

Myria starts, coughing on the dried fruit in surprise. After a brief choking fit, she takes a slow sip of wine to clear her throat while Olympe waits. Myria wrings her hands, casting about for an answer. "I knew I would be competing to marry the prince, but I never expected to come close to winning. I still don't, but I came here for other reasons."

"Your grandmother's inn and your magic lessons," Olympe says.

"I thought I got along well enough with Leor that I could be his friend." Myria chews on her lower lip, unsure of how to continue.

"And now?" Olympe presses.

"I'm a *barmaid*," Myria sighs desperately. "I have no business competing to be the queen of Avalion."

Olympe folds her arms, scowling. "How you were raised matters very little. Noble lineage relies on blood connections, which you have. The rest of what the other ladies have? You can learn it just as well. You belong here."

"The point is, I never expected to come this close, but Cressida sees me as a genuine threat. Emiri told me last night how much the prince cares about me."

"Is that so bad?"

"I..." But the words escape her. She tries something else. "At the joust, Lady Eulalia told me how arranged marriages work. Any noble lady would be grateful to marry someone like Leor, and not because he's the prince. He's kind, thoughtful, and generous. Is that the standard for noble marriages? To hope someone is *nice*? Is there really no such thing as love in court?"

Olympe's brows crinkle. "Is that your concern? Finding romantic love at court?"

Myria's eyes fall to the hearth instead of answering.

Olympe reaches out, but she stops herself and lets her hands fall to her sides. "Love is not a goal we dream of. Not because it is unattainable, but rather because we, the nobility, have other goals on our minds."

"Power and wealth."

Her aunt nods.

"These are not my goals. I care only about enough wealth to ensure the safety of my family."

"Leor sees these qualities in you; he probably knows they would make you the best queen for us."

Myria flinches, recalling how Emiri voiced a similar sentiment last night.

"And we are your family as well. Care about our safety, if you can. Geffrey appears calm, but the state of our coffers frightens him. It petrifies me."

When Myria looks up to meet Olympe's gaze, a hollow echo rings in her ears. Geffrey and Olympe are her family, like Grandma Iris. If she does not secure their financial future as well, she has all but damned them for her own selfish pursuits.

Olympe braves a step closer and grasps Myria's hand. "Yes, love is possible, even here at court. I never expected to fall in love with Caspian Bramble. Still, I was absolutely mad for him by the time of our wedding. I can see Leor has that same fire for you. I have no doubt of his affection, or his ability to make you happy."

Myria allows herself a moment to picture the future her aunt envisions. A royal couple wreathed in velvet and furs. Happy Myria, fulfilled Myria. Happily married. The Brambles restored to their former glory, and Grandma Iris no longer clawing a meager survival on the fringes of Everhaven. The room tilts and elongates, and Myria has to blink a few times to ground herself to the present. The images are incompatible.

Even if she did want to marry Leor, the chance is too slim to rely on. Myria knows House Nocturnus is the only sure option, even if Geffrey and Olympe didn't see that.

Her aunt retrieves a small parcel from the other side of the room. Myria, not comforted by her words, follows sullenly as Olympe reveals a pair of ice skates made from white leather and polished whalebone. "Another gift," she explains.

Myria nods, accepting it. The leather is stiff and new in her hands, sure to create blisters during a sport she is wholly unprepared for.

Olympe eyes her. "I would never advocate for you to do something against your wishes. Your mother took her life into her own hands, and I shall never know why. I suspect she felt smothered or unable to leader her own life, and I can only learn from my mistake since then. I do not wish the same thing to happen to you. Speak to Geffrey about your desires. He will come around."

Myria remains unconvinced of Geffrey's receptive nature, but as they make their way outside Dawnmourne Keep, she mentally prepares arguments to sway him. Cressida's dress proves warm and flattering against the icy breeze that ruffles the fur of her hood, protecting her nose from a red-stung chill. She follows Olympe down the trodden snow path, walking some distance away from the imposing castle to where the river empties into a vast lake. Other nobles have already gathered, most converging on the banks while others glide across the ice in graceful circles. Myria scans the crowd until Olympe nudges her toward a group of noblemen.

"Geffrey is there," she whispers. "Take him aside and try talking to him again. He would not dare blow up in front of the court."

"Or," Myria counters, "that will make him even angrier."

Regardless, she approaches her cousin with leaden footsteps. Geffrey makes a show of laughing at something Lord Sigurd says, and doesn't acknowledge Myria as she taps him on the shoulder. She attempts to capture his attention again by tugging on his elbow.

Lord Sigurd notices her first, smiling his bright smile which feels like looking into the sun. "Duke Bramble, I believe you have a guest."

Geffrey turns around in a slow, exaggerated motion, which makes Myria realize he was merely ignoring her. His smile is obviously forced. "Ah, dearest cousin. Received your new ice skates, did you?"

Myria, not to be deterred, arranges her expression into one of pure determination. "I need to speak with you."

The strength of her words garners the attention of a few nearby nobles—Lord Godric, Count Alanis, and even the king, standing a short distance away. Geffrey's face reddens, but he dares not refuse. He grabs her arm, again too tightly, and leads her several paces away until they are alone and out of earshot.

"You should be talking to the prince," he hisses. "Need I remind you we are trying to win a competition?"

"That is precisely the matter I wish to discuss with you," she says through clenched teeth. "You shouldn't refuse Cressida's alliance. It's the best thing you can do for your house."

"Our house's fate rests within *my* leadership. The decisions alone fall to me. If I agreed to this alliance with Cressida and she became queen, she would have the power to change our alliance's terms. We would be at her mercy. She could decide to let House Bramble fall into ruin with our debts, removing a potential rival altogether."

"I don't think she would do that," Myria says.

"And you're making that judgment based on a single dinner conversation? I've known her my entire life. I know how cutthroat she is, and I understand that Nocturnus *honor* is as worthless as—"

"A Bramble coin?" Myria asks.

Geffrey flinches at this. His face flushes with anger and his eyes grow wide. He opens his mouth to retort and his hand wavers as if to rise, but he stops short on both counts.

Myria does not draw back, instead taking a step closer and meeting his eyes as she continues. "Why are you acting this way? This deal is the safest path."

His face flushes a deeper red. "I disagree. Our best chance is Leor picking you as his bride."

"And what if he doesn't? What happens to our house then?"

For the first time since he stormed out of her room, Geffrey smiles, but it's an unsettling sight, curling with a threatening expression. "Rumors are swirling around the court. We are closer to victory than you think."

This third affirmation of Leor's preference makes Myria's stomach sink. She switches tactics. "When you asked me to accompany you to court, I told you I was unsure about marrying I wanted to marry the prince."

The smile vanishes. "Are you telling me you are still uncertain?"

Myria looks away. It is not the first time someone has asked her directly about her feelings for Leor, but the thought of admitting them... Images flood her mind. Everyone she cares about destitute: Geffrey, Olympe, and Grandma Iris. She feels so much guilt. She cannot meet his gaze. Instead, her eyes find the figures skating on ice. Lady Eulalia twirls gracefully with Lady Brigid in hand. Duchess Cressida stands near the bank with Prince Leor.

And then, Geffrey's voice lowers to a pitch she's never heard from him. He murmurs into her ear, a dangerous sound that makes the hairs on her neck rise. "You might remember the bargain *we* struck before you make new deals with Cressida. If you do not want to marry the prince, then I can help you no longer. You are an investment, Myria. I have devoted what little money our coffers have into funding your grandmother's inn and paying Emiri to teach you magic."

Myria's face smooths over and her mouth presses into a thin line. She keeps her eyes focused on the frozen lake, but a tightness pricks her throat. She tries reinforcing her voice with steel. "I'm aware."

"If I took Cressida's deal, then I can no longer continue to fund either of those endeavors."

Geffrey says nothing else; he has no need to. Despite the heaviness that bears down on her chest, Myria maintains her composure. "I will inform the duchess that we must decline her offer."

He nods, and they return to the rest of the court without a word. The sounds of conversation and laughter reach Myria's ears, but it imbues her with no sense of joy. As Geffrey splits off to return to his group of noblemen, her mind whirs through her limited options. Myria marches to edge of the lake, where Cressida notices her approach. The duchess offers a bow to Leor before excusing herself, grim lines and wariness etching her face at the sight of Myria's stony expression.

"Good morning, Lady Hawthorne," she says, remaining on the ice with her skates. "I trust your evening went well."

Myria steps beyond the safety of snow-capped land, the new skates still hanging from her shoulder. She does not entertain pointless niceties, getting straight to her message. "I explained the terms of your proposal to my cousin."

Cressida smiles wryly. "He refused, did he not?"

"Yes."

The duchess nods slowly. "I suspected as much. How unfortunate. I actually looked forward to our new friendship. Very well." She makes a move to skate back to the prince.

"Wait, please!"

Cressida turns to her, an expectant eyebrow raised.

"While I do not have Geffrey's approval, I would still like to assist your goal." This takes her by surprise. "You want to help me... marry the prince?"

Myria nods.

"You are suggesting that you sabotage your own chances to become queen despite your cousin's wishes." Cressida is incredulous, as if she cannot believe Myria would stoop to such deceit.

"I do not want to be queen," Myria insists.

"Why?"

Myria takes a deep breath. "I want to decide my future for myself, not let others make it for me."

Cressida's sharp eyes travel up and down Myria's frame. "I will consider this, Lady Myria. However, I question how you can help me without the approval of Duke Bramble."

"I will find a way," Myria promises with fierce determination burning in her eyes.

As if to offer her an opportunity, Prince Leor skates up to Cressida, a disarming smile already equipped for Myria. "My lady," he says, "it is lovely to see you this beautiful morning."

Not missing Cressida's eyeroll, Myria dips into a quick curtsy. "The honor is mine, Your Majesty."

Leor nods to the pair of skates hanging from her shoulder. "I see you have the appropriate attire. You should join us on the ice."

Myria hesitates, a finger tracing the curve of the skates' smooth, pale leather. "Yes, these were a gift from the generous duchess here. She was very thoughtful in offering them to me. However, I'm afraid I must return them. I have never ice skated and would only make myself look a fool out there."

Cressida lifts her chin in intrigue before she beckons a nearby servant. "How unfortunate, Lady Myria. Perhaps I will invest in a different gift, one more accommodating to your interests."

Leor looks between them. "I would be happy to teach you myself, Lady Myria."

Myria's eyes widen in alarm. "I couldn't impose. You would spend too much time with me when you should be seeing to the rest of your court. I would only injure both of us with my clumsiness—"

A slight movement from Cressida catches Myria's attention, an almost imperceptible shake of her head. The meaningful expression that accompanies offers a subtle message: *you cannot refuse the prince.*

"You would never," the prince promises in a low, thick voice, much too fervent for their rather public setting.

So, plastering on her diplomatic smile, Myria finally agrees. She laces the leather skates with stiff fingers. Cressida even kneels to help, securing them with deft movements. Before Myria rises, Cressida issues in a quiet voice, "This is precisely why an arrangement will not work without the duke's consent. You cannot refuse what the prince wants, and it just so happens that what he wants is you."

Myria says nothing as Cressida steps back. Prince Leor offers a helping hand, which Myria demurely accepts before he leads her out onto the ice. The minutes pass by as she desperately tries to maintain her balance. Leor's fingers are warm and steady at her hips, on her shoulders, and sliding down her arms. The other ladies of the court do not miss their closeness as they watch with rapt, jealous interest. Even Eulalia, to Myria's dismay, has tight eyes.

She is suddenly reminded of her vision—standing by Leor's side as his chosen queen, wreathed in luxurious furs. A chill unrelated to the climate works down her spine. The image is only disrupted when Leor turns them again and her eyes instantly connect with Emiri's amid the crowd onshore. Her practiced courtier's smile slips, replaced by a grimace that she hides behind a curtain of hair.

18

BLOOD

THE COURT TAKES ITS leave of Dawnmourne Keep the following day. Servants rush in and out of the castle, hauling luggage to carriages. nobles issue sharp commands to their staff, hurrying things along so the court might be out of the mountains before nightfall. They take a different route than before, heading for the western coast.

Myria once again chooses to ride, and is overjoyed as a Nocturnus groom leads Jadis to her. She pats the mare on the neck, and Jadis responds with a nuzzle of her shoulder and an appreciative snort. Myria laughs, then says, "I'm pleased to see you as well, my friend." She mounts the horse with no further delay, and is soon following alongside the train of carriages and wagons.

They arrive just after dark at Solis Abbey, a sizable convent at the base of the mountains. In the evening, as the procession settles into their temporary lodgings, Myria roams the abbey's grounds in peace. With most of the court occupied in the central dormitories, she wanders through the vineyard and the orchard in the lingering twilight. In this tranquil silence, she attempts to settle her racing mind by coming to terms with her impending future and the likely chance Leor will choose her as his wife. The familiar, uncomfortable squirm of her stomach accompanies the thoughts, and when she retires for the evening, her mind is far from soothed.

With limited space, the royal family takes priority in the assignment of rooms, followed by a few noble families. Most of the court must sleep in tents hastily erected by their servants in the abbey's great courtyard, inside its protective walls, while the servants themselves make do with sharing space with the horses in the cramped stables. Myria is one of the lucky few offered a room, but when she discovers it means her aunt will not have a bed, she gives it up for Olympe and sleeps in the House Bramble tent instead. Geffrey, being a duke, was given priority in choice of rooms, saving Myria from a night of uncomfortable silence after their recent confrontation and giving her the tent to herself.

Sleep greets her with restlessness, and is interrupted far too soon by a voice calling her name in a half-whisper at the tent's flap.

Having slept in her only pair of worn leather pants and a linen tunic, she quickly ties the tangled mess of her hair up before pulling back the flap.

The visitor is none other than Emiri, standing outside in the pitch black of night. Myria blinks blearily at him as she tries to make sense of his presence. "It's not even close to dawn," she says after a few silent moments.

He chuckles, but the sound is tense. "Imagine your aunt's surprise when I woke her up looking for you. What are you doing here? Prince Leor arranged for you to have a room."

"And let my aunt sleep out here?" she says, her voice thick with sleep as she rubs her eyes. "The more appropriate question is, what are *you* doing here?"

"Did you think you could miss a lesson just because the court is on the road?"

"It's not dawn."

He shrugs with a sly smile, glancing off into the distance. "I couldn't sleep, so today we're doing something different."

"Tonight, you mean." She has no qualms about being difficult when he's interrupted her evening.

Emiri turns his face up to the sky, as if to read the position of the moon and the invisible sun through the dark blanket of night. "I'd wager it's the early hours of morning." His words attempt a levity that does not quite match his tone, which is sill tense, pinched like a coiled spring.

Something about his manner bristles Myria, and her frustration with Geff and the Summer Courtship bubbles to the surface, dragging with it the memories of their last lesson. "If I go with you, can I expect an impossible task that would drain me of energy again?" Though she does not intend it, the sharpness of her accusation is satisfying.

His cringe is even more so, but his voice adopts that soft, somber murmur. "I... apologize for how our last lesson transpired. You're right; it was irresponsible of me to ask so much of you when you've had very little practice with that branch of magic."

The bristles soften, and she folds her arms. "Go on."

He sighs. "I did not consider your needs. My mood was sour from... the previous night."

Her arms drop at the reminder.

Emiri continues. "And I admittedly took that frustration out on you, which I should not have. Our lesson this morning—"

"*Tonight,*" Myria reminds him.

He chuckles. "Tonight, it will be an easy one. No chance for unforseen consequences."

He holds out a hand as if to help her out of the tent, or perhaps it is a peace offering. A request for forgiveness. She only waits to keep him in suspense; she has long since forgiven him. "As far as apologies go, that was rather decent."

Myria follows him through the slumbering campsite, and they enter the ancient dormitories carved from the mountain base. The architecture reminds her of Dawnmourne Keep, making use of the natural stone as a base for their structures. Inside, she tilts her head curiously since their lessons usually take place outside. Instead of asking why this night is different, she waits to see where he takes her. The corridor steadily slopes downward until they reach the balneary, the abbey's indoor bathhouse. A circular pool of water sits in the middle of the room, steam curling from its surface. The air is thick with the humidity, the temperature warm and rising. Olympe mentioned during the journey that natural, underground hot springs supplied the abbey with constantly heated water. Emiri skirts the edge of the pool, his footsteps carefully treading the slick, wet stone, and Myria follows suit.

In the back, there is a small crevice in the wall, large enough for a person to squeeze through. Emiri grabs a nearby torch and ducks inside. Myria hesitates, peering into the darkness, before doing the same. Their path takes them deeper into the mountain, the air growing thick as the trail continues to slope downward. Myria wonders why Emiri uses the torch to illuminate the way instead of summoning an orb of light. Or better yet, why he doesn't ask her to summon—

She quickly pats down her pockets. "I don't have my moon crystal." Her voice echoes off the rock walls.

"You won't need it," he says over his shoulder without slowing his pace.

After a few more minutes of walking, the narrow passage empties into a more expansive room of smooth stone. It is difficult to discern its precise size in the darkness, even with the flickering light of Emiri's torch. He leaves it on a sconce beside the entrance and braves a few steps into the blackness.

Myria watches him with trepidation as he sweeps his arms about and spins in a slow circle. "Where are we?" she asks. "What are we doing down here?" She peers up, trying to glimpse the ceiling. Her eyes fail her, but her voice echoing around the chamber gives her the impression it must be cavernous. She cannot imagine the original intent of whatever space they're in.

"Try casting a spell," he says, his deep voice reverberating.

She expects him to offer an energy crystal. When he does not, she asks, "How?"

"How did you cast a spell when you fell into the frozen river?"

She considers the question. "I reached for the sunlight above me, like when you had me meditate in our first lesson."

She barely makes out his nod in the dim light. "Find an energy source here."

Myria steadies herself with a deep breath before closing her eyes and reaching out with her mind to find one. The cavern is deep underground with no access to the sky, and therefore, no moonlight. Emiri carries no crystals on him, and there is not even a single plant she can use instead. She and Emiri are the only living creatures there. "I can't find anything," she complains. "It's as if you chose a training spot intentionally isolated from any source of energy."

His light chuckle resounds around them. "You're not far from the truth."

She sighs, trying not to become impatient with her lack of sleep. "I don't understand."

Emiri's tone grows serious, his chuckle and any other sense of mirth suddenly cast aside. "I don't know what your connection to the Perennial Stones means. While my father had visions, I don't understand the nature of yours. I want to help you, but this is the only way I know how. Perhaps you can find a way to interpret the visions. Perhaps they are a warning of things to come or a reminder of the past. The best thing I can do is teach you specific forms of magic to protect yourself. Do you remember the different energies I told you about? What fills the crystals we use?"

"Sun and moon energy."

"And the third type?" he presses.

This gives her a moment's pause as she struggles to remember. "Energy from eclipses. Destructive magic."

"Correct. This is called celestial magic, where energy is harvested from the heavens."

"And what about the plants I would use at my grandmother's tavern?"

"Natural, or terrestrial magic. Energy that comes from the earth and living things. The people of Caliburn pride ourselves on our connection to nature; it is how we discovered magical energies in the first place, many centuries ago. To do that, we had to develop our understanding of how the energy which fuels life moves through the cosmos."

"How does that relate to us being underground? There's no energy here."

"Search again," Emiri says with a measured, patient tone. "You must find it yourself."

She closes her eyes a second time, stretching her mind to its limits. She feels the deep rumble of the earth, subtle vibrations in the stone, but nothing to use as a magic source. Once more, the only signs of life are Emiri and herself. She nearly gives up again when she makes a startling realization. Focusing on Emiri's form,

Myria notices how waves of heat seem to emanate from beneath his skin. Curious, she reaches out with her mind to touch his cheek.

This elicits a soft, surprised gasp from him. Immediately, Myria's eyes fly open to see Emiri touching the same spot on his face. "I'm sorry!" she says quickly. "I didn't know anything would happen."

His parted lips offer a gentle smile. "It appears you've found your energy source."

"People?"

He nods, his face turning grim under the shadows. "It is called blood magic. All magic comes with a price. Most of the time, we can control that price. But there are other times when we are left with no other option. Blood magic is not a common practice since it uses your own life energy. I recommend using it *only* in an emergency."

"Why are you showing this to me, then?" she asks. "Didn't our last lessons demonstrate that I don't know my own limits?"

Emiri considers her for a moment before answering. "You were very resourceful in creating a lifeline when you fell in the river, even if it benefited Cressida. I hope you never have to use this method ever again, but if ever you are in danger, you should be aware of all your options."

He draws something from his pocket and the reflective sheen of his copper knife glints in the torchlight.

"How many times have you used blood magic?" she asks.

"Outside of training? Only once."

"What happened?"

His voice tightens. "It didn't go well."

Before she can ask anything else, he steps closer, the knife taking a clearer shape in his hand.

"Watch carefully," he instructs. "I'm going to show what you should do if you ever need to cast blood magic." Emiri slices a thin red line into his palm with the knife, then clenches his hand into a fist. Thick droplets of blood run through his fingers.

"It is unnecessary to draw blood when casting blood magic. However, by doing so, you have easier access to your source. The energy is easier to tap into with blood flowing."

He opens his hand, the revealing the scarlet fluid coating his palm and fingers with a metallic luster. Then, he makes deft drumming movements with his fingers, materializing a small red orb hovering above his palm. It casts a ruddy glow between them. Myria steps closer as the blood on his hand dries to a dark brown. The orb floats for a few moments before it blinks out of existence, leaving them in the long shadows of the distant torch.

Emiri wipes the blade with his sleeve before holding the handle out for her. "Your turn."

She takes the knife from him, holding the tip against the crease of her palm. Her hands freeze in that position as she takes slow, deep breaths.

Of all the things, *this* makes her lose her nerve?

Myria is glad for the darkness that hides the embarrassment on her cheeks. She sheepishly looks up to Emiri. "I don't think I can—"

Without a word, he circles around behind her. He places a hand over each of hers. His grip over her own on the knife is secure, and his fingers cradle her open palm. His touch is scorching, like fire on her skin. His cheek is only a hair's breadth from hers. His breath is hot on her neck, and she is overwhelmed with a sharp scent of earth and juniper that makes her thoughts swirl uncontrollably. His chest radiates the same stifling heat through the thin shirt on her back, beckoning her to lean against him. It is all she can do to suppress the intuitive shiver that courses through her entire body, leaving her weak and breathless in its wake.

If Emiri notices her visceral reaction to his closeness, he does not show it. He holds her hands together, the edge of the knife barely scraping her palm. "Ready?"

She does not trust herself with words, so all Myria manages is an awkward nod. Her entire body tenses in preparation, but she does not know what she anticipates more—the pain of the knife or the fire of Emiri's skin against hers.

It's over in a single, fluid motion. She feels no more than a sting that draws out a thin stream of blood. Emiri steps back but does not let go of her bleeding hand as he moves to stand in front of her. He holds out his wounded hand, palm up, next to hers.

"Use your energy to heal my wound," he says.

Myria blinks a few times as she clears her mind of her muddled thoughts. "Why healing? Why not summon a light, like you?" she whispers, more to create a few extra seconds to compose herself.

"You were using magic to heal long before I taught you anything. It's what you are most familiar with."

She nods before concentrating on Emiri's cut, healing it as she did in her first lesson. The magic feels different this time, as does the energy that is drained from her. It is not some distant buzzing or dull ache behind her eye. This magic is almost painful, like pulling a deep splinter from her skin. The slight effort leaves her exhausted and sore.

A new light erupts from Emiri's palm, but this time, it comes from her, brilliant and white. It shapes itself into long tendrils that weave around Emiri's hand in undulating motions. When the spell ends and the light fades, no trace of the wound lingers on his skin, not even a remnant of dried blood.

They release each other and take a step back, Emiri inspecting her handiwork and Myria catching her breath.

"I didn't try to make the lights happen," she explains in a shaky voice. "I don't know what that was."

Emiri looks up, his bottom lip quivering slightly before he forces a smile. When he speaks, he sounds hoarse. "The light from your magic. My father used to tell me that blood magic shows your natural aura."

"So that means my aura is white? And yours is red?"

"Sometimes it changes color, but yes, mine is red."

"Do the colors mean anything?"

Emiri tilts his head at her, looking suddenly uncomfortable. "Do the colors of our hair mean anything?"

She looks away, unconvinced with the shifty explanation. "I suppose not."

"Give me your hand."

Myria glances at the open wound on her palm before realizing why he's asking for it. "You want to heal it?"

"It's the least I can do after slicing you open," he says as his familiar, lighthearted grin returns.

She holds her hand protectively to her chest. "It's fine. You don't need to heal it. I understand why you had me do this; I understand the sacrifice it requires. Casting blood magic is an awful feeling I wouldn't want you to experience again. I can deal with a small cut."

Standing her ground, Myria's mouth forms a resolute line as she returns Emiri's piercing gaze. She nearly loses herself in those dark, unwavering eyes, as if the ground falls out beneath her. Breathless, she does nothing as he reaches out and grasps her hand, pulling it away from her chest and holding it between them. His firm grip around her wrist makes fire dance beneath her skin again, inflaming her from her hand to her neck in a consuming, sweltering heat.

"This is precisely why you would be the best queen for Avalion. You put others before yourself. You would serve the *people*." He holds his free palm over hers as he speaks, and the red light reappears between their hands. Myria does not look at its shifting form, her eyes instead remaining on his patient face, illuminated by the ruby light. The stinging in her hand vanishes completely, enveloped by the same cooling, embracing sensation she felt when he healed her at the joust.

But the reminder of competing to be Leor's future queen shatters the magnetism between them. When the healing spell ends, Myria draws her hand back, cradling it to her chest once more. "Thank you, Emiri. I wish I shared your high opinion of me."

He nods. "I look forward to when you prove yourself wrong." He remains still, even seeming to lean closer, as if savoring the closeness between them. "As promised, this was a short lesson."

Myria takes a hesitant step back, drawn against her own desires by the bonds of duty. The space is necessary. Without the intoxication of his earth and juniper scent, she can think clearly and remind herself of her current position. Emiri, perhaps realizing the boundaries they have strained, avoids her eyes and scratches the nape of his neck.

She is competing for *Leor's* hand, and unless she can convince Geffrey otherwise, it seems nothing will change about that. She looks back up to Emiri. He must feel her attention because he halts his fidgeting and meets it. A long moment of tense silence passes between them.

"We should return to camp," she finally says. She turns back to the torch, grabs it, and leads the way back up the passage.

They make their way outside, and Emiri escorts her back to the Bramble tent just as the first rays of the sun peek over the horizon. Myria squints against the brightness, then looks back over her shoulder, but Emiri is gone. His sudden departure creates such a painful, hollow pang in her chest that Myria decides to take advantage of the early hour.

She gathers some clothing and heads back to the balneary Emiri led her past. The bathing room is vacant, as before, something she is grateful for as she steps out of her clothes and slips into the water. She gasps at the water's temperature at first, then sighs as the scorching water of the hot spring embraces her. She submerges herself to scour the grime from her body and the anxiety from her mind—along with the fear and the anger at being trapped in this political game she has no desire to continue. But she is most thankful just how well the warm water hides her tears.

19

SEASICK

THE ROYAL PROGRESS WASTES no time in reaching Goldeport, the glittering port city of House Rosenford. Myria peers through the carriage window at tall wood and stone buildings flanking either side of the street before they reach the harbor. Endless faces meet hers between doors and alleys. Street vendors, market stalls, food peddlers, and running children fill the vibrant city, bringing a smile to Myria's face.

The ships waiting at the harbor are another sight to behold. Living in Everhaven, she has never seen a boat or any other water transport. The royal galleon anchored at a distance is a magnificent display of power, wealth, and influence. Even from afar, the red and golden lion flag billows proudly at its mast. It is so massive, Myria learns, that it cannot dock at the harbor, and everyone has to be ferried over on rowboats. The royal family and House Rosenford naturally take precedence, while lesser families and nonessential luggage are loaded on other boats that will accompany the royal ship to Westhaven. Myria bids goodbye to Jadis for the time being.

Duke Aelric, Sigurd and Brigid's father, waits for the court at the harbor. He greets King Uriel with a low, humble bow. Lord Sigurd all but skips up to his father, his animated movements making Myria think he is restless to be on the water.

"Rosenfords spend most of their time at sea after all," Brigid explains in a low murmur.

Myria nods in kind, as if this is the most natural piece of information she's ever heard.

"Your Majesties," booms Duke Aelric in a deep voice, gesturing to the royal ship behind him. "I am proud to present your new vessel, and I thank you for trusting House Rosenford with its construction."

"Does she have a name yet?" King Uriel asks, appraising it with admiration.

Duke Aelric inclines his head toward the queen. "I was thinking *Eloria,* for her grace?"

Queen Eloria gives Aelric a thin smile, waving his platitudes away as if they are smoke. "Please, I have had countless ships named after me. Perhaps Leor can find a suitable name? After all, he is the focus of the summer."

Duke Rosenford responds in such a manner that suggests this is the best idea he's ever heard. Myria hides a snort behind her hand.

While they wait for the rowboat, Brigid pulls Myria by the arm, nearly bouncing with excitement as she drags her toward Aelric. "Father, this is Lady Myria."

Myria curtsies as she feels the duke's eyes assess her. "A pleasure, my lord."

There is a shine of recognition in the duke's eyes. "Yes, Lady Myria of House Bramble, correct?"

Myria nods.

"I have heard much of your exploits this summer, most notably a riveting joust and aiding my injured son. I also heard you are the lady to watch out for at court. I regret not making your acquaintance sooner."

"Both Lady Brigid and Lord Sigurd have been pleasant companions this summer. I am eager to see more of their home."

Duke Aelric flashes a smile at the compliment, one that is just as blinding as any grin she's seen from Sigurd. "You flatter me, Lady Myria." He turns back to the royal family. "I received the guest list count for lodging and meals, but is there anyone else we can expect? Rumors are going around about the spymaster—"

King Uriel shakes his head. "I received some correspondence, but the spymaster will meet us when we disembark at Westhaven."

As the conversation continues without her input, Myria turns to Brigid. "Who is the spymaster?"

"An agent of stealth and secrets who works in the employ of the king. The spymaster helped save the king from an assassination attempt a few years ago. No one knows who they are except the king himself."

The first rowboat sets off with King Uriel, Queen Eloria, Duke Aelric, Lord Sigurd, and two members of the royal guard. Prince Leor steps down into the second rowboat with Captain Rozenna. Lady Brigid follows, pulling Myria along.

Myria is surprised at the inclusion. "This is *your* time with the prince," she points out with mild panic. "I couldn't impose on that."

Brigid offers a meek smile. "I told my father you were my guest. I never know what to say around Prince Leor; I get so flustered. A friend to help with my nerves would be most welcome."

With no other recourse, Myria allows Lady Rosenford to drag her toward the rowboat, waiting her turn as Brigid gingerly steps down, skirts in hand. Myria considers the distance a few stiff, rueful moments before moving, hoping to avoid catching Leor's eye.

A familiar voice behind hurries her along with light amusement. "Please board at your leisure, Lady Hawthorne."

Myria does not need to turn around to identify its owner, but she frowns at the title. "I've threatened you not to call me that," she growls over her shoulder. Still, she carefully steps down into the rowboat without meeting his gaze.

"Sir Emiri!" Brigid says, shielding her eyes from the bright sunlight as she looks up to him. "Are we to have the pleasure of your company?"

As Myria pointedly refuses eye contact with him, she can almost hear the wry smile in his tone when he says, "Only as a special security detail." The boat rocks slightly as he steps down, taking a seat beside Leor and in front of Myria.

"I am not sure what would require special security on our way to the ship, but I am grateful for the added protection," Lady Brigid muses. Myria notices that while her father's and brother's brightness manifest in their smiles, her brilliance embellishes her words. She might be shy around Leor, but with no stakes in Emiri, Lady Brigid seems perfectly at ease.

Knees pressed close together to take up as little space as possible, Myria struggles to hide a smile. "I assure you, Lady Rosenford, Sir Emiri is here for the prince's protection, not ours."

Brigid giggles while Captain Rozenna, surprisingly, gives a hearty laugh.

After an amused smile, Prince Leor turns to Brigid, inquiring about her singing. She offers a few polite responses, to which Leor requests a song. Brigid declines, insisting she has not performed the necessary vocal warm-ups. Whenever the conversation lulls, Myria attempts to steer it back to Brigid—her talents, her interests, her history with singing. By the time Brigid can contribute to the conversation unaided, the rowboat pulls up next to the royal ship. Captain Rozenna and a Rosenford sailor work to get their small vessel attached to the pulley system that lifts the boat from the water. Emiri uses magic to help support their weight by controlling the water beneath, which Myria watches with acute interest.

Once on deck, Myria cranes her neck at the complex rigging and sails. Brigid delves into a detailed description of the planning behind the vessel's creation and the years of work that went into its design and construction. The wood shines beneath Myria's feet, and the pungent smells of oil and tar fill her nostrils.

Brigid offers a tour for them while their cabins are being prepared and the other nobles arrive. Myria follows her to the prow and then to the rear quarterdeck with the captain's wheel. As Brigid discusses its detailed history of shipwright commissions and purchasing agreements, Myria wanders to the stern and leans over the railing at the rippling blue waters. Then, she turns to gaze out over the horizon, and the immense expanse of water gives her such a feeling of serenity she feels she can forget everything else for just a moment.

"I find the sea comforting, like being at home."

Myria spins around to find Brigid and the others have disappeared with Sigurd materialized next to her. She offers him a small smile. "This is the first time I have seen it."

Sigurd approaches the railing next to her. "I apologize that the company of the court has marred the experience."

She laughs. "If only we were not counted among them."

He blushes, as if realizing his place. "I do not mean to be so discourteous of our stations, but I have always felt more at ease exploring the world than cooped up in castles."

"I feel very much the same way. Do you have any outlandish tales from one of your adventures?"

"Of course, my lady," he says, his expression becoming animated. "You might have heard of my mermaid tale?"

She cannot help but laugh, relishing how it feels to do so in his presence. He does not present the same pressure or expectations as other nobles. "I am positive I have not."

He shrugs it off, as if suddenly bashful. "Probably for the best. Everyone thinks me ridiculous."

"Do not leave me in suspense, Lord Rosenford. I must know more."

"I am not sure if Brambles have any sort of rites of passage, but Rosenford lads often captain a crew on their first sea voyage. Much... indulgence is involved."

"Indulgence?"

"Imbibing of drink," he explains.

"Ah. You were drunk."

"Not the entire time, I swear. By dawn, I was quite sober, so much so that I discovered a mermaid floating at a distance, just as the sun kissed the horizon. I swore I was in love at first sight. Then she waved, winked, and disappeared. Never saw her again."

"Truly a tragic love story. Only a moment, then gone forever?" Myria laughs again but does not mention how Sigurd has already demonstrated a history of easily falling in love.

He shrugs. "Aye, but my broken heart has healed by now. Most people believe me a liar or mad. But I know what I saw. Mermaids are real."

Myria finds something endearing about the way his voice thickens with his conviction. "Have you seen any other mythical creatures?"

He shakes his head.

"Have you ever heard of a minotaur?"

He has, and the revelation of the beast hiding in Talking Tree Forest fascinates Sigurd to no end. She offers to introduce him when the court reaches Fairthorne just as movement on the lower deck catches her attention. More nobles arrive, among them her cousin and aunt.

"Is everything okay, Lady Myria?" Sigurd asks. "You appear rather distracted."

Still reeling from Geffrey's temper, Myria turns a gracious smile to the Rosenford lord. "Will you show me to my cabin? I find myself suddenly weary from our journey."

Sigurd nods and offers his arm, wasting no time as he leads her below deck, circumventing the crowd of nobles. Myria sees Brigid, distracted by the arrivals and flanked by Leor and Emiri. Both instantly spot her, their eyes darting to Sigurd's arm. Leor frowns and seems to struggle to hide it. Emiri looks away, his head snapping with a sudden shift of his hair. Myria tries her best to hide behind Sigurd.

Her cabin is somewhere below the captain's quarters, facing the boat's stern with a single arched window that allows her to look at the silvery sea. The bed sits inside the left wall, surrounded by thick, red curtains.

"I apologize it is not the most glamorous room. You do not have a balcony like the royal family," Sigurd says as she crosses the room to the window.

"I find it absolutely perfect," Myria says with a smile. "And my aunt and cousin?"

"Their quarters are just next to yours. If you need anything—" Sigurd reveals a small, tasseled cord by the bed. "This will summon a servant."

Once she's alone, Myria opens the window and sits on the bed, obviously new and untouched with a soft feather mattress and fresh linen sheets. The alcove it sits in is small and dark, but she can stretch out her arms and legs comfortably. After some time passes, a knock at her cabin door alerts her to the arrival of her trunk.

When the attendant leaves, she locks the door behind him and returns to the window, resting her chin on her arms as the sunlight warms her skin. A bell chimes in the distance, ringing through the air, and Myria feels the ship take a slow, cumbersome lurch. Shouts from the main deck reach her window as sailors bark commands to each other. Soon, the boat is moving, and Myria can feel the rocking waves rolling in her stomach.

A voice drifts to her ears from above. "You really should make an attempt to be more hospitable. Come to dinner with us."

Myria holds her breath, realizing the admonishing tone belongs to none other than the queen.

"You know how seasick I get," the king huffs. "Besides, as you have already so eloquently pointed out, this season is all for Leor. He is the one who needs to remain in the public eye. My presence is hardly required this evening."

Something deep in Myria's gut insists she should not eavesdrop, but she cannot deny her curiosity. She remains at the window and holds her breath to listen.

"After all the work the Rosenfords went through to give us this incredible flagship?" Queen Eloria says, her voice like a sharp prickling of needles. Her annoyance makes more sense when Myria recalls the queen is originally from House Rosenford. "Surely you can respect our hosts better than that. Your absence would insult them."

There is a heavy sigh, but King Uriel puts up no further argument. "It would serve him right," he grumbles. "How did he know about the spymaster? And have the gall to inquire about them in public?"

"I suspect these rumors are your spymaster's doing. It seems as if they enjoy the stir they cause in court."

"Of course, because any time the spymaster is summoned to court, it is usually followed by a hearing, maybe an execution."

Myria's stomach clenches at this news.

Queen Eloria expresses a similar concern, her voice lowering so much that Myria must strain to hear. "Why has the spymaster been summoned? Is something wrong?"

King Uriel is quick to dismiss any concerns. "Nothing of the sort. The spymaster is investigating a matter of their own accord. They have not yet revealed anything to me."

The king and queen fall silent as another pair of footsteps enter their room. The third voice is muffled, so Myria backs away from the window, returning to her bunk.

As she waits for Olympe and Geff to discover her hiding place, Myria stays in her cabin. Although a large vessel, the ship remains a cramped space that allows little room for exploration. She doesn't want to risk running into Geffrey or Leor, so she avoids emerging with the others. Around dusk, she hears Olympe outside her door.

"Myria, open up. It is time for dinner."

She does not move from her bed, feeling comforted by the gentle sway of the ship. She thinks back to the king's words from earlier. "I don't think I should attend. I've fallen ill. Seasick." She waits with bated breath for her aunt's response.

"Seasick?" she repeats.

"Yes, it's awful."

Another pause. "Do you plan to stay locked up in your room this entire boat ride?"

Myria's tone adopts a sharp annoyance. "If it keeps me from embarrassing myself in front of the prince and the other nobles, so be it."

There is a muffled exchange of words on the other side of the door, and Myria realizes another person is with Olympe, probably Geffrey.

"The prince is going to name the ship tonight," the new voice points out. Definitely Geffrey. "And everyone is saying he is going to name it after his preferred suitor."

"And how would it look if he named the ship after a girl who can't stop puking up her insides?" Myria shoots back.

Geffrey pauses at this argument. "He will want to visit you if you do not make an appearance."

"Absolutely not!" Myria calls out. "Lady Myria is not accepting any visitors at this time."

Geffrey emits a loud, frustrated sigh, but he doesn't argue the point anymore.

"Shall we get you anything?" Olympe asks. "Perhaps you would like some company—"

"Oh, no," Geff hisses. "You are not going to skip out on me just so you can stay here and drink. With Myria absent, we *must* uphold the Bramble presence among the court."

Myria stifles a victorious laugh with a pillow.

"Fine," Olympe says with a dejected sigh. Then, louder through the door, "A servant will bring you something later, Myria. If you start to feel better, at least try to make an appearance."

"I will," Myria promises, already knowing it's a lie.

She keeps her window open, allowing sounds from the main deck to drift inside. Leor's strong voice articulates a speech to the court as he names the ship, but Myria cannot discern his exact words, much less what name he picks. The decision is met with rounds of praise and applause. Another bell rings as the sun sinks below the horizon, and footsteps resound on the wooden planks, heading deeper into the ship for dinner. Myria waits for the footsteps to recede before braving the world outside her cabin, thinking the entire court would at least be occupied for several hours with their meal.

She finds her way onto the upper deck and to the prow of the ship, relishing the smell of the salty breeze whipping through her hair. Being outside makes her feel lighter, and her body buzzes with energy. The waxing half moon hovers serenely above her in the starry night sky, illuminating much of her surroundings. The waters below oscillate in the breeze, hitting the sides of the ship with a spray of white foam.

Myria glances over her shoulder to confirm her privacy. A few sailors tend to the rigging and other duties, and an officer stands at the wheel on the rear quarterdeck, but none seem to pay her any mind. She looks back down at the water, an idea coming to mind.

When she calls upon it, the power of moonlight comes to her with ease. With it, Myria draws images on the surface of the seawater, as if it's a crystal clear looking glass and her fingers a paint strokes on a canvas. Practicing her skills with illusion, she reasons.

The water's surface flattens like a window and lights dance across it. First, she casts a likeness of her home, the Morning Glory. The image is clear, like she's standing right in front of it. She maintains the illusion for a few moments, a faint smile on her lips as she thinks of her grandmother. Then, with a wave of her hand, the scene dissolves back into dark, rippling saltwater.

Another gesture conjures the minotaur in Talking Tree Forest, a specific memory involving peaches and a prince. The minotaur kneels with his battle horn, and the others look on with surprise. Myria does not linger long on this image, erasing it with a single swipe of the hand. She is surprised to discover there is no dull, throbbing pain behind her eyes like when she usually performs magic. Instead, she senses the moon supplying her with a renewed wave of energy that makes her feel empowered and tranquil, her mind sharp.

Then she tries something different, a new image that is not a memory, but instead a dream. She starts it off as a memory—her first night at court, dancing with Leor. Only, she makes a minor modification, exchanging his face for another—

"Myria?"

She whirls around, splashing the image in the water away with a whiff of magic, to find none other than Emiri approaching her. His expression is curious, but she is relieved he is not close enough to have seen her illusion.

"What are you doing out here?" he asks, a small smile crossing his features.

Myria clears her throat, glancing over her shoulder to ensure that the illusion is completely gone. A faint ringing echoes in her ear as she disconnects from the magic. "Enjoying the fresh air," she says, forcing a casual tone.

He does not respond as he joins her at the railing. He peers below at the water, causing Myria to wonder if he knows, *somehow*, what she was doing, but his eyes drift back to her face as if the sea disinterests him. "You're not at the banquet," he observes.

"Neither are you."

"There is only a small galley on board; I wasn't invited. There *was* a special seat reserved for you."

Myria, not wanting to think where that special seat was placed, looks away from Emiri's penetrating gaze and out to the horizon. "I... was not feeling well," she says; the tone in her voice increases to an unconvincing pitch. It sounds like a question even to her own ears.

Emiri does not seem to notice. "The prince named the ship earlier."

"Oh?" Myria struggles to keep her voice even. Her heart hammers loudly into her own ears. She does not want to know, yet her curiosity cannot be denied. "And what name did he choose?"

"*Nocte.*"

This isn't at all what Myria expected, and a momentary rush of relief washes through her, calming her heart rate. "*Nocte?*" The name sounds like homage to House Nocturnus. The comforting thought makes her sag against the side of the ship, her knees going weak from her spent tension. "I am sure House Nocturnus is pleased."

Emiri hesitates, which only makes her trepidation return. "The duchess was," he says in a halting voice.

She narrows her eyes at him. "But?"

His voice adopts a stiff and formal edge. "The prince later informed me of his reasoning behind the name. *Nocte* means midnight, which he says is in reference to meeting his true beloved at midnight."

The blood drains from Myria's face, and her fingers grow cold, understanding the reference well. She turns from Emiri and moves away to head back to her cabin without a word. Her future has one clear trajectory now, the decision already made for her. Her mind is in too much of a haze to muddle through it.

"Myria, wait..."

Emiri's voice holds her back as she is about to go below deck. When she looks back at him, he is close, and she keeps her hands tethered in place by crossing her arms. She waits for him to speak, his mouth falling slightly agape as his eyes dart around in a frenzy. The longer he stands there, the more of the familiar heat she can feel swirling beneath her skin again. "What is it?" she asks, interrupting his lingering silence.

"I..." His voice goes hoarse with the single syllable, so he clears his throat, takes a deep breath, and starts anew, his words coming out with his familiar, forced formal tone. "I wanted to let you know there will be no lesson in the morning. I have to run a special security detail with Captain Rozenna."

Myria looks away, knowing Emiri had something else in mind to tell her. Still, it matters little. She even wonders if he is telling the truth about skipping their lesson, but doesn't dwell on the implications. She nods to him. "Good night, Emiri."

And this time, he lets her go without a word.

The *Nocte* arrives at Westhaven the following day. Myria would be relieved to see it if it did not signal being closer to the summer's end. She arrives on deck in time for a last, parting glimpse of the shimmering sea. Her cousin and aunt are there, waiting to disembark, their faces marred with strange expressions. She expects Geff to be resentful, but even he seems meek, almost apologetic this morning.

"What is it?" she asks.

Olympe casts a worried look at her son, her mouth hanging open in stunned silence. Myria looks to Geffrey.

"How's your stomach?" Geff asks instead. He looks over Myria's shoulder, avoiding her eyes.

"Much better this morning."

"Good, because you are about to get some bad news."

She waits for him to elaborate, and when he doesn't, she prods. "And that is?"

Olympe intervenes. "The spymaster has arrived at court earlier than expected. They were brought to the ship before we made port in Westhaven."

"And why is that bad news?" Myria asks, becoming impatient.

Geff inclines his head toward a group of nobles near the longboats. "The bad news is who escorted the spymaster to court."

Myria turns to look in the indicated direction. The crowd's central figure is tall and cloaked entirely in black, the hem cut in ridges to mimic feathers. Their face is obscured below a hood and behind a pointed mask with a hooked nose. She quickly guesses that this is the spymaster. However, her stomach sinks as she recognizes the noble right next to them as none other than Aryn Stirling.

20

HUNTING

THE COURT MOVES ON the road to the Kinggrove, an ancient and revered forest of the kingdom within Runewell lands. The tree line indicates the border of the duchy. A small encampment of brightly colored tents heralds the welcoming party of Duke Mathias, Eulalia's father. He greets them with a stony, smooth face, his expression stern despite the polite smile he offers to the royal family. Eulalia stands, looking radiant, next to her mother. Duchess Euphemia, tall and regal as her daughter, shares her husband's stern, forced smile. Prince Leor approaches the Runewell duchess and kisses her hand, which earns him a slight softening of her features.

"The Runewells, while quite cordial, are not known for their excessive warmth," Olympe whispers to Myria.

Her chest tightens as she watches Eulalia carry all the light and kindness of House Runewell on her shoulders.

Servants lead the noble families to designated tents, the Bramble one appropriately decorated with golden pennants which sway in the gentle breeze. Geffrey follows Myria, and behind him two servants carrying her ever-present trunk of dresses. They deposit it heavily on the ground inside the large tent before departing. Geffrey throws back the lid, and Olympe rifles through its contents. Myria waits on a bench for their decision, resigning herself to the fact that there will be no escaping the court this time, not like she was able to do on the ship.

"What are we doing?" she asks, watching the flurry of activity outside through the open tent flap.

"The Wild Weald Hunt," Geffrey says. "House Runewell appoints our quarry, and the family who can trap the creature without killing it is declared the winner. Then, we reconvene at Oakhaven tomorrow for dinner."

"Is there a prize?"

"I imagine Duke Mathias will announce one, perhaps similar to Cressida's in honor of the Courtship: a private dinner with the prince."

"Do we have hounds?" Olympe asks, selecting a gown from the collection.

Geff turns sheepish. "We do *not* have hounds," he answers, as if this is a great source of shame. "I applied those expenses elsewhere."

Olympe meets his eyes, her face thin with displeasure, but she nods in understanding all the same. "Very well. We shall do what we can."

The chosen gown is thin for the sake of agility and smooth for comfort. It comes with a black cape that matches the black skirt, but the bodice is a dark brass color, representing House Bramble. A thick leather belt cinches the waist. As Olympe helps Myria into it, she marvels at her reflection in the mirror as her aunt pins large hawk feathers in her braids.

Outside the tent, other ladies gather in similar hunting gowns, capes, and corsets, the predominant style for the day. Duchess Cressida appears in a bright red ensemble, making her quite visible through the trees. Wearing muted silver and black, Theodora Stirling stands on the periphery of the assembly, speaking to her brother in a low voice. Myria notices her knitted brow, as if they are disagreeing. She wants to learn more, especially about Aryn's sudden return to court accompanying the spymaster, but someone pulls at Myria's elbow, drawing her to the side.

Eulalia approaches, bearing a sad, apologetic smile. "Hello, Lady Myria."

Despite the apparent bad news her friend is about to share, Myria cannot help the pleased grin that stretches across her face. "Lady Eulalia, I'm sorry if it seems I've been avoiding you—"

"Please. There is no need for you to apologize. We were destined to be rivals from the start."

"Rivals?" Myria's smile fades.

Eulalia nods. "You know this. Perhaps I was the foolish one by letting my guard down around you."

"How is that foolish?"

"As callous as Duchess Cressida may appear, at least she makes no attempt to hide her intentions. Her honesty remains a rare virtue. With you, I am not so sure now."

When Myria first opens her mouth, words fail her. She tries again. "Lady Eulalia, I have hidden nothing from you."

Eulalia takes a deep, even breath, her eyes wandering to the distance. "Perhaps, perhaps not. It makes little difference now. My parents do not think it wise to ally myself with House Bramble any longer. I am to ride with the royal family during the hunt today. While House Rosenford has treated you as an honored guest, House Runewell cannot offer the same courtesy."

She pauses, swallowing hard.

Myria pieces together the formality of her words. "I understand."

When Eulalia looks back, her eyes are gleaming with what may be pity or condescension. "Do you understand, Myria? I *must* win the prince's hand this season. Nothing else matters."

"I understand," Myria repeats, her voice thick and her nose stinging as the realization sets in that as long as she's embroiled in the politics of court, she will never be able to have any genuine friendships.

"You are the obvious contender, and I can no longer be around you during these social events. It would only... sabotage my chances."

"I hope you realize..." Myria's voice breaks off. She clears her throat and tries again. "I truly want you to win."

Eulalia hesitates before reaching out to grasp Myria's hands. "No matter where our paths take us now, I once counted you a true friend."

Lady Eulalia Runewell releases her hands before stepping back and leaving Myria alone with her constricted throat and swirling thoughts.

The court assembles in a clearing in the middle of the camp. The sounds of nickering horse and yipping dogs make Myria restless. Next to her stands Lady Brigid, absorbed with the words of Count Alanis on her other side. King Uriel and Prince Leor ride up to the front of the court on their regal stallions in shining new hunting leathers. Through the crowd, excitement rustles, mirrored even in the king's gaze, usually dull and uninterested, now bright with anticipation.

"The king does love a good hunt," Brigid whispers.

Myria is about to respond when she realizes her words are directed toward Eulalia's cousin instead.

"Find me someone who does not," Count Alanis says, voice taut with eagerness.

Brigid's brow creases and her nose wrinkles in disdain. "Truth be told, I am not one for hunting. I cannot stand the thought of hurting another creature. My father even stopped taking me on his fishing trips because I would get so upset."

"Fortunately, the Wild Weald Hunt requires the animal not be injured," Alanis points out, shifting from bloodthirsty hunter to concerned, empathetic noble. Myria smiles at his switch in tone.

"Do you know what your uncle has planned for us today?" Brigid asks, her voice absorbing some eagerness from the gathering.

"He has not said a word, but I suspect it will be quite the quarry."

Eventually, Duke Mathias rides into the clearing with Eulalia and his wife behind, all three on matching black steeds with glossy coats. Duke Runewell does not silence the court with an announcement; instead, he waits for the clearing to fall silent of its own accord. The noblesse oblige quickly, their enthusiasm palpable.

"I know you have waited with much patience to discover your prey this year, and I am more than pleased to acquiesce to the court's desires."

Mathias nods to his daughter, who lifts her hands in front of her face, drawing a specific pattern with one hand that summons a glittering image in the air above them. In her other hand, Myria sees the distinct shape of a moon crystal.

"The goldhorn!"

The declaration is met with a series of gasps and nervous whispers. Myria studies Eulalia's illusion, the shape of a glistening white deer or antelope, its most distinctive feature a pair of lustrous, golden horns. It appears every bit as magical as the minotaur Myria knows.

"We are to hunt a myth?" someone cries out from the crowd.

"There is one wandering the Kinggrove," Duke Mathias confirms for all to settle their skepticism. "The first hunter to capture the creature without harming it will receive the goldhorn's weight in gold *and* a private evening with the prince for your family's designated suitor."

Soon, Myria is mounted on Jadis with Merek, the Bramble valet, beside her. Although Jadis is not trained in hunting, Merek is confident she will navigate the forest landscape with ease. Geffrey commands Merek to remain by Myria's side in case the estimation of her horse's capabilities is wrong.

"All of House Bramble's riders will be working in your favor," Geffrey whispers to her. "Your safest bet is to stick to another group of nobles to represent us."

Myria nods, her eyes scanning the clearing for the assembled groups. She is immediately drawn to the royal family's crimson swath, interposed by the green flash of Eulalia's hunting garb. Myria looks away once she realizes her eyes search for a different face she knows will be riding with the prince.

By the time the starting bell echoes through the camp, Myria has settled on riding with Lady Brigid and Count Alanis, who start off at a leisurely pace. They seem not to notice her presence as Jadis ambles behind them.

"What do you know of the goldhorn, Lady Myria?" Alanis asks, looking back at her.

Myria offers a wry smile and shakes her head. "Very little, Count Alanis."

"I heard the goldhorn is a magical creature, just as rare as a unicorn," Brigid says, her voice filled with excitement, "and their horns are made of solid gold."

"Its blood is known to contain magical properties," Alanis says. "Some think the horn does as well, but my uncle forbids any harm to the creature, so no one is certain."

"Have you seen the goldhorn before?" Brigid asks.

Alanis smirks. "Aye, I have."

"Then, I daresay we are at an advantage for having you with us," Brigid says with a delighted giggle.

"Do you need anything, my lady?" Merek asks Myria, drawing her attention away from the pair in front of her.

She smiles at him. "Nothing at all, Merek. Do you know how long the hunt usually lasts?"

The teenage boy offers a rueful smile. "Last year, Aryn Stirling trapped the prize a few minutes before dusk."

Myria peers up at the sky, trying to discern the sun's location through the thick canopy of leaves. It is still low in the sky, confirming only a few hours have passed since dawn. She releases a resigned sigh, urging Jadis further along the path. "Do you have a map, Merek?"

Merek does, in fact, have a map of the forest with him. Myria charges him with the task of ensuring that they don't get lost, deciding her best course of action would be to head straight for Oakhaven. Merek also finds this plan agreeable.

"Tis the same strategy the Dowager Duchess employs," Merek admits with a light chuckle.

When Myria looks up from the map, she realizes she has lost the others in the trees. This troubles her little, glad to be mostly alone with her thoughts. She continues along the path with Merek trailing faithfully behind.

After riding through the morning, an uncomfortable pain rumbles in Myria's belly, so she stops next to a babbling creek for lunch. One of Jadis's saddlebags is packed with food, and Myria pulls out a loaf of bread and some dried pork to share with Merek. At first, the boy refuses, but she convinces him to accept half of her share. In exchange, Merek insists he refill their waterskins, and bounds up the riverbank in search of the best spot.

At first, Myria sits on the ground to wait for his return, but her legs grow restless. She stands, brushing the dirt and leaves from her dress, believing that exploring the area nearby would not be remiss. She follows the current downstream to examine the foreign surroundings.

The trees have long, thin trunks, taller than the ones in Talking Tree Forest. It would be impossible to climb them, but the landscape is not as flat, the ground sloping at frequent angles with a plethora of moss-covered rocks and mounds of animal dens. Myria has to step carefully to not lose her footing.

By the time she has worked up a sweat, Myria considers returning to Merek. Then voices reach her ears, making her hesitate. She holds her breath and listens for the source. Exhaling slowly, she walks toward the voices, her path carrying her away from the river. The voices become more distinct as she approaches a sunny glen. She stays well back, hidden in the undergrowth, and cannot see who is speaking. But soon, Myria recognizes the voices as belonging to Captain Rozenna and Emiri.

Every fiber of her body screams for Myria to turn around and leave. She should not eavesdrop, especially on Emiri. The last time she spied on him did not go well. What if she discovers something worse, like some sort of intimacy between him and Rozenna? But this thought only compels her to crouch in place, pressing her back against a tree while her limbs refuse to take her away.

"I don't understand why the spymaster is here," Emiri sighs in frustration. She hangs onto every word he says, listening intently to the baritone of his voice.

Rozenna matches her volume to Emiri's, but Myria can tell she sounds anxious. "From what I've seen, they are investigating all the suitors, making sure there's no unsuitable match for Leor. No secret lovers or other unsavory details for a potential queen. Spotless suitors only."

"But we both know there is one suitor unfavorable by court standards," Emiri says. Myria does not miss the strange inflection that wraps around his words, and she knows from the chill on the back of her neck that he means *her*. It is not the same chill she had when he had called her a dirty barmaid; this is a new thrill that makes her heart skip. Emiri sounds protective.

"If I were you, I'd worry less about the spymaster and more about Aryn Stirling. His return to court is not a good sign in my eyes."

Myria perks up at this. She wonders what makes Rozenna nervous about Aryn.

"He belongs here at court with the rest of these snakes," Emiri growls.

"Well, he's the biggest, most venomous snake of them all. You saw the same as I did how he—"

Emiri hisses, as if to silence her. Myria wonders what the captain was about to say. Her calves burn from crouching behind the tree.

Rozenna continues, this time her voice so low Myria has to lean and strain to catch her words. "He should not be left to his own devices. You know how dangerous he is."

"Lady Myria!" Merek's calls out in the distance, shattering the tension in the air, causing Myria to jump. Rozenna and Emiri, alerted to interlopers, immediately fall silent as their footsteps fade away. Myria shakes off her surprise and stands to return to the creek side.

She finds the valet kneeling over a spread-out blanket topped with their bread, dried pork, and the newly-filled waterskins. He looks up with relief washing over his face. "There you are. I thought I'd lost you. Lord Geffrey would have me flayed if something were to happen to you, my lady."

"I'm sorry, Merek." Myria casts a glance over her shoulder, partly to ensure she was not followed, but also in longing to hear more of what Emiri and Captain Rozenna have to say about Aryn Stirling. She sighs as that opportunity fades with their distant footsteps and turns back to Merek. "Thank you for preparing lunch."

The lad flashes a proud grin despite the sweat of fear still beading his brow. "Of course, my lady."

After their meal, the afternoon drags on with seeing little of the other nobles. Myria, despite enjoying the solace, grows uneasy and frequently requests that Merek check their map. He does each time she asks, waving off Myria's apologies. When he confirms that they are, indeed, headed in the right direction, they continue on their way.

As they plod along through the forest, Myria asks Merek about his family and his dreams. Merek is shy at first, due to his reverence as a House Bramble servant, but eventually speaks animatedly about his mother and father, his brothers, and his hope to some day joust in the tournament. Myria thinks perhaps he is given few chances to speak freely.

"I want to joust, like you did, my lady. Fearless and unyielding. I would carry your house colors well."

"Why not carry your own house colors?" she asks, realizing her mistake a moment too late.

Merek wavers. "Because my family does not have their own colors. Besides, the only way I could joust is if it was for a noble family."

Myria frowns before a new idea comes to mind, replacing it with a grin. "What if I knighted you?"

Merek scoffs, but he is smiling. "You can't knight me, my lady. Only royalty do that."

"In case you haven't noticed, Merek, I am well on my way to becoming queen," she says, jutting her chin high and hardly suppressing a giggle. "And my first act as queen would be to knight you properly. I would give your family their own estate and horses, and you could fight in the tournament to your heart's content."

Merek laughs at the thought, but the joyful sound trails off. "I believe you would be a wonderful queen, but you should save your first act on the throne for something a bit more fitting."

"Oh? What do you propose?"

Merek shrugs his shoulders. "Lower taxes?"

Myria nods with a carefree laugh. "Fewer tax collections it is."

But her laugh also falters as she realizes the playful suggestion is a more likely reality. Emiri, Cressida, *and* Eulalia already think Leor's choice is made. That she,

Myria Hawthorne, will become the next queen of Avalion. The prospect makes her grimace, and the smile fades from her face.

"My lady?"

Myria glances up to see Merek watching her. She forces a smile for him. "Everything is fine, Merek."

He doesn't look convinced. "May I speak freely, my lady?"

"Of course."

Even with permission, he pauses. "Sometimes, I see you at court, with the prince, and you do not look very happy."

"Many people are unhappy in the world, Merek. A few frowns from me should be no concern to you."

"I know, but it's *okay* to not want to marry the prince."

She looks at her hands. "Sometimes, we don't get a choice."

"Why don't you have a choice?"

"Duke Bramble is taking care of my grandmother," Myria says, taking a shaky breath. "If I go back on my promise now, we would owe him more money than we would ever earn. We would be destitute."

Merek considers this for a moment. "Your grandmother is Iris Hawthorne?"

Myria nods.

"When I delivered your last letter, I met her. I know your grandmother is a foul-tempered woman, but her face had this lovely smile when I gave her your letter. She loves you very much. She wouldn't say this, but I think she wouldn't mind going destitute for you."

This makes Myria laugh.

When she recovers, Merek offers a meek smile. "You know, we are near Everhaven, and we're only getting closer every day. I could always—"

Myria holds up a hand to stop him and snaps her head around, a sudden instinct sharpening her senses as she stands alert.

"Lady Myria?"

The skin on her right cheek prickles, and she instinctively grabs Merek's shoulder and pulls them off their horses. As she falls, something whizzes in the air above them, followed by a soft *thunk*. Myria looks up to find a wobbling arrow embedded in a tree.

Myria straightens, her face blazing with fury, as she looks around for the culprit.

Aryn Stirling emerges from the treeline on horseback, a smirk on his face and a bow in his hands.

Sabine appears behind him, her expression stricken as she looks between Aryn and Myria. "My lord, you should not be shooting your bow," she says. "The duke said the animal is not to be harmed."

Aryn does not glance at Lady Valenrence, leaning back in his saddle as he appraises Myria with smiling, cold eyes. "My apologies. I thought I saw an opportunity to hunt for some other game in this forest."

Myria's shoulders shudder with rage as she realizes Aryn deliberately fired at them. Captain Rozenna was not mistaken about how dangerous he could be. But with Merek quavering next to her, Myria schools her expression, forcing a condescending smile that is more than the snake deserves. She turns to Sabine. "I think we can forgive Lord Stirling for his mistake. Surely, it takes a master huntsman to catch their quarry without attempting to maim it and we cannot expect him to achieve the impossible."

Her words are just enough to dissolve his smirk. He urges his horse forward, towering from his vantage. "I merely saw an opportunity to practice my aim," he says in a low, dangerous voice, out of earshot from Sabine.

Myria doesn't waver from his threatening glare. Her jaw clenches. "Maybe you should practice more so you don't miss me next time."

His mouth flickers at her words. "Bold, brave, or foolish?" he muses quietly.

She arches on her toes to appear taller. "I don't expect one who must hide in the woods and take shots at an unarmed woman to understand bravery."

The knuckles on his hands go white as his grip tightens on his horse's reins. They remain still for what feels like ages, measuring each other up. Myria is fully cognizant of her disadvantage, aground and with no weapon in hand. But she refuses to back down. Her mind goes to Emiri's lesson on blood magic. *Emergencies only.*

His eyes don't leave hers. "Perhaps you should run while you still have a chance. Get as far away from court as you can before something *unfortunate* happens to you."

Aryn breaks the tension with a jerk of the reins and a shouted command to his horse as he turns and gallops away, the speed ruffling Myria's hair and cape. Sabine follows without looking back at them.

Once they are gone, Myria realizes she was holding her breath. She lets it out and draws in a deep gasp before pulling the arrow from the tree trunk. As she examines the intricate designs carved into the shaft, she considers just how dangerous Aryn Stirling truly is. His arrow would have hit Merek, injuring him or worse, if she had not intervened.

But how she was able to intervene so quickly remains an absolute mystery to her. That strange prickle on her cheek warned her of the arrow, but surely before it was even loosed. What could possibly cause that?

Trying to shake off the encounter, she snaps the arrow in half and stomps it to the ground before they continue toward Oakhaven. After some time, a bright color on the ground catches Myria's eye, vividly standing out from the greenery of their forest surroundings. Approaching it, Myria notices a small line of flowers growing in jagged, random patterns. They are deep crimson and wet with dew, glistening brilliantly in the streaks of sunlight that reach the forest floor. They seem to create a path. Although the direction of their growth diverges from the route to Oakhaven, Myria decides to follow it.

With each patch of flowers, the same acute awareness that warned her of Aryn's attack urges her onward, tugging her along with a singular focus. It reminds her of the pull of the Perennial Stones. Soon, they reach a break in the trees, and lying on the grass before them is none other than the elusive goldhorn.

For a moment, Myria is too stunned to move, making strangled noises from her throat. Merek says, "It's injured!"

The goldhorn pants heavily, its side rising and falling with labored breaths. An arrow protrudes from its ribs and a thin stream of blood trickles down its snowy side. A large bed of the crimson flowers supports its prone form. Myria realizes the blood dripping from the goldhorn's side is sprouting the flora. It isn't just lying on a bed of flowers, it is lying in a pool of its own blood.

Myria dismounts, startling the beast. It turns its liquid black eyes to her, and its legs twitch as if it wants to bolt.

"Hey there," Myria says out in a soft voice, trying to calm it. "I see that you're hurt. We just want to help."

She makes slow, deliberate movements as she reaches inside her saddlebag to remove her moon crystal. Her fingers also brush against a second item that catches her attention—her wooden flute. With an idea forming, she grabs that too.

The goldhorn's eyes are still trained on her, unblinking as Myria lifts the flute to her lips. She plays the same melody she did for the minotaur the last night she saw him, and the soft harmonies make the animal's ears flicker and twitch with interest. As the pitch climbs, Myria takes closer steps to the creature, kneeling once she is right next to it. It makes no sound other than its labored breathing, its eyes still fixed on her.

Finishing her chord, Myria lowers her flute. "You like music? I have a friend back home who likes it as well."

Of course, the goldhorn does not respond. Still, Myria talks to it as if it can understand her perfectly, a strategy that has always worked on the minotaur. She lays the flute down, her eyes assessing the arrow. The markings on the shaft are familiar. Her tongue tastes metallic bile as she recognizes it as Aryn's, matching the one he shot at Merek.

"I am sorry this happened to you," Myria says in a low voice. "I suspect I know who it was, and *he* is deserving of the very worst of punishments for this crime."

The goldhorn's next breath is accompanied by a sharp snort.

"I need to remove it before I can help, and it's probably going to hurt. Is that okay?"

Myria has always made it a habit to ask a creature for their permission and wait for some indication of it, no matter how silly it may seem. Miraculously, the animal makes the tiniest of movements, a quick jab of its snout that mimes a nod.

Myria nods back, aware of how ridiculous she must look to Merek. She wraps her fingers around the shaft of the arrow all the same, bracing the creature's shoulders with her other arm. After counting to three, she releases a sharp breath and pulls the arrow, extracting it from the goldhorn's flesh.

The creature protests against the pain but does not attempt to run away. Once the arrow is removed, the sheen of the creature's blood transforms into red vines and petals that cling along the weapon's side. Myria sets it next to her flute and reaches for her moon crystal.

"This will be the easy part," She hums in a soothing voice as she holds the crystal against the wound. "I've been healed a few times with moon energy, and it's always a pleasant feeling."

Calling upon all her healing lessons with Emiri, Myria focuses her magic on the goldhorn's body. She studies the patterns of the tissues around the wound to determine how best to close it. With a plan outlined, Myria tightens her grip on the crystal and the icy sensation flows from her hands to mend the torn flesh.

The process is over in a few minutes, and leaves her gasping as she severs the magical connection. A cold sweat beads across her brow, unrelated to the summer heat. Myria smiles at the creature, patting its neck.

"There we are," she says, a little out of breath. "Good as new."

"Um, my lady?" Merek says.

Myria stands and turns to see that they are not alone. Eulalia, Captain Rozenna, and Emiri are all there, frozen still and watching her with incredulous faces. Another icy chill runs down Myria's spine as she realizes the implication of her position—her next to the subdued quarry. She had only wanted to reach Oakhaven, not win the hunt. The goldhorn was far from her mind, and when she encountered it, her only thought was to save it.

"I can explain," Myria stammers, as if she needs to explain herself out of trouble. "The goldhorn was injured..."

Eulalia steps forward, her mouth hanging open in utter shock. She struggles for words. "How did you... My mother said..." She shakes her head, giving up on repeating whatever her mother told her. Her voice is stiff. "I suppose I should congratulate you."

Myria shakes her head. "No, no. Please don't." She gathers her flute and crystal—and even Aryn's arrow—and stuffs them in her saddlebags. "I didn't mean to upstage you. I wasn't even hunting for her."

"Her?" Emiri asks.

Myria had been avoiding his gaze, but she involuntarily meets Emiri's eyes and regrets it. His face makes her mind go blank as she struggles to explain herself. "The goldhorn is female."

"How do you know?" he asks.

She cannot even relish in his surprised expression, one of complete awe and amazement. Any other time, that face of impressed wonder would make her heart flutter. But Myria knows she must make her escape now. "I just know."

With a single, smooth motion, she mounts Jadis, hisses for Merek to follow, and bolts away from the clearing.

21

TREASON

MYRIA SQUINTS AS SUNLIGHT sparkles against the magnificent, white wood walls of Oakhaven. The setting sun casts brilliant orange shafts of light through the trees and seems to set everything ablaze. She has arrived just as Lady Eulalia announces the winner of the Wild Weald Hunt. The prized goldhorn paces restlessly in a wooden cage for all to see. Myria can practically feel the creature's eyes on her, but she slips through the crowd to avoid her attention.

Servants scurry about, preparing tables for an outdoor feast. The nobles are seated on benches at a single, long wooden table. The arrangement places Myria in the middle with her aunt and cousin, across from Lady Brigid and Lord Sigurd. She is surprised to see Theodora and Aryn near the table's head, next to the royal family and the Runewells.

"I had an interesting conversation with Lady Eulalia," Geff whispers as he takes his seat.

Myria freezes, a forkful of roasted pork halfway to her mouth. "What did she say?" she asks, attempting nonchalance.

"She gave me the Hunt's prize money instead of keeping it for herself." Geffrey arches an eyebrow at Myria.

She chews the meat, taking her time to swallow it as she thinks of a plausible explanation. "Probably a conciliatory measure. Her parents will no longer allow her to maintain an alliance with us."

Geffrey considers this news, but he shrugs as if the information is of no consequence.

Myria narrows her eyes at him. "Doesn't that concern you? Our list of allies grows short."

His second shrug is also casual. "It confirms they fear you. They know you remain the prince's favorite."

"There's no other reason?" she asks with a scoff.

A third shrug. "It matters little. They gave us a sizable prize, which will go a long way toward hosting the Eventide Ball. We end the social season at Fairthorne, making a lasting impression on the prince in whatever beautiful gown we put on you, and then you shall be crowned queen before the year is out."

"There are too many assumptions there," Olympe mutters into her wineglass.

Geff scowls at his mother. "Forgive me for remaining optimistic about our futures."

Olympe takes a long draught of the berry wine, making several audible gulps that catch Brigid's attention, and sets the goblet down with more force than necessary. "There is nothing wrong with optimism unless it borders on treason."

"I have said nothing treasonous."

"It is fine to believe the prince will select Myria as his bride. However, it is a different matter to assume she will be *queen*. In case you have forgotten, we already have a queen. For the prince's bride to become queen, something unspeakable will have to occur to our current monarchs. Therefore, it is not advisable to imagine differently."

Geffrey rolls his eyes, looking as though he is about to argue. Myria intervenes before he can. "What's next for us at court?"

Olympe brightens considerably. "Honeyridge."

Her reaction earns a chuckle from Geff. "Mother's favorite place, other than home. The Valenrence estate, surrounded by apiaries for their mead and vineyards for their wine."

"The mead and vintages are how they made their fortune before climbing into the nobility," she explains.

After an uneventful dinner, they spend the night in the grand rooms of Oakhaven. The wide open rooms promise warmth, unlike the austere Dawnmourne Keep. The mattresses are soft and large; the blankets are warm and clean. Even then, they prove insufficient to lull Myria to sleep. She tosses and turns fitfully, her dreams a series of concerning images. A glint of Aryn's arrow, a flash of white hair, and the ominous shape of the Spymaster's mask. Otherwise, racing thoughts of Leor, her future, and an unknown, mysterious figure plague her minutes awake. Her night is so restless that the customary knock at sunrise is a welcome reprieve from being left alone with her mind.

She hurries to dress, disappointed to find that Olympe took her pants for washing. She settles instead on a basic blue linen dress that offers room for movement. When she finally answers the door, her heart stutters at the sight of Emiri.

Turbulent shadows line his face. His eyes flicker to take in her room before he looks away. "Ready?"

The halls of Oakhaven are lined with large, airy windows that welcome an abundance of light, even at dawn. The sun casts fiery rays that force Myria to squint when she looks outside. Emiri leads her down a winding path that seems endless. He passes through a walled courtyard, pausing momentarily to consider it before shaking his head and continuing back inside. Myria does not speak for fear of interrupting his stormy thoughts.

Once inside again, he takes a sharp turn. They climb a spiraling staircase and Myria struggles to keep up with Emiri's agitated pace.

He does not stop until they reach a dust-covered door at the top of the stairs, which looks unused. He shoves his weight against it before it creaks open. Stepping through, Myria quickly realizes where they are.

"The roof?" she asks, peering down at the estate's vast gardens.

Emiri does not comment on his chosen location as he turns to face her. "I apologize for neglecting your lessons recently."

There is an odd quality to his voice that sounds muted, almost distracted. She frowns at him. "You had your security detail," she says. "I assume you were retrieving the Spymaster?"

He nods without meeting her eyes. "We will leave for Honeyridge today, which means you will be closer to demonstrating your magical abilities to the court."

"The illusions?" she asks.

Another nod. "Therefore, I think it's in your best interest to practice them."

"But you don't know what type of illusion I'll need to cast."

He shakes his head. "House Valenrence has revealed little."

"Why magic?" Myria asks. "I have seen few of the other nobles show off their abilities."

"House Valenrence is new in the ranks of nobility. Often, they try to prove their place in the upper echelon with elaborate displays of wealth and magic."

Myria offers a thin smile, understanding. "Magic is a privilege for the upper class."

"Precisely, at least in Avalion." Emiri steps closer to the edge of the roof, where a low wall rises to guard them against the steep height, and surveys the surrounding landscape. "Do you have your moon crystal?"

Myria joins him at the edge, keeping a careful distance away, and pulls out her crystal to show him.

"I want you to create an illusion over there in the courtyard." He points to the same locale they passed through earlier. "Something small. I've already seen you cast large ones." He makes a noise somewhere between a scoff and a chuckle.

She presses her lips together, thinking. "What sort of illusion?"

"Just one thing. An item or object. Perhaps an animal. People may be a bit more complicated, but then again, you have a knack for *exceeding* expectations." The lilt of his voice suggests something beyond humor, but she cannot quite name the tone.

Tightening her grip on the moon crystal, she focuses her attention on the courtyard. The magic is more difficult for her to access during the day, nothing like that night on the *Nocte*. Nevertheless, it feels eager when she summons it, and she conjures an image of the goldhorn. With a small flash of light, the animal appears, standing in the center, turning its head this way and that. It looks real and alive, nothing like the shimmering vision Eulalia created the day before.

Emiri says nothing at first, so she maintains her focus. When his silence drags uncomfortably, it breaks her concentration. She turns to look at him, worried she has done something wrong. However, she finds him gazing at her, regarding her with intrigue, brows knitted together as if solving a difficult puzzle.

She feels the goldhorn illusion fade back into nothingness as her face warms, and she returns his gaze. "What?"

"We didn't have time to talk about the other day." His voice is low, like a whisper, and she leans closer.

"What is there to talk about?"

He smirks, but there is no humor in his eyes. "You found the goldhorn before anyone else."

"And?"

"And few people can boast about an encounter with one magical creature, let alone two."

His concern surprises her. She thought he would comment on her throwing the hunt to Eulalia. She swallows and looks away. "Well, you can boast the same thing, since I know you've seen two as well."

"Only because of you."

Braving another glance at him, she folds her arms around her chest, as if to prevent herself from being scrutinized too closely. "What's your point?"

"You don't think there's a reason for that?"

"Do you?" she asks. Her tone bears a sharp edge, scraping her throat raw like a knife on a whetstone. "I'm not sure what you're implying."

When Myria blinks, she realizes how close they have shifted to each other, and her stomach flips at the discovery. Her entire body tenses with an urge to bridge that gap, but before she can act upon the impulse—or *suppress* it, as she rightly should—Emiri steps back. He walks a few feet away and paces erratically, his former agitation resuming.

Emiri counts the events on his fingers, his words spilling out faster than he can control them. "You are friends with a minotaur, of all things. You already tapped into rudimentary forms of magic before I ever knew you. You excel at every form of magic you're introduced to at an alarming speed. The way you healed Sigurd—"

"Did I do something wrong?" she asks, raising her voice to be heard over his raving.

It does not work. He continues. "Your visions. The connection to the Perennial Stones. The illusion in Dawnmourne. Your white blood aura. And now the goldhorn?"

"You said the aura didn't matter. And what's special about the goldhorn?" she demands, her face growing hotter.

He stops his pacing, turning his wild, dark eyes on her. "The Runewells will never admit to this, but only someone with a deep magical connection can seek a hidden goldhorn. Everyone else would be blind to it. Minotaurs are the same way. It's the only reason we had Aryn with us that first night we met."

She doesn't understand why, but his voice sounds accusing. "What does that mean? What are you saying about me?"

Emiri takes an involuntary step closer to her as he emphasizes his words. "It means *I don't know how to teach you anymore.*"

The revelation disarms her, leaving her stunned as the heat and the anger completely deplete her body. "What?"

He passes a hand over his face in defeat. "I'm beginning to think your skill far exceeds mine. What could I possibly offer you? My father would have been able to help you, but I'm not my father. And I don't know what to do anymore." His voice breaks off, those wild, dark eyes practically pleading with her.

Anger propels her a step closer. "You promised Geffrey you would teach me. He's *paying* you." Her voice rises in pitch, heedless of anyone who might hear. "You have to keep teaching me. *You promised.*"

"What is there for me to teach you?" he asks.

Myria has never seen Emiri this way before, and it seizes her chest with panic and desperation. The magic lessons are her return for bargaining her future away with a prince she doesn't want to marry. This is supposed to be her one silver lining, and if it goes away... She cannot even imagine. What other purpose could she forge for herself?

She grabs Emiri by the front of his shirt, the rough linen bunching in her hands as she drags him down to eye level with her, their noses almost touching. "He's paying you, and *you promised,*" she growls.

He stares at her with eyes widened in fear, watching as if she were some wild animal loosed from a cage. He does not move from her grasp. "This means a lot to you."

"How much has he paid you already? How much have I been worth to you so far and yet deemed not enough?" she yells.

"*Why* does it mean so much to you?"

"I have *nothing* else!" she exclaims, her voice growing hoarse as what little control she had over her emotions vanishes. "Nothing, Emiri Magnus. You were right. A decision has been made for me. And dammit, you are not taking this from me—the one small thing I have left where I can pretend to control some aspect of my life before *everything else is taken*."

She pants, her chest rising and falling as Emiri considers her words. His eyes soften as he murmurs, "Myria."

She takes a deep breath to calm herself, and her next words are hardly a whisper. "There are things you can still teach me." She tightens her grip on his shirt despite lowering her voice, refusing to let him go.

His warm hands cover hers. Her skin flushes under his touch as the moment drags into what seems an eternity. "I... I am sorry."

She doesn't know if he's apologizing for considering giving up on her or because he has, but she allows him to pry her stiff fingers from his shirt. With blood rushing through her ears, every second is punctuated by the drumming of her heartbeat.

Emiri distances himself again and clears his throat. "Very well," he says. "Let's try another illusion, then." He resumes their practice as if nothing has happened between them. For the remaining hour, she practices her goldhorn illusion. She struggles to concentrate the entire time, her mind a whirlwind of emotions she cannot even begin to control. Anger that Emiri would give up on her. Astonishment that he thinks she's more powerful than him. And something else burning deep within her when she remembers the warmth of his skin on her hands. His face only inches from hers, his warm breath caressing her lips, and what that made her feel despite her trembling rage. She focuses on the goldhorn, though. She focuses on the magic, the only thing that she has, as she told Emiri. The creature prances through the courtyard, seemingly alive and thriving even though she knows it's only a phantasm.

"Beautiful." Emiri says, breaking almost an hour of silence with a hoarse whisper.

Satisfied at his praise of her skills, Myria dismisses the illusion and glances over. His eyes are on her, not the courtyard, and she wonders if he was referring to the illusion, after all.

He looks away, clearing his throat. "That is enough for today. You should go pack. We will be setting out again soon."

With a curt nod, she leaves the roof and returns in time to pack for the court's journey to Honeyridge.

The road to House Valenrence's estate is not long compared to the other legs of the journey. Myria enjoys the ride on Jadis, appreciating the summer countryside in all its glory. Despite the warmth of the sun though, it does little to thaw the icy feeling in her chest as she pays little attention to the plans Geffrey outlines for her.

By midafternoon, Emiri surprises by riding up next to her. She glances at him, reassured by his characteristic, stoic manner.

"How are you, Lady Hawthorne?" he asks without looking at her.

That damned title again. "The ride has been agreeable," she says, her tone also cold and withdrawn.

"Has Aryn Stirling troubled you?" he asks in a lower voice. "I know many were not fond of his return."

She shrugs. "I have not seen him today, but I suppose I had my fill of Aryn Stirling when he shot an arrow at me yesterday."

Emiri's detached demeanor disappears with a flash of anger. "He *shot*..." But, remembering his place, he shakes his head, swiftly composing himself. "I will remain vigilant of him," he swears in a gruff voice.

Myria cannot help the teasing smile that rises to her face. "I appreciate your concern for my safety."

He hesitates. "The prince's concern," he corrects. "If you recall, he asked me to watch out for you."

Myria stares straight ahead, not quite finding *that* reassuring. "Of course."

Emiri lingers only a few moments more before spurring his horse ahead.

Just before sunset, they arrive at Honeyridge. It is a massive manor, fitting for a noble abode even if modest compared to the ducal capitals. The ivory stone walls rise imperiously on a hilltop, overlooking the vineyards that stretch around the property. Gardens surround the manor like a palisade of hedges and ivy, lending the structure a rustic, floral appeal. Low stone structures circle this perimeter, home to the Honeyridge apiaries that produce honey for mead. The rolling hills surrounding all this are covered in wildflowers in every color imaginable. The sour smell of yeast from the downhill meadery follows them up the path to the front entrance of the manor.

Duke Cirrus Valenrence, who has traveled with the court across Avalion, sends a servant inside before turning to the king and queen to welcome them. "Welcome again to beloved Honeyridge—the flower which produces the sweet nectar of the kingdom. Your rooms are being prepared as we speak. May I interest you with a few new meads to sample in the solarium while we wait?"

"That sounds lovely," Queen Eloria says. "Lead the way."

Duke Cirrus says nothing to his other guests, gesturing for Sabine to take over in his stead. She nods in acknowledgment, turning to face the rest of the court with a brilliant smile. "How about a tour?" she suggests as if she would rather do nothing else.

Prince Leor bows to her, offering his arm. It is a political move, like every other event of the social season, as he pays respects to the host family by recognizing their suitor. Myria does not want to imagine his courtesy when it comes time for the Eventide Ball.

First, Sabine takes them on a procession of the grounds, weaving them through the hedgerows and ivy-covered trellises. Interspersed in the gardens are small pools of water filled with vibrantly colored fish. Myria can swear their scales sparkle in the sunlight.

Sabine leads them quickly through a secluded courtyard surrounded by climbing roses in a multitude of colors. She enters the estate through an arched doorway where the tour crams into the corridors to see the drawing rooms, parlors, chapel, oratory, and not least of all, the great hall. Myria lags at the end of the crowd, sacrificing the clarity of Sabine's descriptions for the privacy of observing the estate on her own. Lady Brigid and Count Alanis have a similar idea, slowing their pace to converse in hushed tones.

The basement includes an extensive wine cellar, filled to the brim with dark glass bottles in green, burgundy, and some rare blue ones. From the whispers echoing Sabine's words through the crowd, Myria learns they have glass artisans in their employ to design their signature mead and wine bottles.

Then, Sabine leads them outside once more, circling the other side of the house to a stone amphitheater. She waits for the crowd to gather around her before she makes her announcement.

"I am excited to announce the challenge that House Valenrence has designed for the suitors of the Summer Courtship. My mother, Duchess Theia, has always been a fan of the arts. Therefore, each lady from the noble houses will participate in the Art Faire, a celebration of artistic talent that will also test your magical prowess. I am sure that you have heard by now how illusion magic will be required of you. The ladies will perform their art for the entire court, whether it is singing, dancing, or painting. However, illusions must accompany your performance to show that you can be a bride for the crown that is as creative as you are resourceful. Prince Leor will select his favorite performance, and that fortunate lady will have the opportunity to dine with him privately."

Myria would roll her eyes at the unoriginal prize if she were not so alarmed by the challenge. She cannot imagine herself talented enough in any form of art to display it for the court. Intrigued and excited whispers roll through the nobles around her. It is difficult to focus on any single person as panic bubbles in her chest and her pulse rushes in her ears.

Sabine dismisses the gathering with a complimentary wine-tasting promised nearby. Myria lingers, staring at the amphitheater with terror. She does not need to conjure an illusion to imagine herself standing before the court at center stage, looking like a bumbling fool. Geffrey would never withdraw her from such a challenge.

She recalls the wooden flute packed with her belongings. She knows a few melodies, but nothing sophisticated enough for royalty. Perhaps her illusion skills will make a difference; something appropriately impressive to distract from her mediocre musical ability.

With this not-so-comforting thought, Myria turns away from the amphitheater, wandering back through the hedgerow gardens. She does not immediately make her way inside, instead roaming about to ease her anxious mind. She loses track of her path as she wanders, mostly aimless, through the various shrubbery.

But then she turns down a path only to stop in her tracks. Standing before her are Lady Brigid and Count Alanis, embraced and lips pressed together in the throes of passion. Myria knows she should flee from the vicinity and not intrude upon their privacy. However, she is so stunned it takes a few moments for her body to obey. By the first twitch of her foot to turn around, it is too late. She has lingered too long. They catch sight of her and break apart suddenly.

Myria does the polite thing and runs away.

She does not get far before Brigid calls after her. "Lady Myria! Please, wait!"

Myria stops but does not turn to face her, feeling just as embarrassed as if she were the one caught kissing in the garden. Brigid is puffing and panting by the time she catches up. Count Alanis is nowhere to be found.

"Lady Myria, I can explain," Brigid says between gasps for breath, her cheeks bright red. "It's the summer season, you see. It's so easy to get caught up in the social engagements and the courtly flirtations."

Myria blinks at her, thinking about the number of times she's seen Brigid absorbed with Alanis. "You don't have to explain anything to me, Lady Brigid."

Brigid continues, regardless. "I got so caught up in the politics of everything, making alliances, complimenting... *gentlemen*." She stalls awkwardly, refusing to name the specific gentleman in question.

Myria holds her at arm's length, fully gauging the panic on Brigid's face. "It's okay if you have feelings for Alanis."

Brigid's eyes widen as if that's the last thing she wants to hear. "No—no feelings," she insists. "I got carried away."

Myria narrows her eyes. "You don't have to lie to me. I won't tell anyone."

Then, for the first time ever, Myria watches as Brigid's face twists with anger and suspicion. "Then why were you running away?"

Taken aback, Myria releases her, holding her hands back in defeat. "I wanted to give you privacy—"

"Why would you do that?"

"So you could kiss without an audience. Is that wrong?"

Brigid sighs, her body going limp as the anger washes away. "You are new to the court. You do not understand."

"Understand what?"

"You *cannot* tell anyone what you saw. Swear it on your mother's grave."

Myria arches an eyebrow, having never before sworn something on her mother's grave. "Why would I tell anyone?"

"Because it would make this courtship easier for you if I was eliminated. Do you not see? I could be arrested, imprisoned, or worse."

The prospect horrifies Myria. "For a kiss?"

"*Treason*, Myria. Our families have offered us to court the prince, to be his suitors. It doesn't matter that he's only going to pick one of us. Right now, we are all his by right. To... entertain other pursuits of passion is to betray Prince Leor, the royal family, the crown, and all of Avalion."

Myria processes this, accepting Brigid's demand to swear herself to secrecy. After, she stays by the rose trellis courtyard as Brigid returns inside. As her eyes trace the swimming fish patterns, Myria considers all the interactions she shared with Emiri and how many times she was close to committing treason herself.

.

22

ART

PREPARING FOR THE ART Faire takes up most of Myria's days. With the performance looming at the end of the week, Geffrey insists she wastes not a single valuable moment. Her mornings are spent practicing illusions with Emiri, who continues to maintain his safe distance, and afternoons are spent practicing music.

"Are you sure I should play the flute for the Faire?" Myria asks Geffrey. "I'm mostly self-taught, and I don't know any formal compositions."

Her cousin squints at her. "Are you hiding some other talent of renown? An ability to paint? Stunning vocals?"

Her silence tells him everything.

"You will be fine. If you can tame a minotaur with that wooden thing, the court will be no problem. All you need is practice."

The next day, he arrives with a tutor and a new instrument—a golden flute. Myria tests the weight with her hands, uncertainly placing her fingers over the keys. "I don't know. I prefer my wooden one."

Geff sighs, attempting to hold on to whatever patience remaining with him by pinching the bridge of his nose. "We cannot have the court see you playing that thing. Besides, this one has such a beautiful sound. Beade here agrees this instrument is of the finest quality offered in the kingdom."

The tutor, a bearded, eager youth ready to prove himself, nods in assent, settling the matter once and for all. Beade spends the following hours coaching Myria on simple matters instead of music. He criticizes her posture, the angle at which she holds the flute, her grip, and her inconsistent note fingerings. Beade is even more aghast she cannot read sheet music. He drills her on intonation, weight distribution, embouchure, and quality of airflow. Tempo markings, articulations, meter, flats, and sharps. By late afternoon, Myria is so fed up, she snaps at both Beade and Geffrey.

"I *only* have a few days to master this. I simply don't have time to relearn the way I play music. If you want to help, then teach me a piece I can play at the Art Faire so I can master it in time. At this rate, I won't accomplish anything."

Beade gasps, offended, but Geffrey nods at the sensibility in her words. "Very well. Beade, tomorrow, you will teach her a specific piece to master."

Defeated, Beade agrees. "I will bring a selection for her to choose from."

The next day, he brings three for her to consider. Knowing the sheet music would be lost on her, he pulls out his own silver flute to demonstrate them. The first is patriotic in nature, hammering out repetitive beats that praise the glory of Avalion. The second is a lively tune with complicated fingerings and wild rhythms. Beade explains it is a popular dance song played at festivals and would pair nicely with an illusion of a dancer.

The third selection is entirely different, not known by the nobility since it is his own composition. When he plays it, the notes are lingering and mournful, sprinkled with some sweetness in between. When Myria asks for the inspiration behind it, Beade pauses before saying, "A tragic love story, my lady."

She chooses the third one, which earns a small smile from the ever-frowning Beade. Then, they begin the arduous practice of Myria mimicking the fingerings and sounds that Beade illustrates. He mutters on several occasions how ill-advised it is to learn a musical piece on muscle memory alone. The complaints fade when she repeats the refrains in perfect harmony by the second day. He also offers suggestions on illusions she can create to pair with the music.

"I didn't write any lyrics to accompany the piece," he explains. "Therefore, the story it tells is open to interpretation."

While she still meets with Emiri in the mornings to practice magic, she practices the illusion specific to her performance in the afternoons once she is alone with Beade. She discovers the difficulty lies in concentrating on the two tasks—music and magic—at the same time. Beade offers some helpful tips, instructing her to walk around the room while she plays the piece. "Walking should be second nature, yes? If you truly rely on muscle memory for the music, that can be second nature while the magic holds your focus."

"Are we advocating muscle memory now?" she asks him with a grin.

A slight twitch in his face is the only sign of defeat he'll allow her.

The next morning, Emiri inquires about her performance. "Are you playing the flute?"

She clasps her hands behind her back. Geffrey and Beade are the only ones who have an idea of her performance. She kept it a secret from everyone else, even Brigid, who asked to pair her singing with Myria's talent. "Can you not imagine me singing?" she teases.

Ever since the morning on the Oakhaven rooftop, Emiri has not stepped closer to her than several paces. In light of everything, Myria realizes this is practical, no matter how it makes her crumple inside. He crosses his arms, looking at her curiously with lowered eyebrows. "I have never heard you sing. I *have* heard you play your flute."

"You've seen me dance, as well," she points out. "But I suppose it's not one of my strengths."

He chuckles, an airy sound. "Not one of mine either."

Myria wrinkles her nose, thinking about every social function she has seen Emiri take part in. Then, Rozenna's words from Dawnmourne come to mind. "I can't rightly judge that since I've never seen you dance."

"And, with any luck, that will never happen."

She isn't sure if their conversation is straying too close to the personal side, but Emiri shakes his head and continues with the lesson. Myria follows his instructions, but a part of her speculates on his actions with some insecurity. Had he imposed these unspoken boundaries because he also felt the fire dance in his skin when they were close together? Or were the boundaries because he didn't feel the flame at all?

On the day of the Art Faire, Myria dons a simple lavender dress made of lace and chiffon, light and airy for the summer heat. She heads outside behind Geffrey with the court, the golden flute and a collection of charged moon crystals secure in a bag carried by Merek. When they reach the amphitheater, the shoulder-to-shoulder crowd makes her nervous, and she wrings her hands as she takes her seat.

Geffrey remains positive for both of them. "You shall perform exceptionally. People will love you like they did at the joust."

"All I had to do at the joust was not fall off a horse," she hisses. "This is a bit more complicated than that. This is art and music. I've never formally trained in those areas like the other nobles."

"I, however, have," he says, "and you have done better than anything I could accomplish."

She continues to wring her hands as she scans the crowd of faces, noting many she's never seen before. The Valenrence family appears to have opened the Faire to the commoners. The nobles sit apart from them, the royal family in the center of the front row. With her daily practices taking up most of her time, Myria realizes it's been some time since she has seen the other nobles. A crimson entourage of Nocturnus figures surrounds duchess Cressida. The Stirling siblings linger close by, Eulalia sits with her parents, and the Rosenfords gather in seats far away from the Runewells. The spymaster stands on the fringe, observing as much as they can.

As Sabine stands on stage with her parents, Myria realizes it is the first time she has seen Duchess Theia, a tall woman of regal stature with prominent cheekbones. Her dark hair curls down her back, and her skin is smooth and dark like Sabine's. The latter steps forward, addressing the crowd in a confident and clear voice. "Welcome to the Valenrence Art Faire, a celebration of creative and magical talent. We would like to thank the noble houses gathered here for their participation. We look forward to each of your performances."

Polite yet exuberant applause ripples through the audience.

"The social season will dictate our order. First, we have Lady Theodora Stirling."

Sabine and her parents take their seats next to the royal family as the crowd falls silent. Theodora strides on stage with several attendants behind her. They shed matching robes to reveal form-fitting leather bodices and pants that cling to their forms. The sight elicits a wave of astonished whispers from the crowd. When they pull out slender rapiers, Myria realizes they will be dueling.

"Is swordplay an art form?" Myria asks Geff in a low voice.

Geff shrugs, just as confused and intrigued as she is. "Some say there are fighting forms steeped in dance."

With a scraping of metal that rings through the amphitheater, Theodora begins the duel. Myria watches, mesmerized, as the combat plays out less like a fight and more like a dance between partners. Theodora meets each attendant as an opponent with practiced movements. With every blow that lands, colorful sparks fly from her blade. A flash of light in her sword hilt accompanies every strike and burst of color, and Myria realizes that is where Theodora keeps her moon crystal.

The coordinated movements and lights swirl into a mosaic of colors hovering above the combatants. After Theodora has bested each combatant, she takes a bow for the exuberant crowd. The royal Avalion crest floats overhead, a sparkling red background with a shimmering silver lion. Much like a flag, it ripples in an unfelt breeze before a wave of Theodora's hand sends the lion charging toward the crowd. Shrieks of terror and delight fill the audience moments before the beast explodes into a shower of sparkling motes of argent light.

Theodora walks off the stage to animated applause, a wide grin splitting her face. Duchess Cressida feigns a polite smile and congratulates her as they pass each other on the stage's steps. She takes long, purposeful strides to the stage, also followed by a swarm of servants whose primary job appears to be maintaining the long silk train of her ruby dress. Then, hands on her hips, Cressida waits for the crowd to fall absolutely silent. It does not take long to oblige. The five attendants smooth out her train before taking positions in a semicircle, each holding something above their heads. Myria squints and can barely make out several large moon crystals, smooth and lustrous, unlike the jagged shapes she carries.

Cressida clears her throat, clasping her hands before her sternum, and her voice fills the air with a powerful projection. "In the beginning, a shadow rippled across infinite darkness."

Geff heaves a dramatic sigh beside her. "Oration," he explains. "Cressida has always liked the sound of her own voice."

The duchess continues her story, detailing the birth and origins of the goddess, the Lady of Light. With every mention and reference, a burst of light erupts from one of her attendant's moon stones and a visage of the Lady of Light shimmers into existence.

"The shadow was selfish; it knew no other way. Lonely, bereft, it stretched and grasped in search of anything." A dark cloud shrouds the duchess's feet.

"A small flame breathes new life. Such a beautiful phenomenon mesmerized the shadows." A single flame births into a divine woman.

Myria thinks she recognizes the story from her mother, or maybe the patrons of the Morning Glory. It is a long a narration, but thankfully, Cressida provides an abbreviated ending, raising her hands to the heavens in praise of the goddess. "The Lady of Light is always near. Even where shadows lurk, light must always stir nearby to cast them. Even if, in the end, only flame crackles." She lowers her hands slowly, and the assembled images all dwindle to flickering flames just above the moon stones, then a dramatic sweep of Cressida's hands wisps them away.

Again, applause echoes from the stones of the amphitheater, and Cressida takes her bows with a self-satisfied smile before clearing the space for the next contestant.

Lady Brigid steps on stage in a sparkling white dress that contrasts against her dark hair. Her face is drawn with calm composure, but Myria can tell she is nervous by her agitated hand movements. She squeezes her eyes closed and begins by humming a subtle tune, almost too quiet to be heard over the rumbling of the audience. But as the melody is established, it rises in volume and pitch, her voice stepping to a higher octave along one long note in a seamless transition. The tune sounds like a sea shanty, describing forlorn sailors and dangerous waters, but the tone is more refined and haunting.

As her beautiful voice serenades the crowd, the salty smell of the ocean wafts through the arena, accompanied by the crackle of thunder. Occasionally, light flashes over the amphitheater like lightning. Through the course of the song, Brigid's dress fades from white to a stormy blue, flashing white again with each flash of lightning, and then settling on a placid aquamarine as she sings her last note. Her piece finished, she opens her eyes to thunderous applause. She heaves a sigh of relief and smiles for the first time since walking on stage, curtsies, then hurries away from the center of attention.

Eulalia twirls to the side to avoid being bowled over by the fleeing Brigid, then skips onto the stage with either carefree abandon or a reasonable play at appearing as such. Her green, billowy dress has a long train that sweeps behind her. She carries only what appears to be a paintbrush. Keeping her back to the crowd, she holds it poised in midair, seemingly pausing for dramatic effect. When she moves, something glows at her ears, and Myria realizes she is wearing moon crystals as earrings. Eulalia drags a vertical line through the air, and a fully formed tree trunk follows in its wake. She does this several more times, creating a small forest, then adds the leafy details with a quick flourish of her hand. She turns around revealing another moon crystal hanging as a pendant from her neck, and a magical breeze flows across the stage. Painted branches sway in the wind and the sound of rustling leaves filles the air.

"Illusion painting," Geffrey remarks, impressed. "I have never seen that done before."

Lady Eulalia paints the likeness of a river running across the stage, and the body of water flows and bends at her command. The painted water bubbles over stones and the sounds of a babbling brook is accompanied by a refreshing, cool mist that flows over the audience. They gasp in awe with each new creation as the brushstrokes come to life as Eulalia twirls across the stage with the grace of a dancer. For her final creation, Eulalia draws out the shape of a magical winged creature, a hippogriff. It prances to life, and she hops on its back to be carried through the air above the crowd. Myria puzzles over this use of magic, thinking it beyond the skills of illusion. It matters little to the crowd, though. The exceptional ending is met with roaring applause and the chanting of Eulalia's name.

Sabine steps out next, wearing a purple swaths of fabric that reveals the skin of her waist, back, and glimpses of her thigh. Gold chains hang from her shoulders and waist, clinking every time she moves, and a matching gold headdress weaves through her hair. She waits for the spectators to fall silent, then reedy music plays from no discernable instruments. As Myria realizes the music is her illusion, Sabine begins to dance, twisting her limbs and body with sensual movements to match the lilting melody. As the music continues, more figures materialize around her, mirroring her movements exactly. Images of people, Myria realizes. Emiri said they were more difficult to cast. With every new phrase of melody, two more figures accompany Sabine. Even with the added dancers, the eyes of the male nobles are transfixed on Sabine.

"Interesting strategies from everyone," Geffrey whispers.

"How do you mean?"

"Theodora appeals to kingdom loyalty with her magic, showing physical might with her duel. Cressida shows an element of piety, which is strange because I never pegged her as particularly religious. Eulalia demonstrated her skills as a magician, while Sabine appeals to the strength of physical attraction. All important characteristics the prince needs for his bride."

"What about Brigid?" Myria asks.

Geffrey shrugs, not as impressed. "She performed well, but she did not really emphasize any important qualities, nothing to draw the attention or memory."

"And what qualities will I be showing?"

"You have a more difficult job. You have to show them that you *belong*—that you have all the skills of a noble magician and a refined taste for the arts."

Myria says nothing, going back to wringing her hands. While she does not care to win the Faire's prize, she does not want to make a fool of herself in front of the entire court.

Lost in her concerns, she doesn't realize Sabine's performance has ended until the crowd erupts into applause and Geffrey drives an elbow into her ribs. All too soon, her moment has arrived. Myria stands to make her way to the stage on legs that could buckle beneath her. She feels every eye boring into her back. Merek hurries after her, carrying the gold flute and a collection of moon crystals. The former he hands to her, the latter he places around her in a circle. Myria is not deaf to the speculative whispers from the crowd. Once Merek returns to his seat, Myria warms up the glorious instrument by playing one low note and one note an octave higher. The frequencies waver in key, like Beade taught her. Then, remembering the work from her practice, she begins.

She emits the lowest note the flute can withstand, the vibrato wavering solemnly. At the same time, the sky over the amphitheater darkens to night. The court gasps in awe as they crane their heads to watch. Slowly, the notes climb in pitch, each one illuminating a smattering of stars across the darkened sky. Reaching the highest note, the full moon appears.

Then, the melody takes off in earnest, hitting sweet pitches and somber chords. A new swath of trees surrounds the amphitheater, assuming the image of the minotaur's glen in Talking Tree Forest. Then her story unfolds in a series of pictures—the minotaur steps out from his cave to greet a female flutist. They dance, and he transforms into a human, his original form. They kiss. Subtle titterings from the crowd show the audience's investment in the story.

The tale takes a tragic turn. The flutist is killed in a bloody attack as Myria's notes turn mournful. Her lover finds her body, sacrificing his own humanity to bring her back. The ending refrains take a hopeful yet bittersweet pitch as a prince discovers the flutist, falls in love, and marries her. The minotaur remains alone in the forest.

Myria lowers her flute as the night sky fades away. In the reemerging daylight, colorful roses adorn everyone, which disappear under the light of the real sun. It takes a few moments before Myria realizes the crowd is on their feet, and the exuberance of their applause is overwhelming. However, she is deaf to the noise as her eyes inexplicably meet with Emiri's in the crowd.

Despite the boundaries they have silently agreed to, he does not look away, and Myria is too afraid to blink. He watches her intently, his dark eyes piercing and unreadable. She wonders if he *knows*, and the prospect makes her cheeks warm. Although nothing has been said or passed between them, she feels singularly exposed and hopes he understands the depth of her feelings. She yearns for one moment to understand exactly what he's thinking.

The moment is interrupted when Geffrey approaches her, clapping her on the back in congratulations. The deafening applause sharpens into awareness, drowning other thoughts and sounds. When Myria looks back, Emiri is gone.

With Prince Leor the sole judge of the performances, he seems to err on the side of political decorum by showing favor to the hosts of the competition, and Sabine is declared the winner of the Art Faire. She announces an outdoor celebration of food and wine at dusk.

Myria attends the evening gathering at Geffrey's behest, wearing the same lavender dress as she did for the Faire. Many nobles who had never before acknowledged her presence take great efforts to introduce themselves as she stands next to Geffrey in the gardens. They shake her hand, offer compliments, and Geffrey's grin seems to become a permanent fixture on his face.

"You have outdone yourself, Myria," he whispers in between introductions. "The joust is nothing compared to this. They *know* you are a force to be reckoned with."

The muscles in Myria's face ache with the continued exertion of non-stop smiling. "I hope you've compensated Beade fairly. It was his song I played, after all."

Geffrey waves off her concern as a lesser noble from House Runewell approaches. Myria does not remember many names, and the mental exhaustion of her performance is overwhelming. Her eyes stray to the edges of the courtyard, where those not as pleased with her success gather. Aryn sulks next to his sister. Eulalia casts worried looks at her from afar. It is impossible to read the spymaster's expression through their mask, even if they have become an enduring yet looming figure. Sabine's courtly smile fades when Leor momentarily leaves her side to congratulate Myria.

"You put on an excellent show," he says, reaching for Myria's hands with a heavy warmth. Instinctively, she wants to pull back, but a reminder of Cressida's words—a warning not to deny the prince anything—keeps her in check.

"You are far too kind, but thank you," she says, her cheeks aching as she forces yet another smile.

He compliments her skills in music, magic, and storytelling. Myria nods at the appropriate times with movements that feel mechanical and practiced in nature.

By the time Prince Leor returns to Sabine, Geffrey has also disappeared into the crowd, probably to gloat on Myria's behalf. Myria takes a seat on the edge of the nearby fountain, sipping a horn of a sweet, floral mead that does little to soften the bitter edges of her night. Olympe called it blood mead, the nectar stained red by hibiscus flowers. When Myria scans the crowd for her aunt, she cannot find her.

After several long hours, the celebration wanes as nobles search for their beds with clumsy, drunken footsteps. Few remain awake, their heads hunched together in deep conversations. Myria weaves through the gardens, looking for her aunt again. She rounds the corner of another hedge and almost collides with Captain Rozenna.

Myria jumps back, and the guard offers a helping hand to steady her. "I'm so sorry," Myria says, her mind working sluggishly through her exhaustion.

"No harm done," Captain Rozenna says with a slight chuckle. "If you were your aunt, the front of my clothes would be drenched in wine right now."

Myria laughs, recognizing the likelihood. "Have you seen my aunt, by the way? I lost track of her for a while now."

Captain Rozenna nods. "I saw her heading inside a few minutes ago."

"Thank you, Captain." Myria turns to follow her aunt's direction, but Rozenna calls out to her.

"Lady Myria, please be careful."

She looks to the captain with knitted brows, noticing an intense light in her eyes. Myria struggles to read the message there. "I will," she promises slowly before leaving in the other direction, heading back through the arched doorway in the courtyard.

The inside of Honeyridge is empty in the late hour. Myria's footsteps echo on the stone floor. She pauses for a moment, stepping out of her tight, toe-pinching slippers to relieve her aching feet on the cold tiles. The bright moonlight streaming through the arched windows illuminates everything in sharp relief, helping Myria find her way to the staircase without trouble. Shoes in hand, her foot barely grazes the first step before a voice halts her.

"*You.*" The snarl drips with contempt. Myria turns to find its owner—Aryn Stirling.

She straightens herself to meet him as he marches toward her at an alarming pace. She forces a few furious blinks, instinct insisting she be more concerned at his presence. He does not slow when he reaches her, his hand wrapping around her throat and slamming her against the wall, feet dangling in the air.

"And what exactly do you think you proved today with that little act?" he growls through clenched teeth.

Dropping her shoes, Myria claws at the unyielding hand around her neck, quickly losing air. "Get. Off. Me," she croaks between gasps for air.

He moves his lips against her ear, hissing, "Not on your life." His grip tightens, constricting her airway even more. "Not when you think you can ruin everything by making your pathetic appearance at court. I told you to *run.*"

Myria gasps, unable to utter anything else. Her mind flounders around for an escape. She remembers the blood magic Emiri taught her. She tries to summon the energy to push Aryn away. To burn his fingers. Anything.

Nothing happens. With no open wound—no blood to draw power from—no magic submits to her summons.

Myria gathers her remaining strength and rakes her fingernails across Aryn's face. Long scratches open his flesh and blood seeps out. He cries out in pain, releasing Myria as he reaches for his face.

She crumples on the ground, gasping for air as her head feels like it's about to explode. She blinks unbidden tears away and looks up just as Aryn reaches out to grab her again.

Her eyes fixate on the blood dripping down his face. Her jaw clenches as she focuses, grinding her teeth together with the exertion. She draws power from the blood, then feeds power back into it, imagining the crimson liquid transforming into a black, noxious acid.

Aryn reels back a second time, shrieking in surprise as the skin on his cheek sizzles and pops. The sickly sweet, acrid stench of the acid mixed with his bubbling flesh fills the air, turning Myria's stomach. Aryn furiously rubs at his face to wipe away the burning liquid.

She hopes he burns, boils, and crumbles to ash. Her fury ignites something in her chest.

Aryn's screams intensify, matching the rage Myria projects at him. As his flesh burns under the acid, more blood pours forth. Without thinking, Myria draws additional power from the crimson flow before the acid can eat it away. Magic, eager for action and greedy for power, flows into her. She feels overwhelmed by the power, but is thirsty for more.

But new energy swells—she feels him reaching for his own magic with a sudden high-pitched buzz. He stomps for her again, his eyes livid and blazing. She considers how to respond as the energy swells within her. Perhaps she might turn *all* his blood into acid.

Before she can decide, a familiar figure rushes into the hall, planting themselves in front of Myria and facing Aryn. "Don't touch her," Emiri commands, his voice deep, rumbling, and quaking with rage.

Aryn laughs out in a raspy voice. "And you will stop me? The prince's pet?" Emiri is dauntless. "Yes."

Myria pushes herself off the floor. Aryn notices her movement, his eyes wild with what Myria can only describe as hunger. He lunges for her, but Emiri sidesteps to block his path. Aryn's fist connects with flesh, and Myria watches with horror as Emiri staggers back.

The power of the blood magic, still coursing through her, burns to be released. Her head swims, buzzing with promise and exhilaration. Emiri turns to her, wiping his own blood from his lips on the back of his hand. His eyes meet hers and hold them for a long moment, then he shakes his head. "Don't do it," he whispers, as if he knows what horrors she was only moments away from committing.

Aryn steps back in turn, seeming to assess the situation before him.

Emiri turns back to him and straightens as if the punch caused him no pain at all. "*Leave.*"

But Aryn makes one more attempt, this time diving at Emiri and tackling him to the ground. Emiri counters, rolling them over until he's on top. He jabs at Aryn, connecting with the noble's nose. Aryn's head lolls back, bloody and unconscious.

The skirmish over, Emiri shakes out his hand and climbs to his feet. At first, he stares down at Aryn's body, saying nothing. Myria watches him, shocked and unable to move for a few moments, her hands shielding her sore neck. The boiling fire of the blood magic fades with the danger passed, and a sudden wave of exhaustion threatens to overwhelm her.

She breaks the silence with a trembling voice. "How did... how did you know to come here?" Her words sound breathless to her own ears, but she doesn't trust herself to speak louder.

"Rozenna saw him follow you inside. She couldn't leave Leor, so she sent me." His voice is careful, methodical, betraying no inflection.

He takes a step away from Aryn's body, and when Myria sees him wince, a new strength surges through her, bringing clarity. "Come," she orders. "My room is nearby."

Her tone allows no room for argument, and he does not draw back when she takes his hand to lead him up the stairs. Brigid's warning of treason hovers in the back of her mind, and Myria is relieved when they step out onto a deserted second floor. She opens the door to her room and all but pushes him inside. With a final sweep of their surroundings to assure no one else is around, Myria closes the door behind them.

23

TEARS

MYRIA'S ROOM AT HONEYRIDGE is spacious enough to please any noble. On one wall, a fire crackles in a hearth before a plush seating area. The same arched windows seen throughout the manor line the opposite wall. Emiri hovers in the center of the room, pressing a hand against his side. Myria approaches him after closing the door, and he turns slowly to face her, his eyes wide and alarmed.

He begins to object. "I shouldn't be—"

"You are hurt," Myria says. "I am going to heal your injuries."

He must read the commanding urgency in her eyes and relents, stiffly lowering himself onto the bench in front of the fireplace. The bag of moon crystals from her performance sits by the door, which she grabs before taking a seat next to Emiri.

"Move your hand so I can see." When he hesitates, she says, "If I remember correctly, you've seen me in a worse state."

It is difficult to discern in the darkness, but Myria swears she sees him blush at the memory of her tournament injuries—how her bloodied dress was in tatters and he politely averted his gaze. Finally, Emiri yields, lowering his hand so Myria can pull up his shirt to inspect his chest.

She tries to remain clinical as she traces the dark bruises forming over his ribs. She feels him struggling to not recoil beneath her touch, and she draws her hand back. "I think you have a bruised rib, maybe more." She stands. "Take off your shirt and lie down on your back."

To her surprise, he does not protest, complying with her instructions. She helps him pull the shirt off over his shoulders, and the effort leaves him gasping for breath. As he lies down, he strains against the pain by biting down on his bottom lip, then gasps as he bears down on where it was split by Aryn's blow. She runs her hands down his side, feeling for swelling under the bruises which are growing warm.

For a moment, her face quivers. She whispers, "I'm sorry."

"No," he says in a strained voice. "This is not your fault. You did nothing wrong."

"I was the one Aryn—"

"Please," he whispers. "Don't say his name. Not here."

Myria obliges, setting to work. Holding an energized moon crystal next to his chest, she focuses on relieving the swelling around his ribs. Emiri sighs with relief as his pain subsides. The bruises fade, and she turns her attention to his face, mending the cut on his lip and reducing the swelling from his jaw before she withdraws her hands, her work completed.

Emiri sits and reaches his arm high above his head, stretching with careful movements, then rubs his chin and runs a finger over his lip. "Thank you," he sighs. He appears more clear-headed, but does not move to put his shirt back on. Instead, his eyes fall to her throat, and she wonders if there are bruises there from Aryn's grasp. She passes Emiri the crystal and pushes back her hair to aid his inspection.

The firelight glows on one side his smooth face while casting the other half in darkness, accentuating the anger brewing in his eyes. He is silent as he brushes his thumb across her throat. While his touch is cool from the healing magic, it sparks a fire in her chest and her focus falls from his eyes to his shirtless form. When Myria realizes she is staring at the hardened planes of his chest, she averts them even lower to the ground.

By the time he pulls back, the soreness is gone. She clears her throat in the ensuing silence, hoping it will also clear her mind of any intoxicating thoughts. It does not seem to work, and she struggles to adopt a courtly tone. "Thank you for being there. I don't know why... why any of it happened. I'm sorry you got hurt at my expense, but I am grateful that Leor asked you to watch over me."

The silence that follows is thick with pointed hesitation. She looks back up at Emiri, who has his mouth open as if he struggling to articulate his thoughts into words. Eventually, the battle in his mind ends, and the guarded walls he's maintained the entire summer collapses.

"You know... you know that's not the reason."

She says nothing, too afraid to interrupt him.

He seems to force the words out in a painful struggle. "Myria, I have feelings for you."

A hollow ringing fills her ears. Her heart leaps to her throat as she stares at him, unblinking and confused. "What?"

His words flow forth as if from a broken dam. "I know it's wrong, that I shouldn't give in, but I don't know how to hold back anymore that I *care* for you much more than I've ever cared about anyone."

Her entire body tingles and burns as if engulfed in flame. Her heart thrums in her chest. "Emiri, I feel the same way."

Her confession must disarm him, as he peers into her face with astonishment. He glances down at the hand in her lap, then reaches for it with shaking fingers. They brush against the tops of her knuckles with the slightest caress, warm and tantalizing. She wants nothing more than for him to take her hand in his, but as she turns her palm to meet his, resolve seems to overtake Emiri. He pulls his hand back with a growl, his features marred with anger.

"*What am I doing?*" he hisses. "This is a mistake. I shouldn't be here. I'm sorry." He shoots to his feet, grabs his discarded shirt, and storms to the door.

Myria hurries after him, gripping his arm before he can reach the handle. "Wait. Please stay."

She feels Emiri's entire body tense at her words. He does not pull his arm from her grasp as he turns to look at her, his brows drawing together. "I can't."

"I'm not asking you to do anything inappropriate. I only want to talk about this."

"There's nothing for us to talk about. There can't be. Leor is in *love* with you."

The room seems to freeze. Myria can't breathe in the ensuing silence.

Emiri continues. "I hear it from him all the time. He wants you for his queen. Your beauty and your kindness are everything he's imagined, everything he's ever desired in a woman. Every day, he sings your praises. Only, he does not know how those words *torture* me."

He falls silent, and Myria's chest aches to hear his voice. She wants to reach for his face, but settles on tightening her grip on his arm as tears well in her eyes. "I don't want to marry Leor. I don't want to be queen. I don't want to be part of the court. All I've ever wanted was to help my grandmother and to learn magic, and when I met you—"

Her voice catches in her throat, and she releases a trembling breath, slowly releasing him.

"All I have ever cared about since then is learning magic from *you*."

With a single, deft movement, Emiri pulls her into his chest. Wrapping one arm around her waist, he grips the back of her head with the other. He buries his face in her hair and inhales deeply.

She entwines her arms around his neck, and he trembles in her arms.

"I have *nothing* to offer you," he whispers into her neck.

His breath is fire against her skin, stifling and suffocating. She looks up at the ceiling as if gasping for air. "I don't care about that."

Emiri embraces her for another moment before letting go and stepping back to put the shirt back on. "We shouldn't be doing this. Otherwise, we will go somewhere we both regret," he mutters, his walls stacking back up.

Disconnecting leaves her dizzy, and she no longer has the strength to argue or fight back. He moves toward the door, and Myria feels much remains unsaid between them. He casts her one last, furtive glance before slipping out of the room. Alone, Myria sinks onto the mattress, curls herself into a ball, and waits in futility for the stream of tears to end.

Throughout the sleepless night, an indescribable heaviness weighs on her chest, and her breaths are shaky, labored. By daybreak, weak, gray light filters through the arched windows. Then, a sharp knock shatters the stillness. She forces herself to rise and dress in her only pair of pants and shirt before answering the door.

Emiri stands in the hall, surprising her. After the night before, she expected him to avoid her like death. However, duty prevails, as it always does with Emiri.

He refuses to look at her as he leads her to the site of their morning lesson. She sneaks a few glimpses at his stony face. The dark, oppressive bags beneath his eyes suggest sleep eluded him, as well.

The courtyard with the climbing rose trellises proves a serene sight. A foggy mist clings to the ground. Emiri steps back to create even more distance between them. More boundaries. Safe. Her chest aches as he backs away.

When he speaks, his voice is even. His words are slow and deliberate. "Considering last night's events, I have decided to teach you magic often used in combat, so you might defend yourself. *Without* blood magic."

She recalls the greedy thirst that nearly consumed her and the unbridled power coursing through her veins, fueled by her hatred. An image of Aryn drowning in acid, boiling from within his own body, fill her mind until she shakes them away. She tells herself she never would have taken things so far, yet remains unconvinced. "Should we talk about last night?"

He flinches, and Myria realizes they may not both be considering the same series of events from the night before.

"The blood magic with Aryn," she clarifies.

He focuses on a rosebud. "What you did was dangerous, you already know that. But it was necessary. He attacked, and you had no other recourse. In the end, you kept it under control."

Her tongue thickens against the roof of her mouth. She does not wish to admit that the burning in her chest felt like the very opposite of keeping things under control. Were it not for Emiri's timely arrival, she's sure she would have embraced the power and done something unspeakable.

"My hope is this lesson will offer you a safer method of defense, should the need arise."

Her tongue turns sharp, working with the speed of a whip to propel a torrent of words. "But *why* would the need arise? Why did he attack me? Would he have gone so far as to kill me?"

Emiri seems to lose interest in the rosebud as his eyes shift to his hand. His frown seems almost rueful. "I do not know the answer. I would say he hates you because you are a commoner, but it is obviously more than that."

Previous conversations snake into her thoughts. "Does it have something to do with the spymaster? He returned to court with them in Westhaven."

His frown deepens. "It seems likely. I will find out."

His decision ends the conversation about Aryn Stirling, and as he delves into the lesson, Myria struggles to concentrate on his words. Emiri explains how to create invisible wards for shielding oneself from attacks both magical and physical, and how to summon different methods of attack. There are various offensive forms of magic available to her. Flames of every sort imaginable. Icy, sharp projectiles. Concussive blasts. Emiri explains that the challenging part of combative magic is maintaining one's shield, especially if attacking at the same time.

As Myria contemplates the possibilities, she nearly misses Emiri's next words. "This will be our last lesson."

The heaviness in her chest transforms into panic. "*What?*"

He refuses to meet her eyes or answer her question, instead plowing through the rest of his explanation on magical wards. She summons one at his command, and when he tests it with his hand, it dissolves immediately.

"Stronger, Lady Myria."

She flinches at the title and tries again, reaching through the fog for the sun's rays in a half-hearted attempt. Her jaw aches from the constant clenching of her teeth. She is torn between a desire to annoy him into speaking and proving she can make suitable wards.

This time, it holds up against his hand, and he continues testing it by throwing several small stones at her with magic. She deflects the first half dozen, then the next several strike her, leaving painful bruises.

Emiri shakes his head and stoops to gather more stones from a flowerbed. "You're draining yourself by holding the ward. Summon it only when I attack."

She can't focus. Her heart drums in her ears. She struggles to calm her breathing and relax her clenched jaw. He throws another stone, and her ward coalesces too late. The next stone strikes her thigh, eliciting an unbidden yelp of pain.

With each toss, she's a moment behind. She staggers back under the onslaught, struggling even more as each blow serves only to enrage her further.

He stops, tilting his head. "You're distracted. Focus."

She snaps her head to glare at him. Her pulse quickens, the sleep deprivation pumping adrenaline through her body. "Why should I focus if this is our last lesson?" she demands in a shrill voice.

The ferocity of her words does not seem to startle him into submission, as she hoped. His face remains closed off. "Are you intentionally sabotaging yourself? Because you don't want—" He stops, unable or unwilling to finish the accusation, and looks away in a huff.

"Why not? You said in Dawnmourne that you cannot teach me if I'm not honest with myself. What about you? Are you being honest with yourself? With me?"

His face remains guarded, but his ears redden. Good, a reaction. "I don't know what you mean."

She wants to scream at him for denying everything between them. "You said you had feelings for me, but your actions say the opposite, as if you're trying to avoid me. You want to stop being my teacher. You can't even look me in the eye—"

"You *know* why," he growls.

Her heart hammers as he riles up. "Would you deny everything you said last night, then?"

"What I said last night doesn't matter. It changes nothing. Leor is in love with you," he repeats as if those words mean everything.

Engulfed in anger and frustration, the whims of the prince mean nothing to Myria. "I do not love him. I will *not* marry him."

"And what can you do to stop that?"

Myria doubles down, ignoring the logic of his question. "I am in love with *you*."

At last. The words work, disintegrating his stony mask to reveal the crack in his armor. "Myria, I—"

"If you have feelings for me, why abandon me?"

Emiri takes a furious step toward her.

"Why give up any chance and surrender me to Leor?

Another one, closing the gap.

"You have never even kissed—"

One more step, and his hand closes around the back of her neck and draws her close. His lips press into her with a burning hunger. She presses her hands into his shoulders, instinctively struggling to escape his unexpected advance, then she surrenders and slides them around his back to pull him tighter. His muscles shudder under her touch. The agitation in her mind fades as she relishes in, the salty taste of his mouth, and his earthy scent. He threads a gentle hand through her hair while the other hand pushes the small of her back into him with surprising strength, bringing her chest flush with his. The fire in her belly roars to life as he consumes her in his embrace. Nothing else in the world matters as Emiri crushes his mouth against hers. Every movement of his mouth, his hands, and his body are urgent, hungry, and desperate.

As he breaks the kiss, Myria clings to his neck, as if Emiri is her only solace in a raging sea.

He does not let go of her, holding fast as his eyes, dark and flickering, fix on hers. "You asked how I can claim to have feelings for you when I have never kissed you?" His voice is hoarse and husky. "It is because I'm afraid. How could I ever kiss you, knowing it will be our last?"

His voice shakes, and Myria presses her forehead to his, squeezing her eyes shut against fresh tears. "It doesn't have to be our last."

"We both know it does. You're going to marry—"

"No."

"You're still in the Summer Courtship, and he *will* choose you."

He detaches Myria's hands from his neck and lowers them to her side with a sudden gentleness, then separates from her with three steps that echo against the stone with an awful finality. She pleads with him in a toneless breath, "Don't."

He suffers a smile that breaks Myria's heart. "I cannot continue this lesson. I am however confident you will be an accomplished mage and a wonderful queen for Avalion, Lady Myria. I'm sorry."

He turns on his heel and escapes through the hedgerows, disappearing from sight. Myria stares at the leaves as they shudder in his passing, feeling even worse than before. Her knees threaten to buckle under her. She runs her tongue over her lips, and she can still taste Emiri. She feels exposed in the garden, alone with her tears and broken heart. She turns to head back to her room.

Olympe bars her way, standing in the arched doorway with her fists planted on her hips. Her aunt regards her with hooded eyes. At first, Myria cannot move, speak, or breathe. She recalls Brigid's explanation of treason.

"How long have you been here?" Myria asks in a guarded voice.

"Long enough to understand why you do not want to marry the prince."

Myria looks away, chewing on her lip.

Olympe seems to have no patience as she grabs Myria's arm and drags her through Honeyridge to her room. Once inside, she sets to work with an uncharacteristic speed. First, she selects a riding dress for Myria to wear, throwing it to her as she stuffs the rest of Myria's belongings into her trunk—her flute, the moon crystals, *everything*.

"Aren't you angry?" Myria asks behind the privacy screen.

"Not here," Olympe hisses.

24

COMPROMISE

Bramble servants arrive immediately, as if on cue, to carry the luggage away. Olympe wastes no time in dragging Myria along again, stopping only when they reach the stables. Merek is already there with the horses. Together, the three of them set off on horseback down the eastern road, Olympe briefly explaining that the carriage will follow behind with their trunks.

"We must reach Fairthorne to prepare. The court will arrive this evening for the Eventide Ball. Geffrey already left last night," she explains breathlessly as their horses settle into a canter.

"I don't understand," Myria calls to her over the rushing wind. She understands the schedule of the Eventide Ball; she doesn't understand her aunt's reaction.

Olympe looks around at their surroundings. There is nothing but farmland for miles, and not a soul other than Merek to hear them speak as they approach the East Harridan River. Still, she waits until the ferry pushes them and their horses across the river, marking their arrival in Bramble territory.

"I stand by what I said before, at Dawnmourne," Olympe reveals at length, slowing their pace to rest the horses. "Forcing you into a decision you abhor is not worth the risk of losing you. Were you truthful about your love for Emiri?"

Myria stammers, balking at her aunt's frank word choice. She looks over her shoulder to Merek, who is looking off over the countryside with the practiced feigned ignorance of a professional servant. She considers her response for a moment before settling on a nod.

"Then we will withdraw you from the Summer Courtship," Olympe says. "Geffrey is the head of household, so he is the only one with the formal ability to do so. We will talk to him once we reach Fairthorne."

"He won't do that," Myria says. "I tried talking to him before."

It does not sway Olympe. "Then we will talk to him again, *together*. And this time, we are going to be truthful about what we want."

"And what if he still refuses? I cannot possibly pay back his investment in the Morning Glory."

"You underestimate the prize money House Runewell gave us. That should be enough to cover your debt alone. However..." Her voice takes a severe turn. "We will find a way. I swear it."

It is not much, but as her first sign of hope, Myria allows it to swell in her chest, making the heaviness there feel lighter. On their way to Fairthorne, Myria recognizes a familiar road and a small sign with the name *Everhaven* carved into the board, along with an arrow pointing south. Myria stares at it as they ride by, remembering Merek's offer to deliver a letter. The opportunity has been missed, as she has no letter prepared. She shakes her sudden homesickness away as they pass the sign, then focuses her attention on the road ahead to Fairthorne.

The Bramble estate boasts a manicured lawn with an impressive white gravel path leading to a front entryway flanked by white stone columns. The manor's front side is tall, with three stories in the main structure and an additional tower rising higher in the center rear. Above the entry, a long balcony that doubles as an open-air corridor breaks up the second floor. As Myria and Olympe climb the long, flat steps to the front door, Merek leads their horses to the stables.

An attendant, a young woman, is there to greet them as they arrive. "Welcome to Fairthorne, my ladies." She bobs a quick curtsy.

Olympe strides inside with purpose, not slowing her pace. "Jessa, do you know where my son is?"

Jessa catches up to Olympe with ease. "He arrived late last night, my lady, and left early this morning."

"Where to?"

"He did not say."

Olympe nods. "Very well. Alert me when he returns. In the meantime, I want a bath drawn for Myria. Nice and hot, please. And show me the preparations we have completed for this evening. We can expect the full court, including the Stirlings, so I do not want a single detail overlooked, be it the food or security."

Jessa leads Myria upstairs, across an open-air balcony, and to the chambers set aside for the returned scion of the Bramble family. The massive size surprises Myria, and she can barely wrap her head around it being *her* bedroom when Jessa interrupts her thoughts.

"My lady, if you'll wait here a moment, I'll see to that bath."

"Of—of course," Myria says.

Jessa walks to the wall opposite the door, covered in white panels trimmed in gold, apparently a dead end. Then, she pulls open one of the panels to reveal a small washroom.

"That's amazing," Myria says as she peers inside.

"Oh, yes, My lady. It is," Jessa says as she ignites a fire in a small hearth, under a large pitcher of water. "There are doors like this all throughout the manor. The first Duke Bramble, your cousin's great grandfather, preferred a simple aesthetic and wished for doors inside chambers to blend with the walls, hence the paneling." After giving the fire a satisfied nod, she steps out of the washroom and waves for Myria to follow her. "You'll find a wardrobe here as well. Lady Olympe ensured it was well-supplied prior to your arrival. In fact, we've been acquiring and altering items all summer while you've been away."

Jessa pulls open another panel to reveal what could have passed as a bedroom in the Morning Glory, but is filled with chests and trunks, with cloaks and other assorted garments hanging from pegs in the walls.

"It's too much," Myria says around a gasp.

"Just wait," Jessa says with a mischievous grin, then leads Myria past the enormous bed dominating the center of the room. On another wall is a modest bookcase, also painted in shimmering white with subtle golden scrollwork around the trim, resembling barbed vines. Jessa steps to the side of the piece and leans against it. Remarkably, it glides along the wall with little effort and only the subtle sound of tiny metal wheels rolling across the stone floor. Beyond this, a narrow passage opens into a shadowy corridor devoid of torch or window. "This connects to other passages that run throughout the manor between the walls. You can reach almost any room in the manor through these." Jessa adds with a hushed tone and a giggle, "Even the kitchen."

Myria stands in shocked silence as Jessa pushes the bookcase back into place.

"Enough sightseeing though, my lady. Your water should be warm. What say we get you in that bath?"

"Of course," Myria says.

Between the private space, the hot water of the bath, and the amiable company of Jessa, Myria soon feels refreshed and renewed. Then, the two of them head to the kitchen through the passages, with Jessa pointing out a few points of interest along the way. By the time Myria finishes a light lunch, Olympe joins her in the dining hall, seemingly satisfied with preparations for the Eventide Ball. However, with less than an hour until the court's arrival, Geffrey remains missing.

"He did say it might take him a while, my lady," Jessa says.

This seems to do little to alleviate Olympe's unease, but she shakes her head and turns an encouraging smile to Myria. "No matter. We still must host the ball. Come, let me show you the final dress for your social season."

Olympe explains as they make their way back to Myria's chambers that their finest tailors and seamstresses worked on the dress for days, a special order she placed to cater to Myria's distaste for the restrictive designs normally favored by the nobility. "There is no corset," she explains. "Instead, there is specially crafted boning sewn into the bodice to provide full support where necessary."

Myria examines it, speechless, running her fingers through the lightweight fabric. The sleeveless gown is a deep emerald green. "Why not gold for our house colors?"

Her aunt shrugs, as if this is an unimportant detail. "I thought green would best match your skin tone and your eyes."

With Jessa's presence, Olympe does not need to help Myria dress, but she does so anyway. When everything is in place, Myria spins in front of a tall mirror standing in the corner of the room, running her hands down the darker green, embroidered flowers covering the bodice and straps. The back opens at a sharp angle, exposing a substantial amount of skin, reminiscent of the dress she wore at Dawnmourne.

She stops spinning and watches in the mirror as Olympe styles her hair, twisting it into a braid then pinning it up before adding fresh, colorful flowers.

Myria's sense of excitement and amazement around arriving at her family's manor and all the warmth of her reception begins to fade, however, and the reflection in the mirror is soon frowning back at her.

Noticing her forlorn expression, Olympe pauses. "What is it?"

Myria picks at her fingernails. "It's beautiful, but..." How does she explain that she only wants to look beautiful for Emiri? "I'll have to dance with the prince. With this being our social event, he will refuse to leave my side. Where is Geffrey? Leor's decision will be made *tonight*. How many hours left until Geffrey can withdraw me from consideration?"

"Calm yourself," her aunt chides. "A dance with the prince will not harm you. And withdrawals are expected—"

"Who else would withdraw?" Myria snaps, but her mind goes to Brigid and Count Alanis.

"Some families would rather not risk the embarrassment of losing the prince's proposal, so they will respectfully retract their claim. It is not unusual. They would wait until the final night, to do so gracefully. I know of two families who plan on doing such a thing."

This takes Myria by surprise. "Who?"

"It is not official yet, but Houses Rosenford and Valenrence."

Rosenford does not surprise her, but Myria wonders at the implications of Sabine's withdrawal. She has hours yet to ponder this and other things after Olympe and Jessa take their leave. Left to herself and only the company of her thoughts, Myria passes the time until the ball pondering a great many things.

AT DUSK, MYRIA AND Olympe stand in the estate's grand foyer to receive their guests. The royal family is the first to arrive with their entourage. Myria and her aunt descend into a humble bow before straightening to greet them.

Olympe, naturally, takes charge of the situation. "Your Majesties, it is so wonderful to welcome you to Fairthorne once again. We hope you enjoy the Eventide Ball."

King Uriel looks around with curiosity. "Where is Duke Bramble this evening?"

Myria wishes she knew, as well.

Olympe betrays none of her worry. "My son is presently occupied with another matter, but he will make his appearance shortly."

The king and queen head into the ballroom with their royal guard while Leor hangs back with Captain Rozenna. He steps up to Myria, grasping her cold fingers. Despite the heat of his hands, his touch does not warm her.

"Lady Myria, I have been looking forward to this evening, and I hope you will grant me the courtesy of a dance later."

Myria's presents a polite smile in return, in no way reflecting the fear hammering in her chest. "It would be my honor," she says in a formal tone.

It seems enough to assuage him, as he moves into the ballroom behind his parents.

"Captain Rozenna," Myria calls.

The guard hangs back, turning slightly.

"Thank you for what you did last night," Myria says.

Rozenna says nothing, only offering a hint of a smile and a slight nod of her head in acknowledgement.

Myria turns her attention to the rest of the court as they funnel into the foyer. Duchess Cressida and Lord Godric of House Nocturnus enter next. Only Lady Theodora arrives to represent House Stirling. Myria breathes a sigh of relief at Aryn's absence and wonders if anyone discovered him unconscious at Honeyridge. House Rosenford approaches with Duke Aelric, flanked by both his children, Sigurd and Brigid. Behind him is House Runewell with Duke Mathias, Duchess Euphemia, Lady Eulalia, and Count Alanis. The last of the prominent noble families to greet is House Valenrence, with Duke Cirrus, Duchess Theia, and Lady Sabine in attendance. The lesser nobles that follow are given polite introductions. Myria recognizes a few of their faces from the Art Faire, but none of their names. Notably, the spymaster is absent.

Their guests properly greeted and ushered inside, Olympe sweeps into the ballroom pulling Myria along to see it for the first time since her arrival at Fairthorne. It is immense, rivaling the ballroom in the Ilona palace. The domed ceiling consists mostly of large glass windows which reveal the purple twilight sky above. The far wall is not a wall at all. Instead, it is a row of marble columns that open to the gardens beyond, illuminated by torchlight.

As if the nearby gardens did not offer enough flora to appreciate, the walls and tables are adorned with white flowers—roses, lilies, and chrysanthemums. They create a gentle, sweet aroma that wafts through the twirling dancers. A band of musicians plays a lively dance at the far edge of the room, their string and wind instruments trilling out spirited melodies.

Myria keeps to her aunt's side as much as she can, participating in mundane conversations about trade exports, courtly flirtations, land disputes, and other political topics. But the reigning subject of discussion is speculation over who the prince will choose for his wife. A few whispers discuss the withdrawal of Brigid and Sabine.

Prince Leor dances with all the ladies in the name of fairness, while Myria successfully avoids dancing with anyone under the guise of playing hostess. Occasionally, her eyes wander to the prince and the royal family, searching for a specific guest. When this yields no results, she glances toward Captain Rozenna, but to no avail. Emiri is nowhere to be found.

"Has there been any sign of Geffrey?" Myria whispers to her aunt.

Olympe continues to plaster on a forced smile, but Myria can see she looks worried. "Not yet."

"The prince will announce his decision at midnight," Myria says, struggling to keep her voice calm.

"We have time," Olympe asserts before signaling to Jessa. The handmaid hurries over without delay. "I need you to find my son," she whispers. "I do not care where he is. Bring him to me... *now*."

Jessa nods and darts away. Myria returns to feigning interest in the words of other nobles.

Lady Eulalia appears before her, a bright smile on her face. "Lady Myria, I wanted to thank you for hosting such a wonderful event."

"It is my pleasure," Myria replies, presenting yet again a practiced, formal smile which hides the maelstrom of emotions she struggles to conceal.

"I cannot help but notice you are the only one who has not danced with Prince Leor this evening."

Myria continues smiling, but steels herself further at the observation. The practice lie rises easily enough to her lips. "Unfortunately, my duties as hostess have kept me distracted, but the evening is still young."

Eulalia struggles as if she wants to say more. Instead, she curtsies and says, "It has been a pleasure meeting you this summer, Lady Hawthorne." Myria watches her leave with a hollow longing to rekindle their friendship.

"Can I offer you a pastry, my lady?"

Myria blinks in surprise as Merek, dressed in a formal serving uniform, offers a silver tray of desserts. She smiles at him. "I thought you spent most of your time outside."

Merek returns her smile, smoothing back his oiled hair. "Normally, you'd be right, but Olympe asked me to help inside tonight. It's not every day I get to go to a fancy party, even if I'm just working." He gestures toward the tray again. "Pastry?"

Myria holds up her hand as if to ward off the temptation of the sweet deserts. "No, thank you. I'm not hungry, and everything seems to upset my stomach today."

Merek fetches her a goblet of water instead, which she accepts and drains in short order before returning the empty cup to him. As he disappears into the throng of nobles, the current song ends and Myria scans the dance floor. Prince Leor steps back from his partner, Lady Theodora. He looks around the ballroom with an air of expectation, seeming to search for his next partner. Myria hides behind her aunt before he can spot her.

Olympe arches an eyebrow. "Walk the room. Ask our guests how they are enjoying the evening; that'll keep you busy."

Myria watches as Leor revolves on his toes, still searching the room. Luckily, Lady Eulalia approaches him and asks for the next dance, which he naturally obliges to just as the next number starts.

Myria breathes a sigh of relief as she takes her aunt's recommendation and circles the room. She approaches Duchess Cressida, then Lord Sigurd. They both offer polite praise, commenting on the room's beauty, the delightful music, and the delicious food. However, Duchess Cressida complains about the excessive florals, but Lord Sigurd offers compliments on Myria's dress. As the musicians draw the current song to an end, Myria ducks through the columns and heads outside to avoid being spotted by Leor.

None of the nobles in the gardens spare her a passing glance. She finds an isolated corner and draws into herself, cradling her arms around her chest and trying to rub some warmth into her chilled, exposed arms. She looks into the sky, raising her head to stymie a flow of tears as she considers what the future holds for her.

Pull yourself together. Would it really be that bad to marry Leor? There are certainly worse options.

The maestro makes an announcement inside the ballroom, asking couples to select partners for a romantic dance. The few nobles in the garden hurry inside to see who the prince chooses. Myria does not move, tightening her arms and pressing herself deeper into the cold stone corner as she clings to the last shred of privacy she may find for the rest of her life.

"Myria?"

She starts at the sound of Emiri's voice, thinking it a figment of her imagination. When she turns, he is indeed real and standing before her in a fine, red tunic with gold brocade. His shoulder-length hair is smoothed back, with one side braided behind his ear. Despite the dashing figure he cuts, his shoulders are slouched and his eyes dart around, not daring to meet hers.

"What are you doing out here?" she asks.

He takes a deep breath and holds it, then finally looks up to meet her eyes. "I... came to say goodbye."

The words seem as difficult for him to say as they are for her to hear.

"Will you dance with me?" he asks.

The question surprises and delights her, but she searches for a way to break the tension between them. "I thought you didn't dance," she says, poking fun at his reaction to Sabine's invitation in Dawnmourne and his remarks in Honeyridge.

His smile is rueful. "There hasn't been another person I *wanted* to dance with." He holds out an inviting hand.

There is no hesitation as she takes it. The chill of the night and dread of her future melt away under the warmth of his fingers curling around hers.

Despite his purported lack of experience, Emiri brings her body flush with his in a single, smooth motion, one hand finding the exposed skin at the small of her back as the other grasps hers. Myria drapes an arm over his shoulder and presses her cheek against his. He does not shy away, there under the starry night sky. As Myria closes her eyes, she feels his heartbeat thrumming through her body as he leads her in a slow pattern, tracing a square beneath their feet, turning ever so slightly with each sequence of steps.

"You look very elegant tonight," she whispers against his ear.

"And you are breathtaking." His low, raspy response makes her skin flush. He clears his throat. "We can take this inside, if you wish."

"No," she forces out in a whisper. Being close to him is painful enough without the intrusive eyes of the court. "Is this really goodbye?"

He swallows, and it sounds like he is choking back more than an unsteady breath. "Everything will change tonight."

"Yes," she says. "I'm withdrawing from the Summer Courtship."

Emiri hesitates, both in his words and in his movements, bringing their dance to a sudden, lurching halt. "Has Geffrey agreed to that?"

This time, Myria hesitates as she looks down at his shoulder.

"You're too late, anyway. The announcement is in an hour."

"And if I'm not?"

He sighs, and Myria feels the rigid line in his shoulders slacking as he entertains her question. They resume their slow circles in the garden. "Would Geffrey send you home to your grandmother? Would he force you to stay at court until he can arrange another marriage for you to profit House Bramble?"

Myria stiffens with indignation. "I would lead my own life."

"And what would that look like?"

"I would close my grandmother's inn and take her somewhere she wouldn't have to work so hard." She smirks into his neck. "I would take you away from the court and bring you back home to Caliburn. Maybe grandma Iris would like it there."

He chuckles, his fiery breath tickling her earlobe, and his arm tightens around her waist. His fingers trace delicate circles on the exposed skin of her back. "One day," he muses.

Suddenly, he twists, spinning her under his arm and catching her around the waist before dipping her back. He holds the position a moment longer than necessary. His warm hand braces against her stomach, arm around her waist, the tip of his nose hovering over her collarbone. His blazing breath blooms across her chest in alluring swirls. Slowly, he lifts her back up, leaving her breathless as they resume their dance.

"My place," he begins in a thick voice, then clears his throat again. "My place is by Prince Leor's side, always, protecting him in a way not so different from Rozenna. But when he picks you tonight—"

Myria shakes her head. Her eyes bore into his, pleading silently for him to carry her away from all of this.

Emiri continues, his voice barely above a whisper. "I will be proud when you are queen, but I don't know how..."

His voice breaks, he swallows, and he tries again.

"We won't be able to do this anymore. I cannot dance with you as queen, I cannot meet you in secret. I cannot... *compromise* you like that."

The music inside clashes to a halting end, and only one long, mournful note from a single violin fills the silence as Emiri's steps slow to a stop. His hands linger a moment before the one on her waist falls. The other runs a thumb down the crease of her palm, igniting a scorching trail on her skin that sends shudders echoing through her body like the thunderclaps of a summer storm.

The murmur of nobles draws closer, and Emiri releases her hand as he steps back. "I don't know what I'll do—what I can do—but I'll always be here for you."

The night breeze returns to chill her body in the absence of Emiri's touch. Myria opens her mouth to protest—becoming queen, his decision to avoid her, everything—but no words come to her lips.

"My lady?" a timid voice interrupts.

Myria whirls around. Jessa stands before them, her eyes on her feet. "Yes, Jessa?"

The handmaid keeps her face pointed to the ground. "Duke Bramble is waiting for you and Lady Olympe upstairs."

Relief floods through Myria. The moment she can finally be rid of the Summer Courtship is upon her. And if he doesn't agree... Myria's thoughts trail off as she forces out her ever-present, aching smile. "Of course, I'll be right there."

Jessa curtsies before heading back into the ballroom. Myria offers a parting glance to Emiri. She wants nothing more than to kiss him before parting. The urge burns her lips and pulls at her feet to step closer, but she knows she cannot. Not yet. "Tonight, everything changes," she says with a genuine smile.

Then, gathering her skirts, she follows Jessa in search of her aunt.

25

SUMMONS

IT ONLY TAKES THEM a few minutes to find Olympe mingling with the guests. After informing her of Geffrey's summons, she leads the way up the grand staircase, taking a sharp left turn to march down the balcony corridor. They stop before a door flanked by guards wearing royal Avalion surcoats over their armor, which gives Myria pause. The guards' presence can only mean one thing—a member of the royal family is inside. Her mind first goes to Leor, which makes her stomach flip with dread, but she remembers seeing him dancing downstairs.

Her aunt knocks. Myria can tell from her white knuckles that she also has misgivings.

"Come in," Geffrey bids.

As they enter the dark room, Myria is met with more confusion. Inside, King Uriel and Geffrey are seated at a worn, wooden table. Geffrey's stricken expression worries her the most.

"Ladies," he says in a deep, troubled voice.

Myria feels another presence, and peers around to find a man she's never seen before. He is dressed in black velvet with silver threading. His face is long, angular, and smooth, bearing a condescending smile. Olympe seems to recognize him with a glare, making Myria all the more apprehensive. Her mind immediately goes to the courtyard in Honeyridge that morning. Perhaps someone else witnessed her and Emiri kissing, and she has been summoned to be accused of treason.

"Please, have a seat." The stranger swings his arm in a wide arc, gesturing to the table.

Geffrey cocks his head to the side, annoyance painted across his face. "Jessa, you may go. Attend the guests, if you will."

Everyone wordlessly complies. Jessa dips into a hurried curtsy, then nearly runs down the hall as one of the guards swings the door closed. Myria sits beside Geffrey, with Olympe on her other side. The stranger takes his place next to the king.

307

Uriel begins, clearing his throat. "Lady Myria, this is Duke Theobald, the seat of House Stirling and Lord Militant of Avalion. Lady Olympe, I'm sure you are already familiar."

Her aunt gives a single, curt nod. Geffrey remains silent, and when Myria glances at him, he refuses to look at her.

"I believe you have heard about our spymaster," Uriel says.

Myria's stomach turns in knots and her pulse throbs in her temples. If this has to do with the spymaster, then surely she's being accused of treason. She looks again to Geff for some reassurance, some guarantee of her safety, but he still refuses to look at her. She clears her throat to address the king. "They arrived recently to court, when we were at Westhaven."

"The spymaster has been here the entire time. They were ensuring the validity of the suitors' bloodlines."

Rozenna's description of the spymaster's investigation echoes in her head, something about looking into the suitors. Myria squeezes her hands together.

"As it so happens, Duke Theobald has arrived because of your confirmation. He will explain."

Olympe narrows her eyes, glaring at the duke.

"Thank you, Your Grace. His majesty is correct in describing this as a matter of bloodlines. Simply put, House Bramble has committed a great offense by entering Lady Myria for the Summer Courtship."

"This is absurd," Olympe says, looking to her son. Geffrey does not intervene. "Myria has a noble right to court; she *is* our blood."

Duke Theobald inclines his head. "I have no argument with those claims, Lady Bramble." He reveals a faded, yellow document, smoothing it out on the table for them. "In fact, it is the nature of her noble blood itself that makes her ineligible for the Summer Courtship."

Olympe snatches the document, her eyes darting over the words. "This is... a marriage contract? Between—"

Her aunt pales suddenly and her words are choked off by a gasp.

"What is it?" Myria presses.

Olympe meets her with horrified eyes. "A marriage contract between Callia Bramble and House Stirling, signed by my late husband, Caspian."

Myria's brows knit together. "I don't understand. She was engaged to the king. She was engaged to *you*." Myria jabs a finger in King Uriel's direction.

"I thought the same," Olympe says, her voice trailing off.

Duke Theobald clicks his tongue. "It really is unfortunate the late Duke Bramble did not share this information with you. Perhaps it would have prevented this whole misunderstanding."

Myria feels a flash of anger, clearly seeing the familial connection between the supercilious duke and his children. "What happened then? And what does this have to do with me?"

Theobald leans back in his seat, regarding her with intrigue. "It would be improper for me to suggest King Uriel made a mistake the summer he selected his bride. It would be more appropriate to say Callia Bramble deceived the king. While she and the late Duke Caspian shared a father in the late Duke Caedmon, they were truly only half-siblings. After his first wife perished, Duke Caedmon remarried a woman named Vivienne, a foreigner... a citizen of Caliburn."

Myria's eyes widen at this information. "Caliburn?"

Theobald continues. "While it is not unheard of for Caliburnians to enter the ranks of the nobility, they can only do so by marriage into a noble house. Even so, this causes concerns regarding impurities in the bloodline. Thus, as a foreigner's daughter, it would have been most inappropriate for Callia Bramble to become queen. She required a more suitable union to ensure her station remain within the noble class, and that the blood of her offspring might be further cleansed by such a pairing, and so this contract was created." Duke Stirling jabs a finger at the document still in Olympe's hands, but his eyes never leave Myria's. "Your mother was promised to *me*."

"Being the daughter of Duke Caedmon was not enough?" Myria asks, grinding her teeth.

Theobald's smile is thin. "Perhaps, but Vivienne already passed away by the time of the last Summer Courtship. Her marriage to Duke Caedmon was performed in secret and was not consecrated by the crown before her death. Thus, she was never even recognized as a proper duchess. For all intents and purposes, and by the letter of the law, your mother was a bastard born out of wedlock. She was no better than some..." he pauses, as if searching for the appropriate station for such a mark of shame, then his grin grows wide. "No better than some dirty barmaid."

Myria rips the document from Olympe's hands and tosses it on the table. "But my mother obviously never married you," she hisses.

His smile curls more, and he glances at the guard standing inside the door. "Bring him."

The guard leaves, but Myria's chest heaves as she continues glaring at the duke. "So, you stopped my mother from marrying the king for a chance to bed her yourself? And now what? She defied you, so you're looking for revenge against her daughter?"

Olympe's icy hands find Myria's under the table, as if to restrain her temper.

Theobald chuckles, a dark rumbling sound that echoes in the dark room. "I suppose it would be easy for you to think that, but the contract specifies that there must be a marriage, *any* marriage, between House Bramble and House Stirling. Even if it's a Bramble bastard, or the daughter of one. Your mother is no longer available to satisfy that role, so the responsibility falls to you."

Myria stops breathing for a moment as his words sink in. Her voice wavers with anger. "You want me... to marry your son, *Aryn?*"

Theobald claps softly. "Sharp intellect for such a common upbringing."

Heat surges to her cheeks, and Myria jumps to her feet, her chair scraping across the floor. "For what purpose?"

Theobald shrugs. "To purify noble bloodlines, of course."

"How convenient that you provide this document at the eleventh hour before the prince makes his decision. How *convenient* that everyone else it involves—my mother, my uncle, my grandparents—are dead and can't challenge the validity of these absurd claims."

The duke nods toward the crumpled contract. "If you look at it again, you will also find the king's signature to support these 'absurd claims.'"

Myria looks at the king in a new light, her rage making her hands shake. For the first time, she understands the king's role at court as he avoids her wrathful gaze in favor of inspecting the wood grain of the table. She realizes he has remained silent this entire time. He appears weak next to Duke Stirling. "You knew?" she demands.

Geffrey finally comes to life, pulling at her arm. "Myria, he is still the king."

King Uriel looks at her evenly, his face impassive. "While I cared for your mother, as the king, I am required to put personal feelings aside. My duty is to all of Avalion."

"But you knew about me? That I would have to marry a Stirling? Yet you've watched me all summer and said *nothing*?" She all but spits her words.

The king averts his eyes once more. "At the time, I did not realize that the contract would be so enduring. I was young, hot-headed, so I did not realize the contract extended beyond Callia and Theobald."

Myria eyes dart around the room like a caged animal, searching for some strand of hope or support, but finding none. Not in Olympe and Geffrey's defeated expression. Especially not in the patronizing grin of Theobald. This must be a ploy, some desperate attempt to remove her from consideration for the Summer Courtship. "I don't even want to marry Leor." Geffrey and the king stir at this revelation. "If I withdraw from the Summer Courtship, there will be no need for you to exclude me as competition for Theodora by forcing me to marry Aryn."

Theobald appears amused by her attempt to bargain. "The contract exists whether or not you're in the contest."

"You *cannot* expect me to agree to this. What is to stop me from fleeing court like my mother did?"

Another careless shrug from Theobald. "You can certainly try, I suppose. But now, there will be consequences to such actions. When you joined court this summer, you inherently agreed to uphold House Bramble's responsibilities, including this marriage contract. To refuse this would mean open war between our houses."

Myria turns to the king, outraged. "You would let him do that?"

Once more, Theobald answers in Uriel's stead. "It is not the His Majesty's responsibility to intervene. After all, he authorized this contract. Are you so selfish you are willing to permit innocent bloodshed on your behalf? Avalion has not seen a civil war in centuries. Most Bramble citizens are simple farmers. I cannot imagine they would be prepared to march off to war simply because a selfish girl refused to fulfill her obligations."

Myria grinds her teeth together, and she feels the heat of her anger materializing in her balled up fists. She looks at the king once more. "My mother didn't abandon you or break your heart. You betrayed her, utterly and completely turning your back on her. I'm glad she never married you."

Theobald threads his fingers together on the table. "The ability to compromise is a valuable skill in the nobility."

compromise to prevent you from attacking us?" Myria hisses.

A new voice enters the room. "I told you to leave."

The chilling tone of Aryn fans the flames threatening to burst from Myria's fingertips. He sets a dripping, putrid bag on the table and takes a seat, coolly surveying Myria. One half of his face is covered in bandages seeped through with brown, dried blood. Olympe, Geffrey, and the king cover their noses at the stench coming both from the grisly parcel and the man who delivered it.

"I was unhappy with the arrangement as well," he admits. "'Tis why I tried to convince you to leave. You refused, so here we are."

"You knew as well," she snarls.

"Yes, but I finally accepted this outcome. It would be a shame if you did not do the same. Your grandmother would be so disappointed to learn we canceled our wedding. The news seemed to excite her."

The mention of her grandmother confuses Myria. She first thinks of the newly-revealed Vivienne. But when she realizes Aryn is referring to Grandma Iris, the fire burning within her threatens to burst forth. "What. Did. You. Do."

Aryn stands, reaches for the leather bag, and shakes its contents onto the table. "I paid her a visit to deliver the news in person. Meanwhile, I hope you appreciate my engagement gift to you."

It takes Myria a few seconds to process the bloody mess Aryn has brought. When she realizes what it is, she bolts from the room, her stomach convulsing in fear, hatred, and disgust. But even with it out of sight of, she cannot flee the image of the bloody, severed minotaur head rolling across the table.

26

MIDNIGHT FLAME

MYRIA'S EYES BURN WITH tears. She presses a hand over her mouth to stifle her heavy breathing. Outside Geffrey's study, she leans over the balcony railing, attempting to control her racing thoughts. The night breeze caresses her tear-stained face, but offers no relief.

The minotaur is dead. *The minotaur is dead, and Aryn killed him*. For what? He could have threatened her without murdering the minotaur. *And I'm to blame for leading the bastard right to the creature the first night I met him.*

She scrubs at her face, struggling to calm her breathing.

Aryn Stirling killed the minotaur, not because he had to, but because he *wanted* to. He attacked her in a dark stairwell, unprovoked. Wanton violence drew him like a moth to a flame.

A pained wail escapes her lips, and she covers her mouth again. She does not have time to grieve over the minotaur. She barely has time to consider the true purpose of that meeting.

Another smothered whimper escapes, barely muffled by her hands.

She has to marry Aryn Stirling. If she doesn't...

"Myria? Everyone is waiting."

She whirls around to see Emiri approaching. There is no hiding her tears or her despair. His eyebrows knit in concern, his steps slowing as he takes in her distraught state. Lowering her hands, she whispers, "I can't."

She attempts to move past him, but he catches her hands in his, turning to hold her back, keeping her tethered to him. "What happened?"

The feel of his touch around her hands is a slight reprieve, a small comfort that alleviates some of the festering ache she feels ripping apart her chest. Her mind fumbles to find the right words. "My mother—the *Stirlings*—" is all she hiccups into life.

He pulls her closer, his eyes peering into her face as his thumbs rub soothing circles on her hands. "It's okay. You can tell me. We'll take care of it. I'm right here."

Myria runs the tip of her tongue over her chapped lips, salty from her tears, and swallows. She opens her mouth to speak when movement above Emiri's shoulder catches her eyes. Aryn and his father exit the study.

Myria's eyes meet Aryn's icy glare for a moment, creating a hollow ringing in her ears as she realizes something. The minotaur head was proof Aryn had been to Talking Tree Forest, that he had been to the Morning Glory.

That he had seen Grandma Iris.

And he is using that connection as leverage for his threat. He is threatening the people she loves. Myria knows he will not stop with the minotaur or with her grandmother.

He would threaten Emiri as well.

She backs up suddenly, ripping her hands from Emiri's, hoping the others hadn't noticed them so close. "I have to go," she says, her voice stronger. She must protect Emiri from Aryn, but right now, she needs to find her grandmother.

Emiri looks over his shoulder as Geffrey approaches. Myria takes a step back, poising herself on the balls of her feet. Her eyes bore into Emiri's as he turns back to her, begging, pleading. He nods with a sad smile, then spins around and confronts Geffrey, barking something about complaints from the guests in the ballroom, giving Myria enough time to make a run for it.

She dashes for the stairwell, pulling off her shoes to run barefoot. She does not stop for a change of clothes, she does not wait to hear Leor's decision in the ballroom. She cannot stop for anything, heading straight for the stables. The sight of Merek feeding the horses treats from the kitchen is a small victory for her.

"I need a horse," Myria calls to him. "I need the fastest horse we have."

The panic and urgency in her voice push Merek into action without question. He quickly saddles a steed, and when he leads the horse to her, she recognizes Stefan, the noble creature who helped her at the joust.

Myria jumps on, heedless of a ripping sound in her skirt. Her bare toes curl around the stirrups as she squeezes the reins and spurs Stefan into a gallop. As she passes the front steps of Fairthorne, she can hear someone calling her name, but she does not stop to see who it is.

The route between Fairthorne and Everhaven is less than a half-hour's ride. Still, as the wind blows through her hair, unpinning the braid and ripping out the flowers, Stefan cannot move fast enough for her. No thoughts race in her mind, just the deafening wind in her ears and the imminent terror boiling in her stomach.

At some point, she thinks she hears hoofbeats behind her. They are so distant, she pays them no mind. She reaches Everhaven before the midnight bell tolls, but she does not stop to examine the dark windows and quiet streets. She pushes Stefan further. Harder. His hooves ring out on the cobbled streets as they cross town to reach a hard packed dirt road leading southeast.

As Stefan's hooves dig into the soil of the new road, a dreadful odor hits Myria's nose. As she approaches the inn, the acrid stench grows stronger, clouding the air with smoke and ash.

Stefan rounds a bend, revealing a harrowing sight. Myria pulls back the reins, halting the panting horse as she surveys the scene before her for several helpless moments. A blaze illuminates her face in orange light, searing her watery eyes. The Morning Glory is in flames.

The second rider catches up, stopping just behind her. Myria slides out of the saddle and leaps to the ground, then bolts for the burning wreckage.

"*Myria, no!*"

Emiri's reaches out from behind to grab her waist, pulling her against him just before she dashes into the fire. They twist and spin until he positions himself between her and the Morning Glory, a buffer, a shield, an *obstacle* to her objective. She struggles in his arms, flailing about until he pushes her to the ground.

"I have to see. I have to find my grandmother!" she screams, pounding against his arms and chest.

"Your grandmother isn't here," Emiri says. "They would have taken her somewhere else." He wraps his arms around her and presses his weight atop her, seemingly oblivious as her fists pound his arms, shoulders, and face.

Myria stops struggling for a moment, gasping for air as her chest rises and falls against his. Thick, churning black smoke curls in the sky like a storm cloud gathering over the forest. Her back digs into the ground, every bump in the dirt, every bundle of grass roots, every rock digging into her like spear thrusts. But none of this is as painful as the thought of her grandmother burning alive in the blazing inn. "How do you know that for sure?" she rasps out in a broken voice.

Emiri wraps his hands around her wrists in the momentary respite from her struggles. His chest crushes against hers as she heaves with wracking sobs. He buries his face into her loose, windswept hair, pressing his lips against her ear. "Because it would be the best way to control you. They would gain nothing by killing her, but they can use her to manipulate you. I know that's not easy to hear right now, but she is alive. Take comfort in that right now, and I swear to you we will find her. We will get her back."

Myria's eyes burn with tears, smoke, and the stinging heat of the flames, and she looks up to the moon. She stared at the same moon earlier, just a few hours ago, considering a very different future. As the celestial body watches over them, uncaring and indifferent to her suffering, an overwhelming rage festers inside Myria.

Her shaking hands form into fists, and she rips them from Emiri's grasp before bashing them against the ground, letting go of one final, frenzied scream. She releases all of her distress and hysteria in a single moment. With it, a sudden rush of energy leaves her body, rolling from her in a wave of pressure. The torrent of energy washes over the clearing, blowing back the trees and extinguishing the inn's flames.

In the lingering darkness, they stare at the smoldering ashes of the Morning Glory. Emiri says nothing. Myria buries her head in his shoulder as exhaustion overwhelms her.

"What an impressive display."

The voice jolts Myria to alertness. It is familiar, and that familiarity makes the hairs on the back of her neck rise. Emiri leaps to his feet, and Myria rises to stand beside him.

A retinue of riders has joined Stefan and Emiri's horse by the road. Most are masked guards, holding up flickering torches. The lead rider dismounts, the signature cloak of the spymaster swirling around them.

The figure reaches up and removes their mask as they approach, revealing a shock of long, white hair and dark-painted lips.

The woman from Myria's visions.

"Who are you?" Myria asks, keeping her voice even despite the shaking in her legs.

The woman steps closer, an amused, haughty smile curling those dark lips. "I can see you have inherited a special gift from your mother, and her mother before her. It's time you learned more about it. My name is Oriana Stirling, your future mother-in-law."

Myria's heart nearly stops beating and her breath is caught in her chest as if her lungs refuse to let the moment pass. Aryn was only the spark that lit the fire that destroyed her home. Myria realizes, despite all the secret plots and dangerous enemies she's faced up to now, this woman in front of her will ignite the true flame in the palace.

27

EPILOGUE

Leor's eyes endlessly search the night, scanning the sea of faces in the ballroom. Most eagerly return his gaze, but his search bears no fruit, making his stomach turn with unease. After a gracious bow to his dance partner, Duchess Cressida, Leor excuses himself for refreshment. As if on cue, several attendants swarm him with gleaming silver trays of water, ale, mead, and wine. The prince elects for an ale, a reminder of his last visit to Bramble lands.

As he sips from his cup, Captain Rozenna emerges from the shadows to linger by his side. "Enjoying yourself, my prince?"

"I have had several beautiful women to dance with tonight," he replies with a forced smile.

Seeming to sense the strain in his voice, she turns to look at him. While the captain is adept at protecting his physical presence, her experience also lends her an uncanny ability to see through any of his charades. "Most men would consider that a lucky evening, indeed. Of course, you are not like most men."

His smile turns wry. "All the beautiful women in the world cannot compare to the one woman I have yet to dance with this evening."

Rozenna nods. He knows she understands, having already heard his praise of this certain woman. "Nothing compares to what the heart truly wants."

"Have you seen Lady Myria? I cannot seem to find her."

Rozenna's eyes flicker toward the outside gardens by way of answer. She frowns, seeming apprehensive.

Leor laughs at her expression, moving toward the gardens. "I am sure Bramble security would ensure my safety out there, but you are welcome to join me."

"It is not your safety I fear for, Your Majesty," she says in a hushed tone, keeping close to his side as he weaves through the room.

The outside air cools Leor's flushed face. He takes a deep breath and sweet floral scents greet him. He squints through the darkness, searching for the woman who has bewitched him all summer, but there is no sign of her tantalizing emerald dress. Instead, his search yields an unexpected sight—Emiri.

His friend stands in profile, staring up at the sky with a distracted, faraway look on his face. While Emiri is no stranger to melancholy moods, Leor cannot help but think there is something particularly askew with him this evening.

"You joined us for the Eventide," Leor says as he approaches.

Emiri jumps at the sudden noise, then hurries over. "My prince, I am sorry. I did not see you." He descends into a customary bow.

Leor roughly clasps his friend to his chest. "There is nothing to apologize for. I am glad you are here tonight. I cannot believe how nervous I am."

Emiri's smile is thin and pained. "It is a very momentous decision."

Leor does not respond at first, looking at Emiri with worry. "Is there something wrong? You seem more out of sorts than usual."

Emiri looks to the ground, avoiding his eyes entirely. "It is kind of you to be concerned, but I am fine. Was there anything you needed, my prince?"

Leor clears his throat. "Actually, I was looking for Lady Myria. Captain Rozenna indicated she may have come outside."

Emiri's eyes flicker from the ground. "She just returned inside. Geffrey has returned, and he summoned her upstairs."

Leor nods at this information and is about to turn away, but the shadows of Emiri's face keeps him tethered. "Something ails you or eats at her mind," he says, crossing his arms. "Tell me."

Leor knows Emiri would rather keep his thoughts to himself, as he always has, but whatever clouding thoughts plague his mind loosen his lips for a few reluctant words. "It's not my place to speculate."

"Please," Leor bids. "Share what is on your mind, always."

Emiri draws a slow breath. "The Lady Myria has been... *withdrawn* from court lately. It is possible she does not share a mutual interest."

Leor sighs, resigning a part of himself to this truth. "I have noticed this as well. It is precisely why I wanted to speak to her alone tonight before my announcement."

Emiri's eyes appear to tighten. "Have you given any thought to this announcement?"

"Yes, very much thought."

"Do you have any alternatives in mind?"

Leor blinks, repeating, "Alternatives?"

Emiri nods, refusing to repeat or clarify his question.

Leor's throat goes dry. He had not considered such a possibility. Since the night he first met Myria, she has been perfect in every way. Since their first kiss, he has not been able to stop thinking of how her soft lips felt against his own. The lingering memory of her hands on his chest thrills him day in and day out. His voice threatens to break. "Why do you ask?"

Emiri's eyes flicker to the side. "What if she is in love with someone else?"

The ground quakes beneath Leor's feet. The world tilts and shimmers at the edges. The dryness of his mouth cracks with sharp thirst that cannot be quenched. It takes him a moment to see Emiri. Emiri, Leor's longest and closest friend. Emiri, who avoids meeting his gaze. He stares at the strained muscles in Emiri's arm, the white skin taut over his knuckles as he musters the courage to ask, "Who?"

Emiri offers no answer. Leor returns inside as he hears the music shift for another dance. His princely smile remains in place as his mind swirls through the possibilities, knowing Emiri would never suggest such an idea without a grain of truth behind it. His feet carry him to the closest suitor, Lady Theodora, who accepts his invitation for a dance. As he spins with her, his eyes sweep the ballroom for potential candidates that could have captured Lady Myria's attention.

Lord Sigurd is the most obvious of choices. It is no secret the Rosenford heir was on the precipice of a marriage proposal to Myria at the tournament. Their closeness on the *Nocte* was also quite evident. Then, of course, there is Lord Godric, a potential marriage plot engineered by Duchess Cressida. Also, Count Alanis remains a notorious flirt. Would he have been able to capture Lady Myria's heart?

Leor blinks down at his partner, a noticeable absence occurring to him. "Where is your brother this evening, Lady Theodora?"

She averts her eyes, her dark lashes fluttering seductively against the pale contrast of her cheeks. "Lord Aryn was running late this evening. He should be here soon. It is very thoughtful of Your Majesty to ask."

Leor looks away, struggling to swallow past a dry lump in his throat. He does not *dare* to imagine that Aryn Stirling holds Myria's affections. He had been singularly vehement and vocal in his contempt for her. Could that have been a ruse to hide his true passions? While Leor does not think it likely, he cannot deny his sudden wave of insecurity.

The hour of the evening draws near, and Leor stands stiffly at the head of the ballroom in anticipation. His face is smooth and stony like marble. He keeps his hands clasped behind him. Neither Myria, nor anyone of House Bramble, returns to the ball, which makes his muscles tense with dread. Emiri never wanders far from his side, standing faithfully and just as stiffly nearby. It is a slight comfort in the face of this newfound uncertainty.

His mother approaches, a gentle warmth in the stifling heat of the room. "My dearest son," she bids. "Is it not time?"

The music lowers, and the twirling dancers stop to train their eyes on him. Leor's glances to the door, and seeing no one entering, he looks back at his mother. "It appears everyone is not yet here," he whispers in a tight voice.

Queen Eloria smiles at him, still warm but not without its condescension. "Your decision cannot wait for anyone," she says.

Her words curl patronizingly, but Leor does not need another lecture on her disapproval of Myria. "It is not quite midnight. Father has not yet returned."

She acquiesces to this with a slight nod before sweeping away into the crowd. Leor releases a sigh at her absence before turning to Emiri. "Will you..." Leor clears his throat before speaking again, trying not to betray his desperation. "Please, find Lady Myria for me."

There is a unique shine in Emiri's eyes that Leor cannot identify—perhaps it is pity for Leor's naïve hopefulness, his unfounded optimism marred by newfound warnings. But loyal as ever, Emiri bows. "Your word is my command."

His friend strides from the room. For a few minutes, Leor waits for him, wildly searching the crowd of dancers for an impossible hope. When the eyes of the court become too much for him to handle, Leor steps forward, an incandescent smile in place, and announces, "We shall have at least two more dances! Then, once the bell tower strikes midnight, I will name my future bride!"

The court responds with excited applause. The minstrels begin a new song in celebration, and Leor ducks into the main foyer to wait for the momentous hour.

The entrance hall is refreshingly quiet. While the sounds of music and conversation still drift to Leor, the peace of mind he finds alone is undeniable. It gives him time to sort through his muddled thoughts without being in the center of attention, even if for a few minutes. Captain Rozenna follows at a respectable distance, clinging to the shadows to at least give him the illusion of privacy. Other members of his guard linger nearby, unseen.

The peace is interrupted when anxious voices descend the staircase. Leor turns to find Emiri and Geffrey, deeply engrossed in hushed, animated voices. Geff's mother, Olympe Bramble, hovers close behind them. Leor's heart clenches at their troubled expressions.

"What is going on?" he demands. "Where is Lady Myria?"

Geffrey looks up at him with pity and shame painting his reddened face. Duke Bramble appears to not have the strength to answer, so Emiri looks up to meet Leor's gaze and explain instead.

His friend's face is drawn and *angry*, quickly reddening to match Geffrey's. His voice is thick and guttural, like rocks scraping together. "As of tonight, Lady Myria is engaged to Aryn Stirling."

Emiri continues with an explanation, but Leor does not hear the rest of his words. He is not even aware when his friend hurries outside. Movement at the top of the stairs finally catches Leor's notice as his father descends, accompanied by Duke Theobald Stirling. Neither of them holds the prince's attention for long. Instead, a third figure captures Leor's focus entirely.

Aryn Stirling, his face covered in bloody bandages, smirks in triumph. Leor fears the torchlight gleaming in his narrowed eyes hint at what horrors may brew within his mind.

NOCTURNUS

Nightson

Goldeport

Dawnmourne

Elmground

ROSENFORD

Westhaven

Thitis

Silver coast

STIRLING

Ilona

Kinggrove

Oakhaven

Fairthorne

VALENRENCE

Talking Tree
Forest

Everhaven

RUNEWELL

Honeyridge

BRAMBLE

THE MAP OF
AVALION

Acknowledgments

Another book, another set of acknowledgments. This is my first book under this name, so I'll try to keep things short and sweet here.

Thank you to Brian, my editor, who was a great and necessary push and means of support for getting this finished in a legible manner. He goes by B. K. on a lot of platforms, and it's my understanding that this means Book King. Thanks to his vigilant efforts, this book stands to have a substantial less (fewer? Idk, I'm not letting him edit this) amount of em dashes, italics, and adverbs. Thank goodness. It was obscene.

Thank you to my Twitter Writing Community and Discord friends, namely Gwyn, Madeline, and Gabrielle. I have plenty of other Twitter friends and mutuals; that list is far too long to include here. But, come follow me and be friends! @SelunaDrake

My early Beta Readers who offered insight and feedback when it mattered: Ola & Kaitlyn. Your support was truly invaluable in the early stages. As well as my first readers on Inkitt and Wattpad. I promise you—this final version is MUCH better and I hope you give it a try!

To Arbor, whose name draws up memories of couch naps and Goat Simulator.

Koletta, for the illustrious artwork. (Twitter: @charoncreates)

The Patreon group: Jenifer & Jeri. Your undying love and support cannot be overstated.

Every student I have ever had in my classroom. Each of you (yes, everyone) has taught me something, including how to care, empathize, and maintain the patience of a saint. Truly, I would not give up my day job because of how rewarding it is to be your teacher.

To the family always there—Martha & Levoy.
But chiefly, to my Sanctuary. Without you, I would not be alive. I love you.

.

ABOUT AUTHOR

Seluna Drake (she/her) is a high school English teacher, author, poet, and artist. Most of the time she passes as a chaotic creative who spends way too much time on video games and not enough time talking to her therapist. She also considers herself a witch, INFP, and an advocate for youth and marginalized voices. Black Lives Matter. LGBTQIA+ Lives Matter.

You can find her primarily on Twitter: @SelunaDrake.

Made in the USA
Columbia, SC
13 May 2022